P9-CQV-596

GET ALL THIS FREE
WITH JUST ONE PROOF OF PURCHASE:

$50 VALUE

◆ **Hotel Discounts** up to 60% at home and abroad ◆ **Travel Service -** Guaranteed lowest published airfares plus 5% cash back on tickets ◆ **$25 Travel Voucher** ◆ **Sensuous Petite Parfumerie** collection ◆ **Insider Tips Letter** with sneak previews of upcoming books

You'll get a FREE personal card, too. It's your passport to all these benefits–and to even more great gifts & benefits to come!

There's no club to join. No purchase commitment. No obligation.

HPT-PP5A

Enrollment Form

□ **Yes!** I WANT TO BE A *Privileged Woman*.

Enclosed is one *PAGES & PRIVILEGES*™ Proof of Purchase from any Harlequin or Silhouette book currently for sale in stores (Proofs of Purchase are found on the back pages of books) and the store cash register receipt. Please enroll me in *PAGES & PRIVILEGES*™. Send my Welcome Kit and FREE Gifts -- and activate my FREE benefits -- immediately.

More great gifts and benefits to come.

_____
NAME (please print)

_____
ADDRESS   APT. NO

_____
CITY   STATE   ZIP/POSTAL CODE

PROOF OF PURCHASE ONLY

NO CLUB!
NO COMMITMENT!
Just one purchase brings you great Free Gifts and Benefits!

Please allow 6-8 weeks for delivery. Quantities are limited. We reserve the right to substitute items. Enroll before October 31, 1995 and receive one full year of benefits.

Name of store where this book was purchased_____

Date of purchase_____

Type of store:

□ Bookstore   □ Supermarket   □ Drugstore

□ Dept. or discount store (e.g. K-Mart or Walmart)

□ Other (specify)_____

Which Harlequin or Silhouette series do you usually read?

_____

Complete and mail with one Proof of Purchase and store receipt to:

U.S.: *PAGES & PRIVILEGES*™, P.O. Box 1960, Danbury, CT 06813-1960

Canada: *PAGES & PRIVILEGES*™, 49-6A The Donway West, P.O. 813, North York, ON M3C 2E8

HPT-PP5B

▼ DETACH HERE AND MAIL TODAY! ▼

OUTLAWS AND HEROES

TAMING THE LONE WOLF Joan Johnston

A lone wolf like Stony Carlton wasn't easy to tame. Unless, of course, the right woman came along. Then wolves mate for life.

GABRIEL'S ANGEL Dallas Schulze

Sexy rancher Gabriel Taylor knew there were worse ways to spend a heavenly evening than with a beautiful woman in a one-room cabin during a blizzard. But when that beautiful woman was pregnant Angie "Those-can't-be-labor-pains!" Davidson, Gabe knew he was in for one hell of a night....

DANGER AND DESIRE Mallory Rush

The FBI was after renegade Clay Barker, and Melissa Lovelace was the bait. A rookie agent, Melissa had something to prove, but she never thought she'd find herself siding with Clay...against the law.

About the Authors

Joan Johnston knows the law. As a lawyer, Joan is no stranger to right and wrong, and she has a strong love for the West. Joan writes contemporary Western romances and historical Western romances. As a result, she was a natural for the **Outlaws and Heroes** collection. Moreover, Joan has won several awards for her work, including Best Western Series Author in 1989 and the Lifetime Achievement Award in 1991, both from *Romantic Times*. Joan has two children, and enjoys football, sailing, camping and riding horses.

Dallas Schulze loves a happy ending. Dallas is a prolific and talented writer whose growing number of published novels rivals the number of dolls in her ever-increasing collection. Born and raised in Colorado, Dallas now lives in California, where writing is one of her many creative outlets. She has won several *Romantic Times* Awards, including Best Harlequin American Romance in 1989 and Storyteller of the Year in 1991. Dallas hopes that readers have half as much fun with her books as she does! Dallas loves to hear from her readers, and you can write to her at P.O. Box 241, Verduge City, CA 91046

Mallory Rush believes sensuous books open up readers' minds to new experiences. Mallory's sizzling, innovative story lines earned her the *Romantic Times* Career Achievement Award for Most Sensual Series Writer in 1993 and she often speaks at conferences on the topic of sensuality. Continuing this theme, Mallory penned "Harlequin's sexiest story ever," *Love Game,* available from your bookstore. Mallory lives in Wisconsin with her husband and their five children.

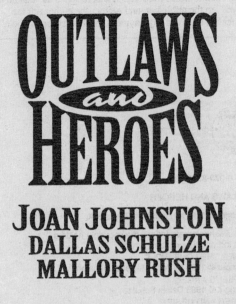

OUTLAWS and HEROES

JOAN JOHNSTON
DALLAS SCHULZE
MALLORY RUSH

Harlequin Books

TORONTO • NEW YORK • LONDON
AMSTERDAM • PARIS • SYDNEY • HAMBURG
STOCKHOLM • ATHENS • TOKYO • MILAN
MADRID • WARSAW • BUDAPEST • AUCKLAND

ISBN 0-373-83311-3

OUTLAWS AND HEROES

Copyright © 1995 by Harlequin Books S.A.

The publisher acknowledges the copyright holders
of the individual works as follows:
TAMING THE LONE WOLF
Copyright © 1995 by Joan Mertens Johnston
GABRIEL'S ANGEL
Copyright © 1995 Dallas Schulze
DANGER AND DESIRE
Copyright © 1995 by Olivia Rupprecht

CONTENTS

CONTENTS

TAMING THE LONE WOLF

Joan Johnston

Dear Reader,

Northwestern Wyoming has to be one of the most beautiful places God ever created, but it takes a special kind of person to endure the harsh winters, the desolate isolation to be found there. I think the mountains, the forests, the primeval nature of the lands draws a certain kind of man—unrelenting…uncompromising…dark and dangerous.

Dark and dangerous. Tall, dark and handsome. A dark, mysterious stranger. We have lots of expressions that suggest the more dangerous a man is, the more attractive he is to a woman. Maybe it has something to do with proving our feminine power by taming the savage beast.

A lone wolf like Stony Carlton is another kind of challenge. He doesn't seem to need anyone, but introduce him to the right woman and he'll give up his roaming ways and take a mate for life.

That's the fantasy. What is it *really* like to fall in love with a dangerous man? I suspect most of us would find it exciting for a little while, but someone steady and dependable might be more comfortable to live with for the long haul.

That's why I like reading and writing romances. I get to vicariously fall in love with and tame a dangeous man by simply turning the pages of a book. I hope you enjoy my venture into the world of dangerous men.

Happy trails!

Joan Johnston

Chapter One

STONY CARLTON took a bite of his hamburger and tried not to listen to the scene unfolding behind the counter of the Buttermilk Café between the waitress and a guy who seemed to be her boss. For a man used to solving other people's problems with his wits—and now and then a gun—it was impossible not to eavesdrop, given the agitation in the woman's voice.

He looked around the empty café. No one else was there to come to her rescue except him—and he wasn't exactly the knight-in-shining-armor type.

"Come on, Bud, I've told you I'm not interested," the woman said.

"Aw, Tess, just one little kiss."

"I said no."

"You oughta have a little more gratitude, seein' as how I let you leave so early in the day."

"You let me leave early because I come in two hours before everyone else," the woman replied with what Stony considered amazing composure.

"Yeah, well, you owe me for givin' you a job when you had no experience."

"I've got experience now, Bud, a whole year of it. I've got work to do, so if you'll just let me by—"

Stony heard muffled sounds suggesting a struggle. He set down his burger, wiped his hands on a paper napkin and threw it down as he left his booth headed for the counter. The man, Bud, had the woman, Tess, backed up against the wall beside the coffeemaker. She was fending off his attempts to kiss her, turning her head away and shoving vainly at his burly shoulders.

"Hey, Bud," Stony said.

Bud turned and glared, clearly irritated at being interrupted. "What?"

"Let the lady go."

"Butt out, mister."

"Afraid I can't do that," Stony said.

"Yeah? So what are you gonna do about it?" Bud snarled.

Stony was over the counter in an instant, as though it wasn't there. He grabbed Bud by the scruff of his food-stained T-shirt and slammed him against the wall, holding him there with his arm rigid, his palm pressed against the center of Bud's chest.

The waitress shot out of the way and stood at the kitchen door, hands clutched together, green eyes wide with fright.

Stony ignored Bud as though he were a bug on the wall and turned his attention to the woman. "You all right, ma'am?"

She nodded her head jerkily.

Stony had been in the Buttermilk Café probably once a month in the past year, yet he hadn't paid any attention to the waitress. Since he had sworn off women a couple of years ago, he had made it a point not to spend his time looking at the pretty ones, so he wouldn't be tempted to go back on his promise to himself.

Tess was definitely pretty.

In fact, she was the kind of woman it was hard to dismiss. Her auburn hair was pinned up off her neck, but it had that mussed-up look, with lazy curls at her temples and ears and throat, as though she had just gotten out of a man's bed. The green eyes that stared warily back at him from a heart-shaped face were curved at the outer edges, like a cat's. Her nose was small and straight, her chin dainty. She had an alabaster complexion, which suggested she didn't get outside much, because the Wyoming sun burned the hide off you summer and winter.

He had avoided looking at her figure because he found it so alluring. She had a bosom—about big enough to fit his hands—that drew a man's eye, a tiny waist and feminine hips. And she was small enough to incite a man's protective instincts. He was tall, over six feet, and he suspected her head would barely reach his shoulder.

"I'm all right," the woman said. "You can let Bud go."

Stony had completely forgotten about the man against the wall. He turned to Bud and said, "What is it going to take to convince you to leave the lady alone?"

"What I do in my own place of business is none of your concern," Bud retorted.

Stony glanced at the woman. "Do you welcome this gentleman's attentions, ma'am?"

He watched the dark flush start at the V neck of her peach-colored waitress uniform and skate up her throat to sit like two roses on those alabaster cheeks. Her green-eyed gaze flitted from him to Bud and back to him.

"I...uh...no," she said. "But—"

He cut her off by turning his attention to Bud. "The lady wants you to leave her alone."

"There's nothing you can do to stop me," Bud said smugly.

"I can testify in court when the lady files a harassment suit against you."

"Why, you— She won't have to file no suit, because she's fired!" Bud said heatedly.

"Bud, no!" Tess exclaimed.

Stony glanced at Tess and was surprised to see she was angry—with him!

"Now look what you've done!" Her fisted hands found a perch at her tiny waist. "I was handling things just fine on my own before you showed up."

His eyes narrowed. "The man was pawing you."

Her chin lifted mulishly. "I've been putting Bud off for a year, and—"

"This has been going on for a whole year?" Stony said incredulously. He turned back to Bud, who was still pinned against the wall. "You've been mauling this lady for a year?'' He gathered up a bigger handful of Bud's T-shirt.

''Wasn't doin' nothin' she didn't want,'' Bud said. ''Widow-woman needs a man more'n most.''

''A widow?'' Stony's glance darted to Tess.

''My husband was killed a year ago,'' Tess said in response to his cocked brow.

He saw from the flash of pain in her eyes that it was still a raw wound. Her boss hadn't done anything to help it heal. Far from it. Stony resisted the urge to slam Bud against the wall again. He forced himself to let go of Bud's T-shirt and take a step back, afraid he would hurt the man if he held on to him much longer.

Stony wasn't sure he had solved anything. Maybe he had made matters worse. He refused to ask Bud to keep the woman on, when it was clear if he did that Bud would continue to press unwanted attentions on his waitress. But Tess apparently wanted—maybe needed?—the job.

''What will you do now?'' he asked Tess.

''Get my job back, if I can,'' she answered with asperity. She walked over and straightened Bud's rumpled T-shirt. ''Come on, Bud. What do you say?''

She managed a crooked smile, but Stony saw her chin was trembling.

Bud shot a malicious look at Stony, then said to Tess, ''You're fired, honey. You can pick up your check at the end of the week.''

''But, Bud—''

Bud jerked his thumb toward the door. "Out." Bud turned to Stony and said, "Now get out from behind my counter."

Stony went back over the counter the way he had come. He glanced at the woman from the corner of his eye as he made his way back to his booth and sat down. He picked up his hamburger and took a bite, but it was cold, and he had trouble swallowing it.

He watched Tess argue in whispers with Bud and saw Bud vehemently shake his head. He watched her take off her apron and drape it over the counter before she headed for the kitchen. He waited for her to reappear. He wanted a chance to talk to her, to make sure she was going to be all right, to see if there was anything he could do to help. Although, with the kind of help he had offered so far, he wouldn't be surprised if she turned him down.

He waited maybe two minutes. When Tess didn't return, he threw some money on the table to cover his check, grabbed his shearling coat and Stetson off the antler coatrack and hurried outside to the snow-covered sidewalk to see if he could find her.

Stony wasn't thinking about his vow to stay away from pretty women. He wasn't thinking about anything except his need to make sure Tess would be able to make ends meet until she got another job. That should have been his first warning. Not that he would have paid attention to it. Stony was the kind of man who would stand bare-assed in a nest of rattlers just for the fun of it.

He stopped dead once he was outside and looked both ways. The snow was still coming down in large, windblown flakes that made it difficult to see very far. She was nearly to the end of Main Street, which was only one block long in the tiny town of Pinedale, walking with her head bent against the wind and her winter parka pulled tight around her.

"Hey!" he called. "Wait for me!"

She took one look at him and started to run.

TESS WAS TRYING HARD not to cry. For the past year she had been deflecting Bud's attentions with flip humor. Only, last night her three-year-old daughter, Rose, had been sick, and Tess hadn't slept much. When Bud had approached her, nothing witty had come to her tired mind. Then that awful man had interfered and made everything worse!

She had been fired.

The desperate nature of her situation was just now sinking in. She had no savings. She had no job. In a town this small in the middle of the off-season there wasn't much likelihood of finding another. Especially if Bud kept his promise to make sure none of his friends in the restaurant business hired her. She didn't even have the money for a bus ticket to somewhere else.

Damn you, Charlie Lowell! How could you lie to me? How could you be a thief when you knew what would happen to us if you got caught? How could you go and get yourself killed like that? And for rustling cattle! I hate you, Charlie! I hate you for dying and leaving me alone.

She should have taken one of the marriage offers she had gotten over the past year from the cowboys who came into the Buttermilk Café. Or the Pinedale police chief, Harry DuBois, who had proposed to her for the second time only last week. At least then she and Rose would have been sure of having a roof over their heads.

She liked Harry, and he was good-looking in a rugged Harrison Ford sort of way, but she hadn't been able to feel anything—let alone love—for any man since Charlie had died. Besides, she wasn't sure she wanted to be married again, not after what had happened with Charlie. She had been deliriously in love when she had married at sixteen. She was barely twenty, but she felt much older and wiser. She no longer gave her trust so freely or completely.

But if she wasn't going to let a husband support her, she had to do a better job of it herself. She had barely been able to cope with her disillusionment and grief over Charlie's death during the past year. She hadn't done much planning for the future.

It seemed the moment was upon her. She was going to have to make some plans, and fast, or she and Rose were going to find themselves out on the street in the middle of a Wyoming winter.

"Hey! Wait for me!"

Tess glanced over her shoulder and saw it was that man from the café. He was coming after her! She wasn't sure what his intentions were, but she didn't plan to stick around and find out. She took off at a run, headed for Harry's office. He would protect her from the madman following behind.

Maybe she would have made it if the sidewalk hadn't been covered with a fresh dusting of snow that concealed the treacherous ice below. Or if she had been wearing a decent pair of snow boots instead of the cheap, leather-soled shoes she wore for work. Tess hadn't taken three steps when her feet skidded out from under her. She flailed her arms in a vain attempt to catch her balance and reached out with a hand to break her fall on the cement walk. It turned out to be a fatal error.

Tess heard the bone in her wrist crack as soon as her weight came down on her arm. She cried out in agony as her body settled on the cold, hard ground.

The interfering stranger was beside her a moment later, down on one knee, his dark brown eyes filled with concern.

"Now look what you did!" she accused.

"What I did?"

"If you hadn't been chasing me—"

"I wasn't chasing you. I was coming after you to—"

"This is all your fault!" she cried, hysterical with the realization that with a broken wrist she wouldn't be able to work for weeks. Not to mention the fact that she had no health insurance and no idea how she was going to pay a doctor to fix her up.

The tears she had so ably kept under control through her most recent disaster could no longer be contained. She fought the sob that threatened, but it broke free with a horrible wrenching sound. Then she was crying in earnest.

She felt the stranger pick her up, being very careful of her wrist, which he settled in her lap, and stand, cuddling her against his chest.

"It's all right, Tess. You're going to be fine. I'm going to take care of you."

She should have resisted. She should have told him in no uncertain terms that she could take very good care of herself. Instead she turned her face to his chest and surrendered to his strength, thinking how good it felt to give her burdens over to someone else, even if it was only for a few moments.

"I'm taking you to my Jeep," he explained as he began walking. "I'll drive you to the hospital, where someone will take care of your arm."

"I don't have money to pay the doctor," she mumbled against his coat.

"Don't worry. I'll take care of it."

They were such wonderful words. She had been in charge of so much lately, and the burdens had been so heavy. She was more than willing to hand everything over to someone else for a while.

"What's going on here?"

It was Harry. Harry must have seen what happened from the picture window in his office.

"She fell and broke her wrist," the man said. "I'm taking her to the hospital."

"Tess?" Harry said. "Do you want Stony to take you to the hospital?"

Stony. So that was his name. And Harry knew him, so maybe he wasn't a madman, after all.

It took too much energy to answer, or even to turn around and look at Harry. She nodded.

"All right, Stony," Harry said. "I'll follow you there."

"I can take care of it," Stony said, his voice rumbly against her ear.

"I said I'd follow you," Harry insisted. "My patrol car is parked down the street."

Stony didn't argue; he merely turned and headed for his Jeep.

Tess was feeling drowsy, which wasn't surprising, considering the amount of sleep she had gotten last night. She had also hit the back of her head against the pavement when she fell, but it was only beginning to hurt because all her attention had been focused on her throbbing wrist.

"Stony?" she murmured.

"What, Tess?"

"My head hurts."

"You must have hit it when you fell. I'll have the doctor check it out."

"Tess?" Harry said.

Answering took too much effort.

"Looks like she fainted," Harry said, hop-skipping on the dangerous surface to keep up with Stony's long stride.

"Knocked out by the fall, I think," Stony replied.

"I only closed my eyes," she mumbled. "I'm still awake."

"I'll be right behind you," Harry said, sprinting—insofar as that was possible considering the icy walks—for the police car parked nearby.

Stony set her in his Jeep and buckled her in. She heard the engine rumble, and things got a little hazy. Behind her closed eyelids she was seeing a picture of the tall, lean, broad-shouldered man who had come to her rescue in the café, his dark brows lowered, his eyes feral and dangerous. And the man who had looked down at her as she lay hurt on the ground, concern etched in his granite features.

His face was weatherworn, with deep brackets around his mouth and a mesh of crow's feet around his eyes that evidenced a life lived out-of-doors. His straight black hair needed a cut. It hung at least an inch onto his collar, and a hank of it was forever falling onto his forehead.

When he looked at her, his dark brown eyes held her in thrall. They were lonely eyes. Or, at least, the eyes of a man used to being alone. They offered sympathy. They asked for nothing in return.

She had seen him in the café before, but not regularly, so he lived around here somewhere, but maybe not right in town. There were lots of cabins along the river in this isolated place where a lone wolf could find solace from the world of men.

She wondered what he did for a living. Judging by his Western shirt, jeans and boots, he could have been another cowboy. But a mere cowboy wouldn't have taken on Bud, who was big enough, and meaty-fisted enough, to be downright intimidating. Stony hadn't blinked an eye at confronting him. So he was probably a man used to being in charge, rather than one who took orders, a man who knew his own strength and used it when necessary.

But he wasn't a cruel man, or he really might have hurt Bud. She had seen how angry he was, but he had kept his rage on a tight leash. He was agile and strong and—

Stony jostled her broken wrist when he picked her up to take her inside the hospital, and the brief agony jolted her awake. But she couldn't seem to get her eyes open. Tears of pain seeped from her closed eyelids.

"Sorry, Tess," Stony said. "Hang on, and the doctor can give you something for the pain."

Tess drifted in and out of consciousness, aware of the murmur of voices, the sting of an injection, the buzz of the X-ray machine, the warm wetness of the cast being applied around her thumb, from the middle of her right hand halfway up her arm.

She heard the word "concussion" and realized that was probably why she felt so woozy. So it wasn't only the lack of sleep that made her feel so impossibly tired. She heard the doctor say she would have to stay overnight so she could be watched. But she couldn't stay, because she had to go pick up Rose from Mrs. Feeny.

"No," she muttered. "Can't stay. Have to go home."

"Be reasonable, Tess," Harry said. "You're in no condition to leave the hospital."

"Have to get Rose."

"Who's Rose?" she heard Stony ask.

"That's her daughter," Harry said.

"She has a daughter?"

The shock in Stony's voice made her smile. She wasn't sure if the expression got to her face.

"An elderly lady keeps the little girl for Tess while she works. Mrs. Feeny, I think," Harry explained.

Mrs. Feeny was very strict about Tess picking up Rose on time. Otherwise the old woman charged her triple. With all the extra she was going to have to dole out for the doctor, she needed every penny she had.

"Have to pick up Rose." She tried to get up, but a palm flattened her.

"I'll do it," Stony said.

"The kid doesn't know who you are," Harry said.

"I'll do it."

"I said I'll do it," Stony countered. "After all, this is my fault."

Tess wanted to smile again. Stony sure had changed his tune. Maybe he was feeling guilty. He ought to. This *was* all his fault!

She welcomed Stony's offer to pick up Rose. For some reason, Rose had taken an instant aversion to

Harry. Her daughter had a way of making her feelings known. Tess licked her dry lips and said, "Okay, Stony. Pick up Rose."

"Tess, you don't know a thing about the man," Harry said. "He—"

"Don't interfere, Harry," Tess murmured.

"You heard the lady, Sheriff. She can make her own decisions without any help from you."

Tess realized she hadn't told Stony what to do with her daughter. "Take Rose home," she added.

"I'll do that," Stony said. "Don't worry, Tess. She'll be safe with me. I have lots of room at my place."

His place?

She had meant take Rose to her own home. Of course, he didn't have the key, and Mrs. Feeny, who was also Tess's landlady, was hardly likely to let a stranger into an upstairs apartment in her own home. So maybe it was better this way. Only, she had no idea where Stony lived. How would she find him when she wanted to reclaim her daughter?

She managed to force her eyes open a crack and sought out Stony's face. "Take me, too," she said. "Rose needs me."

"For heaven's sake, Tess," Harry said irritably. "You're in no condition to do anything but lie flat on your back in bed. Stay here in the hospital where you belong."

The situation was desperate. She reached out and grasped Stony's hand. It was big and warm and callused. His strength made her feel safe. "Rose needs me," she repeated. "Take me, too."

"All right," he said. "I'll take you both to my place."

"Promise?"

"I said I would."

He didn't sound too happy about the situation, Tess realized. But she wasn't about to let him out of his promise.

"Thank you." Her eyes sank closed again.

If she could rest for a couple of hours, she would be fine. Stony could pick up Rose and come back for her. She would rescue her daughter from the clutches of the interfering stranger...as soon as she could get her eyes open again.

Chapter Two

"WHERE AM I?"

"You're at my place, a cabin along the river about twenty miles from town. Don't you remember the ride here in my Jeep?"

"I . . . sort of. It's all kind of fuzzy."

Tess's gaze darted from the male face bathed in shadows beside the bed, to the natural pine log walls, to the wedding ring patterned quilt that covered her, and back to the face made even more attractive by a night's growth of beard. The faint mauve light filling the window across the room suggested it was nearly dawn. The snow had stopped, but it weighted down the branches of the Douglas firs outside the cabin, creating a real-life picture postcard.

She reached for her head with her right hand before a sharp pain and the weight of the cast reminded her that her wrist was broken. She switched to the left and gingerly touched the lump on the back of her head.

"Does it still hurt?" Stony asked.

"My scalp's a little tender, but my head doesn't ache like it did." She realized what was missing and sat up with a jerk that made her dizzy. "Where's Rose?"

"Still asleep."

"Where?" she insisted, reaching out to clutch Stony's forearm. It was as hard as a rock. She realized what she was doing and let him go.

He gestured with his chin. "Right there beside you."

Tess realized why she hadn't seen the child. The bed was huge, and Rose was curled up in a pile of sheets and blankets on the other side. Tess took another look around at the heavy pine chest, the rocker with clothes thrown over the back, the man's wardrobe, and realized she must be in Stony's bedroom.

"I thought you said you had plenty of room," she accused. "Rose and I are in your bed, aren't we?"

"It was the only one in the house big enough for the both of you," he admitted with a crooked smile. "Rose refused to sleep by herself."

Tess turned back to her daughter and leaned over to brush a red curl from her daughter's cheek. "Did she give you a lot of trouble?"

"No more than two or three green-broke broncs."

"Oh, dear. I was a little afraid of that."

"We got along fine, once she figured out I wasn't going to give up or give in."

Tess flushed. "She is rather strong-willed. I suppose I let her have her own way too often."

"She's spoiled rotten," Stony said flatly. "And she has a temper."

Tess opened her mouth to defend her mothering tactics, then realized Stony hadn't been completely successful in controlling her daughter, either. After all, Rose had ended up sleeping in the same bed with her.

"Perhaps she is a little spoiled," Tess conceded, brushing at the stubborn curl that had found its way back to Rose's cheek. "But she's had to cope with an awful lot over the past year."

Stony shifted from the chair beside the bed to a spot on the mattress near her hips. Tess tensed at the intrusion on her space. However helpful he had been, Stony was still a stranger. And she was in his bed wearing no more than—Good Lord—one of his T-shirts!

"I've been wanting to talk to you about that. I mean, about how you and Rose have been getting by," Stony said.

His voice had that rusty gate sound, as though he hadn't used it much lately. It rumbled over her, sending a shiver up her spine. She wasn't sure whether it was the threat he presented, or the temptation, that had her inching away from him.

"We've been just fine," Tess said.

"Don't bother lying."

"I—"

"I spoke with your landlady."

Tess sighed. "I'm only a month behind on the rent."

"You had to give up your phone two months ago. And I didn't see much in the cupboards to eat. How the hell you two have managed to make it this far, I'll never know."

Tess felt the anger rising and struggled to control it. Rose hadn't learned her redheaded temper; she had inherited it from her mother.

"I'd like to know what your plans are now that you've been fired," Stony said.

"I don't see how my future plans are any of your business," Tess retorted. "I'm sure I'll find something—"

"You can work for me." Stony interrupted her.

Tess was speechless. "Doing what?" she managed to say at last.

He made a broad gesture around the bedroom. "I could use a housekeeper, and I know you can cook. I couldn't pay much, but I could give you free room and board. It would give you somewhere to stay and food in your mouths, at least until your wrist is healed."

Tess took a second look around the room. This time she noticed the layer of dust on the wardrobe, the stack of dirty, rumpled shirts on the rocker, the horse magazines strewn across the floor, the empty beer can on the chest. It was clear the man could use a housekeeper. But if he had really wanted one, he could have hired one long ago.

Her gaze shifted back to Stony's face. "Why are you willing to do this for me?"

He frowned and rubbed his thumb along his lower lip. "I don't have any designs on you, if that's what you're thinking."

She flushed. Because the thought had occurred to her. "I never—"

"Don't bother lying again. You've been itching to get out of here ever since you woke up."

She heard the irritation in his voice. His thumb never stopped that lazy trail from one side of his mouth to the other. She felt a surprising curl of desire in her belly and jerked her gaze away from his mouth back to his eyes. That was no better. They were dark and fierce and feral. They made her feel hunted. She lowered her lashes to hide from him but felt her body quiver in anticipation of the need to fight or to flee.

"The way I figure it, I owe you a job," he continued, apparently unaware of her agitation. "I'm the one who got you fired—even if you should have quit a long time ago."

"And worked where?" she demanded, incensed at the implied criticism. "There aren't too many waitress jobs in Pinedale."

"Couldn't you do something else?"

Her anger died, consumed by frustration at her lack of education. She had a high school equivalency degree, but she had believed that was all she would ever need. She had never considered the necessity of any further formal education because she had been perfectly happy being a wife and mother. She had been very good at her chosen profession.

"I had a job I was happy with, until it was taken away from me."

"Well, there you go. What was it?"

"Housewife."

She saw the stricken look on Stony's face and realized she shouldn't take out her bitterness over Charlie's death against him. "I'm sorry. Ever since Charlie got himself killed, I—" She took a shuddering breath. She wasn't used to speaking aloud about Charlie, and the sudden lump in her throat surprised her. She had believed she had come to terms with Charlie's untimely death. Apparently not.

"Was Charlie your husband?"

"Yes. Charles Lowell. He was a butcher at the local grocery store. Or so I thought. He was caught rustling cattle and was killed in the gunfight that followed."

She looked up and discovered Stony staring at her grim-lipped. His face had paled, and his eyes narrowed to slits. "It's not a pretty story," she admitted. "I was devastated, because I was caught off guard. I had no idea Charlie was involved in theft of any kind. I'm afraid I wasn't myself for a long time after that."

"Didn't you have any family who could have taken care of you?" he asked.

"I'm an orphan. And Charlie's parents are dead. It was—and is—just me and Rose. The sheriff's office collected some money for us. Looking back, I suppose it was strange for them to do such a thing—but it got us through the first few months. When I was myself again, I looked around and realized I would have to get a job. Bud was the only one who would hire me without experience.

"I think he did it because he thought he could pressure me into sleeping with him. I'm sure he had no idea I would resist his advances so long or so completely." Her lip curled up on one side. "I guess he finally ran out of patience."

Stony grunted in sardonic agreement. "Will you take the job I offered you, or not?"

She twisted the sheet in the fingers of her good hand. She didn't have any choice. It was take his job offer or starve. But she didn't like it. Stony made her nervous. He made her skin tingle. He made her feel things she didn't want to feel.

Nevertheless she said, "I'll take the job." And then qualified her acceptance. "But only until my wrist heals, and I can decide what to do with my life."

Or until the day came when it was no longer safe to remain with the lone wolf whose den she had invaded with her cub.

HE HAD KILLED HER HUSBAND.

Stony wished he had inquired about Tess's last name sooner. He had been shocked to hear her husband was Charles Lowell. He had been tracking that particular gang of rustlers for several months before he finally caught them in the act, and he had been forced into the gun battle that ensued. He had performed his job with the ruthless efficiency that had earned him his reputation, and Charles Lowell had died.

His identity as a range detective who hired out to large cattle spreads wasn't generally known, and Stony needed it to stay that way in order to infiltrate the roving bands of rustlers that plagued the vast Wyoming ranges. The police had cooperated and kept his name out of the local paper. For some reason, Tess Lowell had never asked the identity of the man who killed her husband, or she would have known who he was.

Stony knew he ought to confess immediately and give Tess the chance to spit in his face. But she didn't have anywhere else to go, and he was afraid she wouldn't stay if she knew the truth. At least he could give her a place to live until she was well again. She and the kid needed him, and he owed them something because he was personally responsible for the loss of both husband and father, even if the man was a felon.

But he resented the intrusion on his solitude.

He was thirty-three and had lived alone in this five-room cabin, which he had built with his own hands, for the past ten years. He liked the quiet. He had spent many a long winter night before a flickering fire with nothing to disturb his peace but the wind rustling in the pines or the buildup of snow sliding off the steep blue tin roof in thunderous clumps.

When he needed a woman, he sought out one who only wanted the same brief physical satisfaction he desired. Lately he had decided even that sort of relationship wasn't worth the risk it entailed. His isolation had become complete and comfortable.

Until this redheaded woman and her redheaded child had invaded it.

His attention was drawn to the child, who woke suddenly and popped upright in bed like a jack-in-the-box.

"Mama!"

"Don't be frightened, Rose. I'm right here," Tess said, holding out her good arm.

The little girl scuttled across the bed and flung herself across her mother's body as though she were being attacked by ravaging wolves. She peered up at Stony with green eyes a shade darker than her mother's and said very distinctly, "I want to go home."

"I know, sweetheart," Tess replied, brushing at the mass of bright red curls—shades lighter than her mother's deep auburn—that tumbled over her daughter's forehead. "I do, too. But we can't, not for a little while."

The child sat up abruptly. "Why not?"

"Because your mother's arm is broken. She needs to rest and recuperate," Stony said.

"What's reputerate?" the child said, her brows knitted in confusion.

"Get well," Stony amended, amused at the child's mangled effort to repeat the grown-up word.

The little girl's eyes widened, and her gaze slid to the cast covering her mother's arm. She reached out tentatively to touch it. "Mama's hurt bad?"

"The cast is there to protect the broken bone so it can heal," Tess explained.

Tears filled the child's green eyes and spilled over. Her lower lip stuck out, and her chin trembled. "Mama's hurt."

Stony was amazed at the instant transformation. How did the kid do it? He watched her mother fall for the act.

"Oh, sweetheart, I'll be fine," Tess said with a hitching sob as she gathered the child to her breast.

Stony snorted. He meant to convey disgust at the ridiculousness of sentimental tears over something that was done and over. He believed the little girl was simply manipulating her mother, for reasons he couldn't imagine and didn't care to figure out. Two sets of long-lashed, accusing green eyes settled on him, and the sound in his throat changed to something more contemplative.

"Is anybody hungry?" he asked.

"I am," Rose said.

Stony's lips twisted cynically when he saw how instantly the child's tears stopped. One clung to her lashes and skidded down her check when she gave him a wide-eyed blink.

"I'll make some breakfast," he said.

"I'll do it." Tess slipped her legs out from under the covers before she realized the T-shirt bared her all the way from her toes to her hips. She flushed and scooted back under the covers.

"Where are my clothes?" she asked.

"I had Mrs. Feeny put some things in a suitcase for you. It's there in the corner. You can get the rest of your stuff from her later."

Stony was still having trouble catching his breath after the eye-stopping exhibit he had just witnessed. The woman wasn't tall, but she had incredible legs, long and silky and perfectly formed. He fought off the image of those legs wrapped around him. His genitals drew up tight in response to such mental titillation.

"I'll go make breakfast while you get dressed," he said, backing his way out of the room. He felt perspiration dotting his forehead, even though the bedroom was far from hot. It disturbed him that his thoughts had taken such a decidedly lascivious turn. He had cast himself in the role of guardian. So long as Tess was under his roof, he had to resist any temptation to seduce her. He owed Charlie Lowell's widow that much consideration.

The whole wall of the house that encompassed the combined kitchen and living area contained French doors that opened onto a large elevated patio. The view included a forest of evergreen pines and fir interspersed with aspens that had lost their leaves earlier in the fall. The light and empty space immediately brought him comfort.

"Is this your house?"

Stony whirled from the refrigerator door and stared at the sprite who was standing barefoot not three feet away from him.

"You should be wearing slippers," he said to the child, aware of how parental he must sound, when the last thing he ever wanted to be was a parent.

She looked down as she wiggled her toes on the polished hardwood floor. She glanced coyly at him from beneath lowered lashes. "Mama's getting me slippers for Christmas."

Not without money, she wasn't, Stony thought grimly.

"Your feet must be cold," he said, scooping the child up and carting her back toward the bedroom. She didn't weigh as much as a case of beer. "You can wear a pair of socks."

"I'm not supposed to wear socks without shoes," she said soberly.

He met her gaze and frowned.

Her chin trembled. "Mama says so."

"I'm not going to bite you," he snapped.

Rose burst into tears. "Mama!"

"What's going on?" Tess said, hurrying from the bedroom.

Stony was dismayed to see she had left his T-shirt on and merely added a pair of worn jeans. It wouldn't take much to have her naked. She was barefoot, too.

"I told the kid she shouldn't be running around barefoot on this cold floor." He watched Tess's bare toes curl against the wooden floor. His gaze skipped back to her face, and he saw the blush was back in her cheeks.

"I don't have the money for slippers," she murmured.

"Put on a pair of socks."

"I think I'm capable of judging whether my feet are cold," she retorted.

He shifted Rose to one arm and bent down to touch Tess's bare feet. "Your toes are like ice," he said flatly. "Put on some socks."

"I don't wear socks without—"

"Shoes," he finished. "Then put on some socks and shoes."

"Is that an order?" she asked.

He wanted to say yes, but the mulish tilt of her chin advised against it. "A suggestion."

"Very well. I'll be right back."

"Bring some socks and shoes for Rose," he called after her. He looked down at the little girl who was peering at him wide-eyed.

"I don't like you," she announced.

"I don't like you, either," he said.

Rose didn't seem phased by the insult. "I'm hungry," she said.

"So am I," Stony muttered. "That's probably why I'm in such a foul mood." It couldn't have anything to do with the two females who had invaded his lair.

"I can help cook," Rose said.

"Can you now?" Stony set her on the counter beside the fridge so she would be off the floor while he rooted around for breakfast fixings. He set the eggs on the counter while he hunted out the bacon and English muffins.

A moment later he heard a tiny "Uh-oh," followed by the sound of eggs cracking on the floor.

He whipped his head up and caught it on the refrigerator shelf. He grabbed at the painful spot and turned to find the eggs spilled from the carton and creating a gooey puddle on his floor.

The little girl's eyes were wide with fright. "I'm sorry."

Stony fought down the urge to yell at her, remembering how quickly she could summon tears. Besides, accidents could happen to anyone. He was willing to give her the benefit of the doubt. This time.

"Are you going to spank me?" the little girl asked, her chin aquiver.

"I didn't think parents spanked their kids anymore," Stony said. "It's against the law, or something."

"Mama says she's going to spank me. But she never does."

"I'll bet," Stony said. That explained why the kid was spoiled rotten.

"Mama loves me," the little girl said solemnly.

Stony took in Rose's big green eyes, her unmanageable, curly head of hair, the chubby arms and legs, and felt an uncomfortable tug at his heart. Rose was lovable, all right. He had to give her that.

He looked down at the chaos she had created with a box of eggs. Lovable. And messy.

"Oh, no!"

Stony looked over his shoulder at Tess, who was eyeing the broken eggs on the floor with dismay. "I'm so sorry."

"No problem. We can have a bowl of cereal instead. No cooking. Saves on dishes."

"I'll clean up that mess," Tess volunteered.

"I'll do it," Stony said, eyeing the arm she had arranged in the sling the doctor had given her. "You're incapacitated."

"What's 'pacitated?" Rose inquired.

"Means she can't do anything with that broken arm," Stony explained to the child. He caught Rose around the waist and, stepping around the broken eggs, hauled her over to the far side of the breakfast bar, where he sat her on one of the two stools there. He grabbed a handful of paper towels and began sopping up the eggs and dropping the shells into the disposal in the sink.

"You must not get much company," Tess said, settling on the second stool.

"I can stand on this side of the bar," he said, rinsing his hands and drying them. He grabbed some bowls from the cupboard and dropped them with a clatter on the breakfast bar. He only had one box of cereal, a healthy wheat flake, and he began pouring it out into the three bowls.

"I don't like that kind," Rose said.

"It's all I've got," Stony replied.

"I want the kind with marshmallows," Rose insisted.

"Rose, darling—" Tess said.

"Eat it or go hungry," Stony said.

Rose moved her bowl just as Stony began to pour milk, and it spilled across the counter.

Stony set down the milk carton as softly as he could, using his last bit of patience. "It's time we had a talk, young lady," he said to Rose.

"I don't like you," Rose said, her chin tilted in a mulish imitation of her mother.

"I thought we settled that," Stony muttered, glaring back at the little girl. "I don't like you, either."

"Rose—"

"Stay out of this, Tess," Stony said.

"I will not," Tess said, rising from her bar stool, her green eyes flashing. "You seem to be forgetting who you are. And who we are."

"I'm an idiot," Stony muttered. "And you're interlopers."

"What's 'lopers?" Rose asked.

"Intruders," Stony snarled.

"What's 'truders?" Rose asked.

"Unwelcome guests," Tess answered before Stony could speak. "I think we can save you and ourselves a great deal of unpleasantness, Mr.—I don't even know your last name," Tess said, astonished at the realization. "I'm sorry we've intruded on your peace. If you'll allow me to use your phone, I'm sure Harry DuBois will be willing to come and get us."

Stony shoved a hand through his hair, catching the wayward curl on his forehead, which immediately tumbled back down again. "Look," he said. "I don't want you to leave. Besides, you have nowhere else to go."

Tess sighed. "Unfortunately, what you say is true. But I don't think this is going to work, Mr.— What is your last name, anyway?"

"It's Carlton, but call me Stony."

"Very well, Stony. As I said, I don't think this is going to work."

"I'm not used to having people around."

"Especially not children, it seems."

"I don't like kids," he said flatly.

"Why is that?" Tess challenged.

Stony thought of his father and his father's very young new wife and their new family that had excluded him. He had to admit his half brother had been cute. His father had been fascinated by his second son. That kid had gotten all the attention Stony had always craved from a father who had always been too busy working to play with him. Thirteen-year-old Stony had felt sick with guilt and shame at his uncontrollable envy and resentment of the time and attention his father gave his newborn son.

He couldn't tell Tess any of that. "Kids are a lot of bother," he said instead.

"I shall make certain Rose is not a bother," Tess said crisply. "Is there anything else?"

"Just keep her out of my way."

Tess looked around the small cabin. What Stony asked was unrealistic, considering the size of the place. "I'll do my best."

"I want to go home," Rose said to her mother.

Stony watched as Tess hugged the child. "I wish we could go home, too, Rose. We have to stay here."

"I don't like that man," Rose said.

Stony met Tess's gaze over the child's head. He wasn't proud of his behavior. But he couldn't help his feelings, either. However, there was something he could do to ease the situation for all of them.

"I've got another job up around Jackson Hole," he said. "I'll be leaving this afternoon, so you'll have the place to yourself. I have groceries delivered on a regular basis from town. If you need more, call the supermarket and give them a list."

He hadn't been meaning to take on more work right away, but it seemed best to put some distance between himself and Tess—for whom he felt too great an attraction, and the little girl—who didn't like him.

"What is it you do?" Tess asked.

"I find cattle rustlers. And bring them to justice."

Tess stared at him openmouthed.

He turned on his heel and left the room before she had a chance to ask if he knew the man who had apprehended and killed her husband.

Chapter Three

STONY HAD SPENT most of the past six weeks on horseback or in his Jeep tracking a bunch of winter rustlers that had proved particularly elusive. He hadn't been home once since he had rescued Tess Lowell, spending his time instead at a place he kept in Jackson Hole within sight of the Grand Tetons. It was two days before Christmas, and he wanted to be in his own home for the holiday. Even if he had to share it with strangers.

He wondered if they had already left. Maybe Tess had figured out some other way to support herself, and she and the little girl were gone. Perversely, he found himself wishing they were still there.

Tess had been on his mind a great deal lately.

He figured it was simply that he hadn't had a woman in a long time, and he had found the sight of her green cat's eyes staring back at him from an alabaster face surrounded by wispy auburn curls especially attractive. He couldn't help remembering the look of her long legs slipping from under his covers. Or the soft weight of her breasts beneath one of his worn T-shirts.

He wanted her. There wasn't anything rational or reasonable about his desire. It was purely primitive. Like a male beast in rut. He had to have her.

He planned to have her.

His heart beat a little bit faster when he saw the smoke coming from the chimney of his cabin as he traversed the narrow, winding dirt road lined with ten-foot mounds of county-plowed snow that led up the mountain where he lived.

She was still there.

He left the Jeep outside rather than putting it in the garage and let himself in through the front door, anxious to see her again.

He was stunned when he stepped inside. His place didn't look the same. Not that it didn't look nice. The Western furniture had been rearranged to create a cozy sitting area around the wood stove in the fireplace and everything sparkled with cleanliness. She had brought evergreen boughs inside and strung them across the pine mantel, adding splashes of red with small velvet bows. And she had put up a Christmas tree with homemade decorations and lights. There were even presents beneath it.

It felt like a home. But not his home.

He hadn't celebrated Christmas since he had left his father's house at eighteen. It conjured too many memories of his father and the wife and child who had usurped what little place he had in his father's life. He had decided he didn't need anybody to love him. After college, instead of going into his father's lumber business, he had escaped to this mountain hideaway to be alone, renting a place in town until the house was done.

The Christmas tree brought back painful memories of being shut out, of feeling lonely and alone. Only he wasn't alone this Christmas. Not if the fire in the chimney meant what he thought it did.

His nose led him to the stove, where a savory stew was bubbling, apparently intended for supper later in the day. He used a wooden spoon to take a taste. It was delicious, tangy with sage and bay.

The house was quiet. Normally he liked the quiet. Now it irritated him. Where was she? Where was the little girl?

He went hunting for Tess and found her in the guest bedroom, sitting on the side of one of the twin pine beds, reading *The Three Little Pigs* to her daughter. He stood in the doorway, listening to their laughter as Tess huffed and puffed and blew the house down. It made his chest constrict for no good reason he could discern.

He knew when she felt his presence. Her shoulders tensed, and she stopped reading in midsentence. She could likely smell him, feel his heat. He felt hers.

"Why did you stop, Mama?" the child asked. "Did the big, bad wolf blow the brick house down?"

When Tess turned to look at him over her shoulder he felt a shiver of raw sexual hunger roll down his spine. The hairs stood up on his nape. His nostrils flared, and his body tautened.

She recognized the danger. He saw it in the way her pupils dilated, the way her mouth fell open to gasp a breath of air, the way her body readied itself to fight—or to flee.

She couldn't run from him. Not without the child. And the two of them hadn't a chance of escaping.

He saw the anxiety in her eyes, along with an unnaturally heightened awareness. She moved slowly, cautiously, standing and laying the children's book down on the bed.

He suddenly realized the cast was gone. Her arm was healed. But she was still here. He felt a surge of triumph, almost of euphoria. He had the oddest feeling she was going to walk right into his embrace.

He took a step, opened his arms to her, and found them filled seconds later as an exuberant little girl launched herself at him from the bed. He caught Rose only an instant before disaster.

"You came back!" Rose chirped, clinging to his neck like a limpet. "Mama said you would. Mama said you're a nice man. Mama said you're taking care of us."

He scowled. "I thought you didn't like me."

Her tiny brow furrowed uncertainly, and her worried glance skipped to her mother. "Mama?"

"I believe Rose is willing to give you a second chance," Tess said in a voice that shuddered over him.

He met her eyes. "Thanks to you, I suppose."

She smiled, and a spiral of desire drew his loins up tight.

"I might have had something to do with it."

Her smile faded as sexual awareness rose between them.

Rose grabbed his cheeks between her palms to turn his attention back to her. "I like it here," she said. "I can play in the snow, and chop limbs from trees and stuff. Mama said you might let us stay if I'm a good girl. I'm not supposed to say I don't like you anymore," she added naively.

Stony's glance shot to Tess and caught her blush of embarrassment. So that was how she had gotten the girl to change her mind about him.

"I promise to be good," Rose said. "Will you let us stay? Have you seen our Christmas tree? Mama made some presents for you. Do you want to see your presents?"

"Rose," Tess said, "give Stony a chance to catch his breath."

His breath was caught already—somewhere in his chest.

Rose wriggled to be let down, and he set her on her feet. She grabbed his hand and headed toward the living room as fast as her tiny legs could carry her. He glanced helplessly over his shoulder at Tess, who gave him a winsome smile as he was led away. He held out his hand to her at the last possible moment, and she laid her slight palm in his, allowing herself to be tugged after him.

Electricity shot up his arm as he made contact with her flesh. If it hadn't been for the hold the little girl had on him he would have taken Tess then and there. He flashed her a look that told her his intention and saw the trepidation rise again in her eyes. She recognized the trap too late. She had been caught, and he would not let her go until he had assuaged the powerful need in him to have her beneath him, to put himself inside her and make her his own.

TESS HAD REALIZED the danger too late. She had known Stony was attracted to her, felt it all those weeks ago when she had woken up in his bed. She had assumed he was civilized enough to control his impulses. She should have known better. No man was civilized where sex was concerned.

Harry had warned her. "He's dangerous. Stony Carlton is a lone wolf who doesn't live by anyone's rules. Watch yourself around him."

She had laughed at Harry and reassured him that after a year as a waitress at the Buttermilk Café she was perfectly capable of quelling the pretensions of a too-forward man.

She felt a frisson of excitement skate up her arm as Stony's hand tightened around hers. She had known she would have to deal with the attraction between them sometime. She just hadn't thought it would be this soon.

"Mama made you a—" Rose cut herself off, putting tiny hands in front of her mouth. Wide-eyed she confessed, "I'm not supposed to tell. It's supposed to be a surprise."

Stony led Tess to the sofa she had angled in front of the fireplace and drew her down on it. An instant later Rose was in his lap chattering again. Because her daughter asked a question she wanted answered herself, Tess didn't bother shushing her.

"Where have you been?" Rose asked. "What have you been doing?"

Stony's thumb caressed Tess's wrist. Her blood began to thrum, and goose bumps shot up on her arms. She stared at him, mesmerized, as he spoke.

"I've been chasing some bad men up near Jackson Hole."

"Did you catch them?" Rose asked.

"Not yet."

"Why did you come home?" Tess asked.

"For Christmas," he said simply.

Tess and Stony's gaze met over Rose's head. He might profess not to like children. He might have cut himself off from other people by living on this mountain. But Christmas was a time for families. And he had come back to spend it with them.

"I see you've been busy." Stony gestured with his free hand at the decorations and the tree. "Where did you get all this stuff?"

"The greenery I found on the mountain. The rest is ours," she said. "Harry DuBois brought it out here for us."

He frowned. It obviously hadn't yet occurred to him that she would have had to call someone to take her in to the doctor to have her cast removed. She saw the moment it did.

"I never thought about you needing a way to get around," he said. "I guess I should have."

"Harry was wonderful about helping me out when I needed to run errands. I could have called 911 in an emergency," she said.

His hand tightened on hers. It was an act of possession.

"You're hurting me," she said quietly.

His hold instantly loosened. But he didn't let her go.

"How soon before that stew is ready?" he asked.

"A couple of hours. I was just putting Rose down for a quick nap before supper." She smiled ruefully. "I'm afraid that's out of the question now."

He arched a dark brow. "What if I read to her? Do you think she'd lie down then?"

"You'd do that?"

He gave her a roguish grin. "How long does it usually take Rose to fall asleep?"

She realized suddenly why he wanted Rose in bed. So he could take her to his.

"How would you like for me to read to you?" he asked Rose.

"Will you be the big bad wolf?" Rose asked.

"How's this?" Stony growled menacingly in his throat.

Rose shrieked in mock fright and raced for the bedroom.

Stony winked at Tess and headed after the little girl. "I'll see you in a few minutes."

Tess suspected Stony's estimate was optimistic. As excited as Rose was, it would be a little longer than a few minutes before he returned. But she had better use whatever time she had to decide how she was going to handle the situation once she and Stony were alone.

She chewed on her thumbnail worriedly. She didn't believe Stony would force his attentions on her. Unfortunately he wouldn't have to use force. She had felt her body respond to his mere presence in the bedroom doorway, to the heat of him, the scent of him, the predatory look in his dark brown eyes.

To be honest, she had fantasized over the past weeks, as she had slept in the twin bed next to her daughter, what it would be like to spend the night in Stony's arms. If he beckoned, it would be difficult to refuse him.

But they would be two strangers having sex, not two lovers making love. It was tempting to imagine herself lying beneath Stony in his bed, but she wasn't sure she would be able to face herself in the morning. Her husband had been the only lover she had ever had. And though they hadn't been married when they made love for the first time, she had been deeply in love with him.

It had happened on a hot summer night, on a blanket laid out on the prairie grass with the sky and stars above them. She had been so frightened and so very excited, because she loved Charlie so much. She had trusted him not to hurt her. Only, it had hurt that first time, and it had never been as good for her as it was for him. But she had wanted to please Charlie, wanted him to love her as nobody else ever had. He had been a cowboy for one of the ranches in the area, much older than her—twenty-three—and, she had thought, much wiser.

But Charlie hadn't used any protection, not that first time, and not later. She was equally responsible for what had happened. She accepted that now. But her foster parents had been sorely disappointed in her when she told them she was pregnant and had kicked her out of their house. If Charlie hadn't married her, she didn't know what she would have done.

She understood the male need for sex because her husband had possessed it. She had not understood that a woman could feel the same...hunger. That was the only word that described what she was feeling— had been feeling over the past six weeks—for Stony Carlton. She was surprised because she knew she couldn't possibly be in love with him. She hardly knew him. But she was attracted to him in a way she had never been attracted to any other man, even her husband.

She had heard it said that for each person there was a perfect mate, that somewhere in the world the other half was wandering, waiting to be found. She felt that way about Stony, that he was her other half, and that she had to fit herself to him, make him a part of herself, or she would never be complete.

Yet she shied from joining herself with a man she didn't love. It seemed...ruthless, heartless, unfeeling.

Not unfeeling. She was feeling entirely too much. Her body sang with excitement. Her skin tingled. Her breasts felt achy. Her belly curled with desire.

She stood and paced the living room, like a mountain lion in a cage. She wanted him. But she would be damned if she would give in to such animal urges. She was a rational human being. She should be able to act in a cool and rational manner.

She would tell him no. And she would mean it.

She turned abruptly as Stony appeared in the hallway that led into the living room. He stopped where he was, and she had the sense of being prey, of being hunted. She looked around and realized there was no escape. She had to go through him to get to the front door of the house. Not that she could leave without Rose. And he knew it. Knew she was trapped. She saw it in the merciless smile that curled his lips.

"Hello, Tess," he said.

His rumbling voice skittered over her spine and made her shiver. "No," she said.

He quirked a dark brow. "I haven't asked for anything. Yet."

She shoved a wayward curl behind her ear and huffed out a breath of air. Her palms were damp, and she rubbed them down the sides of her jeans, then curled her arms around herself protectively.

"You feel it, don't you?" he said.

"No."

His eyes crinkled at the corners as his smile broadened. "I can hardly believe it myself," he confessed. "I swore off women a while back. You've made me rethink my decision."

"We're strangers," she said pointedly.

He shook his head slowly, the smile suddenly gone. "We've never been strangers, Tess. We've known each other forever."

So he felt it, too. Whatever it was. That strange connection between them, urging their bodies together, promising a wholeness, a joining of souls.

Yet, she fought it. Because it couldn't possibly be right to have sex—it could only be sex—with this man she hardly knew.

"I want you," he said as he took a step toward her.

She held her ground.

"I haven't been able to think of anything but you." He took another step.

She searched for an escape route, a means of avoiding him. There wasn't any. Her body quivered as she stood still, waiting.

"I need you," he said, his voice guttural, animal. His eyes were lambent, lit by a fire that heated her inside. He took the last step that brought them into contact. "I have to have you."

She moaned as his arms slid around her and pulled their bodies together. She felt her breasts crushed against his hard chest even as his palm curved around her buttocks and lifted her until her hips fit into the cradle of his, against the hard, thick length of him.

Her hands rested on his shoulders, yet she couldn't summon the strength of will to push him away. It felt so good to be held by him, so impossibly right!

"This is crazy," she said at the same time she laid her head back so he could more easily kiss her throat. His lips and teeth and tongue feasted on her flesh, sending shivers of sensation shuddering through her body.

She grasped his hair, intending to free herself, but clung to him as his mouth captured hers, his tongue probing until she let him inside.

And then she was lost.

His hips thrust against her in time with the movement of his tongue in and out of her mouth. She groaned and arched her body upward, needing to be closer, resenting the layers of denim and cotton that separated them. His hand slid between her legs, and he lifted her nearly off the ground. His thumb caressed her until she gasped, as he found the spot he had been seeking.

She reached for him with her mouth, needing to be closer, to be connected to him. Then her tongue was in his mouth, tasting him, teasing his inner lip, biting at his lower lip until he growled deep in his throat.

They began tearing the clothes off each other, couldn't get them off fast enough. Buttons popped, clattering across the hardwood floor, zippers came down, T-shirts were ripped off until they stood naked before each other.

His eyes were heavy-lidded, his gaze feral, the pupils huge, making his eyes dark black pools into which she might fall and never return. His body was surprisingly tanned, lean, but muscular, with sinews visible in his arms and shoulders. His belly was flat, his chest furred with black hair that became a narrow black line leading to the curly bush that surrounded his genitals.

Her gaze rose to his. She was panting, unable to catch her breath. Frightened. And exhilarated.

It was going to happen. He was going to claim her. He was going to make her his.

She felt her knees weaken, nature's way of making sure the female was prone, so the male seed could take root. He caught her before she fell and lifted her into his arms, holding her tight against his chest.

She hadn't given a thought to where they were, the fact that her daughter could waken and come upon them.

He carried her to his bedroom, to the king size bed that hadn't been slept in since he had left. He pulled down the covers and laid her on the cool sheets, following her down until he lay atop her. He nudged her legs apart with his knees and put his hand between her thighs to touch her.

She flinched at his touch, though it was gentle. It was almost embarrassing how wet and ready she was. His touch made her even more so.

She stared up at him, wondering what it was about this particular man that made her so vulnerable to him. He reached into the bedside table and found the protection she hadn't thought about.

He really doesn't like children, she thought.

But she was grateful he was taking the precautions that had been the farthest thing from her mind. She knew better. She knew the consequences of being foolish and in love.

Well, she was certainly foolish, anyway.

He spread her hair on the pillow around her face, playing with it, caressing it between his fingertips.

"It's softer than I thought it would be. Because of all those curls," he explained with a smile that made her heart beat faster.

She slid her hands through his hair. "Yours is soft, too." She tugged his head toward her, wanting his mouth on hers.

The kiss was long and slow and deep. Her body arched upward into his, an itch seeking to be scratched.

His hand curved around her breast, and she made an animal sound at the feel of his callused fingertips on her flesh. He cupped the soft mound and held it steady for his mouth. He sipped at her, licked and bit and licked again. Then he suckled her, drawing her nipple into his mouth.

She nearly came off the bed.

He spread her legs with his knees once more and placed himself at the entrance to her. She expected him to thrust quickly, but he took his time, entering her a little way and then backing off, only to return and probe a little deeper, until at last she reached up with her legs around him and urged him inside to the hilt.

He gave a satisfied sigh as he sank into her that was matched by a guttural sound of her own.

Then he turned her face up, so she would be looking into his eyes and began to thrust, in and out, slow at first, and then faster, as his thumb played with her between their sweat-slick bodies.

She began to writhe beneath him, and her eyelids floated downward. She had never felt like this. She couldn't seem to control her body. It began to contract, to spasm in a way that was both frightening and immensely pleasurable. She fought the lack of control, fought the loss of self.

"Look at me, Tess," he commanded. "Come with me," he urged.

She opened her eyes and met his gaze, fierce and intense, deep and dark as a well. She began to slide into the darkness where there was nothing but joy, the two of them no longer separate but joined as one euphoric being.

"You belong to me," he said triumphantly. "You'll always be mine."

It was the last thing she heard before the darkness consumed her.

Chapter Four

THE LOVEMAKING Stony had just experienced far surpassed anything he had ever known with a woman. But he had no idea what had possessed him to utter those unbelievable words at the moment of climax.

"You belong to me. You'll always be mine."

He had to be out of his mind. For years he had been a loner who didn't need anyone. He had no reason to marry, because he never intended to have children. What had made him stake his claim on Tess Lowell—a woman who came packaged with a three-year-old imp?

He hardly knew the woman.

He felt like he had known her all his life.

It had to be lust that had prompted his behavior. He had desired her, so he had taken her to bed. Now that his need was slaked he would be fine.

Only, he wanted her again already, and they had just finished a bout of lovemaking that was indescribably satisfying. He couldn't imagine not wanting her tomorrow and the day after that. So maybe it was something more than lust. But what?

He raised himself on his elbow so he could watch Tess while she slept. The curls around her face were damp with sweat, and her lips were swollen, pouty from his kisses. He had left a love bruise on her throat. He slowly trailed the sheet away, so he could look at all of her.

It was, after all, only another female body. He had seen his share of them. Why did he find this one so exquisite? Nipples the pink of prairie roses. Breasts full and exactly the right size for him. A slightly rounded stomach. The deep russet curls between her legs. And, oh, those legs! He liked the way she had wrapped them around him, her heels digging into his buttocks, demanding to have him inside her.

He was aroused again merely looking at her.

He wasn't sure what he should do about the situation. He had never wanted anyone to love him because he had no intention of giving love in return. Loving left you vulnerable. He had vowed when his father abandoned him never to give anyone the chance to hurt him that way again. It was safer not to ask for love. It was safer to be alone. Even if it was occasionally lonely.

Good Lord! Did he want her to love him?

No, of course not. Though she didn't yet know it, he was the one responsible for making her a widow. Better not to let his thoughts wander in a hopeless direction.

But he had no intention of letting Tess go anytime soon. Even though he could never let himself love her. Even if all they could ever have together was fantastic sex.

Her eyelids fluttered open, and he watched her eyes fill with tears. He kissed away the first salty drop before it could reach the pillow. "What's wrong?"

"I . . . I don't understand what compelled me to do such a thing. I hardly know you." She suddenly realized she was naked before him and scrambled to cover herself.

"Don't," he said, catching her wrist and preventing her from drawing the sheet back over her. "I like looking at you. You're beautiful."

"I'm not. I have stretch marks. And my legs—"

"Are perfect." He smiled. "All of you is perfect." He hadn't noticed the stretch marks. He searched for them and found them along her hips, silvery lines where her flesh had stretched to accommodate a baby. He had a fleeting picture of her grown huge with his child and brushed it away.

"We have to get dressed," she said. "Rose will be waking soon."

"Don't worry. I locked the door. She can't get in."

A rueful smile appeared before she said, "You don't know Rose. She'll stand at the door and yell until we let her in."

"All right. We'll get up. Soon."

She started to rise, but he levered himself over her and kissed her deep and hard. It only took a moment before he was protected and inside her again. He saw her flush and realized she had been wet and hot and ready for him.

She had wanted him again, too.

He threaded his fingers through hers and held her hands prisoner above her head as he slowly thrust into her. He stared into her eyes, willing her to accept his claim. Her chin trembled, and her eyes grew liquid with feeling.

"This was meant to be," he said. "The two of us together. Don't fight it, Tess."

She groaned and arched upward, raising her breasts to him, an offering fit for the gods. He supped, drinking the heady wine she offered him.

"Please," she begged. "Please."

He knew what she wanted. He gave it to her.

Himself. All of himself, enough to make two halves into one whole. Enough to fill them both full. Enough to take them to paradise again.

I NEED HIM. I want him. I never want to leave him.

They were the first thoughts Tess had when she surfaced from a deep well of pleasure for the second time in as many hours. They frightened her.

All she had ever wanted her whole life was to be loved, to belong to someone who would need her as much as she needed him. She had needed and loved each set of foster parents who had taken her in. But the most she had ever received in return was adequate care. She had never been mistreated; but she had never been loved, either.

She thought she had learned her lesson: not to give her love where it wasn't wanted, not to lay herself open to the pain that came inevitably when she had to acknowledge she wasn't loved in return. Even with Charlie—heaven forgive him—she had known her love was not returned.

He had wanted her body, and he had been honorable enough to marry her when she had gotten pregnant. But Charlie had never loved her. He had been incapable of the emotion.

Here she was making the same mistake again. She didn't want to feel what she was feeling. But she didn't know how to stop. She turned and stared at Stony, who was sleeping beside her. She had to get out of here before she let this man sneak past her guard and into her heart.

He didn't like children. He liked living alone. He had no room in his life for her and her child. She would be a fool to trust another man, to give her heart to him. Especially this one.

She had asked Harry about Stony Carlton and gotten few answers. Stony wasn't a lawman, yet he hunted outlaws—rustlers—for a living. She wondered if he knew all about her husband's activities. Her thoughts shied away from contemplating such a possibility. It was better not to know.

Theirs was clearly a relationship doomed at the start. Yet she had let it start. Better to end it now, before she got hurt. Although, there would be hurt, even now. Because, though she wouldn't have wished it, would never have dreamed it, this lonely man already possessed a part of her soul . . . the part that had been missing all her life.

Tess dressed quickly and left quietly, closing Stony's bedroom door behind her. She was relieved that Rose wasn't yet awake and took advantage of the slight respite to spend some time alone in the living room.

She sat cross-legged on the comfortable sofa in front of the wood stove and watched the flames flickering inside the glass door.

She should leave.

Only, where would she go? Her situation hadn't changed one iota since she had accepted Stony's charitable job offer. She didn't want to continue imposing on him now that she was well. But she had tried to find a job in town once the cast was off her arm and discovered there was no job to be had until the season began. She was stuck here until spring.

She felt Stony's presence before she heard him. She supposed a man used to sneaking up on rustlers had to be able to move quietly. It irritated her nonetheless that she hadn't heard him coming. Although, when all was said and done, there was nowhere she could run.

She turned and found him standing right behind her dressed in nothing more than a pair of jeans. He had left the top button undone, and it was plain he wasn't wearing anything beneath them. The aged denim hugged his body like a glove, revealing the vivid outline of his arousal.

She wrenched her gaze away and turned to stare at the fire.

"We have to talk," he said, vaulting over the couch and settling softly beside her, his legs crossed Indian style.

She was aware of him, the heat of him, the musky male scent of him. "I have nowhere to go—"

"—or you'd leave," he finished for her.

"Yes, I would," she said, her chin jutting. "This...thing...between us is...disturbing."

"What if I said I understand what you're feeling?"

She glanced at him quizzically. "You do?"

"Something...unusual...has happened—is happening—between us."

"Something magical," she said quietly, almost wistfully.

His gaze softened as he met her eyes. "You felt it, too?"

She nodded, then ruffled her hair with her hands. "It doesn't make sense."

"All I know is I don't want you to leave right now," he said.

Her lips twisted cynically. "Lucky for you, I can't get another job until the season begins in the spring."

He smiled. "That settles it, then. You'll stay."

"But this...thing...between us... What are we going to do about it?"

"If this is something we both want, I don't see why we can't enjoy each other—take physical pleasure from each other—without letting it go any further than that. I don't want a wife."

"Or kids," she reminded him.

"Or kids," he agreed. "But I do want you."

"And I want you," she admitted. "So we merely take what physical pleasure we can from each other for a few weeks or months without any other commitment between us?"

"I don't see why not," Stony said.

Tess saw more than a few pitfalls in his plan, but she looked at him and realized she wanted to feel again the wholeness she experienced when he held her in his arms. "All right," she said. "Until spring. Agreed?"

"Agreed."

She held out her hand, and he took it. Electricity arced up her arm. She tugged her hand free and stood, needing to put some distance between them before they ended up in bed again.

"When's supper?" he asked. "I'm hungry."

"I'm hungry, too," Rose said, appearing in the doorway to the kitchen.

"You're barefoot again, young lady," Stony admonished.

Rose yelped and raced back toward the bedroom.

"Where's she going?" Stony asked.

"To get socks, I imagine," Tess said with a smile.

"Can she get them on by herself?"

"I'll have to help her. The sock drawer's too high for her to reach."

"You're busy," Stony said, rising from the sofa. "I'll do it."

Tess arched a disbelieving brow. "You don't like kids," she reminded him.

"Yeah, well, I'd like it even less if she got sick. Besides, I'm hungry, and you're putting supper on the table." He winked, a charming gesture that made her heart flutter. "I think I can handle it."

It was impossible not to smile back at him. "Be my guest," she said.

Stony didn't hurry down the hall because he knew Rose would be there waiting for him. He hadn't counted on the little girl's resourcefulness. She had pulled out the bottom drawer of the chest and was standing on it in order to reach the top drawer of the chest, which she had managed to open. The whole chest was in danger of tipping over onto her.

"Rose!" he said, his voice harsh with fear.

She leaned back, startled. Her weight, added to that of the open drawers, was all it took for the chest to begin its tumble.

He snatched her off her precarious perch and caught the falling chest with his hip. He grunted in pain as everything on top came thumping down onto the braided rug.

"What's going on in there?" Tess called from the kitchen. "Is everything all right?"

"Everything's fine," Stony called. "Hunky dory," he muttered under his breath. He clutched Rose tight while he gave his adrenaline-laced heart a chance to slow down. His hip throbbed where the chest had caught on the bone. He leaned his weight back to force the chest upright.

"What's hunk-dory?" Rose asked, apparently oblivious to the danger she had been in.

"It means you nearly got killed, but you didn't," Stony retorted as he shoved in the bottom drawer of the chest with his bare foot. He shifted her onto his arm so he could look her in the eye. "You should've asked for help. You could've been hurt."

"I was getting socks," she said in a small voice, "like you said."

Which made the whole thing his fault, he supposed. It surprised him to realize he cared enough about her to be worried that something might happen when he wasn't around to keep an eye on her.

She pointed to the mess on the floor. "Everything fell down," she said, her chin trembling.

"Yeah, well, nothing's broken," he said gruffly. "We can put it all back again." He knew he was an idiot to be trying to placate a three-year-old, but there wasn't anyone around to catch him at it, so he could do as he pleased.

She wriggled, her sign to be let down, picked up a pewter bookend and handed it to him. "Here," she said. "I can help put it all back."

They worked together over the next several minutes. He picked Rose up at her insistence so she could rearrange everything to her liking on top of the chest. By the time they were done, she was smiling again. Seeing that smile made him feel ten feet tall. It was ridiculous to let her under his skin. Especially when she wasn't going to be hanging around very long. But he didn't call Tess to come get her kid. Hell, he was enjoying himself.

"You still need socks, young lady," he said, folding his free hand around her ice cold toes.

She giggled. "Can you do piggies?"

"Do what?"

"You know. Piggies."

He was afraid he did know. It sounded like fun. But he wasn't going to let her make a substitute father out of him. "You need socks," he repeated.

He opened the top drawer and pulled out a pair of pink socks.

"Not those," she said firmly.

"What's wrong with these?"

"I want the ones with Mickey Mouse."

Stony started to argue with her, saw the mulish cast of her mouth and changed his mind. Tess would be wondering what had happened to them. He searched through the whole drawer and came up empty. "There are no socks in here with Mickey Mouse on them."

"Where are they?" she demanded.

"How should I know?" Frantic to avoid the tantrum he could see coming, he grabbed a pair of socks with white lace and pink bows along the edge. "How about these?"

Her eyes widened, and she said with three-year-old reverence, "Those are only for Sunday school." And then, "They're my very favorite."

"You want 'em, you got 'em, kid." He sat down on the bed and tugged the socks on, despite the resistance of her curling toes.

Rose looked first at the lacy socks and then up at him with something akin to awe. He felt absurdly delighted to have pleased her so well. He took her hand and headed back down the hall. "Come on. Let's go see your mom."

The first words out of Tess's mouth when she saw the two of them was, "Those are her Sunday school socks. She'll ruin them if she walks around in them without shoes."

"I'll buy her another pair," Stony said, exchanging a glance with Rose, who beamed back at him.

"I don't want you spending your money on us," Tess countered.

"It's only a pair of socks," he argued.

"Maybe to you it's only a pair of socks," Tess said, meeting his gaze. "To me it's an hour of work behind a counter." She turned to Rose and said, "Go put on a pair of shoes. Now."

Rose turned to Stony. "Do I have to?"

Stony saw the alarm on Tess's face at this clear sign of rebellion in the ranks. His own mother had died when he was very young, so his father's word had always been law. Now he saw what might have happened if his mother had lived. When there were two adults in a child's life, there was room for appeal. Only, Rose wasn't his daughter, and he had no right to be making decisions that affected her life.

"Do as your mother says, Rose. She's the boss."

To his surprise, Rose didn't argue, just stomped her way back to the bedroom.

He let Rose go, then had an awful thought. "Where do you keep her shoes?"

"On the floor of the closet," Tess replied.

He heaved a sigh of relief. At least she couldn't knock anything over. He realized he was worrying about her—as if she was his responsibility or something. Which she wasn't. And never would be.

But he was plagued with guilt at the thought of how dire Tess's circumstances must be if she had to be careful not to ruin a pair of child's socks. It was small solace that her husband would probably be in jail now, if he weren't dead. Perhaps a good lawyer might have gotten Charlie Lowell off with a short sentence. Perhaps he would already have been out of prison and back helping his family.

They needed help from someone. For a while, so long as Tess and Rose stayed, it might as well be him.

IN THE MONTHS that followed, whenever he went out hunting the ever-elusive rustlers, Stony wore the navy blue mittens and scarf Tess had knitted and given him for Christmas. When he was home, he spent his days playing in the snow with Rose, and his nights loving Tess.

If he let himself think about it at all, Stony had supposed Tess would have less time for him because of the child. It had been that way with his father. Time and attention given to his new family had taken away from time and attention given to him.

Somehow, Tess managed to make him feel a part of the time the three of them spent together. Her warmth and joy enfolded both him and the child. The jealousy he had expected to feel toward Rose—akin to the shameful resentment he had felt toward his half-brother—never materialized. He wondered if it was because he didn't want or need Tess's attention as much as he had wanted or needed his father's love.

Actually the opposite was true. What he needed from Tess far exceeded the care and respect he had wanted from his father. It dawned on him as he lay in bed with her spooned against his groin, his arm under her breasts, that he wanted her love.

The thought terrified him.

What if Tess was like his father? Would he always come second behind the child? Would he always end up with whatever love—and time—was left over after she had given to Rose first. It was selfish to want Tess's love all to himself. But he did.

He was unaware he had made a disgusted sound in his throat.

"What's wrong?" Tess whispered into the darkness. She turned in his arms and pressed herself against him. His body instantly hardened.

"Don't, Tess." He didn't want to need her any more than he already did.

"What's wrong?" she asked.

He heard the caring in her voice. She had plenty of time for him now. Rose was sound asleep. "I don't want to talk about it."

She sat up. "You've been moping around for the past three days. You might as well tell me what's troubling you. Neither of us is going to get any sleep until you do."

"It's nothing," he insisted.

"Fine," she said turning her back on him. "Keep it to yourself."

When he tried to put his arm around her, she shoved him away and said, "Leave me alone."

Here at last was the rejection he had expected from her all along. He refused to accept it.

"Don't turn away from me, Tess."

Tess heard the longing in his voice and recognized the need for what it was.

"Oh, Stony." She turned back into his waiting arms, pressing herself against him. And felt the fire ignite between them as it always did.

She tried not to let her love show, tried not to give too much of herself. When Stony thrust inside her she arched into him. When his mouth captured hers, she surrendered to his passion. When their bodies joined at last, she knew her soul was lost. To a man who didn't want to love her, a lone wolf who couldn't be caged.

Chapter Five

STONY HAD REALIZED over the course of the winter that he couldn't live without Tess. He resented the time he had to spend away from her hunting down rustlers. He was ready to admit he needed her in his life. However, he had some daunting hurdles to get over before that was possible.

He had to tell Tess that he was the man who had killed her husband. And he had to come to terms with the fact that he would always have to share her with Rose, in the same way he had been forced to share his father with a half brother. Both obstacles loomed, seemingly insurmountable, before him. The need to resolve them consumed his waking moments and haunted his dreams.

He knew Tess was aware of his distraction, yet she didn't confront him about it. He was glad, because he had no idea how he could explain why he had kept his part in her husband's death a secret from her all these months. He was living a lie. Unfortunately he knew exactly how Tess felt about lies.

The second time he had returned to his cabin, having left it to return to Jackson following his brief Christmas holiday with Tess and Rose, he had found things achingly familiar, even to the savory stew bubbling on the stove.

At supper he had said, "I don't know when my house has ever seemed so much like a home. Thank you, Tess."

She had blushed, those marvelous roses appearing in her cheeks. "Do you mean it, Stony? Really?"

"I don't lie. Especially about important things."

"That means a lot to me," she said, her eyes downcast. He thought she wasn't going to explain herself, but the rest of it came tumbling out. "I was devastated when I found out that Charlie had been lying to me—about the rustling, I mean. To this day, it's the one thing I can't forgive him."

He had felt a pang of remorse at the lie of omission he was perpetrating. *Tess, there's something I have to tell you. I killed your husband.* The words were on the tip of his tongue. He could hear himself saying them. They remained unspoken.

Surely, when the time came to tell Tess everything, he would find a way to make her understand why he had kept the truth from her. Fear of what she might say and do when she learned his part in her husband's death upset his stomach. He had laid down his fork, the pleasant meal abruptly ended.

During the past four months, the right time had never come to confess. The longer the lie lay between them, the more difficult it became to tell her the truth.

He was running out of time. The snow was melting off the mountain. It was already gone in town. Soon the tourists would begin to arrive, and Tess would leave him to return to her life in town.

Unless he could make things right about what had happened with her husband. Unless he could offer love, even when it meant accepting second place to someone else in her life.

Stony turned on his side in bed and stared at Tess in the early golden light of morning. She was more beautiful to him than ever. And infinitely precious. He should wake her up and confess the truth.

Now was not the right time, either. He had gotten a call last night, a lead on the rustlers who had proved so elusive all winter. He was closing in on them. He had to leave this morning and return to Jackson. He didn't know how long he would be gone.

He lay back down and folded his hands behind his head, staring at the ceiling. He was going to lose her. Deep in his gut he knew it, and he was bone-deep scared.

One second the room was silent. The next, a tornado of energy came whirling in. Rose's pajama-clad behind plopped down on his stomach, and her hands landed flat against his bare chest. He gave a *"woof"* as the air in his diaphragm was pushed out by the weight of her. She rubbed her nose against his and said, "Good morning, Stony."

Her visits had become a morning ritual. After the first nearly embarrassing episode several months ago, he had stopped sleeping naked. It was a small enough sacrifice to enjoy the light she brought with her each morning.

"Hi there, little bit," he said. "What's up?"

"Is it spring yet?" she asked, glancing out the window.

Snow from an early March storm was melting from the tin roof, dripping off the eaves. "Almost," he said.

"You promised to let me ride a pony when spring comes."

"So I did." He rubbed his morning beard. There was no putting it off. "I have to leave for a while, Rose. I have to go chase the bad men again."

She frowned, a ferocious glare worthy of the vilest villain in a penny dreadful. "I don't want you to go."

A sudden lump formed in his throat. He didn't want to go, either. How had Rose become so dear to him when he harbored such resentment against her for the place in her mother's heart she stole from him? It was hard not to be enchanted by Rose, who gave love freely and demanded nothing in return.

She bounced up and down on his stomach. "Don't go. Don't go. Don't go," she chanted.

He grabbed her hips to save his solar plexus. "I won't be gone long. And when I come back, it will be spring."

"Promise? And I can ride a pony?"

"I promise. And you can ride a pony."

"Yippee!" The bouncing started again, as though she were already on the horse, a wild bucking bronc.

"Whoa, there, cowgirl! Wait until you have the horse under you." He slid Rose onto the bed between them, tickling her once he had her down. She giggled delightedly. It was all part of the game between them.

Rose turned to Tess, who by now was always awake and leaning on her elbow with a grin on her face, watching their antics.

"I'm hungry, Mama," Rose said.

"Breakfast will be ready as soon as you put on the clothes I left at the foot of your bed last night," Tess said.

Rose hugged her mother and got a kiss on both cheeks and the tip of her nose before she disappeared into her own bedroom to dress.

Stony proceeded with the next part of the ritual, which involved him and Tess and a few drugging early-morning kisses that occasionally turned into hard, fast and unbelievably satisfying sex. But not this morning.

Tess leaned back and searched his face, looking for something.

"What is it?" he asked.

"Remind me what it is, precisely, that you don't like about kids," she said.

His eyes shuttered immediately. This was forbidden territory, and she knew it.

"Don't shut me out, Stony. Talk to me."

"What is it you want me to say?"

"Explain why you profess not to like kids when I can see with my own eyes how good you are with Rose."

He sat up against the headboard and shoved an irritated hand through his hair. He couldn't tell her about the lie. Maybe he could tell her about this. "It's not something I'm proud of," he admitted, hoping that would be enough to placate her.

"Can you tell me what it is? Will you?" she persisted.

It came out in a rush, before he could stop himself. "My mom died when I was little, and it was just my dad and me. He must have missed my mom a lot, because after she was gone, he lost himself in his work. He never had any time to spend with me. So I spent my time alone.

"When I was thirteen, my dad remarried and started a second family. He changed his priorities. My half brother, Todd, suddenly got all the attention I'd been yearning for ever since my mother's death." He shrugged. "That's it."

He was amazed at her perception when she said, "I see. Oh, I see. Why you profess you don't like children, I mean. You resented sharing your father's love with a baby."

"I don't want to share you," he said, the words torn from him almost against his will.

"Oh, Stony." Tess slipped her arms around Stony's waist and laid her head against his chest, where she could hear his heart madly thumping.

"Don't you know love is boundless?" she said quietly. "It doesn't have limits. I can love Rose and still have more than enough left over for you."

It was an admission of love, of sorts. Even that was more than Tess had intended to say. Yet, she knew Stony had needed to hear her say it.

"Leftovers," he grumbled, pulling her tightly, possessively, against him.

She hesitated only a second before plunging even farther into dangerous waters. "No. Not leftovers. I love you differently than Rose. She's my own flesh and blood. I feel responsibility and delight and devotion when I look at her.

"But you, Stony. You're the other half of me. I've been looking for you all my life. I love you with every particle of my being."

His arms tightened until she thought her ribs would crack. She waited to hear the words from him, needed to hear them. She silently begged the wary wolf to take the few steps necessary to reach the hand she had held out to him.

"God, I love you, Tess."

She felt her nose burn and tears sting her eyes. She clutched at him, a sob of joy clogging her throat. "Oh, Stony. I love you so much."

"What about me?" Rose demanded. She stood beside the bed fully dressed, her shirt on inside out, tugging at the sheet that covered them.

Tess looked at Stony, and they grinned at each other. He reached down and scooped Rose up in one arm and pulled her close to include her in their hug.

"I love you, too, Rose," he said, his dark eyes focused on Tess.

Tess knew what it meant for him to make such an admission. Knew it was only the beginning for them all. There would be no need for her and Rose to leave now. The future loomed before them, bright and shining.

"Are you going to be my daddy?" Rose said.

Tess looked to Stony for his answer, her heart in her eyes. *Say yes,* she willed him. *We come together as a package. It won't mean leftovers. I have plenty of love for both of you.*

He cleared his throat before he spoke, prolonging the moment, a wary wolf until the very end. Then he surprised her, because she had really thought he was going to say yes.

He said maybe.

"We'll see, Rose," Stony said. "We'll have to see."

Tess was startled—almost alarmed—at how quickly Stony extricated himself from their cozy cuddle. "What's the hurry?" she asked.

"I've got to get going," he said. "I have to be in Jackson by noon."

Since it was early morning and Jackson Hole only an hour's drive away, his excuse didn't make much sense. Maybe everything was moving too fast. Maybe he didn't trust her not to give him leftover love. Or maybe he was being forced into a commitment he didn't really want to make. Whatever it was, she felt the lone wolf retreating from her.

"Why don't you go into the kitchen and get out the orange juice," she said to Rose. "Then wait for me, and I'll help you pour it into the glasses."

"Okay, Mama," Rose said.

Tess heard her trotting down the hall. "Can you drop me off in town before you leave?" she asked Stony. "I have some errands to run. I can get a ride back from Harry."

"Why is Harry so willing to give you all these rides?" he said, stepping out of bed and yanking on a pair of jeans.

"Because he's my friend," she said. "Why else?" She got out of bed herself, because that was no place to argue with a man.

"I don't know," he said, plainly irritated as he buttoned up his fly. "Why don't you tell me?"

"Are you trying to start an argument?" she asked, fisted hands perched on her hips. "Because if you are, I'll be more than happy to give you one."

"Am I about to see that famous redheaded temper of yours?" he snarled. "I've been waiting four months for it to erupt. I knew it was only a matter of time."

He was purposely provoking her, but she couldn't seem to stop herself. "I suppose you don't have any foibles."

"My foibles never bothered anybody when I lived alone."

"That can easily be arranged again!" She shot the words back. She was heartsick, listening to herself. She didn't want to leave him. She loved him. But he must want her to leave. Otherwise, he would never have started this argument. Unless there was something else.

"What's wrong, Stony? What is it you aren't telling me?"

Tell her now! Dammit, tell her.

He couldn't. He was too scared. Happiness of a kind he had never imagined was in his grasp. He couldn't take the chance of losing it.

"Dammit, what do you want from me?" he raged.

"I want an answer!" she retorted, easily as infuriated as he was.

He grabbed her arms and pulled her to him, capturing her mouth with his, his tongue thrusting possessively between her teeth. His palms cupped her buttocks, and he dragged her up the front of him until his hard length was pressed against her. She wasn't nearly close enough. He jerked her panties down, tore open the buttons of his jeans and shoved down his underwear until he was free.

He lifted her legs around his hips and thrust inside her, deep and tight. He gripped her buttocks as he drove into her, hard and fast, reaching a climax only seconds later.

He felt the weight of her as his senses returned. She was trembling in his arms. Her breathing was as ragged as his, and he could see the rapid pulse pounding in her throat.

He eased her legs away from his sides and disengaged them, because his knees were threatening to buckle.

It was only then he realized he hadn't used a condom.

He always used a condom. Because he didn't want kids, didn't like kids. Only, Tess had made him realize that was another lie. One he had told himself for years.

"Tess, I..."

"Don't say anything."

"I'm sorry," he said anyway.

Her eyes slid closed, and she clung to him. It took him a moment to realize her knees were threatening to buckle, too.

"Sit down before you fall down," he said, urging her onto the bed. He rearranged his clothing and picked up her silky underwear from the floor where it had fallen and handed it to her. When she didn't take it, he dropped it on the bed beside her.

She sat unmoving. Silent.

He didn't know what had come over him to make him take her like that, without warning. Her continued silence scared him even worse than her anger. "Tess, we'll talk about this when I get back, all right?"

She didn't answer him.

He gripped her chin and forced her to look at him. "You'll be here when I get back." It was an order. One he was afraid she would defy.

She remained mute.

He let go of her chin, and paced before her like an animal in a cage. "Look, I couldn't stand the thought of Harry DuBois pawing you like your boss."

She looked up at him, her brow deeply furrowed. "Harry is nothing like Bud. He's my friend. That's all we are to each other."

"Then you'll come back here and wait for me after you've finished your errands in town?" he asked anxiously.

"You'll have to give me a ride into town first," she said with the beginning of a smile.

"About...about what happened," he said, his hand plowing its way through his hair. "I...I don't know what came over me."

She glanced up at him coyly. "If I didn't know better, I'd think you were jealous of Harry DuBois."

He grabbed at the excuse she had given him for his behavior and managed a sheepish grin. Maybe he had been a little jealous. "You belong to me," he said. "Be here, Tess."

"I'll be here when you get back," she promised.

TESS HAD fully intended to keep her promise to Stony when she made it. She hadn't counted on finding out the dreadful secret he had kept from her for more than four months.

Stony had killed Charlie.

She had gone to Harry's office to ask for a ride home, and he had seen the love bruise on her throat that Stony had put there during their tempestuous lovemaking that morning.

"Why do you stay with him, Tess?" Harry demanded. "I've told you time and again the man's dangerous."

"Not to me," she replied with a smug smile. "Come on, Harry," she said, slipping her arm through his. "Have a piece of pie with me at the Buttermilk Café before I pick up Rose from Mrs. Feeny. Then you can drive us home."

"All right, Tess. Against my better judgment, I'll give you a ride back up to his place."

They were settled in a booth with a slice of the buttermilk pie for which the café was famous in front of them when Harry said, "How soon do you think you'll be coming back to town? There's an apartment coming available in the complex over by the hospital next week."

"I don't think I'll be coming back to town," Tess said.

"You'll have to, once you get a job."

"I don't think I'll be looking for a job in Pinedale."

"What are you talking about?" Harry asked. "What's going on, Tess?"

"I think I'll be staying at Stony's cabin. With him."

"You'd actually consider living with him indefinitely? When you won't even consider a marriage proposal from me. Explain that to me, Tess."

Tess flushed. "He loves me, Harry. And I love him."

"You know nothing about the man!" Harry snarled, keeping his voice down to avoid being overheard by the growing lunch crowd in the café.

"I know everything that's important to know about him."

"Like the fact he killed your husband?" Harry snapped.

Tess's heart actually stopped beating for an instant. "That's..." She started to say impossible, but she had known for months that Stony hunted rustlers for a living. She settled instead for, "Unbelievable."

"Believe it," Harry said. "I don't understand why he never told you himself. I didn't think he had, or you wouldn't be in love with the man."

"He... he was only doing his job." She hated herself for defending Stony, when what she wanted to do was rage at him. She closed her eyes and gritted her teeth to try to stop her chin from trembling.

Why hadn't Stony told her? He couldn't care for her feelings very much, or he would have confessed his part in Charlie's death long ago. He had said he loved her. Had he stretched the truth about that, too? More likely, he just liked sleeping with her, making love to her.

"Stay in town with me, Tess. Don't go back to him. I'll take care of you. You won't have to worry about anything. You can stay at my place and keep house for me."

"Rose doesn't like you, Harry."

Harry snorted. "Rose is stingy with her favors, Tess. Tell me, does she like Stony?"

She hadn't, at first. She loved him now. The thought of how disappointed, how utterly heartbroken her daughter would be if she never saw Stony again, made Tess's throat constrict. It was painful to swallow the bite of pie in her mouth, but somehow she managed it. A tear scalded her cheek as it slid free. She brushed it angrily away. She wasn't about to cry over any man who could so callously lie to her.

She had been a fool again and given her trust to yet another untrustworthy man. Only this time it was infinitely worse. This time the man who had betrayed her held more than her heart. He possessed the other half of her soul.

"Tess, let me comfort you," Harry urged. "Let me take care of you."

"No!" she snarled across the table at him. "The last thing I'd ever do is put my life in another man's keeping. Take me back to Stony's cabin, Harry."

"What for?"

"I want to pack mine and Rose's things."

"Then what?"

"I have a little money saved—my salary for the past four months," she said with a cynical twist of her mouth. "I plan to use it to buy us tickets on the first bus that passes through town."

"Where will you go, Tess?"

"Anywhere that takes me away from here."

Chapter Six

HARRY WAS INCENSED at the way things were turning out. Not only had he lost his chance of getting Tess Lowell into his bed, but it was likely Stony Carlton was going to show up in the wrong place at the wrong time and spoil a real sweet thing. Damn Charlie Lowell for getting himself killed. The replacement Harry had been forced to hire to run his rustling operation wasn't nearly as reliable or as accessible. Every time he had to make contact with the man it increased the danger of getting caught himself.

It had been damn handy over the past four months having a spy in the enemy camp. Not that Tess had known the role she played. But every time she called on him for a ride into town he had known for sure that Stony was out in the field. He had promptly gotten his band of rustlers out of harm's way.

Only, this time, Stony had left home the very day Harry had scheduled a tractor trailer pickup of stolen beef. Harry wasn't sure he could get in touch with his henchman in time to warn him. He had tried phoning his contact in Jackson, but there hadn't been an answer, and he refused to leave an incriminating message on an answering machine.

Harry had no choice except to drive to the rendezvous point himself and warn his man off before it was too late. He didn't want things spoiled too soon. A few more good runs, and he would have all the money he needed to buy himself a ranch someplace nice and warm, like Arizona.

When Harry arrived at the rendezvous, he saw the trailer was already there being loaded. He watched for a long time from seclusion, making sure there was no sign of the range detective before he drove down into the valley.

"Hey, boss," his contact said. "What are you doing here?"

"There's trouble," Harry said. "Stony Carlton is on the prowl. Take what you've got, and you and your men get out of here."

"There's only a dozen more head to load, boss. Then we'll go."

"I said now, and I meant now."

The man opened his mouth to argue before he caught sight of Harry's hand resting on the butt of his police revolver. "Sure, boss. Whatever you say."

It wasn't as simple as it should have been for the truck to make its escape. The rear wheels had stuck in the mud caused by melting snow. Harry had only stayed to make sure the men didn't disobey him, and he was furious when he realized they were going to have to unload the cattle already in the truck in order to break it free.

"Get the damn chute back in place," he shouted into the truck window. "And get those cattle out of there!"

"Not so fast."

Harry whirled and uttered a string of foul expletives.

Stony arched a brow. "Very inventive. Too bad you couldn't have used a little bit of that intelligence to avoid getting yourself into this situation in the first place."

Harry started to reach for his gun.

"I wouldn't do that if I were you," Stony said. "I've already had to kill one man in the past year. I'd hate like hell to make it two."

Stony had to keep an eye on the men in the truck, which caused his gaze to waver from Harry for an instant.

"Don't, Harry!" Stony said as Harry reached for his gun.

"I'm not going to jail," Harry said as he drew.

Stony shot to kill. It was what he had been taught. A wounded man with a gun could still shoot back. Harry grabbed his chest as he fell backward, the gun flying from his hand. Harry's bullet caught Stony's sleeve and ripped through a quarter inch of his arm.

Stony ran up to Harry, to kick the gun out of his reach and to see if there was anything he could do for the man. From the corner of his eye he saw the two men in the truck take advantage of his distraction to shove open their doors and run. They wouldn't get far. Help was already on the way.

"Damn you to hell," Harry muttered, clutching at his chest.

Stony knew the wound was serious. He did what he could to staunch the bleeding, but it didn't look good. He saw from the resignation in Harry's eyes that he knew he wasn't going to make it.

"There's an ambulance standing by," Stony said. "The police will call it in as soon as they get here."

"How did you find us out?" Harry asked.

"I've been hunting you for months, watching your patterns. I took a guess where you would hit next." He shrugged. "I was right."

"How did you know to wait for me?" Harry insisted.

Stony's eyes narrowed. "I didn't. If you hadn't shown up when you did, we would never have known about you. Unless your men gave you up."

"Charlie threatened to do that if I didn't give him a bigger share," Harry said. "That's why I had to kill him."

"What?"

"Shot him with a rifle from the hill behind you."

"But I—"

"Your bullet only wounded him. Mine killed him."

"I don't believe you," Stony said.

"Why would I lie?"

"Why would you tell me the truth now?"

"Because I'm dying. Because I owe Charlie Lowell something. Because I like Tess. Ask the coroner, if you need proof. He'll tell you what kind of bullet killed Charlie Lowell."

Stony's eyes narrowed. "You think this will make a difference to Tess?"

Harry tried to laugh, but coughed blood instead. His voice was weaker, and he had to pause often to catch his breath. "I told her you killed Charlie. She hates your guts. Good luck."

"Damn. Oh, damn."

"She leaving you, Stony. She's taking the next bus out of town."

They could hear police sirens in the distance. But the light was already dimming in Harry's eyes.

"Tell Tess I'm sorry," he gasped.

They were the last words Harry said. Stony closed Harry's eyes and stood to wait for the Jackson police to arrive.

It took an interminably long time to point out which way the two rustlers had gone on foot, get his arm bandaged and explain the circumstances of Harry's death. He excused himself as quickly as he could, pleading a family emergency.

It was an emergency. If he didn't hurry, he wasn't going to have any family. He drove like a crazy man along the treacherous curving roads that followed the Hoback River through the mountains from Jackson south to Pinedale.

Stony was glad he hadn't turned out to be the one responsible for Charlie Lowell's death. It would make it easier in later years when Rose was old enough to be told how her father had died. But he had a feeling his innocence wasn't going to help much where Tess was concerned. He had lied to her. Even though he hadn't known it at the time.

He skidded his Jeep to a stop in front of the Buttermilk Café, where the bus that was headed north from Rock Springs along U.S. Route 191 would stop.

She wasn't there.

For a panicked moment he thought the bus had already come and gone. Then he saw a couple of people with traveling bags drinking coffee and realized he had arrived in time.

Except, if she wasn't here, where was she?

He tried several other restaurants within sight of the Buttermilk Café, figuring maybe Tess hadn't wanted to wait there because of Bud. She wasn't in any of them. He thought of Mrs. Feeny's place, but the elderly woman said Tess had picked up Rose around noon. She had no idea where Tess had gone from there.

Stony was getting frantic. Maybe Tess had hitch-hiked, caught a ride with some tourist passing through town. Didn't she realize how dangerous that was? Surely she would have rejected such an idea, in consideration of Rose. He felt like going from door to door through town looking for her, but he knew the futility of that.

He realized there was one other place she might be.

As he made the last turn up the winding road to his cabin he saw the smoke coming from the chimney and felt his heart begin to pound.

Let her be there. Let her be waiting to hear my explanation. Let her be understanding.

There was no one in the living room when Stony stepped inside. There was a stew bubbling on the stove with the familiar scents of sage and bay filling the room—and making his senses soar.

He followed the hallway to Rose's room, where he found Tess reading *Little Red Riding Hood.* He saw the moment she realized he was there. Her body tensed, and she hesitated ever so slightly before she continued reading.

"What big teeth you have, Grandma," Tess said.

"The better to eat you with," Stony finished in his best big-bad-wolf voice.

"Stony!" Rose cried.

He opened his arms, and she threw herself into them.

"You're home! You're home! I want to go ride a pony. You promised."

"Yes, I did," Stony said. "As soon as you wake up from your nap, we'll go." He paused and added, "If that's all right with your mother."

"Please, Mama. Oh, please," Rose begged.

Tess kept her back to Stony as she put the book between the pewter bookends on top of the chest. She turned to him at last, and he saw the damage his lies had done.

"Stony and I have to talk, Rose. You take a nap, and we'll decide later whether there's still time for a ride before...dark."

Before...they left?

So she hadn't forgiven him. This was only a respite. His work was still ahead of him, convincing her that she belonged with him. That she could trust him with her life.

And with her love.

Rose started to whine. "I want to ride now."

"Do what your mother said, Rose. Lie down and go to sleep," Stony ordered in a voice the little girl immediately obeyed. He couldn't promise her the ride would come later. He had no idea what Tess would do or say. He had no idea whether the two people he loved most in all the world would still be here at the end of the day.

He followed Tess into the living room and sat with her on the couch. The wood stove was lit to take the chill from the room. They watched the flames through the glass door in silence.

"How can I make you believe you can trust me?" Stony asked at last.

"Why, Stony? Why did you lie?"

He took a breath and let it out. "I was afraid of losing you."

She turned to stare at him. "Did you really kill him, then?"

He shook his head, unsure what to say. "I thought I did. It turns out Harry DuBois actually killed him."

"What?"

"I caught the rustlers I've been hunting since the fall. It turns out Harry was the brains of the outfit. Charlie worked for him. He killed Charlie because Charlie asked for a bigger piece of the action."

"Oh, Charlie. Oh, no," Tess moaned.

He reached for her but she jerked herself out of his way. "Please, don't touch me. Not yet."

He had the terrifying feeling she wasn't going to let him back in, that she was going to shut him out. He kept talking. So long as they were talking nothing was settled.

"The rustlers were so successful eluding me because Harry was informing them every time I came hunting for them. Harry knew what I was doing because whenever I was working you asked him to give you a ride back and forth from town."

"Oh, no!"

"Pretty nifty work on his part, I have to admit."

"I'm sorry if I was responsible—"

"If he hadn't been using you, he would have figured out some other way to keep tabs on me. It's harder to catch the bad guys when the good guys are the bad guys."

She shook her head. "I think I know what you mean."

"About us—"

Tess interrupted him. "I want to believe you lied to me because you were afraid of losing me. I want to forgive you."

"But..."

"But I'm afraid, Stony. I gave you my trust, and you let me down. Just like Charlie."

"I'm not at all like Charlie," Stony countered. "I would never purposely do anything to hurt you. I love you, Tess. I want to marry you."

She gasped and turned wide eyes toward him.

He hadn't known he was going to propose until the words were out of his mouth.

"You must be desperate," she said, the hint of a smile teasing at her lips.

His features remained grim. He wouldn't believe she belonged to him until she said yes. "Will you marry me, Tess?"

"I have a daughter, Stony."

"I know that. I love her, too, Tess. Will you marry me?"

Tess had done a great deal of thinking in the hours since Harry had given her and Tess a ride to Stony's cabin. It was a known fact you could never really tame a wolf. Stony Carlton had been a lone wolf for a very long time.

Still, he had come a long way in the months she had known him, from the man who wanted no commitments, the man who wanted no children, who had rescued her in the Buttermilk Café, to the man who had proposed to her and waited now for her answer.

The truth was, there was a great deal of risk involved in loving any man. She had to choose between loving Stony, and spending her life without him. Given those two choices, she knew what her answer had to be.

"I love you, Stony."

Stony let out a whooshing breath and scooped Tess into his lap. "Lord, woman, don't ever leave me in suspense like that again!"

Tess tunneled her fingers into the hair at his nape and pulled his face down for her kiss. "Love me, Stony."

"I do, Tess. More than life."

His mouth came down hard on hers, and Tess willingly surrendered to his strength.

"Are you going to marry me?"

"Anytime you want," she said with a grin.

A small head popped up behind the sofa. "Are you going to be my daddy?" Rose asked.

"Rose!" they both exclaimed together.

Rose stood her ground. "Does it?" she demanded.

They looked at each other and grinned. She was a proper wolf's cub, all right—all spit and fight.

Stony grabbed Rose by the arms and dragged her over the top of the sofa into Tess's lap, so he was holding both of them. "Yes," he said. "I'm going to be your daddy. Is that all right?"

"Do I still get to ride a pony?" she asked.

Stony laughed. "Yep. You might even get one of your own."

"Yippee," she said, bouncing up and down. "I'm gonna have a daddy *and* a pony!"

"You have a nap to finish first, young lady," Stony admonished. "And where are your slippers?" he asked, catching her bare feet in his hands.

Rose slipped out of Tess's lap. "I'm gonna go take a nap," she said. "So I don't need any slippers."

She was gone an instant later.

"Good Lord," Stony said. "Do you suppose they'll all be like that?"

"All? How many did you have in mind?" Tess asked.

"At least one more," he said. "If that's all right with you."

"I'd love to have your baby—as many babies as you'd like."

"Come here, Tess. I want you."

His eyes were feral, dangerous. The predatory beast was back, wanting her, loving her, a lone wolf who had finally found his mate. Some other woman might have tried to tame him, but Tess was perfectly satisfied with the wily rogue who had claimed her for his own.

GABRIEL'S ANGEL

Dallas Schulze

Dear Reader,

Writing about a strong man is both a delight and a challenge. A delight because he's invariably interesting to work with and a challenge because he's likely to step right out of the computer monitor and demand that you do things his way!

Gabe Taylor turned out to be more delight than challenge. A classic cowboy, he's laconic but has a strong sense of humor. He's lonely but won't admit it, even to himself. Once we'd agreed on that much, it was up to me to find a woman to match him. I came up with Angie, a woman whose chatter would fill his silences and whose slightly skewed way of looking at life would appeal to his sense of humor. Then, just to keep him on his toes, I threw in a blizzard, a baby who decides to arrive ahead of schedule and a reason that Gabe thinks he can never fall in love.

I hope you enjoy the resultant sparks.

Dallas Schulze

Chapter One

THERE WAS SOMETHING about the sight of a gun in the hands of a nervous woman that tended to put a real crimp in a man's mood. Particularly when the muzzle of that gun was staring him right between the eyes in a kind of one-eyed glare that made him realize it had been a long time since he'd given any real thought to the hereafter—a location that suddenly seemed much more important than it had a few moments before.

Gabriel Taylor swallowed a curse as he pushed the cabin door closed behind him, shutting out the blowing curtain of snow that had made his arrival here as much a result of luck as his considerable tracking skills. This is what he got for not minding his own business, he reminded himself. You'd think he'd have learned his lesson years ago—it didn't pay to stick your nose into things that didn't concern you. Like as not, you'd get it bitten off.

He stared at the woman holding the gun and debated his options. He could step back out the door, get on his horse, forget all about finding the car abandoned in the ditch alongside the road and pretend he'd never seen the wavering trail of footsteps in the snow. He could just leave this woman, her gun, her soft blond hair and her big blue eyes and try to beat the worst of the storm back to the ranch.

But then, when she froze to death, as she probably would, he'd have that on his conscience. He bit back another curse, disgusted with the situation, the woman, the gun and, most of all, himself.

"I've got a gun," she said abruptly. Her voice was low and husky, the kind a man liked to hear whispering his name in the dark, not telling him she had a lethal weapon.

"I can see that," he said tiredly. "I don't suppose you'd consider putting the damned thing down?"

"Don't move," she ordered by way of an answer.

Her voice was shaking almost as much as her hand, but there was determination behind the fear in her eyes. Moving slowly, Gabe reached up and lifted his hat off. He ran his fingers through his dark hair and grabbed for his thin supply of patience. Trying to look at things from her point of view, he could understand why she might be a little nervous. She was a woman alone, and he didn't look much like a knight in shining armor.

Still studying her, he rubbed his fingers over his chin, wishing he'd taken the time to shave this morning. A full day's growth of beard probably made him look even less respectable than he usually did. But with snow predicted by nightfall, he'd wanted to make use of every minute of daylight to check on the herd. As it turned out, he'd already lost the last hour of daylight, trailing after this woman and her damned gun. The thought of that lost time put an edge in his voice.

"Lady, I don't have any designs on your person except to make sure you don't freeze to death on my property," he told her bluntly.

Her eyes widened in shock, and her mouth dropped ever so slightly open. "G-go away," she told him when she recovered her voice.

"I wish I could do just that, lady. But, like I said, you'll probably freeze to death, and, sure as hell, I'll feel guilty about it. Though why I should, I don't know. Even a damned tenderfoot knows better than to go hiking in a blizzard."

"I wasn't hiking," she protested. "My car died and I thought I could walk to the next town."

"I found your car. If you'd stayed with it, I wouldn't have had to spend the last half an hour trailing you here. The next town is thirty miles in the opposite direction. You'd have been deader than a doornail before you made it five."

"Would you stop talking about me being dead?" she snapped. Some of the fear in her eyes had been replaced by a healthy indignation. "I made it here, didn't I?"

"Blind stupid luck," Gabe summed up.

"Well, I'm here and I'll manage just fine without your help." The fear in her eyes had been replaced by annoyance.

They were very pretty blue eyes, he noted reluctantly. In fact, she was a very pretty woman. Her skin was pale, blushed pink over the cheekbones. Her mouth was a perfect cupid's bow with the lower lip just a little fuller than the upper. Dark brows curved over eyes the color of a Wyoming summer sky, a pure, clear blue that hardly seemed real. With her gold hair curled in soft abandon on the shoulders of her thick black coat, she looked like a picture on an old-fashioned candy box. The coat looked to be about three sizes too big, making it impossible to even guess at her figure. Not that he cared what her figure was like, he reminded himself. She was costing him time he could ill afford, time better spent taking care of his stock.

"Sure, you will." He nodded to the small cast-iron stove and the pile of slightly scorched sticks huddled in the stone-cold firebox. "Where'd you learn to build a fire?"

"None of your business," she snapped, shooting an embarrassed look at the stove. "I'll manage."

"Yeah, right." He took a step toward the stove.

"Stay where you are," she ordered, tightening her grip on the gun as the barrel wavered. "Don't come any closer. I know how to use this."

"Good for you. It'll come in handy if you need to shoot somebody." Ignoring her, he crouched down in front of the stove. Setting his hat on the floor beside him, he began building a fire with quick efficiency. He didn't have to look at her to sense her uncertainty.

"I have a gun," she said, sounding almost plaintive.

"So you said." Gabe flicked his thumbnail over the head of a match and set it to the pile of crumpled newspapers. He waited a moment, watching the flames lick up around the pile of kindling. Pushing the door almost shut, he picked up his hat and stood, turning to look at the woman.

She was staring at him with a mixture of wariness and annoyance that might have amused him at another time. At the moment, he was too concerned with the tasks that remained to be done before the storm got any worse to see much humor in the situation. And he was getting tired of her pointing that .45 at him.

"Are you going to put that damned gun down?"

"N-no."

Gabe's patience ran out. A quick snap of his wrist sent his hat spinning toward her face. Startled, she gasped and jerked back. Before she could recover her balance, Gabe closed one hand over her wrist and used the other to wrench the gun from her fingers. As quickly as he'd grabbed her, he released her, stepping back a pace. Once again, they faced each other across a few feet of scarred wooden floor. But this time, Gabe had the gun.

If she started screaming, he was leaving, he promised himself. He'd take his chances with the snow and let her worry about keeping the fire going rather than deal with a hysterical woman. He eyed her warily.

"That was a rotten trick," she said accusingly. He was vaguely pleased to see that she seemed more indignant than frightened. She had guts. Not much common sense, but she did have guts.

Ignoring her, he flipped open the chamber to empty the bullets out. Only there were no bullets. She'd been holding him off with an empty gun.

"It isn't loaded," he muttered, his voice soft with disbelief.

"Of course it isn't. I didn't want to shoot anybody," she said, her voice cranky as a three-year-old's.

"Did it occur to you that a loaded gun might come in handy? What if I'd turned out to be a mad-dog killer?" Somehow, finding out the gun was empty touched off his anger in a way that having it pointed at him hadn't done.

"I haven't decided you're *not* one," she snapped, rubbing her fingers over the wrist he'd grabbed.

Gabe ignored the twinge of guilt he felt at the thought that he might have left bruises on her pale skin. "I don't think killers are much inclined to build fires to keep their victims warm," he pointed out as he slid the gun into the back of his waistband, letting the weight of it settle against the small of his back.

He looked at her. She looked back, her expression a little sullen around the edges. But she wasn't crying or screaming and she hadn't done anything stupid, like run for the door. Maybe they could make it through the night without too much difficulty. He shifted position and she jumped as if he'd shouted "boo." She was watching him as if he were a hungry wolf and she was lunch. Not that he blamed her, Gabe admitted to himself. He hadn't exactly been what you'd call friendly. He sighed.

"Look, lady, like it or not, we're stuck with each other. The storm is halfway to being a full-blown blizzard. I've been working since before first light. I'm tired, I'm hungry and I'm cold. Right about now, I'd planned to be heading home to a hot shower and a hot meal. If I hadn't come after you, that's exactly where I would be."

"Nobody asked you to follow me," she pointed out irritably.

"Like I said, lady, I don't like people dying on my property."

"Angie."

"What?"

"My name is Angie, not 'lady.' Angie Davidson. 'Lady' makes me feel like a poodle."

Gabe was surprised to feel one corner of his mouth twitch into a half smile. She really did have guts.

"Angie." He moved to touch the brim of his hat, then remembered he wasn't wearing it. He settled for a polite nod instead. "I'm Gabriel Taylor. You can call me Gabe."

"I'd rather call you gone," she muttered.

Gabe's mouth twitched again. "I feel pretty much the same way about you but, like I said, we're stuck with each other, at least until morning."

"Morning?" Her voice rose on a squeak as her eyes widened in shock. "I can't stay here all night. We— *you*—can't stay here."

"I told you. This storm is working itself up into a full-fledged blizzard. Nobody's going anywhere tonight."

And maybe not tomorrow, either. But there was no point in mentioning that just yet. She already looked as nervous as a long-tailed cat in a room full of rockers.

"But I can't stay here," she repeated. "I'm supposed to be in Cheyenne tonight."

"Is someone expecting you?"

"No. Yes—" She corrected herself so quickly that the two words blurred together.

"They'll probably just figure you had the good sense to find a place to stay until the storm blows itself out," he said, pretending to believe there was someone waiting for her in Cheyenne.

"But—" She glanced out the window and swallowed whatever she'd been about to say. Even someone who'd never seen a blizzard could recognize the severity of the storm outside.

"I've got to see to my horse," Gabe said. "Mind if I get my hat?" He gestured to where it lay on the floor just behind her.

Angie turned to glance at the battered gray Stetson hat. Instead of answering with words, she moved out of the way. Gabe stepped past her and picked the hat up. He turned to look at her. Up close, he could see the smudgy thumbprints of exhaustion under her eyes. He caught the slight movement of her fingers as she curled them into her palms, clenching them into nervous fists. But she met his look without flinching.

Guts. Definitely, she had guts.

"Don't let the fire go out," he told her as he settled his hat onto his head. "I'll bring some more wood in when I come back."

Without another word, he turned and strode from the cabin.

Chapter Two

THE DOOR SHUT behind Gabe Taylor's tall figure, and Angie edged closer to the stove. The heat from the tiny fire felt good. She'd been at the cabin a good hour before he'd gotten there and all she'd managed to burn was half a newspaper and her finger. She hadn't realized how cold she was until she felt the warmth of the fire on her skin. Careful not to disturb the small bed of coals, she fed some wood into the stove. She was keeping the fire going because it was the sensible thing to do, not because *he* had ordered her to.

She had the distinct feeling that Gabe was a man accustomed to giving orders and equally accustomed to having them obeyed. But that didn't mean he could bark instructions at her and expect her to jump. On the other hand, the fact that he could build a fire went a long way toward making up for any other failings he might have.

Angie spread her fingers in front of the fire, closing her eyes with pleasure as the heat danced over her skin. Reluctant as she was to admit it, maybe Gabe Taylor's arrival was a good thing. His contempt of her fire-making skills was justified. She'd never built a fire in her life. And she still hadn't, she thought ruefully.

When he came back, she should probably thank him. It was not a welcome prospect. Her reluctant rescuer wasn't exactly approachable.

Her heart had nearly stopped when he had appeared. She'd heard his footsteps on the porch and had grabbed for the gun, praying whoever was out there wasn't dangerous. Her prayers had been answered—sort of. She believed him when he said his only interest in her was keeping her alive. His gruff uninterest could not have been any more obvious. But any man as good-looking as Gabe Taylor was dangerous. If she'd learned nothing else from Ted Sinclair, she'd learned that. Ted had been handsome as sin, too, and he'd turned out to be a total flake.

Angie fed a few more pieces of wood into the fire. Ted wouldn't have had any more idea than she did about how to build a fire, she thought as she watched the flames lick up over the new fuel. So Gabe had already proved himself to be the more useful of the two men. Not that that was much of a compliment, considering just how useless Ted had proved himself to be.

When she heard the sound of boot heels hitting the wooden planks of the porch, Angie was almost grateful for the interruption. She'd already spent more than enough time thinking about Ted the Flake. She didn't want to waste another minute of her life on him.

She settled a pleasant expression on her face as she turned toward the door, determined to try to improve relations with her temporary cabin mate. If they were going to be stuck here together overnight—and she was trying very hard not to think about that—then they might as well be friendly toward one another.

But the door didn't open. Instead, something thumped against it with a blow solid enough to make her jump. Her imagination immediately presented her with images ranging from grizzly bears clawing to get inside to tomahawks embedded in the wood by bloodthirsty savages.

"Don't be an idiot," she muttered out loud. Pressing one hand over her heart in an effort to still its too-rapid beat, Angie reminded herself that grizzly bears did not wear shoes and she had distinctly heard heels hitting the porch floor. As for the tomahawk, her knowledge of Native Americans was culled from watching old Westerns on late-night TV—a notoriously unreliable source of historical information. For all she knew, tomahawks were an invention of some fevered scriptwriter's imagination. And even if they weren't, it was a sure bet they weren't being tossed around these days. Not even in Wyoming, which seemed to have retained more than a bit of the spirit of the old West.

The thump came again, causing Angie to jump once more. Before she could come up with any more wild possibilities, a solidly male roar sounded through the thick wood.

"Open the damned door before I kick it down!"

Gabe. Of course. He'd said he'd be bringing in more wood, so his hands were probably too full to open the door. She hurried across the cabin and pulled the door open as quickly as possible. Gabe strode in and she thought it was a good thing she was standing to the side of the opening. He'd have mowed her right down if she'd been in front of him.

A wave of cold and the crisp smell of snow came in with him. Angie cast one anxious look out at the blowing white flakes and pushed the door shut. If she hadn't stumbled over this cabin, she'd be out in that. The thought sent a shiver down her spine that had nothing to do with the temperature. Gabe was right— it was only blind, stupid luck that had kept her alive.

She hunched her shoulders inside her heavy coat and crept a little closer to the stove. Gabe was crouched in front of the stove, feeding in one of the logs he'd just brought inside. All she could see was his profile, and that was shadowed by his hat. The solid line of jaw did not look particularly inviting, but as he'd said, they were stuck with each other and she was determined to try to make the best of it.

"I'm sorry it took me so long to open the door," she said, trying to sound friendly. "I didn't know it was you."

"Who'd you think it was?" he asked without looking at her. He shut the stove door and stood up, dusting his hands off.

"Well, actually, I considered the possibility that it might be a bear," Angie admitted, aware that it sounded pretty ridiculous now.

"A bear?" Her admission got his attention. He looked at her. He used the side of his thumb to push his hat back on his head as if to be sure that he saw her clearly. His eyes were a clear, deep green and they held a look of pure amazement. "A bear?"

"I know it sounds silly. I mean, I heard your boots on the porch, and bears don't wear boots. Although, as cold as it is out there, I wouldn't be surprised if they'd *like* to wear them." She lifted one shoulder in a self-deprecating shrug. "But that was the first thing I thought of."

"What was the second thing?" He sounded as if he wasn't quite sure he wanted to know.

"I thought it might be a tomahawk hitting the door," she admitted. Her half smile invited him to share the absurdity with her.

"A tomahawk?" He stared at her blankly. "You thought I was throwing tomahawks at the door?"

"Not you. I thought it might be an Apache or something."

"An Apache? In Wyoming? Throwing a tomahawk?" From his tone, it seemed as if he couldn't decide which of the three things was more unlikely.

Angie shrugged. "Hey, the only thing I know about Apaches is that the Rifleman played Geronimo in an old movie."

"The Rifleman? Chuck Connors played Geronimo? His eyes are blue." The last was offered as if it was the one thing he was sure of.

Angie shrugged again. "I told you, I don't know much about the Apaches. Just what I saw watching old movies on TV."

"I wouldn't believe everything you see on TV," Gabe said after a long moment. "Trust me, you don't have to worry about tomahawk-throwing Apaches in Wyoming."

"I trust you." As she said it, she knew it was true. She did trust him. And not just his knowledge of Native American culture. It was crazy, considering her track record when it came to judging men, but she just felt as if she could trust him. He was big, unfriendly and handsome enough to make even her bruised heart beat a little faster, but there was just something about him . . . She felt safe with him.

"I'm going to bring in another load of wood," he said, giving her a wary look. "I'll holler when I get to the door."

"You can kick it," she assured him. "I'll know it's you this time."

"You sure you won't think it's a knife thrower from the circus? Or maybe a soccer player kicking goals against the door?"

Though his tone was perfectly serious, one corner of his mouth twitched upward in something approaching a smile, and there was a glint of reluctant humor in his eyes.

"Don't be ridiculous. Everyone knows circuses spend the winter in Florida and soccer is not played in the snow." She gave him a look of superiority and was rewarded by a deepening of that glint in his eyes.

"My mistake," he said gravely.

"That's quite all right," she said graciously. Her serious expression cracked into a smile that invited him to enjoy the absurdity of the moment with her.

For a moment, she thought he was going to smile back at her, that she might actually get to see what he looked like without a scowl. His mouth almost curved in a real smile. Then he looked at her as if seeing her, really seeing her, for the first time. She saw his eyes widen a little, as if in surprise, then narrow. His expression chilled and his gaze suddenly iced over. He reached up to tilt his hat back down over his forehead.

"Back in a minute," he said, his tone almost formal. He turned away without giving her a chance to say anything more.

Not that she had any idea what she might have said, Angie thought as she watched him leave. What on earth had caused him to poker up like that? For a minute there, he'd seemed almost human and then he'd suddenly turned all icy cold again. She stared after him a minute and then shrugged. Maybe he was shy. It was hard to imagine a man as ruggedly good-looking as Gabe Taylor being shy, but it was possible.

Whether he was shy or just ill-tempered, he certainly did know how to build a fire. She gave the stove an admiring glance. With the door shut, the flames were no longer visible, but heat radiated from the squat little stove. She might be marooned overnight with a man of uncertain temperament but at least she'd be warm. She began tugging open the buttons on her heavy coat.

Tossing the coat over the back of a chair, she smoothed the heather gray cable-knit sweater over the hips of her slacks. It was just as well that the heater in her old car was temperamental. At least she'd been properly dressed for this little adventure in the frozen wilderness.

The sharp thud of boot heels hitting the porch floor sent her hurrying to the door. Unless his personality had undergone a miraculous transformation, Gabe wasn't likely to appreciate a repeat of their earlier exchange. She opened the door just as he reached it.

"Thanks." He brushed past her, and her nose twitched at the smells he brought in with him—snow and pine and an odd musky scent that she associated with horses.

He knelt to arrange the wood along the wall, close enough to the stove to be handy but far enough away to be safe. Angie let her gaze trail down the solid width of his shoulders and back to narrow hips encased in snug denim. It was like seeing a cigarette ad come to life. The man practically radiated masculinity.

"Are we going to need all that wood?" she asked, as much to distract herself as anything else.

"Probably not." He didn't turn to look at her but continued stacking the wood into a neat little pile. "This place is old but it's solidly built. Once it warms up, it'll hold the heat pretty well." He set the last log in place and stood up, dusting his hands off. He reached up to take off his hat as he turned toward her. "I'll keep the fire high for a while and then damp it down a bit and it should... Holy—!"

Gabe nearly choked trying to swallow the second word of his exclamation. His hat dropped to the floor as shock made his fingers go slack. He stared at her as if she'd suddenly grown horns and a tail. Only it wasn't really her he was staring at. It was her belly.

"What?" Self-consciously, Angie smoothed her hands over the solid bulge of her stomach. The way he was looking at her, you'd think he'd never seen a pregnant woman before.

"You're pregnant!" His tone made the words an accusation.

She lifted her chin. "Is that a problem?"

Chapter Three

WAS IT A PROBLEM? Gabe struggled with the answer to that. It wouldn't have been a problem if she'd been a *little* pregnant. But from the size of her, she was a whole lot pregnant, and that was most definitely a problem.

"It's a problem if you're as far along as you look," he answered her after a long pause. "In case you hadn't noticed, we aren't exactly within shouting distance of a hospital."

"The baby's not due for almost three weeks," she told him.

"Good." Gabe felt some of the tension leave him. "I don't want to play midwife."

"Don't worry, you won't have to," she said tartly.

There was an awkward silence. It occurred to Gabe that maybe his reaction had fallen a little short of good manners. From her expression, Angie agreed. He bent to pick up his hat. He turned it between his fingers, uneasily aware that he owed her an apology and at a loss for words.

"I guess I overreacted," he said finally.

"Think nothing of it. I *enjoy* having it pointed out that I'm big as a house." She tugged the hem of her sweater down with a defiant little gesture that drew attention to the swell of her stomach. "If you hadn't mentioned it, I might have thought it slipped your attention."

"It was just that... Well, you looked like..." Gabe stopped, aware that he was probably making things worse. "Sorry," he finally muttered, feeling like a total clod.

There was a brief silence while Angie seemed to weigh his sincerity. She must have decided in his favor because she smiled suddenly. "That's okay. I guess it must have been quite a shock. I didn't realize how well that old coat hid my stomach."

"Very well," he assured her, trying to keep his eyes off her belly. Three weeks? She looked as if she was already three weeks overdue. Maybe it was just that she wasn't very big to start with, which made her stomach seem so enormous. She wasn't more than an inch or two over five feet and she was small boned and delicate looking.

"It belonged to my Aunt Margaret."

Gabe dragged his eyes up to her face. "What did?"

"The coat. She was always very heavy. When she turned forty, she bought herself a membership in a gym. She told the family she wasn't planning on losing weight, she just wanted to be healthier. Only she started losing weight anyway. It's pretty hard *not* to lose weight when you're doing aerobics five times a week. And then she started lifting weights, too. Two years later, she was wearing a size five. She cut her hair in this spiky little crew-cut kind of thing. And then Uncle Al divorced her.''

"Because of the haircut?'' Gabe asked, unwillingly drawn into the story.

"No. He said he didn't mind the haircut or the thong leotards but he drew the line at Boris.''

"Boris? She was having an affair?''

"No. That was later. Boris was her dog. He's a rottweiler. Aunt Margaret bought him because she said she needed protection when she was going to the gym at midnight.''

"Midnight?'' He tried to imagine going out at midnight to lift weights or jump up and down in an aerobics class.

"She belonged to this gym in L.A. that was open twenty-four hours and she was taking two classes a day, one after work and one at midnight. It was because of the one at midnight that she bought Boris. Only Boris didn't like Uncle Al. He bit him. Twice. So Uncle Al said she had to make a choice—him or the dog.''

"And Boris won?''

"How'd you guess?'' She gave him a surprised look.

"I'm starting to see a pattern.'' Which was a pretty frightening thought.

"Well, you're right. She divorced Uncle Al and she and Boris moved from L.A. to New York. She changed her name to Crystal because it was more in keeping with her image. Only no one in the family ever calls her that, so she doesn't talk to us much anymore. Last I heard, she was teaching five aerobics classes a day and living with some guy named Deke who can bench press a gazillion pounds or something. I guess Boris likes Deke. Or maybe he just figures Deke might bite back.

"And that's how come I was wearing Aunt Margaret's old coat," she finished cheerfully.

"Boris didn't like the coat, either?" Gabe guessed. He felt a little like Alice at the Mad Hatter's tea party. There had to be a reason they were discussing her aunt's coat, but he couldn't put his finger on what it was.

"I don't know what Boris thought of the coat, but Aunt Margaret got rid of her whole wardrobe. Well, she had to, really. Even if she hadn't cut her hair and changed her name and divorced Uncle Al, she'd lost all that weight and nothing fit her anymore. So she had to buy all new clothes, of course."

"Of course."

"She threw almost everything out, but my mother rescued a few things that she thought were just too good to let go. And the coat was one of them. I thought it was kind of silly to save a coat that was five sizes too big for anyone in the family, but it came in handy on this trip. I knew I'd need something warm, but I didn't want to spend a lot of money buying a coat that I'd only be able to wear for a few weeks. Actually, I didn't *have* a lot of money, even if I had wanted to spend it. So it turned out pretty handy for me. I guess everything happens for a reason."

"I guess so." But if there was a reason for this conversation, it escaped him.

Gabe shook his head a little, like someone coming out of a dream. The cabin was starting to get dark. Twilight was coming early because of the storm. He tossed his hat on the bed and reached for the front of his coat. "Why don't you sit down? I'll get a lamp lit and then see what we've got to eat."

"I'm pregnant, not sick," she told him a little huffily. "You don't have to coddle me."

Gabe raised his eyebrows and gave her a cool look. "This cabin's barely big enough to swing a cat. If you sit down, it'll give me more room to work."

"Oh." Her cheeks flushed, she abruptly sat.

Gabe tugged at the front of his coat, popping open the snaps. The sound was loud in the suddenly quiet room. Since his arrival at the cabin, silence had been a rarity. Whether she was issuing threats or telling him about her aunt, Angie had talked almost nonstop. Once she'd decided he wasn't going to harm her, she'd turned out to be as friendly as a kitten. And as noisy as a magpie. To a man accustomed to spending a lot of time alone, the sudden quiet should have been a welcome relief. Instead, he found himself wondering if he'd hurt her feelings.

He shot her a quick look as he tossed his coat onto the narrow bed next to his hat. She was sitting in the straight-backed chair like a schoolgirl called into the principal's office. All it needed to complete the picture was for her to twist her hands together in her lap. Except she didn't *have* a lap to twist them in. The sight of her bulging stomach added to his guilt for some reason he couldn't quite define.

He hadn't said anything harsh, he thought defensively. But she was still sitting there, and he was still feeling guilty. He lifted the lantern off its hook on the wall and checked the fuel level. He could feel Angie watching him, saying nothing. He lit the lamp and adjusted it. Damn but she had the biggest, softest eyes, and right now, they held an expression that made him think of a spanked puppy.

He groped for something to say. These past few years, he'd spent more time talking to cattle than he had to people, and his conversational skills were more than a little rusty. He settled for the safely banal.

"Are you hungry?"

"Starving."

Her smile lit her whole face and made her eyes sparkle in a way that took his breath away. He couldn't ever remember seeing anyone look so completely alive. With an effort, he dragged his eyes from her face.

"I'll see what we've got."

He felt her eyes following him as he moved over to the tiny kitchen area. There wasn't much to it—a chipped porcelain sink supplied by an old-fashioned hand pump and a few wooden crates that someone had nailed to the walls years before to serve as cupboards. It was stark but Gabe had made do with less.

"Since you said you didn't want me to freeze to death on your property, I guess this cabin must belong to you?"

"It's on my land but I don't use it much." He got out a can of soup and a can of pressed meat. Did pregnant women eat regular food or were they supposed to stick to some special diet?

"Only when you're rescuing stranded tenderfeet?" Angie asked. Out the corner of his eyes, he saw her dark brows hook together in a sudden frown. "Or is that 'tenderfoots'? Is there a plural for 'tenderfoot' or do they just come in the singular?"

It took Gabe a moment to work his way through the tangle of questions and self-given answers. He sorted through several possible responses and finally decided to skip the whole question, whatever it had been.

"You like tomato soup?"

"Hate it." She wrinkled her nose in a comical grimace of distaste. "But if it's that or starve, I'll eat it."

"How about vegetable beef?" He held up a second can.

"Much better. I don't suppose you have any bread and butter to go with it?" she asked wistfully. "I was going to treat myself to a steak in Cheyenne."

"No steak. No bread. No butter. Crackers are about as close as it gets."

She wrinkled her nose again. "I must have eaten a hundred boxes of crackers when I was having morning sickness. But I'm hungry enough to eat the box right now."

"I don't think we'll have to resort to that. There's plenty of food."

"Good. The best thing about being pregnant is that you get to eat a lot and no one says a word about it. I love to eat. Lucky for me, I've got a fast metabolism so I don't put on weight easily. Not that you can tell it by looking at me now," she said cheerfully.

Gabe suspected a fast metabolism had less to do with it than the number of calories she burned just talking. He opened the can and poured the soup into a battered aluminum pot. While he worked, Angie talked. She told him that she was heading for West Virginia to stay with her brother and his wife; that she'd lived in California her whole life and had decided it was time for a change. She liked what she'd seen of Wyoming so far, but she thought it would take some time to get used to the vast emptiness of it.

Her car was named Bonnie because it was blue. "You know, like in the movie?" She accepted his grunt as assent, and Gabe didn't correct her. What movie? Bonnie? What kind of a name was that for a car? Come to think of it, why name a car at all?

She wasn't sure what was wrong with Bonnie. She'd checked the spark plugs and the oil because her brother had taught her to do that when she was in high school, but that was the full extent of her automotive knowledge. She hoped there was nothing seriously wrong with Bonnie because she didn't have a lot of money to pour into fixing up her car. She didn't plan on staying with her brother and his wife more than a few weeks after the baby was born. She was going to get a job and a place of her own.

"Not that I expect it to be easy, because I know jobs are hard to find." She fingered a chip on the edge of the old porcelain bowl he'd set in front of her. "I have a degree but it's in clothing design. Not much demand for that."

She wrinkled her nose across the table at him, and it occurred to Gabe that he'd like, very much, to kiss her, wrinkled nose and all. He looked down at his bowl of soup and wondered if he'd gone completely out of his mind. He'd obviously been spending too many hours with the cattle when he was finding himself wanting to kiss a woman he barely knew, one who never shut her mouth and was nine months pregnant to boot.

"Where'd you get the gun?" he asked, changing the subject abruptly.

"Mark gave it to me. That's my brother. Mark's a firm believer in people being self-sufficient. His whole basement is full of food in case there's ever a disaster, and he and his wife go out on survival treks every chance they get."

"He planned on you hunting your own food with a .45?" Gabe asked dryly.

Her laughter was so rich and warm that Gabe found himself half smiling in response to it. "No. But when I moved out on my own, he thought I should be able to protect myself. I really *do* know how to use it," she told him very seriously. "I didn't want to leave the gun in Bonnie but I didn't want to dig the ammunition out of the trunk. Besides, I didn't expect I'd need to shoot someone, so I didn't think I'd need bullets."

"Can't say I'm sorry." The memory of the gun's single eye staring him in the face put a slight edge in Gabe's voice. "But you could have been in real trouble with someone else."

"But you weren't someone else, so everything turned out okay." She frowned. Her teeth tugged at her lower lip. "I don't think I'll tell Mark about this, though. He'd think I was an idiot to try and hold you off with an unloaded gun. And I suppose he'd be right," she admitted with a sigh. "No doubt, Marla wouldn't have needed a gun. She'd have had you pinned to the floor in a third nelson."

Gabe choked on a mouthful of hot coffee. "Half nelson. It's a half nelson."

"Whatever." Angie shrugged her indifference to the correct terminology. "Marla would have done it."

"Who's Marla?" He still couldn't figure out how she managed to get him interested in these convoluted stories of hers.

"Mark's wife. Mark and Marla." She wrinkled her nose. "Can you imagine going through life that way? Sounds like a dance team from the Lawrence Welk show." She sighed. "But Mark thinks she's perfect."

"You don't agree?"

"She's okay." Angie lifted one shoulder in a half shrug. She ran her fingertip along a crack in the battered table, her eyes on the aimless movement. "She's tall and slim and gorgeous and frighteningly competent at just about everything. It's a little intimidating."

"Why go live with them?" There was nothing else to do, he told himself, excusing his uncharacteristic curiosity. He might as well listen to her talk.

"Because I need someplace to stay, and they're my best option. Mark and I were born kind of late in our parents' lives. My dad is in his sixties and they want to retire and move to Arizona. A lot of their friends have already moved there. But they can't do that if I'm living with them. And I don't have the money right now to get a place of my own and manage until the baby's old enough for me to find a job. Mark said I was welcome to stay with them as long as I want. I'm not sure

Marla shares his enthusiasm," she admitted with a sigh. "But it's only for a few weeks."

Gabe noticed that there was one glaring omission in her story. She hadn't said a word about the baby's father. He'd noted that she wasn't wearing a wedding ring. But that didn't mean a whole lot these days. She might not like wearing rings or she and the father might not be married. But from the way she spoke, he didn't even seem to exist.

Maybe the guy was dead. And if he wasn't, he ought to be for letting Angie make a trip like this in her condition. Maybe the guy didn't care about her or the baby. It happened all the time, but having met Angie, he found it hard to imagine the kind of man who'd just turn and walk away from her. Gabe was surprised by the depth of anger he felt toward the unknown man. It might be sexist, but if he'd ever seen a woman who needed someone to look out for her, it was this one.

She had guts but she was too damned trusting. Look at the way she'd opened up with him. She didn't know him from a hole in the wall but she was treating him like an old friend. Her trusting nature wasn't his problem, though. With luck, the snow would stop tonight and tomorrow morning, he'd ride back to the ranch, bring back something with four-wheel drive, get her car fixed and get her on her way. She'd go to West Virginia and her brother and his Amazon wife. He'd go back to his ranch and get on with his life. In a few weeks, they'd have forgotten each other's names.

In the meantime, listening to her talk was a relatively painless way to spend an evening.

Chapter Four

SHE WAS TALKING too much. Angie could hear herself going on and on but she couldn't seem to make herself stop. Any minute now, Gabe was going to reach the end of his patience and strangle her.

"I think you're the first real cowboy I've ever met," she heard herself saying in the perky voice of a game-show hostess. "Not that I haven't seen lots of guys wearing cowboy boots and hats, but most of them aren't the real thing. You obviously are—the real thing, I mean."

"I like to think so," he drawled. He looked at her across the table, those deep green eyes holding a faintly questioning look, as if her sanity was in doubt.

Not that she blamed him for wondering. She was starting to have a few doubts herself. *You're the first real cowboy I've met.* Had she really said something that stupid?

"There probably aren't many real cowboys in Los Angeles," she rattled on. "Lots of movie cowboys but not many real ones." She toyed with her spoon, dabbling it in the thin film of soup left in the bottom of her bowl. "We don't have a lot of cows in Los Angeles."

"I'd heard that."

"Too many people, I guess." *Oh God, where was a good case of laryngitis when you needed it?*

"I reckon so."

His drawl seemed exaggerated, but when she sneaked a glance at his face, his expression was completely solemn.

"I guess it takes a lot of room to raise a cow." *Shut up! You sound like an escapee from a mental ward.*

Gabe seemed to give some consideration to his answer. This time, there was no doubting the thickening of his drawl. "Well, it takes a mite more room than raising a dog and a mite less than raising a giraffe. I wouldn't recommend them as pets. They're hard as hell to housebreak."

Angie felt the color creep up from her throat, spreading across her face until her cheeks felt as if they were on fire.

"I'm talking too much, aren't I?"

"I don't mind."

"I don't usually rattle on like this. It's just, when I get nervous, I tend to talk. And once I get started, I just keep going."

"You don't have to be nervous about being here with me," he told her, his tone making the words a promise.

"It's not because of you."

It wasn't exactly a lie. She wasn't afraid of him but she had to admit that she might have been a little more

comfortable if he'd been five foot tall, weighed a
hundred pounds soaking wet, had a weak chin and
wore glasses. But he was at least a foot too tall for that
picture, with the shoulders that filled out a plain blue
chambray shirt in a way that ought to be illegal. The
last word that could be applied to his chin was *weak*
and those deep green eyes didn't look as if they needed
any help seeing clearly. Add to that a wealth of thick
black hair, and you had a package that radiated masculinity. Even in her current, highly pregnant condition, it was a bit much to find herself confined with all
that testosterone.

"It's not you," she said firmly. "I know I can trust
you."

His mouth twisted in something that wasn't quite a
smile. "You'd have a hard time finding many people
around here who'd agree with you."

It was the first piece of personal information he'd
given her, unless you counted his name, and from the
way his expression immediately closed up, he was as
surprised by his words as Angie. She longed to ask
what he meant but knew he'd never give her an answer.

"I've got good instincts about people," she said instead. "I'm never wrong. Well, almost never," she
amended, smoothing one hand over the bulge of her
stomach and considering just how wrong she'd been
about Ted.

"Instincts aren't always reliable," he said, as if reading her mind.

"Maybe not. But if you can't trust yourself, who can you trust?" She refused to let Ted Sinclair make her doubt herself any more than he already had. Trusting him had been a small error in judgment. Okay, maybe it had been a big error, she admitted, feeling the weight of her belly.

"It's not that I'm nervous about being here with you, exactly," she told Gabe. "It's just...everything. This cabin, the snow, my car dying." She waved one hand to encompass the whole situation. She sighed. "I expected to be in a motel in Cheyenne by now."

"You'll be there tomorrow night." He stood and picked up their bowls. "I can open another can of soup if you're still hungry."

"No, thanks. That was plenty." She hadn't really been as hungry as she'd thought, and it had been an effort to force down the last few spoonfuls of soup.

He carried the bowls over to the sink. Angie thought about offering to help, but as he'd pointed out, there wasn't really room for two people to work. She leaned forward a little, trying to ease the dull ache that had settled in her lower back. Maybe trekking through a snowstorm hadn't been the smartest thing she could have done, she admitted. Especially not when she was carrying around all this extra weight.

Smoothing one hand over her stomach, she tried to remember what it felt like to be slim. It seemed as if she'd been waddling around like an overfed duck forever.

"You okay?"

She looked up to find Gabe watching her. "I'm fine." She grinned at his uneasy expression. "Don't worry. I'm not going to be waking you in the middle of the night and demanding that you drive me to the hospital."

"I'm relieved to hear it."

"I was just thinking that it will be nice to have a waist again." Her wistful tone startled a half smile out of him, and she found herself wondering if he ever smiled all the way. So far, she'd only been able to tell if he was amused by that odd little quirk of his mouth and a subtle lightening of his eyes.

"Three more weeks," she said, half thinking out loud. "I should have time to settle in at Mark's house and get a feel for just how difficult it's going to be living with Marla the Marvelous."

"Marla the Marvelous?" That funny almost-smile came and went again as he finished drying the dishes.

"I suppose that isn't a really good attitude," she admitted with a sigh. "It's just hard to warm up to a woman who manages to look good even in camouflage."

"I can see where that might make things difficult," Gabe agreed.

"You can laugh," she said, ignoring the fact that he hadn't even cracked a smile. "But you don't have to live with her. She probably serves army rations for dinner and sleeps with an Uzi under her pillow."

"That could be a problem if she's the kind of woman who wakes up on the wrong side of the bed."

"Ohmigod!" Angie stared at him as if seeing him for the first time.

"What's wrong?" Gabe looked back at her, his dark brows raised in question.

"Are you married?"

His brows climbed a little higher. Angie flushed, realizing how abrupt the question had been. She was batting a thousand tonight, she thought. Yammering about cows in Los Angeles and now blurting out that question as if she were five years old and didn't know any better.

"I'm not married," he said slowly.

"It just occurred to me that, if you were married, your wife would be worried sick about you," she explained. "I'd hate to think that I'd managed to spoil not just your night, but your wife's."

"No wife."

"Good." The single word sounded abrupt, and she hastened to smooth it over. "I mean, good that there's no one to worry—not good that you're not married. Though it could be good that you're not married, too. If you don't want to be married, which I assume you don't or you would be. Married, I mean." Angie let her voice trail off, aware of the dazed look in Gabe's eyes.

"I suppose I didn't explain that very well," she said in a very small voice.

"I followed it just fine," he assured her. The knowledge seemed to worry him.

"The way I'm acting, maybe I should be on my way to Oz to talk the Wizard into giving me a brain instead of going to West Virginia."

"From the sounds of it, Marla the Marvelous has the Wizard beat, hands down."

Angie's smile was weak. He really had been awfully nice about this whole mess. Some men might have held a grudge over the way she'd pointed a gun at him, even if it had been empty. She rubbed the ache in her back and resolved to restrain her rambling tongue. Gabe must be counting the hours until he could get rid of her. She'd caused him so much trouble. The least she could do was make sure that nothing else went wrong before morning came.

ANGIE WOKE from a restless sleep, aware that something was not right even as she opened her eyes. The twinges of pain that had been coming off and on all evening had solidified into something much more powerful. She caught her breath as a giant fist seemed to grab her stomach and squeeze.

It felt just the way labor was supposed to feel, she thought as she swallowed a groan. Only it couldn't be labor because the baby wasn't due for almost three weeks. And first babies were never early. Or was it that they were often early? Damn, why hadn't she paid more attention to that part of the book?

The pain eased and she drew a deep, cautious breath. It wasn't labor, of course. It was probably those stale crackers she'd eaten. It was just a stomach ache. It certainly wasn't...

"Gabe." Her voice rose on the name, turning it into a wavering cry.

Chapter Five

"WHAT?" Gabe came awake with a weary sort of acceptance. What on earth had made him think that she wouldn't talk in her sleep? If he'd learned one thing about Angie Davidson, it was that she could probably talk right through her own funeral. Not that he'd been sleeping all that well, anyway. He rolled onto his back, grimacing at the hardness of the floor beneath him. The cabin was well stocked with old blankets and sheets, but a couple of blankets didn't provide much padding between him and the floorboards.

"You remember when I told you that I wouldn't be waking you in the middle of the night to take me to the hospital?" she asked in a thin little voice.

"Yeah." Damn, didn't the woman ever run out of things to say? Gabe stared up at the darkened ceiling, wondering why it hadn't occurred to him to gag her before he'd lain down.

"I lied."

"About what?" He stifled a yawn. What was she rambling on about now?

"I think my water just broke."

It took a moment for the meaning of her words to sink in. What the hell was she talking about? What water? The hand he'd been running across his face stopped on his chin, his eyes popping wide open above it. Her water? Realization hit him with the force of a blow to the solar plexus, literally knocking the wind from him for a moment.

He bit off a curse as he rolled to his feet and reached for the lamp he'd set on the table before lying down.

"Don't light the lamp!" she shrieked as soon as she heard the clink of metal on glass.

"Don't...? It's blacker than the ace of spades in here. We've got to have some light."

"No. I don't want you to see me."

There was a long pause. Gabe groped for his patience and self-control. The woman had just told him, if he understood things correctly, that she was about to have her baby, the baby she'd promised him wasn't due for another three weeks, the baby she'd sworn he wouldn't be playing midwife to. They were miles from the nearest house and a hell of a lot farther than that from the nearest doctor, or a hospital. They had no electricity, no running water, and he had never in his life so much as held an infant, let alone delivered one. And she was worried about his *seeing* her?

"Are you sure your water broke?" His tone was so carefully controlled that he hardly recognized it as his own.

"Yes."

"Does that mean the baby's on the way?"

"I...I think so."

"You don't think this is a false alarm?" he probed, just to be sure.

"N-no."

His only response was the scrape of a match against the table. A moment later, the little cabin was filled with soft golden light. He blew out the match, dropping it in the dented metal ashtray that sat in the middle of the table. The sight of the ashtray made Gabe long suddenly for a cigarette. He had given up smoking five years ago and rarely thought about it anymore. But a few hours in Angie's company was enough to make him long for the soothing rush of nicotine in his lungs.

"Don't turn around!"

"I can't do much with my back to you!" he snapped.

"I don't want you to see me," she repeated in a very small voice.

"You're not making sense," he argued, struggling for patience.

"I know. I'm too scared to be sensible," she muttered miserably.

"There's nothing to be scared of," he lied. Without giving her a chance to argue, he turned around, carrying the lamp with him as he moved over to the bed. "Everything's going to be all right."

Gabe only wished he could be as sure as he sounded. He set the lamp in its place. He crouched down beside the bed, trying to think of some concrete piece of re-assurance he could offer her.

She looked so small and so scared that he felt all his irritation fade away. He was scared but he wasn't the one about to give birth under less than ideal circumstances. He could hardly have blamed her if she'd been howling like a child. But though her chin quivered a little and her eyes were suspiciously bright, she hadn't given in to her fear.

Her courage touched him in a way that hysterical sobbing wouldn't have. He found himself wanting, more than anything, to erase the fear from her eyes. He caught her chin between his thumb and forefinger and tilted her head back until her eyes met his. "You're going to be fine," he told her firmly.

Please, God, let me be telling the truth.

"Have you ever delivered a baby?" she asked in a tone full of desperate hope.

"Hundreds of them," Gabe said recklessly.

"H-hundreds?" The word rose on a surprised squeak.

"Sure. They just all happen to have had four legs."

"Four legs?" She gawked at him. "*Four* legs?"

"Two legs has got to make it easier," he said with grim humor.

There was a moment of dead silence, and then Angie giggled. It held a watery note but it was definitely a giggle. "Cows? You're talking about delivering cows?"

"They're calves when you deliver them," he corrected her solemnly. "And I've got to admit that the mama does most of the work."

She giggled again. "I've been complaining for weeks about feeling big as a cow, so I guess you've got the right credentials."

"The best," he told her, wishing it were true. "The first thing to do is to get you out of these wet covers."

Before he could move her, Angie's fingers dug into the solid muscles of his forearm. Her eyes were big and round with fear. "I'm scared, Gabe. It's too early."

He racked his brain for something to reassure her. "It's your first baby, right?" She nodded. "First babies are early all the time."

"Are they?" Her eyes brightened. "I thought they were but then I thought maybe the book said they were usually late. You're sure it's that they're early?"

"I'm positive," he lied firmly. What the hell, it might be true. And whether it was or wasn't, this baby was apparently on its way. "Besides, with all that walking you did this afternoon, you probably made the poor kid seasick and he's decided he wants out before you take up aerobics like your aunt and her boyfriend, Boris."

"Boris is the dog," she told him, giggling weakly. "Deke is the boyfriend, and I don't think he does aerobics. He lifts weights."

"Whichever." He didn't care if Deke and Boris both lifted weights. All he cared about was getting this kid into the world safe and sound.

He just hoped to God that there was nothing wrong with it when it arrived.

"I CAN SEE THE HEAD! Just a little more work. Push, Angie."

"You push!" She panted furiously. "I've been pushing for hours. I'm too tired to...Oh, God!" The final word rose into something approaching a scream. Angie's body arched with the force of the contraction.

"That's it. Come on. One more time," he said, coaxing and ordering her at the same time.

"I can't," she wailed, her voice thinned with exhaustion and pain.

"Yes, you can." He looked up, his gaze meeting hers across the swollen mound of her stomach. Her eyes burned like blue flames against the pasty white of her skin. Her hair clung to her face in sweat-dampened strands. She looked on the edge of collapse. But at that moment, Gabe didn't think he'd ever seen a more beautiful woman.

She'd shown more guts in the past six hours than he'd ever have thought possible. In the early stages of labor, she'd hidden her fear with a barrage of words, chattering about everything and nothing. Her conversation had ranged from rap music to the sinking of the *Titanic* and whether or not it was right to bring artifacts up from the wreck. Gabe had listened with half an ear, throwing in a comment whenever she showed signs of running out of topics. God knows, he'd probably needed the distraction almost as much as she had.

She'd watched him make what preparations he could and had uttered not a single word of complaint about the primitive circumstances under which she was about to give birth. From the start, she'd acted as if she had complete faith in his ability to see her through this. His admiration for her had grown by leaps and bounds as he watched her ride out the contractions, helpless to do anything more than offer her his hand to grip when the pain peaked.

Seeing her now, exhausted, sweaty, on the edge of collapse, he would have given anything to be able to take some of her pain onto himself. But he couldn't do that. And soothing words weren't going to do her any good, either.

"Don't wimp out on me now," he snapped. "You're almost there. One more contraction." At least he hoped that's all it would take. "And push hard this time."

Her eyes widened in shock, then darkened with rage. "Push hard this time?" she questioned, her voice rising to a furious shriek. "What the hell do you think I have been doing, you miserable son of a—"

She arched again, her entire body twisting with the force of the contraction.

"That's it!" The baby slid into Gabe's hands, red and slippery.

Working on pure instinct, he wiped his fingers across the baby's nose and mouth to clear away blood and mucus and tilted the tiny body head-down. What the hell was he supposed to do now? Before he could decide whether he was supposed to hang it upside down and slap it on the buttocks, the baby sucked in a breath and gave a thin little cry, protesting its rude arrival into the world.

"Is it all right?" Angie demanded, trying to lever herself up on her elbows to see the newborn. "Is my baby all right?"

"She's fine," Gabe told her. He grinned at her, feeling a wild elation like nothing he'd ever known. "She's perfect."

"She? It's a girl? Oh, let me see."

Holding the slippery infant as carefully as he might have handled a stick of lit dynamite, Gabe eased her up onto her mother's stomach. The baby let out another thin wail and curled into a fetal position. Gabe gave a shaky laugh.

"You can sure tell she's yours. Not more than a minute old and she's already talking."

"Is she all right?" Angie shoved her hair back impatiently and blinked the sweat from her eyes as she tried to get a better look at her daughter.

"She's perfect." Gabe said again, touching his finger to the baby's cheek, light-headed with relief. "She's about the most perfect thing I've ever seen."

"Look at her." Angie's voice was hushed. "She's beautiful."

Gabe looked at the red, wizened little body, the scrunched-up face and the head pushed out of shape by birth and agreed with Angie wholeheartedly. He'd never seen anything more beautiful in his entire life.

Chapter Six

WHEN ANGIE WOKE, she was aware of several things
at once. She was exhausted and every bone in her body
ached. At the same time, she felt a lightness of spirit
that more than made up for the physical aches and
pains. She had a baby, a little girl, perfect in every
way.

Opening her eyes, she tilted her head to peer down
at the tiny bundle snuggled against her side. All she
could see was the top of the baby's head, covered with
wisps of pale hair. Still hardly able to believe the miracle of it, Angie shifted position so that she could see
more of her daughter.

At just a few hours old, she was, in her mother's
completely unbiased opinion, already showing signs of
great beauty. Her face was scrunched up as if sleeping
took a great deal of concentration. Her skin was red
and mottled, and she looked like nothing so much as
a very tiny, very old lady. Angie doubted there'd ever
been a prettier baby born.

Feeling like a child who'd just been handed the
world's greatest Christmas present, she longed to tug
loose the fabric swaddling the baby so that she could
look at her own personal miracle again. But she didn't

want to wake the infant, so she contented herself with rearranging the makeshift blanket, smoothing a wrinkle here and there. Gabe's T-shirt had been the softest piece of fabric available and it made a more than adequate blanket.

Gabe. Angie lifted her head to look for him. He was sitting at the table, sound asleep, slumped over so that his head rested on his folded arms. He'd been tending the fire when she fell asleep. Seeing him lying there, Angie had to blink back tears, her chest aching with emotion. He'd taken such good care of her. Who would have believed those big, rough hands could be so incredibly gentle? Or that he could be so sensitive to her every need? He'd handled even the most intimate details so matter-of-factly that he'd left no room for her to feel embarrassed. She'd had doctors treat her with less sensitivity.

The baby stirred, and Angie's attention was immediately all for her child. Pale blue eyes stared up at her vaguely. Angie had heard all the medical opinions about how babies didn't really focus much at first but she didn't believe it for a minute. Looking into her daughter's eyes, she was convinced that *her* child could see perfectly well.

"Hello, sweetheart." She pitched her voice low, in deference to Gabe. "I don't have to ask how you are, because I can see that you're absolutely perfect."

The baby frowned and wiggled. One hand tugged free of the T-shirt and waved aimlessly in the air over her face. Angie caught it between her fingers, marveling at the tiny perfection of it.

"How is she?"

Angie looked up at the sound of Gabe's voice, her face breaking into a smile. "Did we wake you?"

"No. It was either wake up or be permanently crippled." He winced as he stood up, arching his back a little to work out the kinks. "How is she?" he asked again.

"She's perfect." Angie looked back down at her daughter. "She's absolutely perfect."

"How are you?" he asked, giving Angie a sweeping look.

"I'm fine. A little sore but nothing major." A little sore wasn't exactly adequate, but there was nothing Gabe could do about her aches and pains so there was no sense in mentioning them. Besides, when she looked at her daughter, everything else faded into insignificance.

He ran his fingers through his hair and stifled a yawn. He felt like forty miles of bad road. He needed a shower, a shave, a meal and about ten hours of sleep—none of which was he going to get any time soon. He'd slept longer than he should have as it was. He wanted to get Angie and the baby to a hospital as soon as possible. True, everything seemed to be all right, but he wouldn't be able to relax until he'd heard a doctor confirm that.

A thin wail announced that being the center of attention was not nearly enough to satisfy the baby.

"She's crying," Angie said uneasily. "Do you think she's in pain?"

Gabe sank down on his heels next to the bed and looked at the baby. Her face was screwed up in an expression of supreme displeasure. Her tiny mouth puckered, and her hands waved wildly over her head.

"Maybe she's hungry." This might be his first baby human, but he'd dealt with enough newborns of the four-legged variety to have a pretty good idea of what their priorities were.

"Hungry?" Angie tugged at the sheet that was tucked around her breasts. She flushed. "I guess that's probably it."

"Seems the most likely thing," he said, speaking over the baby's increasingly annoyed wails.

Angie lifted herself on her elbow, and Gabe moved immediately to help her, his strong hands easing her upward until her back was braced against the wall so that she was half sitting up. Before she could reach for the baby, he was there, lifting the tiny, wiggling bundle with gentle competence and depositing her in her mother's arms.

Angie started to lower the sheet and then hesitated, feeling suddenly self-conscious. He immediately sensed her discomfort and recognized its source.

"I'll leave you alone." He started to rise, but Angie's fingers caught at the sleeve of his shirt.

"You don't have to. I mean, it's stupid to feel embarrassed now. Considering everything that's happened, I mean."

"It's okay."

"No, really, I'd rather you stayed." Her cheeks warmed. "I'm not sure I know how to do this."

To his credit, Gabe didn't laugh. His eyes widened a little, as if in disbelief, but he didn't say a word. "I think it's pretty straightforward."

"I know. It's just that I'd feel better if you kind of hung around."

"Sure. I'll...uh...make a pot of coffee," he said after glancing around for inspiration.

"Thank you." She gave him a shy smile. It was ridiculous to feel self-conscious, considering just how intimately he knew her body, but she was grateful to him for understanding—or pretending to understand. He moved away, occupying himself with the task of making coffee while she fumbled her way through the first moments of breast-feeding.

Gabe told himself he wasn't going to look, that he was going to give her complete privacy—as much as was possible anyway. He dumped stale coffee into the metal basket in the dented aluminum pot and then filled the pot with cold water from the pump. Unless Angie asked for his help—and why she thought *he'd* know anything about it, he couldn't imagine—he was simply going to pretend that he was alone in the cabin.

"Oh!" The startled little exclamation jerked his eyes toward the bed without his volition. What he saw held him transfixed.

Angie held her daughter cradled in one arm, her head bent forward as she watched the child nurse. It was a classic pose of mother and child, one he'd seen in paintings and photographs. But no painting or photograph could possibly convey the depth of feeling he saw now.

As if sensing his gaze, Angie looked up, her eyes meeting his. Her smile was both shy and welcoming. It seemed the most natural thing in the world for him to cross the room and sink down on the edge of the bed beside her.

"I guess you were right. She was hungry."

Her earlier self-consciousness had disappeared, replaced by a feeling of rightness. She wanted to share this peaceful moment with him. Gabe had brought her child into the world, had almost certainly, saved both their lives.

"If you hadn't been here . . . I can't even imagine what would have happened to her. To both of us."

"I didn't do a whole hell of a lot," he said, shrugging.

"You probably saved both our lives," she said quietly, determined to say the words even if he didn't want to hear them. "I can't ever thank you enough for that."

"You're the one who did all the work. What are you going to name her?" he asked, effectively changing the topic.

"I don't know." Angie smoothed one hand over the baby's head. "I wouldn't let the doctor tell me whether it was a boy or a girl, because I wanted to be surprised." She glanced up at him and grinned. "I didn't plan on being surprised quite this soon, though."

"So I gathered," Gabe said dryly.

"Anyway, I was so busy trying to figure out what I was going to do with my life that I didn't really spend a lot of time thinking about names. I guess I'll have to get one of those baby-name books."

"There's no rush."

"No. But I don't want to be calling 'Hey, you' when she's heading off to college."

"You've got time."

They sat without speaking for a moment, the silence broken only by the faint suckling sounds as the baby nursed.

"Where's her father?"

Gabe's question startled Angie out of a peaceful haze. She frowned. The last thing she wanted to think of was Ted Sinclair. She hated to let thoughts of him intrude on the near perfection of the moment. Gabe must have seen her frown because he withdrew the question immediately.

"Forget it. It's none of my business."

"No, I don't mind." And she didn't, at least not in the way he meant. She was silent a moment, marshaling her thoughts. How could she explain about Ted? When she looked back on it, she couldn't believe how stupidly naive she'd been, how trusting.

"I went to high school with Ted," she said, deciding to start at the beginning. If she had to admit to being an idiot, she at least wanted him to know that there'd been mitigating circumstances. "He was two years older than me so we didn't have much to do with each other, but I knew who he was. *Everyone* knew who he was. He was the captain of the football team *and* the debating team."

She looked at him to see if he understood the significance of this.

"A jock with a brain," Gabe said, summing it up succinctly.

"A gorgeous jock with a brain," she elaborated. "'Tall, dark and handsome' was invented to describe Ted Sinclair. All my friends had crushes on him. He didn't notice any of us, of course, because we were too young for him. I daydreamed about him all the way through high school. Even when he graduated and went off the college, I daydreamed about him.

"I eventually grew out of my obsession. Or thought I did. I went off to college. I dated. I even fancied myself in love once, only it turned out that he ate peanut-butter-and-onion sandwiches and I knew we'd never be able to get past that."

"That would be a pretty tough thing to overlook," Gabe agreed drily.

"I know it doesn't sound like much, but you don't know what peanut butter and onions does to a person's breath."

"No, I don't," he said gratefully.

Angie smiled but her expression quickly changed. She looked down at the baby, stroking her finger gently across one impossibly soft cheek. "I came home from college and got a job at a local bank. Like I said before, a degree in fashion design doesn't qualify you for much, but I'm pretty good with computers, too, so they gave me a job. It just happened to be the bank where Ted's father has been the manager since before the flood, and Ted just happened to be working there, being groomed to take over his father's job. And we just happened to get involved."

She stopped, remembering her giddy delight at the fact that she was dating Ted Sinclair. She felt a thousand years older than that foolish girl. "We dated for almost a year. Looking back, I think I knew for at least half that time that it wasn't going to work out. I didn't even really like him. His favorite topic was himself. And he spent more time looking in a mirror than he spent looking at me."

"So you broke it off," Gabe prompted when she stopped.

"I wish. But the truth is, I couldn't quite get past the fact that I was fulfilling a childhood fantasy." Her mouth twisted ruefully. "I didn't want to admit that Ted was a jerk, because it would spoil the fantasy.

"He's the one who broke it off because he met someone else—someone who liked watching him watch himself in the mirror, I guess. I found out I was pregnant about a month after we broke up."

"Did you tell him about the baby?"

"Oh, I told him. He'd have found out anyway. After all, we were still working in the same bank. But I assumed he'd want to know, want to be involved in his child's life. I was wrong. When I told him I wasn't going to have an abortion, he promptly denied paternity and said I'd have to take him to court if I expected to get any money out of him."

Gabe made a sound in his throat that sounded suspiciously like a growl. Angie lifted one shoulder in a half shrug, dismissing the hurt she'd felt at the time.

"It's just as well, really. He'd make a lousy father. That's one of the reasons I decided to move. I didn't want him around the baby. You know what small towns are like—the gossip never dies. I didn't want my baby growing up listening to it. So I moved."

Gabe looked at the curve of her cheek as she bent over the baby and the fullness of her breast where the child nursed. He'd never in his life encountered quite so much strength in such a soft package. She was right—the gossip never died completely in a small town. He had firsthand experience of that. He'd thought it took strength to stay and face down the gossip, but maybe it took just as much strength to pull up stakes and move.

"It's his loss," he said finally.

"That's what I kept telling myself. Now, seeing her, I know I was right. It's definitely Ted's loss."

The baby's hand waved aimlessly, and Gabe reached out to touch it. Tiny fingers grasped the edge of his finger. The contrast in size made him smile, and Angie felt her breath catch at the way the expression lit up his face. She remembered wondering what he'd look like if he really smiled. Now she knew and the effect was powerful. She'd been so busy thinking of him as her knight in faded denim that she'd almost managed to forget that he was also a very attractive man.

"She's got a good grip," he said with such obvious pride that Angie smiled.

It was a shame that Gabe wasn't the baby's father. She'd be willing to bet that he'd never allow a child of his to grow up fatherless. She felt a sudden ache in her chest at the thought that her daughter might never have a father. Afraid he'd be able to read the thought in her eyes, she looked down.

The baby was still clutching Gabe's finger in her tiny hand, and Angie's breath caught a little at the sight of his hand so close to her breast. There was something very evocative about the contrast between his hand, tanned and callused from years of work, and the pale smoothness of her breast.

Something in the quality of Gabe's stillness made her lift her eyes to his face. Their eyes met, and she felt the impact of that look all the way to her toes. It was something much deeper than sexual awareness. It was as if they were looking directly at each other's souls. For that single moment, she felt as if she saw everything he was and everything he would ever be and that he saw her just as clearly. She'd never felt such a sense of connection with anyone in her life.

When Gabe leaned forward, it seemed the most natural thing in the world for him to kiss her. His mouth was warm and firm. The kiss was an affirmation of life, an acknowledgment of all they'd been through, of what they'd shared. Angie lifted her free hand, touching the tips of her fingers to his cheek, feeling the roughness of his beard against her skin. She knew, in that moment, that she could spend the rest of her life looking and never find another man who touched her the way this man did.

Her eyes fluttered open as Gabe drew back. She stared into his face, wanting to tell him...what? That she'd just fallen in love with him? That she thought they were meant to spend the rest of their days together? He'd think she was nuts, not without justification. *She* wasn't any too sure about her sanity at the moment.

What had happened just now? Was she the only one who'd felt as if the earth had moved under her? Gabe's expression was suddenly shuttered, revealing nothing of his thoughts. She might have imagined the kiss and those few seconds of silent communication between them. Only she hadn't imagined, she thought as Gabe rose and turned away without saying a word. It had happened and she wasn't going to forget. Not until she figured out what it had meant.

Chapter Seven

Three months later

IT SEEMED TO GABE as if he'd spent most of his life alone. He was an only child, his mother had died when he was young and his father had been too busy trying to run a ranch to have much time to spend with his son. Gabe had never needed someone else's company to feel complete, never craved companionship for its own sake and never felt lonely just because he was alone.

Until now.

These past few weeks, the ranch house had started to seem awfully empty—an emptiness that was echoed somewhere deep inside him. For some reason, he'd begun to look at his life and wonder just where it was going. He was thirty-two years old—not exactly ancient, but he certainly wasn't a kid anymore. He'd been running the ranch alone since his father's death three years before. If taxes didn't go too high or beef prices dip too low, he'd be running it the rest of his life and that suited him just fine. He liked ranching, liked the gamble of it, needed the wide-open spaces that were a part of it. No, it wasn't the ranch that was causing this niggling feeling of dissatisfaction.

It was the aloneness he was starting to feel. He'd watched his father work himself to death trying to fill the empty places left inside after his wife died. It hadn't worked for Bill Taylor, and Gabe was starting to think it wasn't going to work for him any better than it had for his father.

He stared out the window at the moon hovering over the mountains to the west. He cradled an old-fashioned glass in his right hand. The whiskey he'd splashed in it half an hour ago was barely touched. He'd had the vague idea that alcohol might serve to fill the hollow feeling in his gut but he'd abandoned the idea almost as soon as the drink was poured. He'd never been much of a drinker, and it would be stupid to start now. Besides, it would take more than whiskey to cure what ailed him.

Sighing, he turned away from the window and stared at the empty living room. Nothing about it justified his feeling of dissatisfaction. The room was relatively tidy. Aside from his office, he didn't spend enough time in the house to make much impression on it—good or bad. A fine layer of dust coated the table-tops and the hardwood floor needed a good waxing, but a little dust and dull floors never hurt anybody.

His frown deepened. He'd been only nine when his mother died but he remembered what the house had looked like when she was alive. It had been a home then. It had been more than the fact that she kept the place cleaner than he bothered with. There'd been an indefinable air that said that lives were being lived here, that this was more than just a place to sleep and eat. After her death, there'd been no one who cared enough to maintain that feeling, and the old house had gradually ceased to be a home and had become simply a place to live.

"Damn." He cursed his mood softly, hating the echo of his own voice. It was only recently that he'd started to feel like this. He wanted to believe that it was caused by an early mid-life crisis but he knew exactly what had triggered this sudden feeling that time—and his life—were running out on him.

Angie and her baby.

There. He'd admitted it. Angie and her nonstop talking and her convoluted stories and that baby of hers had made him really look at his life. And he didn't much care for what he was seeing.

Gabe took a sip of whiskey. The ice had nearly melted and it was like drinking flavored water, but he hardly noticed. What was Angie doing now? Had she found a job? And if so, who was taking care of the baby? The thought of a stranger's taking care of the baby he'd helped bring into the world didn't sit well with him. He reminded himself that it was none of his business. Angie and the baby—hell, he didn't even know what she'd named it—had been out of his life from the moment he'd left them at the hospital.

He turned back to the window, his hand tightening on the icy glass. Hell, he'd only known her a day. Even if it had been one of the more eventful days he'd ever spent, that was no reason to let her linger in his thoughts the way she had.

He'd half expected to hear from her before now. Maybe even half hoped he would. But since leaving her at the hospital, the only communication he'd had was a polite little note thanking him for everything he'd done for her and the baby, including having her car repaired and brought to the hospital. She'd appreciate it if he'd let her know how much the repairs had cost and had given him her brother's address, where he could send the information.

He'd crumpled up the note and thrown it in the trash. He'd be damned if he'd send her a bill, as if he was a damned mechanic. Even if replacing her fuel pump had put him in the poor house, which it hadn't, he wouldn't have let her pay for it! Once his temper had cooled, he'd fished the note back out of the trash and stuffed it in a desk drawer but he hadn't looked at it since.

Damn the woman, anyway. She was like having a cocklebur stuck to him. She didn't know the meaning of the word *quiet*. She was as trusting as a puppy. Delivering her baby had been the most harrowing experience of his life. You'd think he'd be glad to get rid of her. And he was.

It was just that he couldn't seem to quit thinking about her.

Disgusted with himself, Gabe went into the kitchen and dumped the rest of his drink down the sink before going up to bed. Alone, just the way he'd always been.

"GABE!"

"Dammit, Red, I'm not deaf," Gabe snarled, coming out from under the truck's hood. He rubbed his fingers over the back of his head, which had connected resoundingly with the underside of the hood. "You don't have to shout like the world was coming to an end."

"Sorry." Red neither sounded nor looked sorry. In fact, he looked so pleased with himself that Gabe felt an uneasy twinge. He'd known Red Martin most of his life. Red had come to work for his father when Gabe was a boy. The man was a good cowboy, but there was a streak of mischief in him a mile wide. The last time he'd seen Red look so happy was when he'd coiled up a dead rattlesnake and put it in the oven for the cook to find.

"What have you done?" Gabe asked without bothering to conceal his wariness.

"I ain't done nothing," Red denied, all injured innocence. His faded blue eyes gleamed with pleasure. "Looks to me like you're the one who's done something you shouldn't't've."

"What are you talking about?" Gabe reached for a rag and began wiping the grease off his hands. Replacing spark plugs was not exactly one of his favorite things to do, and he wasn't really in the mood for one of Red's practical jokes. "If you've put a dead buffalo in my bed or filled the bathtub with spiders, I'm going to fire your sorry butt," he promised darkly.

"I ain't done a thing," Red insisted. "I just come to tell you that you've got yourself a visitor."

"Who is it?"

"Nobody I ever seen before, but they's asking for you."

Gabe studied his foreman, trying to figure out what the joke was. What was it about a visitor that had put that unholy gleam in Red's faded blue eyes? Since Red obviously had no intention of telling him anything more, there was only one way to find out.

Gabe stuffed the greasy rag in his back pocket and stalked out of the shed. If this was another one of Red's practical jokes, he was going to strangle the old man with his bare hands, he promised himself. Narrowing his eyes against the sunlight, he glanced at the cloudless blue sky. So far, it had been a clear, dry spring, which had made calving a lot easier on the men and the cattle, but in his experience, Mother Nature usually extracted a price for every gift of good weather. He hoped they weren't going to pay for a nice spring by having a dry summer. Making a mental note to make sure the spring was cleared, he strode toward the car parked in front of the ranch house.

As he got closer, he saw that it was a blue compact. A familiar blue compact. Gabe's stride slowed. There was a woman leaning against the fender. A woman with hair the color of sunlight. Angie. He had the ridiculous idea that thinking about her last night had somehow conjured her.

"Gabe!" Her voice had the same husky edge that he remembered. She hurried toward him, her face lighting up in that smile that had haunted more than a few of his dreams. He'd never known anyone else who put so much of themselves into a smile.

"Gabe!"

She stepped up to him so naturally that Gabe somehow found his arms around her without having a chance to think about what he was doing. She pressed her cheek against his chest, wrapping her arms around his waist in a fierce little hug. She smelled of sunshine and, shampoo—fresh, clean scents that seemed just right for her. Gabe closed his eyes, and for a fraction of a second, it seemed as if the emptiness inside was filled.

The thought shook him, and he released Angie as if she'd suddenly caught fire, stepping back away from her. She was wearing a pair of faded jeans and a rose-colored shirt that reflected the color in her cheeks. Her figure was softly rounded, her breasts and hips fuller than the current fashion. But the rich curves looked just right on her.

"I look better than I did the last time you saw me," she said, apparently reading his thoughts. It was such a blatant play for a compliment that Gabe felt one corner of his mouth kick up in a half smile.

"You look good," he said truthfully.

"Thank you." She grinned, her nose wrinkling in the same way he remembered. "I'd just about have to look better than I did, wouldn't I?"

"You'd been through a lot."

"And looked it. Oh, it's good to see you again," she said, smiling up at him with such open joy that Gabe felt his chest ache.

"What are you doing here?"

Her eyes widened a little at his blunt tone, but her smile didn't waver. "I don't suppose you'd believe it if I said we were just in the neighborhood and decided to stop by?"

"No, I wouldn't. We?" He glanced over her shoulder at the car but saw no one.

"Gabby and I, of course," she said, as if it should have been obvious. "I brought her with me. Well, it's not like I could leave her in West Virginia. Not with Marla the Marvelous buying camouflage diapers and ready-to-order formula from the Pentagon."

"Formula from the Pentagon?" Gabe repeated. He'd almost forgotten this feeling of disorientation.

As if he'd missed a few vital pieces of the conversation, the ones that would have made it all make sense.

"They probably don't make formula," Angie admitted. She turned toward the car but continued to talk over her shoulder, assuming Gabe would follow, which he did. "Actually, Marla wouldn't buy formula from the Pentagon even if they made it. She's not a fan of the military establishment. She thinks they're too liberal. If she had her way, we'd be invading half the planet before you could shout 'Give peace a chance.'"

She pulled open the passenger door and bent over the seat, fumbling with something Gabe couldn't see. Her voice was slightly muffled by her position, but that didn't slow her down.

"I stood it as long as I could but I was afraid Gabby's first word was going to be 'Uzi' so I decided I had to leave. Only I wasn't sure where to go. My parents moved to a condo in Arizona. There's no room there, and besides, I don't think it's really fair to inflict a baby on them at this stage in their life. And then I remembered what you'd said, and it was so obvious I couldn't believe I hadn't thought of it before."

"What I said?" Gabe asked warily. "What did I say?"

"About how it's so hard to get a housekeeper. It's the perfect solution for both of us," she announced cheerfully.

"What is?" He was starting to feel real alarm.

"Gabby and I moving in with you," she said brightly.

Before Gabe could protest, which he intended to do vociferously, Angie straightened and turned away from the car. She held the baby in her arms, and Gabe was caught off guard by the wave of emotion he felt. He'd helped bring this child into the world three months ago. The last time he'd seen her, she'd been a wizened, red-faced little creature. Now, she was a pink-cheeked, blue-eyed cherub. Her wispy, pale gold curls were decorated by a ridiculous pink bow that was tilted drunkenly over one eye.

"She looks better than she did the last time you saw her, too," Angie said, reading his mind.

"She looks fine," Gabe said. It was a hopelessly inadequate response but it was all he could get past the knot of hunger that was lodged in the base of his throat. Seeing Angie and the baby in front of him, he was suddenly, achingly aware of everything that was missing from his life.

"She's gorgeous," Angie corrected him. "Everyone thinks so. Even Marla admitted that Gabby was the prettiest baby she'd ever seen. But if we'd stayed, Marla would have taught her to play encampment instead of house. I think she means well and I know I'm probably setting the women's movement back twenty years, but I like Barbie dolls."

She made the announcement defiantly, as if challenging him to argue with her. Since Gabe had no particular opinion of Barbie dolls, he settled for a noncommittal response. "Okay."

"It's not like I think Barbie dolls should be role models or anything," Angie told him earnestly. "Although when you really look at it, they've had a lot of careers. I mean, they've been astronauts and doctors and just about everything else under the sun. I don't see that Barbie dolls are such bad role models for a little girl. But of course, the measurements are ridiculous, and I'm sure that's part of the reason so many women aren't satisfied with their own bodies, which is stupid really because nobody can have a body like a Barbie doll."

"I guess not," he agreed cautiously. How had they gotten onto the topic of Barbie dolls and their suitability as role models?

"Anyway, I wouldn't want Gabby to grow up thinking that she had to look like a Barbie doll but I'm not too crazy about the idea of her first doll being a G.I. Joe, either. You can't tell me *he's* an ideal role model for a little girl."

He had no intention of telling her anything of the sort. Since he still didn't know why they were discussing dolls at all, he tried to bring the topic back around to something a little closer to the point—at least to what the point ought to be.

"Look, about you staying here. I don't think—"

"Here. You two should get reacquainted."

Before he could form a protest, Gabe found his hands full of soft, sweet-smelling infant. He shifted his hold automatically, cradling her in his arms. She stared up at him with eyes the same clear blue as her mother's. She seemed to be studying him very seriously, weighing whether or not he was an acceptable person to be holding her.

"Gabby, this is Gabe," Angie said. "I told you all about him. If it weren't for him, you and I would have been in a lot of trouble."

The baby continued to stare up at him with those solemn eyes. Gabe's voice was gruff when he spoke. "What kind of a name is 'Gabby'? Sounds like an old man's name."

Angie laughed, a soft, husky rush of sound that made Gabe want to smile with her. "You're thinking of Gabby Hayes. I did not name her after Gabby Hayes. Actually, I probably should have named her after my aunt—my great-aunt, really. She's got tons of money and maybe she'd leave it all to Gabby if I'd named Gabby after her, but I couldn't see settling a baby with a name like Eustacia Eugenia."

"Good God." Gabe looked at her. "Eustacia Eugenia?"

"Awful, isn't it?" Angie wrinkled her nose. "What's worse, she acts like a Eustacia Eugenia, all upright and proper and no sense of humor at all. Of course, I can't really blame her for that. How could you possibly have a sense of humor with a name like that? Can you imagine someone named Eustacia Eugenia laughing out loud?''

''No.''

''Me, neither. So, even though it might have made her an heiress, I couldn't name Gabby that. Besides, Aunt Eustacia is the sort of person who'd let you name your child something horrible just to please her and then she'd leave all her money to a home for underprivileged Harvard graduates or something. And there'd you be with a kid permanently warped by having this awful name and broke on top of it all.''

''So you named her Gabby?'' It was certainly an improvement over ''Eustacia Eugenia'' but it wasn't likely to win any prizes.

''Of course not. I named her Gabriella. After you.''

Gabe stared at her, his eyes startled. He felt as if he'd just been kicked in the solar plexus. ''You named her after me?''

''It seemed like the only possible choice,'' Angie said quietly. ''She probably wouldn't be here if it weren't for you. After everything you did for her—and for me—I couldn't think of any name I'd rather give her.''

Gabe lowered his eyes to the baby in his arms. Gabriella. She was still watching him with those solemn blue eyes but she seemed to come to some decision about him. She smiled suddenly, her face crinkling and her eyes sparkling with pleasure. Like her mother, she put everything she had into her smile. She waved one plump little hand at him, and Gabe's heart dropped right into her fingers.

"You can stay," he told Angie without lifting his eyes from that magical baby smile. "But just for a while."

Chapter Eight

"YOU ARE a very clever little girl," Angie told her daughter. "How did you know that a smile was just what Gabe needed to help him admit that he wanted us to stay?"

Gabby gurgled an acknowledgment of her own brilliance and waved her arms in the air for good measure. She was lying on the bed in the guest room Gabe had shown Angie to. His tour of the house had been perfunctory at best, and Angie knew he was having second, third and fourth thoughts about agreeing to let her stay.

"I suppose, if I had any pride, I'd pack us both up and leave," she told the baby as she began changing Gabby's wet diaper. "I mean, I didn't really play fair, making him hold you and all. He might be able to resist me but how could anyone resist you?"

Gabby made noises of agreement. Bored with the process of a diaper changing, she decided to add an element of challenge by kicking her legs as rapidly as she could, shouting out encouragement to her mother at the same time.

"It's for his own good," Angie said, trying to soothe her conscience. With the ease of practice, she captured Gabby's ankles in one hand and quickly stripped off the soggy diaper. She turned to drop it into the plastic pail she'd placed next to the bed.

"He needs us," she told the baby. "He just doesn't know it yet. Did you see his eyes when he saw us?" Gabby pumped her legs again, trying to avoid the clean diaper her mother had ready. "He was glad to see us. And then he put all those walls back up."

Angie shook her head and captured Gabby's ankles again, plopping her bare bottom down and fastening the fresh diaper in place with quick efficiency.

"You probably don't remember this, but three months ago, I fell in love with Gabe. I thought it might just be circumstances. After all, he did save our lives, and people do tend to think they feel things they don't really feel after something like that. Only I really did feel what I thought I felt because, when I saw Gabe this afternoon, I felt it all over again. Do you understand?"

Gabe would have sympathized with Gabby's puzzled frown. Angie sighed as she picked the baby up and sat down on the edge of the bed with her.

"The bottom line, sugar, is that I love him. He's strong and gentle, and I'd trust him with my life. I'd trust him with *your* life, and that's even more significant. He might not know it yet but he already loves you. And I think, maybe, he could love me, if he'd let himself. There was that kiss..."

Angie's voice trailed off, her eyes darkening to smoky blue as she remembered that kiss. She hadn't known it was possible to feel so perfectly in tune with another human being. She wanted to feel that again. She wanted to feel Gabe's arms around her again, wanted to feel as if she could shelter there forever.

Maybe it wouldn't happen. Maybe Gabe wouldn't fall in love with her. But this was something worth taking a few chances for. She'd wasted a year of her life on Ted Sinclair. Well, it hadn't really been wasted time, she thought, looking down at Gabby. She wouldn't have traded anything for her daughter. But if she could spend a year trying to make a relationship work with a shallow jerk like Ted, the least she could do was devote a little time to something a great deal more worthwhile.

But she felt more than a little guilty about manipulating him the way she had. Handing him the baby had really been a rotten trick.

"But it's not like I can just move into the neighborhood and expect to bump into him," she defended herself to Gabby. "As near as I can tell, there is no neighborhood. So I really didn't have any choice but to get him to invite us to stay."

She nibbled on her lower lip, her conscience nagging at her. "Maybe I shouldn't have exaggerated quite so much about Aunt Marla."

Despite her tendency to look as if she'd just stepped out of the pages of a magazine, even when she was wearing khaki, Marla had turned out to be a good friend and real source of support. It had been Marla who'd encouraged Angie to take a chance by coming back to Wyoming. Mark had thought she was nuts to uproot herself and the baby to find a man she'd known barely twenty-four hours, but Marla's exquisite eyes had misted over with tears as she told her husband to butt out.

"I don't think Marla would mind," Angie said to Gabby, who was busy chewing on her own fist and appeared to have lost interest in the conversation. Angie's conscience continued to nag at her, just as it had done all the way from West Virginia. "It's not like I'm going to force Gabe to do anything. I'm just going to be here—we're going to be here—and we'll see what happens."

She glanced around the room, noting the dust that dulled every surface. "He really does need a housekeeper," she said, remembering the rest of the house. "And he needs us. He just doesn't know it yet."

"I AIN'T NEVER THOUGHT much of babies," Red said, peering toward the house. "But I gotta admit that little one is cute as a speckled pup."

"Yeah." Gabe followed his gaze.

Angie was sitting on the porch swing, a pile of mending in her lap and Gabby propped up on pillows next to her. Even from here, he could hear Gabby talking to herself and laughing, see her hands waving as if to illustrate whatever she was saying. He didn't have much experience with babies but he found it hard to imagine that they were always as sunny tempered as Gabby.

In the past two weeks, he'd almost never heard her cry. She laughed. She cooed. She gurgled. And she talked to anyone who'd pay attention to her. She was a lot like her mother in that respect, Gabe thought, feeling a twinge of amusement. Between the two of them, he'd almost forgotten the meaning of the word *quiet.*

He frowned a little, thinking that he should have minded that more than he did. Actually, he should have minded a lot of things that he didn't. Like the fact that the house was suddenly full of baby things. How one small child could require so much...stuff was beyond him. Gabby came with more accessories than one of those stupid dolls Angie had talked about. The house was cluttered with items small and large, all in bright primary colors. He couldn't ever remember seeing the place look so completely lived-in.

He jabbed the post-hole digger into the ground, biting off a section of dirt and dropping it to the side of the hole. He hardly recognized his own life anymore. Two weeks ago he'd been thinking about how empty the house was, how empty his life was. Now the house smelled of wax, floor polish, baby powder and home cooking. Windows had been thrown open, letting in the smell of sunshine and springtime. His clothes were mended, there were fresh sheets on the bed and hot meals on the table.

"Thought Gabby was a pretty silly name, first time I heard it," Red continued. "Then Miss Angie, she told me she'd named the tyke after you." He shot Gabe a sly sideways glance. "Interesting thing, that. Makes a body wonder why she might want to go and name a sweet little baby after an ornery cuss like yourself."

"No law against wondering." Satisfied with the depth of the hole, Gabe set aside the post-hole digger and reached for a new post.

"Don't have to wonder," Red said smugly. "I asked Miss Angie why she'd want to do a thing like that. She told me a real interesting thing. Said you'd been the one to deliver that baby. Said you'd saved both their lives. Said you were a real hero."

"She talks too much," Gabe said shortly.

Red laughed, a rusty sound like a saw cutting through oak. "Can't argue with you on that one. She sure can talk a blue streak. Never saw anybody talk so much in all my born days. I don't mind, though. Not when she smiles so much. Got the prettiest darned smile I've ever seen."

She did that, Gabe thought, his eyes drawn back to the porch. And she smiled often. He'd never known anyone who could be so happy about nothing in particular. More often than not, when he walked into the house, he could hear her singing to herself. Her voice was hopelessly off-key and she forgot the words most of the time, but the sound always bubbled over with contentment.

"Hand me that sledgehammer," he said, forcing his attention back to the job at hand, which was mending a section of corral fence. Red did as he asked, making a production out of lifting the hammer.

"I'm gettin' too old to be building fences," he said plaintively.

"Don't give me that," Gabe said without sympathy. "Don't think I don't know that you're still the arm wrestling champion around here."

"That's strategy, not muscle," Red protested.

"Well, use some of that strategy to hold this post so I can knock it into place."

Red braced the fence post but he wasn't through complaining. "I still don't see why you couldn't get a couple of the younger bucks to help you with fixing this here fence."

Because he didn't like the way they looked at Angie, Gabe thought. But he wasn't going to say as much to Red. Next thing he knew, the old coot would be thinking he was jealous. The truth was, he was just saving Angie the trouble of dealing with the hands. She was too damned friendly. It was going to get her into trouble one of these days, but not while she was staying on his ranch. He'd make sure of that.

She was his employee, after all. Though he still wasn't sure how she'd persuaded him to give her a job as his housekeeper. It was temporary, he reminded himself. The cool voice of reason questioned just what was going to happen to change the arrangement—it wasn't likely that a job was going to fall out of the sky and drop into Angie's lap.

Gabe's expression was grim as he worked the fence post into place. If he was honest with himself, he had to admit that he wasn't all that anxious to see Angie and the baby leave. He liked having them around, liked the changes they'd made in his life. He was starting to wonder if maybe, just maybe, they didn't have to leave at all.

And that was a dangerous thing to think.

Chapter Nine

ANGIE STEPPED out of the shower and reached for a towel. Running the towel down her arm, she caught a glimpse of herself in the steamy mirror. Frowning, she leaned closer, studying her reflection. She looked the same way she always did. She wasn't a raving beauty but she was reasonably attractive. A bit rounder than she'd like, she thought, frowning at the fullness of her hips. She should have skipped that slice of apple pie after dinner, but it had been her mother's recipe and it had turned out so well that she hadn't been able to resist it.

Gabe had certainly enjoyed the pie, she thought, her mouth curving. He'd eaten two slices. If there was any truth to the old saying about the way to a man's heart being through his stomach, these past couple of weeks should have built her a freeway right to Gabe's heart. He'd shown a flattering appreciation for her cooking.

It was too bad that appreciation hadn't extended to the rest of her. Angie frowned at her reflection again. Hips or no, she wasn't bad-looking. So why did Gabe treat her as if she was his maiden aunt? She knew he was aware of her. She saw it in his eyes sometimes.

She'd glance up and catch him looking at her the way a man looked at a woman he found attractive.

Patience, she counseled herself as she finished toweling dry. She didn't know what had caused it but she sensed that Gabe had put up some pretty strong walls between himself and the rest of the world. She couldn't expect those walls to crumble just because he found her attractive.

Besides, he was at least talking to her now. Really talking to her. Tonight at dinner, she'd coaxed him into talking about his plans for the ranch. He was experimenting with a small herd of buffalo. The demand for low-fat beef had made them an increasingly viable option for ranchers willing to take a risk. Not that any kind of ranching wasn't risky, he'd said, with that funny half smile that made her want to lean across the table and kiss him.

But she'd restrained the urge to do that and they'd had a very pleasant conversation. After dinner, Gabe had gone into his office to catch up on some paperwork, and Angie had put Gabby down for the night and then watched a little TV. He still hadn't come out of the office when she came upstairs to shower and get ready for bed.

Angie shrugged into her robe, belting it snugly around her waist before reaching up to pull loose the pins that held her hair and letting it tumble onto her shoulders in thick golden waves. Patience, she reminded her reflection. She was in this for the long haul. Gabe would come around sooner or later.

And if he took too long, she'd just have to tackle him, wrestle him to the ground and have her way with him.

The thought of her attacking Gabe was ridiculous enough to make her smile. The expression lingered as she opened the bathroom door and stepped out.

She all but fell over Gabe, who'd been walking down the hall. His hands came out and caught her elbows to steady her.

"Careful."

"Sorry. I didn't mean to run you over." She tilted her head back to smile up at him.

"It was just as much my fault as yours," Gabe said absently. She smelled of soap and something soft and gentle that he couldn't quite identify. He drew in a deep breath, trying to place the scent, but it eluded him.

"Are you wearing perfume?" He was surprised when Angie blushed.

"Baby powder," she admitted in a muffled voice. "You caught me stealing Gabby's baby powder."

Gabe felt one corner of his mouth curl. She looked as guilty as if he'd caught her stealing the baby's bottle.

"I won't tell her," he promised solemnly.

"Oh, it's not that. It's just that baby powder isn't exactly on the top-ten list of seductive scents."

"I don't know about that," he murmured, thinking that it certainly seemed to be working on him. Of course, maybe it wasn't the way she smelled. Maybe it was the way her hair seemed to catch the light or the gentle invitation of her mouth or the way her cotton robe clung ever so slightly to the damp curves of her body.

"Not that I'm trying to be seductive," Angie said, apparently concerned that he might misconstrue her remark. "Because I'm not. Not specifically, anyway. I wouldn't mind being seductive exactly but I don't want you to think that I had it in mind or anything."

When Gabe didn't say anything but only continued to look at her, his green eyes hooded and unreadable, Angie gave a nervous laugh.

"I guess I didn't have to say that, did I? I mean, if I were trying to be seductive, I wouldn't be putting on baby powder, would I? I'd put on something called Pulse or Wanton or...or something. Nobody puts on baby powder if they're planning a seduction. Which I'm certainly not. Planning one, I mean."

"Are you nervous?" Gabe asked her.

"Nervous? Me? Why would I be nervous?"

"I don't know." As if watching from outside himself, he saw his hand come up, saw his fingers slide into her hair. "You told me once that you tend to talk a lot when you're nervous."

"Am I? Talking a lot, I mean?" She seemed to have a hard time getting the words out.

"Nonstop." He stepped closer, crowding her back against the wall. *This was all wrong.* Just a few hours ago, he'd been thinking about how wrong this would be. Angie was not the sort of woman who took affairs lightly. He should just step back and walk away and he could pretend there'd never been a moment when he'd been so close that he could feel the peaks of her nipples through the fabric of his shirt and her robe; that he'd never seen the hunger in her pretty blue eyes; never felt her need rise to meet his own.

"I swore I wouldn't do this," he said, talking as much to himself as to her.

"Do what?"

"Kiss you." His fingers slid deeper into her hair, cupping the back of her head. He was standing so close that her body touched his from knee to chest.

"K-kiss me?" Angie's eyes widened until they were huge blue pools of disbelief. And need, God help him. "It's okay," she stammered breathlessly. "I don't mind. Unless you mind. But you shouldn't, because I'd like it. If you kissed me, I mean. I probably shouldn't admit it, because you'll think I'm a brazen hussy. Except I don't think there is such a thing anymore. I think they're out of style but if they weren't I wouldn't care anyway, because I—"

"Shut up," Gabe told her, just as his mouth closed over hers.

Angie melted against him, all soft and warm and irresistible. Her fingers curled into his shirt, clutching little fistfuls of cotton as if they were her only grasp on reality.

Gabe knew just how she felt. He'd been fantasizing about kissing her ever since she'd showed up on his doorstep. It didn't seem possible but the reality was even better than the fantasy. Her mouth yielded to his as if she'd been waiting for his kiss all her life. He could taste the mintiness of her toothpaste and found it unbearably erotic. Toothpaste and baby powder—he'd never realized how seductive they could be.

But it wasn't the toothpaste or the soft powdery scent that made Gabe draw her closer, made him want to absorb her into himself. It was Angie. He needed her. He needed her warmth and her smile, needed to feel her vibrancy, needed to taste her hunger.

"Gabe." She whispered his name as his mouth slid down her throat, his tongue tasting the pulse that beat raggedly at the base of her throat.

"Gabe." Her fingers threaded through his dark hair, dragging his mouth back up to hers.

They kissed again and again, long, drugging kisses that seemed to heat the very air around them. Passion rose swift and hard between them, catching them up in a whirlwind of hunger and need. His fingers tugged at the belt of her robe, and Angie moaned softly into his mouth, pressing herself closer to him.

The very force of his need made Gabe hesitate. It took every ounce of control he possessed to keep from stripping the robe from her and taking her right there and then. Stretched out on the floor or pressed against the wall—he didn't care so long as he could be inside her, could feel her softness surround him.

"Angie?"

"What?" She was pressing quick little kisses along his collarbone, her fingers reaching for his belt buckle.

"Look at me." Gabe pressed his hand over hers, stilling her fingers. She tilted her head back to do as he asked, and the slumberous look in her eyes was almost his undoing.

"Now who's talking too much?" she asked huskily.

"Is this what you want?"

"It's what I want."

"No regrets?"

"No regrets," she promised softly. "Now, shut up and kiss me again."

"Always happy to oblige a lady," Gabe murmured against her mouth.

He bent and swept her up in his arms, carrying her down the hall to his bedroom. Nudging the door open with his shoulder, he considered the idea that he could be making a big mistake. This might be wrong. Might, in fact, be disastrous. But he could no more stop it now than he could stop a tornado. He had to have her. Come hell or high water, he had to have her.

"I LOVE YOU, GABE."

They were lying together in his bed. Angie was pressed close against his side, one leg thrown over his, her head on his shoulder. Gabe had been lying there, eyes closed, trying to remember if he'd ever felt such complete contentment before in his life. Making love with Angie had been everything he'd imagined it would be and more. Who would have dreamed that that curvy little body of hers could hold so much passion?

Her soft declaration shattered his mood, the words rolling over him like thunder rolling in on a summer storm. They shook him to his soul, made him aware of the depth of his own hunger, of how much he wanted to hear her say them again; how much he'd give to be sure she meant them.

"You don't know me," he said roughly.

Angie raised her head from where it had been resting on his shoulder and looked at him, her eyes clear and direct. "I know you."

She said it with such conviction that he could almost believe her. Almost, but not quite.

"You can't. Counting the night Gabby was born, we haven't known each other even three full weeks."

"It doesn't always take time to know someone." She looked away from his face, focusing her gaze on where her fingers were combing through the mat of hair on his chest. "I learned a lot about you the night Gabby was born."

"Despite what you think, I didn't do much that night."

"You kept me from falling apart. I was so scared, and you made me believe that everything was going to turn out all right. And it did."

"No thanks to me," he denied. "I was scared to death."

"But you didn't let me see that." Angie's eyes were clear and warm. "You can argue all you want, but I do love you."

Gabe stared at her, feeling humbled and elated all at the same time. Her courage never ceased to amaze him. Whether it was the physical courage with which she'd faced childbirth or the emotional courage she was showing now. He groped for words but found them elusive. If he told her he loved her, he'd be making himself vulnerable to her. What if she changed her mind? What if she realized how little she really knew him?

"Angie, I—"

She put her fingers over his mouth, stilling his words. Her expression was soft with understanding. "You don't have to say anything in return. I just wanted you to know. It would be a kind of lie if I didn't tell you."

She lay back down, nestling her head against his shoulder again as if the conversation was over. Gabe stared up at the ceiling and felt like the worst kind of coward. How was it that she could find the courage to say those three simple words and he was paralyzed by the thought of them? It would be a kind of lie not to tell him, she'd said. That must make him the biggest liar in the whole damned state, he thought.

Chapter Ten

"I CAN'T BELIEVE we've been here two and a half weeks and this is the first time I've seen Rock Creek." Angie was almost bouncing in her seat with excitement as she contemplated her first trip into town. Even better, her first trip into town with Gabe.

"There's not much to see," he said, sounding more grim than the comment warranted.

Angie shot him a sideways glance, remembering his comments all those months ago about her being the only person in the area who thought him worthy of trust. She found that hard to believe. She'd never met anyone she trusted more. She considered asking him to tell her why he had such a decided lack of enthusiasm for his hometown but abandoned the idea almost immediately. It wouldn't do any good.

She suppressed a sigh and glanced down at Gabby, who was strapped snugly into her car seat between them. Last night hadn't exactly proved as effective as a magic wand when it came to solving all the problems in their relationship. Not that she regretted it. Not for a minute. Making love with Gabe had been even more wonderful than she'd dreamed it would be. But she'd hoped it would open him up a bit more.

She looked back out at the passing scenery, frowning a little. Maybe she shouldn't have told him that she loved him. Maybe it had been too soon to tell him that. But the words had just refused to stay inside another minute. She sighed a little, hoping that she hadn't made a huge mistake.

GABE WATCHED the expressions flit across her face and wondered what she was thinking. He was already starting to regret this trip into town. Waking with her in his arms this morning had felt so good it had scared him. He'd crawled out of bed, careful not to wake her, his only thought to run like a rabbit. But Gabby had been awake early, too, and he'd heard her fussing in the room she shared with Angie. It would have taken a harder man than he to turn a deaf ear to those snuffling little cries.

As soon as she saw him, her tears had stopped and her face had been wreathed in a smile of irresistible sweetness. Gabe had found himself changing a diaper for the first time in his life. By the time the diaper was solidly, if somewhat crookedly, in place, he'd decided that he'd rather hog-tie a full-grown Brahman bull than diaper a baby. He'd also realized just how much he was going to lose if Angie and Gabby walked out of his life.

So he'd invited Angie to go into town with him, the one thing he could damned near guarantee would convince her to leave. Made loads of sense, he thought as he pulled into a parking place in front of Garret's hardware. The best damned thing that had ever happened to him and he was doing everything he could to end it.

AT FIRST GLANCE, there was certainly nothing about Rock Creek to explain Gabe's apparent distaste for it. It was a small town, hardly more than a wide spot in the road. There were two gas stations, a grocery store, a hardware-and-feed store, a café, a tiny post office and three bars. Angie made note of the proportion of bars to other businesses and made an educated guess as to what people did for entertainment on a Saturday night.

Gabe got out of the truck without a word. She had Gabby unstrapped from the car seat by the time he opened her door and she handed the baby out to him so that she could climb down from the truck.

"I've got a long grocery list," she told him, reaching for Gabby. "Why don't I meet you back here in half an hour?"

"I'll go with you," he said as he handed the baby to her.

"You don't have to."

"I'll go with you," he repeated shortly.

Angie gave up the argument. It would have been nice if she could have believed that he couldn't bear to be parted from her. But it soon became apparent that his main purpose in accompanying her was to discourage any attempts at friendliness by anyone they encountered. At least, that's what seemed to be his purpose.

Not that people were exactly rushing up, begging to chat with her, Angie thought as she pushed a cart with one defective wheel through the small grocery store. But then again, considering the icy green of Gabe's eyes, *she* certainly wouldn't have dared to say hello.

She did her best to look unaware of the sidelong glances she was getting. It was harder to ignore the stunned look that came into people's eyes when they saw Gabby resting happily in Gabe's arms. She'd expected people to be curious and they were. What she hadn't expected was the wide berth given them by virtually everyone. By the time they left the grocery store, Gabe's expression was so implacably hostile that he almost made her nervous.

He loaded the groceries in the back of the truck and then turned to look at her. "Wait here. I've got to pick up something at the hardware store. I'll only be a minute."

"Fine. I'll just run across the street to the post office. I want to get some stamps."

"I've got stamps back at the ranch house. You can use those."

"I'd rather buy my own."

"I'll go with you."

"I don't need an escort to walk across the street. There's so little traffic, I could crawl across on my belly and not be in any danger. Go get whatever it is you need, and I'll meet you back here.''

He opened his mouth as if to argue and then, without saying what he'd intended, said, ''Fine.''

Angie was aware of his eyes following her as she crossed the street and wondered if it was her imagination that had put a look of something close to despair in them.

The post office was about the size of a walk-in closet. On one side was a bank of mailboxes, on the other was a bulletin board that held an assortment of notes and a couple of Wanted posters. In the center was a counter, behind which stood an old man wearing a faded gray sweater that almost perfectly matched his hair.

''Mornin','' he offered by way of greeting.

''Good morning.'' Angie smiled cheerfully, pretending not to notice the blatant curiosity with which he was eyeing her.

''What can I do for you?''

''I need some stamps.''

''Come to the right place for them. How many do you need?''

Angie asked for a booklet of first-class stamps and then shifted Gabby in her arms so that she could get to her purse.

''Cute baby,'' the man said as he fished her stamps out of a drawer.

"I won't argue with that," she said with a smile. "How much do I owe you?"

He gave her a total. "Saw you come in with Gabe Taylor."

"That's right. I'm his new housekeeper."

"Housekeeper?" The man's eyes widened, and she could all but see the gears turning as he digested this bit of information. "Known him long?"

"A while." She had no intention of telling him the history of her relationship with Gabe. Especially not when she didn't understand what was going on.

The old man looked undecided and then leaned across the counter toward her, pitching his voice low. "You maybe ought to think about finding yourself another job, ma'am."

"I like the one I have."

"Might not be safe. A woman alone out there on the Taylor place."

"What do you mean?"

"Why don't you tell her what you mean, Delbert?" Gabe's low voice startled both of them. With the door open to let in the fresh spring air, he'd been able to approach silently. Angie turned toward him and was shocked by the cold menace he projected. She wasn't surprised when Delbert mumbled something about having business to take care of and scurried toward the back of the building and disappeared. He left behind a thick silence.

"What was all that about?" Angie demanded.

"Did you get your stamps?"

"Yes. Are you going to tell me what's going on?"

"Not here." Without another word, he turned and walked out.

She stared after him for a moment but she could hardly insist that he stand in the middle of the Rock Creek post office and tell her why he seemed to have a quarrel with the whole town.

They drove most of the way home in silence. Angie was waiting for Gabe to open the conversation, to offer some explanation for Delbert's veiled warnings, not to mention his own peculiar behavior. By the time he parked the truck in front of the ranch house, it occurred to her that he didn't intend to say a word about it.

"Are you going to tell me what was going on, or am I going to have to drive back to town and corner poor old Delbert?"

Gabe had been reaching for the door handle but he stopped. She watched his profile and saw his jaw clench. She was suddenly afraid of what he might say, but it was too late to withdraw her question.

"I'm not exactly a favored citizen in this area," he said finally. "People aren't much inclined to forget past sins."

"What past sins?" she asked, completely bewildered. "What did you do that they can't forgive?"

"I spent time in prison."

Angie gasped. "In prison? You?"

"That's right." His tone was so carefully indifferent that they might have been talking about someone else.

"What on earth for?"

He looked at her then, his eyes cold and flat, his mouth a thin, hard line. "Rape."

The cab of the truck filled with a silence so profound it was almost painful. Angie was so stunned that her mind went completely blank. She just sat there, staring at him. Something flared in his eyes, an emotion that came and went too quickly for her to read it.

"I'll help you carry your stuff out when you're done packing," Without giving her a chance to respond, he jerked open the door handle and stepped out of the truck.

When she was done packing? Angie watched his long-legged stride eat up the distance to the house. Good grief. He thought she was going to leave because of this.

Her fingers fumbled with the straps on Gabby's car seat, but she finally managed to get them loose and lift the baby out. She slid down from the truck with a jarring thump just as Red approached, his bowlegged walk making him look as if he was striding across the deck of a ship.

"What's wrong with the boss? He took off for the house like he'd been stung by a bee."

"I'll explain later. Here." Angie thrust Gabby into his arms. She had a glimpse of his openmouthed expression of terror before she turned and sprinted for the house. She had to talk to Gabe.

He was in the kitchen, making coffee as if he hadn't a care in the world. Angie felt anger boil up in her. She stalked across the kitchen and grabbed hold of his sleeve, pulling him around to face her.

"What makes you think I'm going anywhere?" she demanded furiously. "Didn't you hear me last night? I told you I loved you. Did you think I was kidding?"

"You don't have to pretend it doesn't bother you," Gabe told her. "I saw your face."

"The only thing you saw in my face was surprise. And of course it bothers me. It bothers me to think of you spending time in jail for something you didn't do."

"How do you know I didn't do it?" he asked bitterly.

Angie snorted. "Don't be an idiot. You could no more rape a woman than you could flap your arms and take off flying."

Gabe stared at her, dumbfounded by her unquestioning faith in him. "You can't be that sure."

"Yes, I can. Anybody who believes you'd do something like that just doesn't know you as well as I do."

"The whole damned town believed it. Most of them still do and they've known me all my life."

"I told you last night that knowing someone isn't a matter of time. Are you going to tell me what happened?"

And for the first time in almost ten years, Gabe found himself talking about what had happened. When he got out of prison, he'd promised himself that he'd never talk about it again and he'd kept that promise. He'd offered no explanations, no excuses. The one or two people who'd scraped up the courage to mention the incident had been treated to a stare so cold, they'd backed down immediately.

Now, he found himself fumbling for the words to explain it to Angie. How he'd been a wild kid, a troublemaker in school and out. If there was a fight, he was in the middle of it. If a girl was out past curfew, she was probably out with him. The only place he hadn't screwed up was working on the ranch. He'd been cocky, hardheaded and arrogant as hell.

When a girl in a neighboring town had accused him of rape, it was no wonder everyone believed him capable of committing the crime. Hadn't the girl's father caught him sneaking out of the house after attacking the poor girl? Damned near beat him half to death, and Gabe deserved every blow. They'd always known he'd come to a bad end.

Two days after his twenty-fourth birthday, he'd gone to prison. Six months later, the girl had admitted that she'd lied. They'd met at a party and gone back to her house. They'd slept together. Then, when her father came home unexpectedly and caught Gabe in her bed, she'd screamed rape.

"I was lucky she had a conscience," Gabe finished. "Once she admitted she'd lied, they turned me loose."

"They should have put *her* in prison," Angie snapped, her eyes bright with anger.

Anger on his behalf, Gabe realized. He couldn't ever remember someone being angry *for* him.

"She was young," he said, shrugging. He'd let go of that particular anger a long time ago.

"So were you! You could have spent years in prison." Angie shot to her feet and paced across the room and then back again as if she was too full of anger to stay still.

"But I didn't."

She sat down again, clasping her hands on the table and leaning toward him. "If you were cleared, why would the people in town still blame you? Didn't they care that you were innocent?"

"I doubt if they know."

"What do you mean? You told them, didn't you?"

"The only people I told were my father and Red."

"But... didn't people ask why you were out of prison?" she asked in bewilderment.

"Nobody asked me."

There was a long silence. Angie sat back in her chair, her eyes considering. "Did you look at them like that?" she asked finally.

"Like what?"

"Like you were going to tear their head off if they so much as looked at you sideways?"

Gabe shifted uncomfortably in his seat. "How do I know how I looked at them?"

"Well, if you looked at them all icy cold like you looked at them today, it's no wonder they didn't ask you why you were out of prison. They probably thought they'd be taking their lives into their hands just to say hello to you."

Gabe thought back to those first visits to town, remembering the way the women would cross the street to avoid him; the veiled and not-so-veiled warnings he'd been given by some of the men.

"They treated me like I was a mad dog," he said, unaware of the old pain that laced his voice. "They all thought I was guilty."

"You said yourself that you hadn't exactly been a model citizen," Angie said gently.

"There's a big difference between a barroom brawl and raping a woman," he snapped. He stood up and paced over to the sink, leaning against it.

"Of course there is, but you *were* convicted. And if no one ever bothered to find out why you were let out of prison . . ." She let her words trail off.

Gabe stared out the window, not wanting to hear the logic in her words. He'd been holding on to the bitterness for a long time. It wasn't easy to hear that it might not be completely justified.

"Do you always ˜owl at everyone the way you did today?" Angie asked from behind him. There was a trace of humor lacing her voice, and he knew that she was looking at him with that same humor in her eyes.

"Worse sometimes," he admitted, turning to look at her.

"Worse? Good grief. It's a wonder you haven't turned half the town to salt. Or would it be stone? I guess salt is what happens when you look at something terribly sinful, which I've never thought quite fair. Shouldn't the people committing the sin be the ones who get turned to salt? I mean, why should you become a salt lick just for peeking? It doesn't seem—"

She broke off when he strode over to the table and caught hold of her shoulders, dragging her up out of her chair.

"What?" She looked up at him with those beautiful blue eyes, and Gabe felt his chest swell painfully tight.

"You talk more than anyone I've ever met in my life," he told her.

"And you talk less. So we—"

"I love you," he said, interrupting her ruthlessly.

She stared up at him, her mouth slightly open as if caught in midword. The silence stretched. And stretched.

"Well, I'll be damned," Gabe said softly. "If I'd known that was all it took to shut you up, I might have said it days ago."

"You love me?"

"Isn't that what I said?"

"Say it again," she pleaded breathlessly. "Say it again so I'll know I wasn't having an auditory hallucination."

"I love you," Gabe said obligingly. Funny how it seemed easier to say the second time around.

"You're sure? You're not just saying it because I said it to you? Because if you're saying it just because of that, I'd rather you didn't. I wouldn't want—"

Gabe employed his favorite method of silencing her. When he finally let her up for air, Angie opened her eyes and gave him a dazed look.

"I think you mean it."

"That's what I'm trying to tell you."

"How come?" She cuddled closer to him, her face glowing with happiness. "How come now and not last night? How come you're telling me now?"

"Maybe it's because you believed I was innocent even without me telling you," he said slowly.

"Of course I believed you were innocent. I keep telling you—I know you, Gabe Taylor."

He was starting to believe her.

They stood there without speaking for a little while, wrapped in each other's arms, content just to be together.

Angie spoke first. "I left Gabby with Red. You don't suppose he'll lose her, do you?" She didn't sound particularly concerned.

"Not likely. He likes her. Said she was cuter than a speckled pup." Angie's laughter made him grin. "That's a pretty high compliment from Red."

"I suppose we should go rescue him," she said but didn't move.

"People will think she's mine," Gabe noted.

"As far as I'm concerned, she is yours," Angie said. She tilted her head back to look up at him, her eyes serious. "You're the one who brought her into the world, the first person to hold her. I think she'll be awfully lucky to have you for a father."

Gabe had to clear his throat before he could respond. "When we get married, everyone will be sure she's mine."

"Are we getting married?" Angie asked dreamily.

"As soon as we can arrange it."

"Good."

Angie pressed her face to his chest, feeling the solid thud of his heart beneath her cheek. Who would ever have dreamed that getting lost in a snowstorm could lead to such a perfect ending?

DANGER AND DESIRE

Mallory Rush

Dear Reader,

As we all know, sometimes bad things happen to good people—and vice versa—and by golly, it just isn't fair! Wouldn't it be nice if we lived in a world where justice always triumphed? Even better, if true love always conquered all.

One of the real joys being a writer is the ability to create the kind of world I wished I lived in, and to share that world with readers. But even in fiction, my characters must still grapple with the realities we all face: Moral and ethical dilemmas. Divided loyalties. Fear of failure. Love and the risk of rejection.

How simple it would be if these judgment calls were divided cleanly between lines of black and white, right and wrong, win or lose. But that's not usually how life or good fiction work. *Danger and Desire* gave me the opportunity to explore this fascinating mire of contradictions life can throw at us while we simply try our best to do the right thing.

Just between us, I'm glad I don't have to tread the same high wire Clay Barker and Melissa Lovelace have ahead of them. She's on one end, he's on the other—and neither have a pole to sustain their balance. All they have to guide them are their hearts and mutual determination to see justice done. There are obstacles aplenty in their way—they're working from opposite sides of the law.

I hope you enjoy *Danger and Desire*, and I wish you the sweetest justice of all: May *you* get your man!

Warm wishes,

Mallory Rush

Chapter One

"BAD NEWS, CLAY. *Bad*, bad news."

"Badder than me?" He chuckled, then quickly sobered at his associate's anxious nod. Any news "badder" than Clay Barker himself had to be worse than awful. "Have a sit, Red, and lay it on me." Clay waved to the Queen Anne chair facing the carved antique desk where he played judge, jury and, more often than not, hangman.

Minus the rope, that was. He meted out justice, fair and simple, but executions weren't his job. The way he figured, he might be "the law" at Revenge Unlimited, but that didn't give him the right to play God. To take another life would make him no better than the criminals he cleaned off the streets.

Sitting, Red leaned close and whispered, "You had this office checked out lately?"

"First thing on my agenda every mornin'. No bugs, it's clean. So let's get down to business. What's up?"

Red made a sound that was between a snort and a groan. "You remember that hooker from Austin—the one you took on personally after she had her face messed?"

"Sure, I do. Pretty gal, except for a broken nose, split lip, eyes too swollen to tell what color. Of course, she looked real good in comparison to the john who did it after I let him know that's no way to treat a lady...of the night."

"Turns out that wasn't just any john." Red slapped the desk. "Hell and be damned, Clay, it was a fed!"

"Oh, really?" he drawled. Leaning back in his big leather chair, Clay propped his feet on a neat pile of Barker Imports letterhead. "Does this mean I'm supposed to be shaking in my boots?" He tapped his pair of custom-made ostrich skins together.

"You oughta be, but you don't have enough sense for that. We're in deep trouble, Clay. Our friend at the Bureau sent word that the top dog wants your head."

"The only beef the FBI has with me is for making their job easier," he said flatly, unable to believe even the top dog would "cut off his nose to spite his face," as his mother, God rest her soul, would have put it. "I clean up the streets, no charge to the taxpayers, and deal with the vermin that slip through the legal cracks that keep their hands tied. As for the fed I dealt with personally, if he'd kept his hands off that woman, I wouldn't have had to get mine dirty on him. Fed or no fed, nobody has a right to do what he did. And if he values his continued health, he won't be doing it again."

"You're talking business as usual, and this is anything but. Your client conveniently forgot to tell you that she had a regular who's a major drug dealer and the fed who beat her up got carried away trying to extract some information. It wasn't a mean bit of S and M, like she said.''

Clay finger-drummed the desk and considered the belated facts. Seemed for once he hadn't been thorough enough in checking out a potential client's claim of being victimized by the legal system. Loopholes, deals cut, bail jumping—the reasons people came to him were endless. But every case he took on had a common thread that ran through the shredded fabric of his own life: while the victim was held prisoner to trauma, rage and fear, the violator roamed free. Revenge Unlimited was about justice, not mindless vigilantism.

All things considered, the hooker still qualified.

"Okay, so that makes her a liar—of omission,'' Clay said. "As for the perpetrator, his reasons don't justify his actions. And frankly, I doubt the Bureau suits would condone such overly ambitious methods of persuasion—including the big shot who supposedly wants my head. He must be upset because I'm getting jobs done that going by the book can't, and it's screwing with his Christmas bonus, not to mention his ego.''

"Unfortunately it goes deeper than that. You pissed off the wrong person, Clay. The fed whose face you rearranged just happens to be Mr. Big Shot's favorite nephew. A word of advice? Close shop before you end up doing hard time with the same kind of scum that keeps you in business."

Clay knew for a fact it wasn't his front business that Red was referring to. A man didn't get much more respectable than being a purveyor of fine European imports, and while he wasn't the richest man in Dallas, he did better than okay. Good enough that he could pay his handpicked associates like Red plenty well for their services, despite the fact his organization was nonprofit. A price could not be put on justice. Besides, his real payoff had nothing to do with money and everything to do with needing a reason to live.

Close shop? He may as well put a gun to his head and join Martha and their two children at the graveyard he visited when the days were too empty, the nights too lonely. Hell, seven years and he still couldn't sleep without seeing the mangled remains of his family. Why them and not him? *Why?*

Knowing that was one answer he'd never have, he returned his attention to the immediate concern. "Should I take it that you're putting in your notice?"

"You take it right, Clay. You do a lot of people a lot of good, and working with you these past five years has been a privilege. But I've got a new wife and a baby on the way to think about, and nothing is worth risking what I've got."

Yep, there was the difference between Clay Barker and the others. Most of them had something to lose; Clay Barker had already lost it all.

"If I were in your position, I'd feel the same way. Don't be a stranger, you hear?" They shook hands. "Take good care of that wife and baby. Oh, and Red, you're right. Nothing's worth risking what makes a man well and truly rich."

After shutting the door that separated his legitimate enterprise from the not-so-legit office, Clay tried to sort his mixed feelings. Happy as he was for his friend's reasons to get out while the getting was good, he couldn't deny a twinge of envy.

Returning to the desk where he screwed with the screwed-up legal system—one that had certainly screwed him royally—Clay found himself wishing that he had something to lose again, too.

Chapter Two

SHE WAS TRYING HARD not to sweat. And just her luck that she was wearing a bulky cardigan on this unseasonably warm October day. Prepared as she'd ever be, Melissa Lovelace held tight to the bulging manila envelope documenting her cause. A deep, bracing breath and in she went.

The smell of leather and potpourri and exorbitant prices assaulted her comparatively pedestrian senses. Clay Barker's upscale store was the kind of place that made the rich feel at home and people such as herself feel like imposters pretending they could afford to do more than browse.

Pretending to browse, she silently rehearsed her plea for help from a man whose ruthless reputation was a stark contrast to his obvious taste for all things refined and elegant.

"You're welcome to play it, ma'am," drawled a deep voice that sounded as rich and mellow as the grand piano she was gingerly touching.

Intending to decline and ask to speak to the proprietor, Melissa turned.

And promptly forgot the opening line she'd rehearsed.

If looks could kill, she was a goner. The man was drop-dead gorgeous. She'd seen a picture of him but it hadn't prepared her for this larger-than-life work of masculine art. His clothes were impeccably tailored and surely custom-made to fit his lean but muscle-mean Texas-size frame. As for his face, there was nothing pretty about it, yet that only seemed to accentuate his rare kind of handsome.

Character. It was grooved into every fine line that called him forty, going on a hundred. There was a story in his gray eyes, which were oddly warm, yet haunted. The ghost of a smile played about his firmly-set lips.

Melissa wet hers and recouped as best she could. "Mr. Barker? Mr. Clay Barker?"

"That's what I answer to." A leisurely glance at the envelope she clutched to her chest and he said, "What can I do for you today, Ms....?"

"Melissa Lovelace." Although they were alone, she lowered her voice to a confidential hush. "I was told through a friend of a friend, that you have another business. One that's referred to as Revenge Unlimited."

"No." He contradicted his flat denial with a single, short nod. "Sorry, but I've never heard of it. I do, however, have an opening for a salesperson and if that's your résumé you brought along, I'd be happy to look it over in my office." At her quick acceptance, he raised a finger that had the effect of a snap-to-it snap on the neatly dressed, grandmotherly-looking woman who hurried over.

"Yes, Clay?" she asked, taking Melissa in while efficiently fluffing her gray bangs back into place.

"Hold my calls please, Amanda, while I see to this lady."

In minutes Melissa decided that she'd never been treated like such a lady in her life. From the light pressure of palm to elbow as he escorted her to his tastefully appointed office, to the chair he held out, to the offer of cappuccino—which she accepted and he prepared, then served with a smile—she was captivated by this contradiction of a man.

This was Clay Barker? This was the merciless vigilante with a list of crimes against criminals? Maybe she was too green—barely out of Quantico and on her first important assignment—but her instincts insisted that this was a sting that stank.

More than ever, she wished she'd been given access to his substantial file. As it was, she'd been handed selective information, briefed, and assigned the position of decoy. At last, her chance to redeem the family name after her father, once a top-notch fed, had been outed in disgrace. So much was riding on her performance, and how thrilled she'd been to prove herself worthy of this entrustment. Gone was the thrill. She was struggling to lie through her teeth and do her job.

She had to do her job.

Easing into the chair beside her, rather than behind his desk, he said with the kindness of a benevolent priest, "Now, let's see that résumé of yours."

Despite a sudden reluctance, Melissa handed over the envelope stuffed with mock newspaper clippings on the out-of-town murder of her "brother," along with overwhelming evidence that the suspect was guilty but, thanks to a too-convenient alibi and friends with legal clout, had walked away a free man.

While sipping the cappuccino, she covertly watched as he read. The more he read, the thinner his lips became; a muscle ticked beside his clean-shaven jaw. Halfway through, he turned a gaze on her that was filled with simmering anger and stark compassion.

"My, but what impressive credentials you have."

His whisper was a lethal sound. The wire taped to her ribs—a precaution in case he discovered the bug under his desk—should have picked up his voice. For all the good that would do, since he was talking in innuendo.

Obviously, he knew he was under surveillance and was taking no chances. Like it or not, she had to persuade him to do just that. Reminding herself that her reputation was on the line, she searched for a way to make him say something incriminating.

"There's more," she said, urging him to flip through the threatening letters pieced together from magazine cutouts. "I only brought a few, but this gives you an idea why I came to you. I'm really des—"

He cut her off with a finger pressed to her lips. His own formed a warning frown, letting her know the contact was precautionary, not personal.

But it felt personal.

"Deserving," he said firmly. "These are excellent letters of reference. But I'd like to check them out before making a decision. You don't mind, do you?"

His finger was still on her lips and it was more than a little disturbing to feel her tongue press against her teeth, which denied it a sampling lick. He was slow to remove his silencing touch and looked surprised at his own reluctance to enable her to answer.

"That's... that's fine."

"Good," he said gruffly. "I'll get back to you on this." He reached for a card on his desk, jotted a note, then handed it to her.

Melissa scanned the message. "7:00 p.m. tonight— Iguana Mirage in Deep Elum."

"Thank you, Mr. Barker. I'll look forward to it." She was about to slip the card into her purse when his fingers slid over hers and plucked the card away. Brief as the contact was, she gave a small jump, jolted by the frisson.

On the heels of that unexpected charge came the daunting realization that he didn't want her to have even this minor piece of evidence.

Leading her to the office door, he offered his hand—a warm firm grip of her clammy grasp. They shook on it. In that single gesture she had a piece of evidence that said a lot more than the card: Clay Barker was a man of his word.

Was that in the file she wasn't privy to? Melissa was starting to feel a bit set up herself. And then she had the wind knocked right out of her.

A flick, a tiny flick of his fingertip to her palm, was followed by his engaging smile. Discreet, but the most overwhelming innuendo in this fiasco of a meeting.

After a cordial goodbye, Melissa left with less than she'd come for and plenty more than she'd bargained for.

Clay watched the tempting sight of a long blond ponytail and shapely backside disappear from his shrewd view.

Returning to his desk, he didn't waste time reviewing the envelope's contents. He'd seen enough to know what he was dealing with.

Which was more than he could say for Melissa Lovelace.

She was young, refreshingly naive, and had a voice that was pure molasses. Sweet to the ear and warm enough to heat up a griddle. *Ssss.* He could still feel the chemistry they'd generated and judging from that parting little gasp of hers, Miss Melissa wouldn't be forgetting it anytime soon.

As for himself, he'd gotten past his widower's guilt for borrowing what ease he could from a woman's arms some years ago. But those occasional indulgences were occasional and indulgences.

Melissa Lovelace wasn't that kind of a woman. The effect she'd had on him was an unexpected treat—like the candy bar he unwrapped—but a man like himself had to be careful in his nibbling of something so indescribably delicious.

Even if the candy wasn't laced with poison, too much of a sweet tooth could earn anyone a date with a drill.

Chapter Three

"DAMN, LOVELACE, didn't you see anything we could use for material evidence?"

"Sorry, but unless you can use his interior decorator there's nothing visible in that office worth confiscating."

"Don't be cute," snapped Special Agent Dean. Her Maalox-guzzling boss was chugging away in the borrowed local office decorated with Most Wanted posters.

Clay Barker's wasn't among them. Yet.

Melissa decided she could go for a chug of antacid herself. Not that it would get rid of the butterflies winging around the knots in her stomach.

"I did the best I could," she asserted, knowing that wasn't entirely true.

"You'll have to do better next time. Did you get any sense of how soon that'll be?"

"He gave me..." *Tell him. Tell him about the card. To hell with finding out the real scoop, just do your damn job.* "He gave me the feeling that it won't be long because he was sympathetic and wanted to help."

"Yeah, that sounds like Barker."

"You sound like you know more about the guy than I do and what you know of him is...admirable."

Dean shot her a quelling glance—one that was tinged with regret. It was similar to her father's expression when he'd run off a boyfriend with a wild reputation and suffered a daughter's wrath—a daughter who had some growing up to do before she could appreciate a parent who held the reins tight because he really cared.

Dean wasn't a coddler by a long shot, but he cared in his own way. Though he had a gruff demeanor to match his "been there, done that" middle-aged face that was both wizened and weary, Melissa perceived a really good guy beneath. He reminded her of Andy on "NYPD Blue"—were Andy the color of rich dark toffee. Maybe it was the way Dean mopped his brow a lot with wrinkled handkerchiefs that always needed bleaching; maybe it was his no-nonsense directness of a team player who could be hell on his teammates—especially rookies like her—if they didn't play the game his way.

Then again, maybe it was his paunch that rode just over his belt, testimony to his fondness for beer and french fries. Every now and then she had an urge to poke his stomach and say "Pillsbury," but that surely wouldn't win a giggle. Especially not now while he plowed a meaty hand through his short black hair and fixed her with a warning gaze.

"Look," Dean said with a heavy sigh, "it doesn't matter what either of us knows about him, or what I might personally think about Clay Barker. We've got our orders and if his head doesn't roll, ours will. This is your chance to get a leg up on the ladder earlier than most agents ever have a shot at. Considering your, uh, roots with the force, that's a real vote of confidence. A word of advice? Keep your nose clean and don't blow it."

"Yes, sir," she said with a hint of sarcasm. It wasn't outright insubordination, but she resented the hell out of this subtle twist of the knife she was under.

Dean wasn't mean-spirited, but clearly he didn't want her snooping and turning up anything that would compromise the blind loyalty that set her apart from her father—a good fed gone bad. The payoff money he had taken from a drug lord had been for her. But what did she care about Ivy League tuition when the price was so devastatingly high? For Daddy, the wonderful, doting father he had been, and for herself, pride demanded that she rewrite the past. It was her ambition—had been since their world had collapsed five years ago—to prove a Lovelace still deserved to be trusted with a badge.

Maybe she'd been wrong. It had taken her father years to corrupt his position and here she was, on her first assignment, withholding information and breaking from the legal pack to do some private investigating of her own.

The problem was, a tail would be following Barker and there she'd be consorting with the enemy. No matter that she was compelled to do what felt right, her future was on the line.

"I just remembered something," she said suddenly. "I saw two tickets to the symphony on his desk, dated for tonight."

"It's not much but at least that'll save us the trouble of keeping up with him in traffic. He's damn slippery, whether behind a wheel or doing one of his deeds."

"Misdeeds, you mean?"

Dean scowled. "Yeah, whatever."

A curt dismissal and Melissa took refuge in the nearest rest room. She sat on a toilet, put her head between her knees and battled a wave of nausea.

Whether she was sicker with herself than she was with the smell of a dirty deal, she wasn't sure.

The only thing she was sure of was that Clay Barker had outsmarted the wire she wouldn't be wearing tonight. And glad as she was that she hadn't been able to incriminate him, she was still duty-bound to get what information she could on an enigma who'd made her knees go weak.

THE IGUANA MIRAGE was manic as usual on most any given night. It made conversing difficult and that suited Clay's purposes fine. As did the crowd he concealed himself in to watch how Melissa negotiated her

way through the throng of partyers that ranged from
drag queens to cowboys.

A person with his kind of training could tell a lot
from the way a person moved. Melissa slipped her way
through with street-smart ease, cinched with a natural poise. For not knowing much about her, he was
certain of important qualities: She had guts, and what
confidence she lacked was hidden behind attitude and
a knockout set of baby blues that a man could get lost
in if he wasn't real careful.

Her eyes spoke. And how. A rowdy that'd had one
too many latched on to her arm and before Clay could
jostle his way over to intercede, sweet Melissa had that
out-of-line sucker backing off like a shot with no more
than an innocent blink and two words that surely described what any man with a hormone in his body
would like to do to her.

On she moved through the cloud of bar smoke and
neon lights. She blended in like cream stirred into
coffee, giving him a charge more potent than ten cups
of kick-ass caffeine. Simply watching her gave him a
totally new kind of high.

It was the first time a woman had given him a rush
to rival that of the satisfaction of meting out his own
form of justice. And she'd done it without so much as
a kiss from those lips he never should have touched.
He'd be touching them still, and with more than his
finger, if he hadn't the sense God gave him.

By the time she was close enough for him to see those Marilyn Monroe curves that even a brown bag couldn't hide—much less the short black sweater-dress, purple opaque stockings and black booties she wore—the sense that God gave him was close to deserting him.

With the same phantom movement of a killing machine he'd learned from the SEALs, Clay maneuvered his way behind her.

"You look like a long cool draw of Dom Pérignon poured into a Baccarat flute," he said in her ear, his teeth begging to tug a dangling gold hoop. "Nothing that pricey to be had in this joint besides you, but name your poison and I'll buy."

The shoulder beneath his palm that had initially stiffened, relaxed to the consistency of melting wax.

"Clay," she said with a genuine smile, then quickly amended, "I mean, Mr. Barker. I was afraid I'd missed you."

Glad for the excuse to be so close he could smell the delicate fragrance of her hair, the cologne on her neck, Clay was struck with a pang of longing for a good woman to care enough to miss him.

"I'd rather you keep the Clay and get rid of the Mr., while I do the same with Ms. Glad to see you Melissa. You've been on my mind since you left." He really meant it, and what a twist of difference that was.

Before she could reply or turn, a push from behind had Clay suddenly flush against her. While the press of bodies prevented him from immediately regaining a polite distance, his own body reacted to its intimate fit against her backside.

"Sorry," he said, while not feeling sorry at all.

"No problem," she gasped, suddenly lunging for a just-vacated table beside them.

"Good save!" Claiming two chairs before someone else did, he seated her, then sat down himself.

She leaned across the table littered with glasses and an overflowing ashtray that a harried waitress overlooked as she rushed past. "This doesn't seem like your kind of place."

"Darlin', I've been places that'd curl your toes. Maybe that's why I like that snooty store of mine—kind of evens things out. Now, how about I head for the bar and save us what's sure to be a long wait. What'll you have?"

Melissa wanted to say, "You." He looked even better in a flannel shirt and faded jeans than he had in a smart suit. But she knew better than to compromise herself any more than she already had.

"A beer would be fine." While Clay forged his way through, she noticed he seemed to stand taller than anyone there and it wasn't just his towering height. He emanated power and purpose, like a man with a mission who would stop at nothing to accomplish it.

She had a mission of her own to determine how just or unjust the case she'd been assigned to really was. Somehow she had to get him to reveal the reasons behind the line he straddled, and why the heat was suddenly on.

But if she found him to be more victim than victimizer, what would she do?

"I decided you're too elegant for a draft so I ordered up a couple of imported brews." He placed one in her hand and clinked amber rims. "Here's lookin' at you, kid."

Bogey had nothing on the look he gave her. Or the sexy half smile he wore as fine as his jeans as he scribbled a note on a napkin and pushed it her way.

My office was bugged. I'm under surveillance and it could be close as the next table. Act like we're on a date, okay?

When she nodded, he turned over the napkin and wrote: *Do you think you were followed?*

"No." She wanted to tell him that neither was he, since he was supposedly at the symphony.

The napkin went into a half-filled glass and she wondered at the lengths he was going to. Then again, he was smart as hell to erase even the most minor of details.

"You're a very elusive man." A fed's observation but spoken like an intrigued date.

"And you're a very appealing woman. One that could spell big trouble for even an elusive man."

Her heart slammed against her chest. Had she said something, done something to tip him off? But then he whispered in her ear, "I'm more worried about the trouble you could be in than the kind you could spell for me. We need to talk but this isn't the place. Let's finish our drinks, then we'll ease out of here.''

Their drinks downed, she grabbed her purse and noted that Clay scanned the room as he cut a sure path to the brimming dance floor.

''It's a jungle,'' he said, skimming her waist, then pulling her against him while everyone else gyrated to the Stone Temple Pilots. ''I've seen more than my share of action, but combat's got nothing on this. I don't want to lose you so hold tight to me, darlin'.''

Hold tight she did while they were bumped from all sides. Clay buffered the crush with his arms around her, his palms sweeping over her back. It felt protective and intimate and so complete he could have been doing a body search.

Was he? she frantically wondered. Was that the real purpose of this dance? Lord knew, he was sealed tight enough against her chest and hips to determine if she was wearing a wire. Of course, it was allowing her to determine that he had a pistol strapped beneath his shirt. A .38 was her guess; she'd left hers behind in the motel room, along with the FBI technicians who were installing a camera and recording equipment.

Fed stuff, and she was trained to use it all. No training needed to realize the gun wasn't the only arsenal he was packing.

If he was suspicious of her, it certainly wasn't impeding the effect she was having on him. As for herself, she was beginning to realize this was indeed a dangerous man—not the least of which was his ability to arouse, body search or no.

"Let's go." His abrupt command contrasted with his smooth move for the emergency exit that led to the alley.

It was narrow and dimly lit but after assessing that it was empty, he cinched her waist and moved with a skillful fleetness into a nook of bricks that sequestered them in darkness except for a slender shaft of moonlight.

"The ambience could be better, but we can talk here. First off, who exactly gave you my name?"

Melissa gave him the name she'd been told he would trust—though obviously he shouldn't.

"Fred Sipple, huh? What's he up to these days?"

Giving you up to save his own skin for something, that's what. "I—I'm not really sure. Like I said, he's a friend of a friend."

"Okay, next question. Why'd you come to me instead of going to the law for your rightful protection?"

This much they'd prepared her for, given her pat answers to the questions he was sure to ask. "You saw the kind of justice that was served my brother. The evidence pointed to Ryan McGee, his business partner, and he got off scot-free. And why? Because Ryan had friends with connections and his father's a respected judge. It never even got to court. They said his alibi held up and a big surprise that was, since it was his sister who vouched for him. But he did it, and all the proof I gave them was dismissed as circumstantial."

"And now he's sending you threatening letters. Is he stalking you?"

She hesitated. "Yes. I'm afraid he'll track me down here. And even if he doesn't, I can't stay in Dallas indefinitely. My job, my home, and what few relatives I have are in Atlanta. But after the way my brother's murder was handled, I can't live there any more than I can trust the system with my life. That's why I came to you."

She waited, her heartbeat on hold while Clay considered the lies she'd fed him. Part of her wanted him to be the kind of man who would champion such a cause. Part of her prayed he would turn her down flat.

Slowly, he gave a nod. "Now that I've got the full story, I'm glad that you did come to me. I've been where you're at and it's people like you that make me think there's a reason I'm still here." Definitely here; here and stirring her senses with no more than his nearness, which exuded confidence, caring and charisma. "I'll take your case, Melissa."

That big step up the ladder suddenly felt like a toppling fall. He'd swallowed the bait but all she could think was, thank God nobody knew it but her. *Why were they doing this?* Maybe Clay Barker worked outside the system, but he worked from a code of honor that clearly transcended this scam.

Still, she had to play it out.

Or tip him off.

Her conscience was deadlocked with duty. "Maybe...maybe I should take my chances with the police. I mean, what you said about being under surveillance—"

"You let me worry about that. As for you going to the police, if I thought they'd give you the proper protection, I'd say that's exactly what you should do. But considering what you've told me? No." He moved closer, braced his palms on either side of her head, against the bricks that were scoring her back. "I don't want to see anything bad happen to you, Mel."

Mel. Only her dad had ever called her that. Her heart broke a little, remembering how good it had been before he'd committed suicide. Really, her father had been dead inside ever since the disgrace he'd brought on his only child. Mel, so proud of her widowed daddy. A daddy who'd let her rub his shiny badge for good luck when she was a child. A child who had wanted to grow up to be just like daddy.

Nostalgia mingled with the bittersweet now. And her heart broke a little more. Clay was so near she could smell the smoke on his clothes, the beer on his breath, the clean scent of his cologne. And she was supposed to be the instrument that would send him to prison and take all that away; reduce this proud man to a numbered shirt behind bars.

She took a steadying breath and was filled with his vital presence. "You're a good man, Clay Barker, and I don't want to be the one responsible for anything bad happening to you."

"Darlin', I'll let you in on a little secret." *Don't!* she wanted to shout. But there were his lips flirting with her temple and making it hard to even think. "What's left of my heart is good but I can be one mean, nasty bastard. There's a reason for that and one I've never shared with a client before." His pause was significant, as was the challenge in his shadowed gaze. "But you're not just any client, are you?"

Chapter Four

"WHAT . . . WHAT DO YOU MEAN?"

"You know exactly what I mean." When she shook her head, he felt the rise of compassion. Poor Melissa, she didn't stand a chance against the likes of him. "We've been setting each other off like bottle rockets ever since you wanted to play that piano in a store that's not half as classy as you. My own hands are itching to get in your hair and, if you don't mind my sayin' so, all over you, to be exact. I have some very stringent ethics when it comes to business—both businesses. Getting personally involved with a client is something I've never done, never even been tempted to do."

"Why are you telling me this?"

For more reasons than I understand, myself, he wanted to tell this woman who smacked of integrity. A woman who had an effect on him that went beyond the physical. Just maybe she'd work some magical miracle and help save his unsavable soul. But given she had more to lose than he did, he deemed it only fair to give her a glimpse of the danger he posed to a woman who'd be foolish enough to care.

"Because I want you to know I'm not the sort who tries to take advantage of anyone who's clearly vulnerable. Which you are. But I'm very close to kissing you, anyway, despite the poison you're sure to taste when I do." Taking a deep breath, he told himself to just say it. "I'm damaged, Mel."

Her eyes in the sparse moonlight were pools of concern but her response was direct. "What happened?"

"You ever see the movie *Death Wish?*"

"Charles Bronson. His family was murdered and he took the law into his own hands to keep others from being victimized the way he'd been."

"That's the one. Suffice it to say the movie was a fairy tale compared to the nightmare I can't close my eyes without seeing all over again. Picture this— There's a man who quit playing soldier after he met one of the best women God ever put on this earth. They started a business and thanks to luck and hard work it took off. Along came a baby, then another one. She took care of the children while he spent more and more of his time in the pursuit of making money."

For a moment he couldn't go on, wishing back all the time he'd wasted on stupid ambition. "So anyway, he's coming home late as usual and he's calling out, 'Honey, sorry I'm late but—' And that's as far as he gets before he drops his kiss-and-make-up flowers on the floor. A lamp's overturned. And there's blood, a trail of it to the kitchen."

"Oh, God. Where were the children?"

"It appeared they must have walked in and he decided to get rid of the only witnesses. So there I am, holding my family like three Raggedy Anns with the stuffings coming out of them. Laid them to rest, then-respectable law-abiding citizen that I was, and put my faith in the system that was sure to see justice done." With a snort of sick disgust, he added, "And my, oh my, what justice I got after they caught the filthy bastard."

"Don't tell me he was given a light sentence."

"Hardly. See, it didn't matter that they caught him with our silverware at a pawnshop, enough to pay for a week's fix. Turned out it didn't matter he was a junkie with all sorts of previous charges that never quite made it to court. Maybe it had something to do with his daddy being a state senator and his brother vouching they'd been cruising that night. Seems they found the silverware dumped on a side street. Guess that butcher got nervous and decided to ditch the evidence."

"But what about fingerprints, hair or skin samples? Surely there was other evidence."

"Sounds like you watch your share of detective shows," he noted. At her quick nod, he slowly shook his head. "For leaving in a hurry, there was an amazing lack of evidence. And just as amazing was that before they could impound his car to search it, it was stolen and never found. After a cursory investigation, a few other suspects were rounded up but there was nothing to pin on them. Within a year my case went the way of my family. Buried."

He smacked the bricks beside her head and demanded, "You hearing all this, Melissa? Is it striking a familiar chord?"

She shuddered. Familiar? More like a blueprint of her own fake case.

"I can't even imagine living with that kind of horror."

"Living?" He snorted. "I died seven years ago, darlin'. You're in the company of a dead man. One who walks and talks and eats out a lot since he can't step into a kitchen without needing to puke. The body's there—make that *here*—" he brushed his chest against hers "—but the soul's as dark as the grave I court on a regular basis. Sometimes I'm not sure if I do what I do for some kind of renegade justice or so I can get my death wish. No such luck. Yet. Want to know what became of that junkie?"

Something told her that was information that could send Clay Barker to death row—give him his wish, along with that of whoever was wanting revenge.

"No. No, Clay, I don't."

"Good," he said with an odd note of approval. "Now, enough about me and mine, it's you and yours we need to discuss before we can get on with more pleasurable pursuits, so let's wrap this up quick. Are you wanting an eye for an eye? As in, murder for murder?''

Was he capable of it? She didn't doubt that for a second. Clay had killed that senator's son and she didn't need to do any homework to confirm what she knew as surely as she breathed. What she did need to know was if he would kill again. Had he turned from being protector of the innocent to self-appointed executioner of the guilty?

"He deserves to be dead," she said carefully. "But I'm not sure if I want his blood on my hands."

"It'd be on mine. On these very hands that are touching your neck and could snap it in a heartbeat." His thumb stroked her jugular. "You're not afraid of me, are you, Mel?"

She was afraid of him like she'd never been afraid before. Scared senseless that this damaged man could damage her heart—and destroy her career in the process.

"Should I be?" she whispered haltingly.

"Oh, yeah," he murmured. "You most definitely should be fearful of a man who's as needy as I am." He smiled then. With about as much warmth as a Canadian winter. "However, special as you are, I wouldn't kill him even for you. I'm in the business of righting wrongs—but two wrongs don't make a right. It's a fine line I walk and this is where I draw it— I'll ensure your safety with an ample reminder that you'd better stay that way. Even a hint of a threat and I'll make sure he *wishes* he was dead."

Melissa breathed a silent sigh of relief. "And just what do you charge for such services?"

"Depends on what you can afford. Seein' that money's no object to me and I like to consider my organization as a nonprofit social service, I prefer to barter. Nice suit I was wearing today, wasn't it?"

"Brooks Brothers, eat your heart out."

"Yep. Even retired tailors can fall on hard times and find out it's not what they know but who they know that calls the shots. I call 'em as I see them. Oh, which reminds me. That envelope you gave me had a phone number where you could be reached and—"

"Did you call there?" she asked anxiously.

"Why do you sound like you're worried that I might've?"

Where was her training when she needed it? Top of her class and she'd been reduced to weighing the price of her failure against the possible miscarriage of justice she'd been given to carry out.

Justice. She had crusaded for it from grade one when the class bully had picked on a classmate half his size. When playing peacemaker hadn't worked, she'd given that bully a shiner that had landed her in the principal's office.

Daddy had been proud. *Pride.* It was as deep in her bones as her thirst for justice. And now the two were colliding. But how high could she hold her head if justice was sacrificed in the name of personal pride?

Oddly enough, she did feel some pride in the simple human decency of giving Clay what warning she dared. "Of course I'm worried about you calling me. If you're being bugged, then there could be a tap on your phone."

"There is," he assured her with a dry chuckle. "And that's why I didn't call but let my fingers do the walking." He walked his down her arm and rubbed her inner wrist. "Your pulse is beating awfully fast. So's mine. Seems you're doing one helluva job at bringing me back to life. Now, about that motel where you're staying…" His lips swept lightly over hers and his tongue made a quick dart before retreating.

"Yes?" she whispered, grateful for the wall's support.

"It's not exactly a Motel 6, but I'd rather you be staying somewhere with a style more suitable to you."

"I'm afraid that's not within my means." Not only that, she was staying where the Bureau had put her up. Which conveniently happened to be where her "stalker" would be spotted, engendering a call to Clay for help; the designated showdown would then take place in her room. And once Clay attacked her supposed stalker on camera, then the feds would burst in and have their man. Caught in the act after he'd managed to log over a hundred cases of retribution without once being pulled in for questioning.

Clearly, he had his supporters. And they weren't limited to the local law, which was playing awfully dumb and showing a distinct lack of support.

"My means are plenty ample," he assured her. "And I'd very much like to expend some on a worthy cause. Let me put you up, Mel. No strings, I swear. I just want you staying in the best place possible for as long as you're here. Given my current situation, it could take a little while to deal with yours. By the time I can manage it, who knows? Maybe you'll decide Dallas has enough fatal appeal to stay for more than a visit."

He was fatal appeal incarnate, and she was ready to take up residence in this alley in exchange for the kiss she was longing for. If only he wasn't who he was. If only she wasn't who she was....

But if-onlys weren't what was. She needed to know more. Things like—could this be some kind of a test, with Clay the decoy, to assure the powers-that-be that she was dedicated to a fault?

No. No, that was ridiculous. She was being paranoid and still carrying megaguilt for the sins of her father, committed on her behalf. But what of Clay's sins? Was he truly as fine and good as she believed him to be—or was he on to the scam and using her to outwit the system? Much as she wanted to shun such a thought, *that* was a possibility she couldn't ignore. She certainly wouldn't be the first woman who fell for a charmer that used them, then discarded them.

Melissa fought the urge to drop her face in her hands and groan. This was all so complex, so confusing, and she hated to be confused. Hated standing here and saying nothing to this man who was patiently waiting while she sorted her jumbled thoughts and finally emerged with a simple truth: She just wanted to do the right thing. But if hell was indeed paved with the best intentions, she could end up getting burned if her instincts were wrong. Those instincts were all she really had to guide her. Between her sheltered upbringing, making Daddy proud with straight A's at Brown, then needing that 4.0 for a scholarship to finish her last two years with a major in political science—big whoop; try to get a job with that—and waitressing before her personal mission drove her to Quantico, she hadn't gotten much experience in power plays or with men who thrived on power.

Clay emanated power, wore the mantle of it with the ease reserved for one who hadn't inherited it by position or money; his was the kind that came embedded in the genes. She was a rookie. He was a hard-hitting, big-league player pitching more curveballs than she could possibly catch. But she was smart, Melissa told herself; she caught on fast. All she needed was time to sift the weevils from the flour to determine if throwing her lot in with Clay was worth sacrificing her personal quest, her reputation and career—hell, just about everything that defined her life.

Question: How much time did she have? Dean had indicated someone wanted Barker badly enough to say, "However long it takes, just make it quick."

Her guess was they were counting on a month, tops.

"Melissa? You're awful quiet. Hope you didn't take offense. I just want to help you. It'd make me feel real good." He leaned in, brushed his hips lightly against hers. "C'mon darlin'," he murmured, "make me feel good."

Chapter Five

MELISSA DECIDED Clay Barker was a criminal, all right. It had to be illegal for a man to be so devastatingly seductive that he could make a woman want to make love in a dark alley.

"You're making it hard to think," she softly accused as he slid his hands into her hair.

"Then, don't. Just say, 'Yes. Yes, Clay, I'll stay where we can meet in more hospitable surroundings and talk without anyone else listening in.'"

It was a tempting offer. His home was being watched. His office wasn't safe. Her motel room was even less so. As for any future meetings like this, she'd have an ulcer to compete with Dean's in less than a week.

Another hotel? It was a viable option—*if* she could come and go off-duty without being spotted with Clay; *if* she could juggle two temporary residences incognito. Not an easy feat, but she'd been trained by the best and had the expertise to throw in a red herring if the FBI decided Clay had more going on than an affair.

They couldn't arrest him on that. Hell, Dean had one going himself, so he probably wouldn't be inclined to point the finger. In fact, Dean didn't seem overly thrilled about this job, either, so he'd probably be more lax than usual despite all his huffing and puffing and Maalox guzzling.

"What if..." Was she actually going to suggest this? She was. "What if I agreed but stayed booked where I am? That could confuse anyone coming after me and—and maybe whoever it is that's after you...?" She let the question hang.

"The law, darlin'. The very law I uphold in my own way when they fall down on their end."

"Do you know why they're after you?"

"Sure do. But the less you know, the better, so I'll be keeping such things to myself. As for your suggestion, I think it's a fine idea for you to keep your current quarters as is and hang your hat at, say, The Mansion on Turtle Creek? Only the best for the best, and I do believe it would be best to have you registered under an assumed identity. My secretary, Amanda Graves, won't mind at all loaning us her name or seeing to the arrangements herself tomorrow."

Tomorrow! He was moving on this faster than she could work out the logistics. Thinking quickly, she said, "I want to be clear that just because you're paying the rent doesn't mean I'm any less independent than I'm accustomed to being."

"But of course not. You're a big girl and perfectly capable of doing whatever you please—so long as it doesn't put you in harm's way. And to be quite truthful, I prefer to be seen with you as little as possible in any surroundings that appear less than innocent. I don't want you implicated, in case the law decides to scrutinize you."

Any screwups on her end and that was a very real possibility. "For being such a mean, nasty bastard you are a remarkably decent man, Clay Barker."

He slowly shook his head. "Not as decent as you think. While I do want to protect you from any taint by association, I'm well aware that the cleaner you appear, the more I can use that to my benefit. I'm hoping you might be willing to lend me a small assist in exchange for a portion of our yet-to-be-agreed-upon fee."

Caution clashed with a true wish to help. It wasn't a long battle—over in the time it took him to stroke her arms when she shivered.

"What do you want me to do?"

"Answer my call when I give you a jingle tomorrow, and play along with the request I'll be making that we meet to further discuss your sterling credentials." His laughter sly, he added, "Who knows? Just maybe you'll land a temporary job out of all this."

At the rate she was going, if any job was going to be temporary it was her current one.

"All right," she slowly agreed. "That covers a portion of your fee. What about the rest?"

His gaze roamed leisurely over her and she shivered even harder while a heady warmth slid through her veins.

"Like I said, you've got a particular something I'm in need of. Been a long time since a woman turned me on without so much as a kiss. What I want from you is...more. Lots more. I want to feel again, Mel. I want to remember what it's like to walk into a room and have a special woman wrap her arms around me and say, 'Hi honey, how was your day?' I want to share dinner and make small talk instead of eating alone as I've developed a habit of doing. I'd love to see you wash your face and brush your teeth, then watch you get ready for bed."

"So there are some strings attached, after all."

His look was one of swift offense. "I beg your pardon? I don't remember mentioning anything about sharing a bed."

"Then you wouldn't want to—"

"No," he said flatly. "When a man's gone as long as me without the very things that make sex truly good, make life worth living, then he's not about to waste a treasure trove on a quick fix. There's a big difference between making love and screwing. Forgive my bluntness, but I'd lay odds that's a difference you're not personally acquainted with. Am I right?"

A blunt question deserved a blunt answer. "You are."

"It can be fun between loving partners," he informed her, "but even then there's some heart mixed in with the heat. Otherwise, it's damn cold and don't I know it, it bein' all I've partaken of since I lost my wife. I've had enough of that shallow crap, Mel. So there, no need to worry I'll be asking for more from you than a good-night kiss. Fact is, I could use one right now to seal the deal. *If* we're agreed on the terms of my fee?"

He waited in absolute stillness until she looped her arms around his neck. And then he moved in like a shadow that covered her without touching.

"We'll consider it a pay-as-we-go plan," she whispered, drawing him close enough to feel the steady beat of his heart against the rapid pounding of her own. "Here's my down payment to seal the deal."

"Then kiss me and make it as substantial as you can afford. I wouldn't want you to overextend your—"

That was as far as he got. Her lips swallowed the remaining words on his and Clay knew the thrill of being overextended for the first time in seven years. It wasn't the bodily thing, although he was way overdrawn in that department, too; it was *feeling* and that feeling was a sense of losing what he'd thought he didn't have to give: himself.

He wasn't all there, not nearly, but the remains of who and what he had been were gasping to life like the spark of a match to tinder. And what a match she was, her tongue questing about for the answers he judiciously parted with as she searched for what truth could be found in his mouth.

This much he shared—that he was generous with those who were deserving. And she deserved as good as she gave. He sucked her tongue, and decided it was as sweet and pliable as the rest of her gathered in his arms. Hungry arms. She fit in them too right, which was dangerous for them both since it damn near stripped him down to the bone.

Bad to the bone he could easily be. And well he let her know it with the plunge of his tongue, deep enough she was sure to taste his ample poison. But she took it. Took it and begged for more with the tilt of her hips, and the whimpers he greedily swallowed.

Yes, oh, yes. How very tasty she was. Pure as baby's breath; earthy as a woman in heat. Lord, much more of this and they'd both be toast.

Clay tore his mouth from hers, and said roughly, "Substantial enough. I'm satisfied."

"Like hell," she gasped, fitting her thighs like a vise to his.

"If I didn't know better I'd think you were wanting to find out what it's like to screw." Unable to deny himself the utter wonder of wanting to make love like there was no tomorrow, he gently cupped her breast and imagined laying his head there while feminine fingers stroked his hair and soothed all his worries away. "I could teach you with the skill of a master, but darlin' that's a lesson you'll have to get elsewhere because it won't be coming from me.''

Her thighs eased their pressure and she laid her forehead against his chest. When he tried to lift her face to his, she resisted.

"Look at me, Mel."

"I don't want to."

"And why not?" he demanded.

Melissa debated, then decided she'd give him the unvarnished truth to clear her conscience of the subterfuge that turned her stomach while he turned her inside out.

"Because if I look at you, I'll want to kiss you even more. And I don't want to do that because I'm feeling foolish for throwing myself at you. And besides not being the type to do such a thing, I'm not accustomed to being rejected."

"Rejected?" he repeated in disbelief. "Lord have mercy, but you are in need of some learning. I couldn't reject you if my life depended on it—such as my life is. I've led a hard one for quite some time and what I need from you is…softness. Your soft voice, the soft spot I saw in your heart the first time you opened your mouth and nothing came out while you tried to remember whatever it was you'd been planning to say. And *this*."

The breast he held endured a rhythmic squeezing. "Lord, but I do need this soft-woman flesh of yours. I need what it makes me feel inside. Something that's like an echo from the past and yet it's here. Right here.''

"An echo from the past," she repeated as he fondled her, making her flesh too warm, her heart quicken and her breast swell in his palm. "Is it me that you're feeling? Or the memory of your wife?"

He didn't readily reply and she knew a sinking sensation. To be a dead woman's substitute for a man who had loved her so completely that he had nothing left for another...

She'd never had her heart broken before; love had yet to come her way. But in that moment Melissa knew that she was courting heartbreak.

In self-protection, she pulled away.

He pulled her back.

"You're nothing like Martha," he said firmly, even as he continued to softly touch her. "But there's a certain purity the two of you share. It's a rare and wonderful quality that I don't want to corrupt. I'm much too old for you, baby doll, and I'm not just talking years. While I am not a robber of cradles, neither am I one to play the saint that I ain't. I need that special something you have and I'll take as much as you'll give. Don't be overly generous, Mel. I have a selfish streak and whatever you give, I'll keep. No equal return from my end. You'll be filling a dry well."

She searched his eyes. And what she saw was a terribly damaged man who was trying very hard not to damage her while he claimed what healing he could.

"For such a dry well, you seem to have more than your share of purity yourself. I think you shoot from the hip, straight and clean. A rare and wonderful quality. I'm sure there's more where that comes from and I wouldn't be a bit surprised if that well's not as dry as you think."

"Should I take that to mean you plan on doing a little digging?"

"Let's just say that scratching the surface of Clay Barker is enough to make any woman want more." She moved into his cupping hold. "Just so you know, I've got a selfish streak, too."

He kissed her neck, bit softly at a nipple, then abruptly stepped away. "Best we say good-night before we give in to our selfish streaks and spoil the spoils I'm after."

More than anything she wanted him to be selfish. So selfish that they'd wake up in a bed as ill-fated as their star-crossed paths that had them on opposite sides of the law; enemies supporting the same principles but divided in their methods for reaching a fair end.

It wouldn't be fair if he was using her to his own ends. But at the moment, it wasn't in her to care.

"You can be as selfish as you want when we're alone."

"Won't be in my office. Or on the phone. Everything we say can and will be held against me. Remember that, Mel. And while you do, remember that I'm stingy with my trust but I do trust you." His words still ringing like buckshot from a gun blowing up in her face, Clay kissed her hard and fast. "Now let's get out of here before I feel more than a breast or—"

She kissed his cheek. He touched his fingertips to where she had kissed him and a slow smile warmed his lips. "That's the kind of kissin' I miss. I'll keep an eye out till you're in your car."

His protectiveness didn't sit well with her knowing the car he assumed to be rented was federal property, unmarked. And then he made her feel even worse, calling after her, "Stay safe now, you hear?"

Even as she cranked the engine and Clay blended into the shadows, Melissa knew she'd never been less safe in her life.

Clay had killed that senator's son. And she knew in her heart that he could, and would, kill again should he ever love someone else enough to die along with them and count himself among the living dead.

Could he love her like that? She wasn't sure, but she could love him. She knew it with a gut-deep instinct to rival that of a baby's first breath.

Scary stuff. Damn scary.

Just as scary as knowing that life was a crap shoot and although she'd bought time for them both, the shit was sure to hit the fan.

Chapter Six

CLAY PARKED HIS "company" car a block from where he should have been ten minutes ago. The souped-up ghetto cruiser wasn't pretty to look at but it ran like hell on wheels. Most important, though, it wasn't traceable to the esteemed Mr. Barker, but was on "permanent loan" from yet another satisfied client.

Substantial enough. I'm satisfied.

Like hell...

He had to get her out of his head and out of his heart. He was alive because he had nothing to live for. Lose that ruthless edge and he could get his death wish before the night was over—save the feds all the painstaking trouble they were going to. All for naught tonight; they were gonna be pissed when they discovered it wasn't really him in his vintage Mercedes, but a trusted ally zapping shut the iron gates and winding down his long private driveway right about now.

Of course if he didn't keep his mind off Mel, then all his painstaking trouble could be for naught, too. Even if he didn't get himself killed, one slipup and he could find himself behind bars. Mel would be better off if he was there already—the equivalent of being dead, most likely his throat slit in his sleep—and taking her chances on any fate that didn't include him.

Too late, she'd already kissed the dice and was gambling on Lady Luck. Mel was gonna need it in spades. Not only was he pulling her into the wasteland of his personal existence, he was using her to toy with the feds and beat them at their own game.

He didn't like using anyone, particularly not a woman he wanted to protect, but Revenge Unlimited had become his very lifeblood. Problem was, Mel had somehow managed to tamper with that blood, had slipped her way into his veins with the ease of a needle through skin.

Mel as a decoy to a sitting duck could be the more apt description. His contact at the Bureau had alerted him that some sort of trap was in the works but given the number of Barker supporters within the agency, the details were being kept top secret. Could Mel be an agent? Absolutely. But if she was, she had come alone, no wire, and had done a damn good job of convincing him she was trustworthy. The particulars in the envelope had checked out—which didn't mean a hill of beans.

Are you an agent, Mel? Are you? he silently wondered as he strode toward his destination. A grim smile twisted his lips as he considered the irony of wanting a woman who may have been sent to entrap him.

She wanted him, that much he knew for a truth. And unless his instincts were way off base, she was of a mind to save him—from himself if not from the feds. Maybe both.

He liked the idea of someone wanting to save him for a change. Liked it too much. It tapped a soft spot inside him that hadn't been touched in so long it gave him the most peculiar feeling. *Feeling.* Mel made him feel. Dangerous stuff—especially when he had to focus on the job at hand.

You can't want her, can't even think about her, he silently commanded himself as he approached the graffiti-sprayed door of a deserted warehouse. With the muted sound of ritual chanting in his ears he slipped on a black ski mask.

You know what you have to do, what you have to see to do it. Be there, hold them. His mind filled with the vision of a macabre family-group hug, he gave a sideways kick to the door.

Willing his anger to be his shield, Clay strolled into the midst of a cult gathering—one of those underground movements that wasn't inclined to let their converts go. As he understood it, the leader was something of a cross between Charles Manson and that wacko from Waco.

Clay spied his target. She was barely eighteen and was trying to back away from a branding iron that would forever mark her as one of theirs. She looked scared, like she'd gotten into something she was desperate to get out of and wanted to go home to the parents who were counting on him to return their prodigal to them. Lucky for that prodigal, she'd told a friend about her latest adventure and that friend had had the good sense to alert the parents. Unfortunately the police couldn't act on heresay and even weird religions were protected by certain rights.

To hell with that—a line had to be drawn somewhere. The officer who'd heard out the frantic parents was sympathetic but couldn't cross that line. He had, however, put them in touch with a certain someone who could.

"Evenin'," Clay cordially greeted the crowd of... twenty, he quickly determined. Making his way to center stage, he carried himself as though he had every right to not only barge in but to emcee the proceedings as well.

"What's this I see?" he blandly inquired as he insinuated himself between the girl and the glowing red iron that was being waved a mite too close to his face. "Surely you weren't planning to use that on anyone. Unless it's on yourself." He nodded toward the serpents and dagger-speared hearts decorating the leader's exposed body parts. "Nice tattoos. Guess you decided you needed an extra, huh? I'll do it for you if you like—though I can't say where it might land—but I'd much rather leave you to your own devices while I escort this young lady out of here."

"She stays here." The decree accompanied a stir of the iron in the smoldering coals of a barbecue pit beside him.

"Then I insist on sticking around, too. What's for dinner? I could really go for a steak, but burgers will do."

"Who are you?" demanded the wild-eyed fanatic who apparently didn't care much for uninvited guests. Especially one who wasn't appropriately intimidated by the threat of getting his chest grilled.

Clay licked a finger and tapped it to the iron poised inches from his sternum. The sizzle provoked an image of Mel melting in his arms, and the squeeze of his heart when she'd kissed his cheek. *Jesus, get out of my head! You're not saving me, you're gonna get me killed!*

While he struggled to grasp back the razor edge of his rage, he bought precious time with more banter. "Who am I? Why, I'm none other than the Devil himself, come to pay a call on all you bad girls and boys. Save me the trouble of putting you all to bed— as in for some time—and let me see this young lady home. Her mama and daddy are just a mite distressed that she got mixed up with the wrong crowd." He stretched as though bored while priming himself for a mass attack. "Now, either back off or do your best to make a convert of me."

"Grab him!" ordered the leader as he lunged with the searing weapon. Clay sent it sailing end-over-end in a flash, its owner right behind. The maniac's startled yelp ended with a solid smack against the wall.

As several followers rushed to their fallen leader, Clay whispered urgently to the girl, ''While I keep them busy, get yourself out of here and wait for me outside the door.'' Then slapping his chest in a ''c'mon, have at me'' invitation, he asked, ''Any other takers?''

They converged en masse. Clay took them on with a blur of kicks and jabs riding on the momentum of over two hundred pounds condensed into each blow. With the cool efficiency that had marked him as one of Uncle Sam's best, he finished the job in short measure.

Bodies littered the floor. A cursory check of each one assured him the damage was limited; restricted to concussions that hopefully had knocked some sense into them but stopped short of a fractured skull.

It was quite a mess he'd made, but just maybe some good would come of it. They'd be in traction for a while, hopefully long enough to recover from their brainwashing. If nothing else, they'd surely realize the merits of keeping clear of the girl.

After making sure there was no evidence traceable to him, Clay paused to consider the wisdom of leaving a single telling clue behind.

This dangerous newfound reason for living warned him not to add more fuel to the bonfire already going. However, he was inclined to rub it in that they needed him.

He strode over to the master of this twisted game and laid down his calling card. No blood or fingerprints, but it represented an indelible mark, as unique as his signature.

Returning to his charge, he hooked a consoling arm around her shoulder. "Time to go home, little girl."

"I—I'm scared, so scared. It wasn't supposed to be scary but it was a nightmare and—and—" A torrent of tears doubled her over. Clay picked her up and carried her to the Chevy, deposited her on the front passenger seat, clicked the seat belt and patted her bowed head.

"In exchange for my services, I want a promise from you."

"Anything, anything," she sobbed.

"Promise that you'll restrict your religious practices to The Golden Rule and do unto your parents as you'd have them do unto you. No more flirting with the dark side. And should those sick souls do so much as call or send you a red-ink letter, tell your folks so I can pick up where I left off. Okay?"

At her quick succession of nods, Clay deemed his job done. Almost. He stopped long enough at a phone booth to make an anonymous call to 911, then returned the prodigal to her parents and left with his fee: a vow of silence should the law pay a reluctant visit, as it most surely would; and come Christmas, a catered party to die for from the most coveted caterers in Dallas.

Assuming he'd still be around to collect.

The idea had never bothered him before. And because it bothered him now, Clay knew his avenging-angel days were numbered.

Chapter Seven

MEL JUMPED AT THE SLAM of the phone's receiver into its cradle. If Dean had knocked the plastic any harder, there wouldn't be a phone to answer when Clay called.

"Now they call us, now they call us! Hell, we'd have known sooner from the morning's paper. Reece, go get one."

"What's going on?" Mel asked apprehensively as Dean paced the floor of her motel room, drinking freely from the Maalox bottle until he whirled on her.

"Guess where Barker was last night."

"I . . . I understand that he blew off the symphony or gave the tickets away, so he wasn't there." She also understood that a tail had been put on him anyway and how lucky she was he'd slipped it.

"He pulled a job last night. Does this make us look bad? No-o-o. It makes us look like a bunch of idiots that don't know our heads from our asses!"

Her stunned reaction was genuine. "He pulled a job? What kind of a job?"

"Broke up some creepy cult get-together with about as much delicacy as God's wrath on Sodom and Gomorrah. What he left of the members had an E.R. hopping all night. The only statement to be had was some crazy mumbo jumbo about a demon in a black mask they could swear was Brandon Lee come back from the dead and thinking he was still filming *The Crow*."

Relieved as she was that their clandestine meeting hadn't been discovered, there was no relief in imagining Clay had put himself at such risk. But had he? Had he actually kissed her like mad, then gone about his death-wish business as though he didn't care that she cared?

"If that's all you have to go on, how do you know it was him?"

"There's no mistaking Barker's work. Clean and mean, he doesn't show a stitch of mercy, then turns around and becomes a Good Samaritan with a 911 call. That's proof enough, but he made sure we knew for a fact who did it. He left his calling card with the leader of the pack."

"I take it this is one of those minor points that weren't included in the information I was given." She let Dean think her subtle accusation came from wanting to be in the know instead of having uncovered enough on Clay Barker to suspect she'd been set up as much as he. No doubt her superiors had thought she'd balk at playing decoy if given the whole story.

Her superiors had thought right.

The immediate one, Dean, blew out a disgruntled snort. "Look, Lovelace, I'm warning you that this man could charm the pants off a nun. Once he makes contact—assuming that he will—don't let that charm get in the way of the job. He's got a weak spot for damsels in distress and you play that for all it's worth.''

"Are you suggesting that I invite more than his interest in me as a client?"

"Take it however you like. Your duties don't include intimate lures, but it certainly wouldn't hurt to appeal to his hormones. Apparently he's got his share, considering the mistress he keeps on the side."

The lurch of her heart coincided with a shrill ring of the phone.

"That could be him," Dean said. "Pick it up and I'll take care of the tape."

Blocking out the tangle of emotions she'd have to sort out later, Mel did as instructed.

Clay returned her "Hello?" with a cheery greeting. "Mornin', Ms. Lovelace. Clay Barker here, getting back with you on the job we discussed yesterday." He paused and Dean nodded in approval as he monitored the taped conversation. "I'd like to meet for lunch so we can work out the details for a mutually agreeable association."

"Certainly, Mr. Barker," she said with a politeness to match his. "What time and where?"

"The Mansion on Turtle Creek has a most excellent restaurant. How's two o'clock? A late lunch, but the rush will be over and we can hear ourselves talk."

With that reference to their secret encounter, he signed off and she barely had time to hang up before Dean growled, "Damn. Damn! 'Hear ourselves talk,' my eye. He's making sure the place is almost empty so he can watch any agents watching him. The man's too sharp, sure to spot any one of us and he's got the balls to wink at our guys in the bargain. You go alone and we'll listen in on the wire you'll be wearing."

"I'll go alone," she said, grateful for that. And disgusted enough to be ballsy herself. "But I'm not wearing a wire."

"Excuse me?" Dean pulled out a wadded-up handkerchief and dabbed at his forehead. She couldn't see any furrows of disapproval, but the squint of his brown eyes and the testiness of his voice let her know she'd better toe the line he was drawing. "I could have sworn you just said you won't be wearing the wire. Surely I misheard."

"Your hearing's fine. Considering the care Barker's exercising, he obviously knows something's going down and sharp as you say he is, he might even suspect me. If so, I don't want to give him any reason to substantiate those suspicions." The hell she didn't. Mistress or no mistress, she hated this assignment. And she hated living out of a suitcase in this bring-your-own-shampoo, cookie-cutter room with tacky pictures, plastic glasses and trash cans, and fake-wood tabletops cluttered with equipment.

No wonder she had no intention of unpacking. Privacy was non-existent with the constant comings and goings of the five other agents on the case, all of them males. They seemed to think she was one of the guys and therefore didn't mind the rank jokes, belching, junk-food discards that made the place smell like stale tacos, and their leaving the toilet seat up.

How she wanted to go home, hole up in her cozy apartment that had been the servants' quarters of a mansion whose glory days were long gone. There she could pour out her heart to the teddy bear Daddy had given her at age twenty to soften the blow of his devastating confession.

She'd brought the bear along for consolation and the urge was strong to hug the stuffing out of him right now. But with Dean watching as she went to the suitcase, she settled for a squeeze of a raggedy arm beneath her underthings. Then she made a show of checking her gun to appear agent-tough, not teddy-bear dependent.

"Even if he's not completely sold on you, no way can he tell if you're wearing a wire," Dean insisted, breaking the taut silence that had the feel of a staring contest.

"Sure there is," she argued, confident in her reasoning. "You said he's a ladies' man and indicated you'd like me to use that to our advantage. Maybe he'll want to extend lunch to dinner and dancing. Easy enough for roaming hands to detect a wire during a slow dance.'' Again she wondered if their dance last night was due to suspicion. No matter. She'd obviously convinced him to bite the bait. Too bad for that. And too bad the bait was hooked and sinking fast.

"Good point, Lovelace,'' Dean conceded with a nod of approval. "With thinking like that, I can understand why you were head of your class. Dress in something classy and try not to enjoy his company too much while making sure he enjoys yours.'' After another swig from the bottle, Dean wiped a white dribble from his chin with the handkerchief before shoving it into his pocket. "I'll expect a full report once you're done working out the 'details' of your 'association.' As for any juicy ones, I'd just as soon not know about them.''

"Why not?'' she quietly demanded, intercepting his hurried stride to the bathroom. Mel blocked the door; she wanted some answers. "Surely it wouldn't bother your conscience.''

"I've got enough on my conscience without adding more manure to the heap.'' He grimaced and hugged his waist. "The sooner we can get this assignment over and done with, the better for my health. I'll owe you for whatever you can do to hurry things along.''

"Sure,'' she said, knowing full well that she was going to hurry about as fast as a snail on downers. "But in exchange, I want in on some of what's been kept from me.''

"Such as?" he asked **warily,** glancing anxiously toward the toilet.

"What's his calling card?"

"Silver." Dean's jaw tightened while her heart did the same. "As in ware."

CLAY PRETENDED TO SCAN the menu while taking note of Melissa's rigid posture in the plush chair. There was a guardedness about her that told him she was disturbed about something and that something had to do with him.

When the waitress came with the wine and left with their orders, he didn't bother with small talk. "What's wrong?"

"Nothing." She hid what looked to be a scowl behind a sip from her glass.

"You're a liar," was his blunt reply. Just as blunt was his grip of her knee beneath the table. "We're alone except for that couple across the room. They've got eyes only for each other so they're certainly not watching us pussyfoot around whatever reason has you sulking and refusing to look at me." She stared back at him. "Much better, darlin'. Now, what gives?"

"What gives is that I give a damn. About you."

"And that's a problem?"

"Yes, Clay, it is. A big problem. No woman with an instinct for self-survival would let herself care about a man who doesn't want to survive himself."

"I take it you read the Dallas *Morning News*." He noticed she hesitated before giving a curt nod. "What makes you so sure I'm the one responsible? No evidence was reported that would link me to a hot spot where all hell broke loose."

"Let go of my knee and show me your hand."

"But I like squeezing your knee... among other things." When she thrust away his massaging palm, he decided he wouldn't get any more squeezes until he followed orders. Lord, but she could be one tough little cookie—maybe even tough enough to keep a hellion like him in line. With his palm up, on the table, he might as well be laying down his weapon.

Stroking the bandage he'd kept concealed with a glove until restaurant manners dictated he remove them, she said pointedly, "I don't think you got whatever's under that gauze by misdirecting your razor this morning."

"It's just a little burn." It had been a long time since a woman had seemed close to letting him have it for risking his health. Even after he'd quit the SEALs, his wife had gotten on him for not going to a doctor over a simple case of strep throat. Clay's own throat tightened when Mel put her lips to the bandage. "What's this? A kiss to make it all better?"

"I'll tell you what this is, Clay Barker. It's me telling you that I'm scared as hell because I give a damn and you haven't for so long that you've forgotten how."

"Then why don't you make it your personal mission to help me remember? In fact, I'd even be willing to let you take your best shot later. Say...eight tonight, the top-floor suite. Amanda's already taken care of it, even passed along the keys. One for you—" He slipped it into her palm before patting his suit-coat pocket.

"And one for me. Private as these surroundings surprisingly are, you never know when unwanted company might put in an appearance. When you greet me at the door I'd very much appreciate your wearing what's waiting in a box on the—" He grinned like the devil he was when she took a gulp of wine.

"On the couch, darlin'. Seeing that this is a pay-as-we-go plan and after last night I'd better lay low for a while, you won't be owing me such things as letting me tuck you in, just yet. Which brings me to an offer of more than my services in exchange for your efforts to restore my lost memory."

"Don't tell me you're actually offering me a job."

"Why, Mel, I knew you were sharp." He went back to squeezing her knee and noticed it faintly shook. "Besides giving us an excuse to spend more time together while I personally see to your safety, it'll give you something to do with your days. And I do like to pay my people well. C'mon, Mel. No reason to say no, and you might as well save me the trouble of convincing you in a weaker moment, so just say, 'Yes. Yes, Clay, I'll work for you.'"

When she hesitated, he spiked the punch. "Worried as you seem to be about me, it would allow you to keep an eye on me and make sure that I behave." Unable to resist, he winked. "And I can do the same for you."

"LESS THAN TWO HOURS and you're back?" Dean's tone implied equal amounts of relief and a total lack thereof. "What happened to dinner and dancing?"

"He must have other plans for the night," Mel reported with the conviction of one who was sure of it. "Maybe he's got a date with his mistress. Smooth operator that he is, I wouldn't be a bit surprised if he's juggling more than one."

"Nothing illegal about that," Dean defended with a hint of sympathy. And admiration, which she supposed came from his unsmooth juggling of his sweetheart of a girlfriend and his queen bitch wife. Oddly enough, Dean could likely empathize with her emotional dilemma more than most. "None of our business what he does in bed. All we're concerned with is his taking the bait. Has he?"

Feeling as though she were on a high-wire and without a pole to sustain her balance, Mel took the plunge. "He has. Sort of. Did he offer to help? Yes. Any time soon? No. For now, you'll just have to play his waiting game while I go to my new job. It seems he wants to keep me gainfully employed until he deems it safe to ensure my safety. I start first thing tomorrow."

"Aw, jeez, is this the pits or what?" Dean looked to be choking on a bowlful of sour cherries. "Okay, he's got your days tied up. What about the nights? Did he give you a number to call, should trouble find you after hours?"

"He did." Though she wanted to laugh at the irony of it, Mel refrained. "The police. He assured me that a single mention of my name would have them over pronto, and certain not-to-be-named detective friends would make sure he was alerted." With effort she managed to sound indifferent. "I guess they have a number he doesn't want to give me—where he can be found in a bed other than his own."

"That bastard. That cagey bastard, too good for his own good and even worse for ours." Dean smacked a fist into his palm and she winced as she remembered the proof of how Clay had spent the midnight hour.

Taking a chance on the lack of ill-will Dean seemed to bear the "cagey bastard," she confessed, "I have some reservations about this assignment. Clay Barker strikes me as a very decent human being whose only real crime is cleaning up the streets. While I can't condone his methods, they're obviously effective. He's fair. But the sting we're working?" She shook her head.

Dean frowned—then concurred with a shake of his own.

It was ample support to induce her to hopefully ask, "Do you think there's a chance things will cool off and we'll pull out of here before I'm eligible for the insurance benefits and pension plan he mentioned?"

"Don't I wish. But he stepped on the wrong toes. We're in this until it's over and out. Either it's curtains for him or we're filing files till I hit retirement."

"There are worse jobs. Case in point."

"Point well taken. But if we get pulled, replacements'll be sent in." Lowering his voice, he confidentially added, "He stands a better chance with us on the witness stand. We might even be able to get his sentence reduced so he can get out before he's got both feet in the grave."

She refrained from saying that he had one there already and hell could freeze over before she knocked out the other foot from under him. A shudder went through her as she added, "You know as well as I do that even a year in the pen is the equivalent of a death sentence. He'll be targeted as the enemy. They'll kill him."

"It won't be easy, him being a top-notch martial-arts expert, among other things. But considering the numbers sure to gang up against him..." With a heavy sigh, Dean downed what remained in the plastic bottle and chucked it into the trash. "You're probably right."

This isn't right! she wanted to scream. But screaming wouldn't do anything besides get her taken off the case, so she said nothing.

"Misery liking company, want to join me for dinner?"

"Thanks, Dean, but I've got other plans."

"Oh yeah?" He raised a brow in question.

"Yeah." For such an evasive answer, she couldn't help but notice how easily Dean let it go.

Chapter Eight

PAUSING BESIDE the suite's door, Clay tapped the entry key to his chin.

There. He'd like a kiss right about there. Then one to each cheek before the cologne he'd splashed on led her to nuzzle his neck. Odd he hadn't broken into a sweat during last night's job—except for when he'd thought of Mel and fully realized the danger she posed—but here he was, wiping his palms on his pants. Was he eager? Way too. And apprehensive? At least a twinge as he let himself in, silent as a shadow.

No Mel in sight but the packages were gone from the couch. Seemed she hadn't the good sense to grab the goods and run since he could hear her in the adjoining bedroom.

For a moment he let himself imagine what all that muffled movement suggested: She was opening the packages, too surprised to do more than stare in disbelief—before she laughed and... She was taking off her clothes and he didn't need to imagine what the sight of that would do to him.

Good thing for them both he knew better than to steal so much as a peek.

Instead he listened and imagined and smiled a forgotten smile, all of it an indulgence that heated his blood and warmed his heart. When he deemed her just about done, Clay returned to the entry door and opened, then closed it loud enough to announce his belated arrival.

"Mel?" he called. "Sorry I'm late but—"

He got no farther as the sight of her stole his very breath. Sucking in a steadying one, he managed, "Hey, lady, you look better than great. A sight for sore eyes if ever there was."

She cinched the pristine white velvet robe, then fussed with the high lacy collar of the matching Victorian gown underneath.

"Hi," she said self-consciously.

"Honey," he prompted, tossing his suit coat onto the couch and rolling up his sleeves. He opened his palms in a glad-to-see-ya gesture when he really wanted to grab her to him and kiss her like crazy while he got rid of what she'd just put on.

It seemed the want wasn't his alone, given her flowing stride and the arms she wrapped around his waist. Her cheeks all rosy, her smile overly pleased and bashful at once—Lord, what that did to him.

"Hi, honey," she said. "How was your day?"

"The truth?"

"Nothing but."

"In that case, it fairly well sucked." He pinched her cheek. "Except for you."

She laughed softly and kissed his chin. *There.* Oh, yes, there. And then she planted one on each cheek before she sniffed at his neck. Not quite a nuzzle, but close enough to convince him she was more inclined to linger than not.

"Hungry?" she asked, just before her stomach growled.

"You bet I'm hungry." As to what for, he let his gaze rest on her lips. "What're you up for from room service? Your call."

"I made one already. Hope you like Chinese since there's a seafood stir-fry for two on its way. And some egg rolls and other stuff that I thought would cover the bases."

"More like a home run," he assured her. "Hope they throw in some chopsticks so I can impress you with my dexterity at working two things at once while I go about feeding my face." My, but her blush was cute. And she blushed even more when he patted her rear before leading her hands to his tie. "Do it for me?"

Do it she did. For him and to him. With her near strangling him, followed by an "Oops, I'm sorry!" before she nearly mangled the damn thing getting it off, Clay was touched by her determined attempt to make him more comfortable.

By the time she'd removed the tie, his comfort level was nearing rock bottom.

A nudge of his hips to the cradle of hers and Clay backed off with the quick intake of her breath in his ears.

"Thank ya, darlin'," he said with all sincerity. "It's been a while since I was so nicely accommodated."

"Oh, really?" Her reply was too quiet. "I would have guessed that you're accommodated whenever the urge strikes."

It was striking him now and in a way far different than on those nights he shelled out to sleep. And he couldn't deny that the urge was all the stronger for what sounded close to jealousy from a woman who wasn't for sale.

"There's a difference between being accommodated and being accommodated *nicely*." Before he could say more, a rap sounded at the door.

Intercepting her, he felt for the pistol concealed against his ribs. "Who's there?" he politely inquired.

"Dinner from Wong's."

Clay nudged Mel from view as he cracked the door open. At the smell of to-die-for Chinese wafting his way, he went for his wallet.

"My treat," Mel insisted, digging into a robe pocket. After paying the deliveryman with an ample tip that declared her one of those who knew the meaning of doing thankless labor to pay the rent, she raced to the bedroom and returned with two plump pillows, which she plopped in front of the coffee table.

"What's this?" he asked, intrigued when she dropped to her knees to divest him of Italian leathers and dress socks.

"It's a fantasy I've had since I saw *Madama Butterfly* in high school. I haven't breathed it to another soul—except to an old girlfriend who was offended by the very idea."

"Something tells me I'm gonna like this a lot more than I would that old girlfriend of yours."

"Probably," she agreed, laughing softly and making him want to hear that laugh again and again. "She was a real bra-burning feminist and couldn't believe I'd actually want to pretend I was a geisha. I tried to explain that there was nothing degrading about lavishing attention on a man. That the way I saw it, the guy would end up on his knees and eating out of my hand. But she didn't buy that."

"I do." Considering where Mel's planted knees positioned her head, Clay knew she could have him begging with a single, well-placed kiss. Hell, she didn't even have to do that. Just looking up at him with those clear blue eyes was enough to make him topple and fall. Fall on Mel and bury her with the weight of his yearning for all she could give him.

He bent low and kissed the tip of her nose. And then the corner of each eye before letting his lips linger on the crown of her head.

"You smell good, damn good. Just wash your hair?"

"I wanted to but didn't have time. So I sprayed some perfume on it."

Such a simple admission, and yet it sparked the past to life and imbued the present with more feelings than he could readily sort. He'd caught Martha a few times doing that trick with her hair and had teased her since it wasn't the type of thing she was inclined to admit—raised as a debutante as she'd been. But Mel? She just told it like it was.

Again it struck him how alike yet dissimilar the two women were. And while he gravitated to their shared qualities, he was grateful for the differences. There would never be another woman quite like Martha. But he'd lay money and lots of it that Mel was in a league of her own, as well—had to be, to do the things she did to him.

Cupping her face, he searched for some understanding of those things that stirred him. But they were simply there; logic had nothing to do with it. As for how she had managed this remarkable feat, he'd likely get that answer as soon as did any man who'd taken one look at a woman and, with the drop of his heart, just *knew*, she was it—"it" being a force greater than reason and one to be reckoned with inevitably.

Clay straightened, aware he didn't feel too steady on his feet. The lingering smell of her hair was messing with what remained of his senses.

Which was clearly not much, since he could hear himself awkwardly confessing, "I thought about you all day, Mel—wasn't able to concentrate on business or anything else, for that matter. I couldn't wait to get here and now that I am..." Hell, he sounded like a gee-whiz farm boy who was thrusting a corsage at the girl of his dreams before heading for the prom. "And now that I am— Aw, crap, what am I trying to say?"

"Maybe that you'd rather be with me than playing the Lone Ranger, Zorro and Batman all rolled into one?" At his decisive nod, she gave him an impish grin that damn near curled his toes. She tickled them before patting the pillow beside her. "Good. Now, sit."

"Yes, ma'am." Gladly complying, Clay found a supreme contentment in simply watching her set the table with nothing but white containers and two pairs of chopsticks. Picking hers up, she tapped them against his hidden weapon.

"Two's company, three's a crowd."

"Seems to me that a geisha would take it upon herself to get rid of any unwanted company." He drank in her intimate smile as she released his shirt buttons, then swept her palms over his chest, leaving it as bare as his feet.

Clay caught her wrist en route to the gun's hilt. "Don't want you to get your hands dirty," he told her before removing the iron himself. With a long reach he slid it under the couch.

"Thanks. It doesn't do much for my appetite."

"Nor mine," he agreed, while his appetite for something other than food was definitely alive and well.

She was efficient with the chopsticks and fed him several generous bites, but Clay noticed her gaze kept darting in the gun's direction. And when he fed her in return, she seemed preoccupied, eating in a thoughtful silence.

"What's on your mind, darlin'?"

"I'm wondering why you didn't use that gun last night." Then she hastened to add, "Assuming it was you."

The precaution of her phrasing gave him to wonder once more if she was an agent—one who was trapped between duty and desire. Or could she be truly in need of his help and didn't want to know any particulars, should she be questioned? Either way, she obviously didn't want him to incriminate himself.

"If one were to make that assumption," he said carefully, "they might also assume that a man who's been trained to survive, shoots to kill. For that reason, he would be very reluctant to use his gun if killing was not his intent."

"But what if . . . what if such a man had also been trained to kill with means other than a gun?"

Clay laid a hand to her throat and stroked her jugular; her pulse leaped beneath his thumb. "Those means could be just as deadly and potentially much more cruel. However, there's something very personal about physical contact, don't you agree?"

He could feel her swallow beneath his palm before she whispered, "Yes. Yes, I do."

"Then perhaps you would also agree that most individuals would exercise more control with a bare hand to a throat than a finger to a trigger. One's personal. The other's not."

And well didn't he know it. Clay removed his hand, feeling as though he were sullying Mel with the taint of blood that could never be washed away. There was no remorse in him for what he had done to avenge his beloveds' deaths, but that dark, dark part of his past was better forgotten.

Mel helped him to forget and he silently blessed her for the ease with which she now did just that—her eyes half closed, her fingers tracing where his had been, lips parted and pouty, begging for a kiss.

Since he knew full well that once he started kissing her he wouldn't be able to stop, Clay quickly slipped the chopsticks into her mouth, wishing he were the tasty fare on the tongue he was aching to touch with his.

They took turns feeding each other but for the most part they ate in silence. A very telling silence, because it was as natural as her lick of a dribble of sauce from his chin.

Pitching in with the cleanup, he admitted, "I like this. Reminds me of when I used to help with the dishes and loved every minute of it.'' What he didn't say was how he'd rubbed his chest against Martha's back while they'd played with the bubbles in the sink.

''You'd better not let that get around or you'll have women lined up for miles, wanting dibs on you.'' Avoiding his distant gaze, she added, ''Of course, even without the dish-duty incentive, there're probably plenty lined up as it is.''

''Why, Mel, sounds as if you think I've got a harem and I'm angling to add you to the she-cats clawing each other's eyes out to pounce my bones in bed.''

Her glance implied that was exactly what she thought.

''That's none of my business.''

''But you want it to be and I rather like that. In fact I like it so much that I'll let you in on what defines my not-so-loving love life. I have a mistress. It's strictly a business deal that doesn't involve anything other than me paying her rent for a few visits a month. No emotional investment, mind you, even after two years. Sounds romantic, don't you think?''

''I think it sounds...sad.''

For it sounding so sad, Mel looked awfully glad.

He pulled her by the robe's lapels until her lips were nearly on his. Because those lips were more dangerous than a gun with the safety off, he didn't kiss her.

''You're good,'' he said point-blank.

''That's funny, considering you make me want to be bad.''

"How bad?"

"This bad!" She threw a fortune cookie at him. It bounced from his nose to hands that just managed a save.

Laughing along with her, Clay chewed on the brittle sweetness while reading aloud: "Says here: 'Beware of nightingales who sing too sweetly at night.'" He ate the message along with the cookie. "What say you to that?"

She sidestepped the question by reading her own fortune: "'Good things come to he who waits. Waiting is over.'"

With a suggestive glance, she handed the message to him, while his own real message—"Good fortune is at hand"—led him to produce the deck of cards he'd brought along to keep his own hands off her.

"Poker." He shuffled and she cut. "You a good bluffer, Mel?"

Examining her cards with a witchy smile, she challenged, "You tell me."

Chortling at that, he didn't mean the pair of kings and queens in his hand when he said, "Two of a kind. Heaven help us both, I do believe that's what we are. But if you want to win, you'd best have a royal flush. How many to get there?"

She laid down a single card. Before he could dole another out, Mel ordered, "Stop right there." Lordy, but she spoke with the authority of one reading a just-caught criminal his rights. Hands on the wall, legs spread—didn't he wish? "Are we betting for pennies or what?"

Hmm. He'd never been one to let opportunity pass him by, and what an opportunity this was to get some goods on Mel.

"How about . . . secrets?"

A bit too quickly she asked, "What sort of secrets?"

Clay didn't readily answer, his attention on the high-necked collar she was suddenly fussing with. A nervous little gesture—as though he'd suggested strip poker instead.

He narrowed his eyes on hers but she met his gaze levelly. For a moment he considered confronting her with the riddle of her behavior; asking her flat out if she was concealing her true identity from him.

Clay quickly discarded that idea. At this point she clearly wasn't ready to admit to any deception—*if* there was one—and cornering her would be a very unwise move. However, there was more than one way to skin a cat. . . .

Brushing her fingers from the button, he dipped his beneath the lacy collar to lightly trace the column of her throat. "I wouldn't want you giving up any secrets you're not inclined to part with. But whatever you're willing to share, you can trust me to take it to my grave."

He watched her reaction closely and noted she cringed slightly at the reference to his grave—which

pleased him in a perverse sort of way. He also noticed
a flicker of…guilt? It was too fast to catch, but Mel's
sudden grin seemed strained.

"Then secrets it is. But no strong-arming or digging for dirt by the winner, okay?"

"Fine by me. After all, you might win and I've got
enough dirt for us both." Unable to resist a little bait-
ing, he yawned as if already bored. "You, however,
probably don't have a molehill's worth of down-and-
dirty skeletons in the closet. Given that, you're already ahead of the game."

"Don't be so sure of that," she informed him with
a haughty little sniff. "Even a 'darlin'' like me can
have her share of skeletons, Mr. Barker. But if you
want to rattle any of mine you'd better be a very patient and tenacious man, since I prefer to keep my
mystique. Now put *that* in your pipe and smoke it."

Whoa, he'd hit a button! The prospect of really
getting her riled was awfully tempting. A "Take this!
Oh yeah, well, take that!" argument would surely put
some kick back into his life. Something to consider
when he wasn't having such a good time soothing her
ruffled feathers while plucking at any errant ones to be
had.

"You've got mystique to spare, Miss Lovelace.
Why, even a tenacious man could wear himself thin
trying to figure you out. I'm plenty tenacious—but
patient?" He shook his head. "When I see what I
want, I go after it."

"Should I take that to mean you see something you want?"

"Let's just say you'd better be an Olympian runner. Or preparing yourself to have more than old skeletons rattled from your mouth to my ear." Running a thumb over her soft, flushed cheek, he quietly warned, "I'm on your tracks and closing in fast. Lady? *Beware.*"

Chapter Nine

BEWARE... BEWARE... BEWARE...

Mel's stomach rolled over and she wasn't sure if it was more from his foreboding whisper or the thigh-trembling effect of his languorous stroke to her cheek. For such an innocent touch it was powerfully, darkly seductive.

She knew that he could seduce her, here and now, take her down without a protest beyond a "Don't stop." And Clay knew it, too; she could see it in his knowing half smile. Something of a cock was in that smile and the fact that his sexual arrogance aroused her was *not* to her liking. But she couldn't really fault him for his confidence when he hadn't so much as made a pass—although that rankled, too.

So why don't you make the first move? she asked herself. It should be easy enough; but it wasn't. Not for a girl whose female influences had been strict-but-kind nuns at an all-girls school. A girl whose over-protective father had preached Books Before Boys—and what boyfriends she'd had, he'd chased off, insisting they didn't have the right stuff, or else they would have fought for her.

Would Clay fight for her? Would he stand up to Daddy, were he still living, for the girl who was now a woman? A woman who had survived hard knocks to emerge with the stuff that made her strong. An equal strength she had yet to find in a man; she'd sent more suitors packing than Daddy had.

Clay had the right stuff, had it to spare, and made the woman feel like a girl again—one who wanted to act like the femme fatale she wasn't and seduce him with the sensual skills she'd elected not to hone. She'd had opportunities aplenty, but temptation had been in short supply.

And now that she was well and truly tempted, pride intervened. Even if she didn't make a fool of herself, she wasn't about to risk Clay's rejection of her advances as he had the night before. Sure, he'd been quite the gentleman about it, but her feminine ego still smarted from the sting.

Mel lifted her chin. "So, you think you can catch me and have all the secrets you want, do you?"

"I do."

"You sound awfully sure of yourself."

"I am. Especially since I can be most persuasive."

She pulled the robe tight, as if it would protect her from hands that could surely be as cold and brutal as they were tender and warm. His hands were like an extension of the man himself, with so many facets, even a lifetime wouldn't reveal them all. Yet she feared how long that lifetime might be; feared he could induce her to expose every lie she'd told him, every secret in her heart, with a moving caress, and certainly, with a promise to close shop and grow old. *With her?*

Aware that even the thought of it was to set herself up for heartbreak, she summoned her defenses and chanced asking, "How would you persuade me? Or is that a secret I'll have to win—or lose—to find out?"

"Consider it a show of good faith that I'm willing to give you a freebie." He goosed her ribs and she jumped. "Tickle torture."

Her laughter was part relief, part dread. If his caresses didn't get him any and all the secrets he was after, then a good tickling most definitely would.

"Thanks for the warning. All the more reason to play to win—which I always do."

"Like I said, two of a kind. Still want that card?"

What she wanted was *him*. On any terms other than those that had been dealt them. Surely there was a way they could both win, a way neither of them would lose in this high-stakes game.

Yeah, right. And cows really did jump over the moon. Someone was going to pay big, and the mounting evidence was pointing to her.

Mel tapped the deck and silently groaned when her royal flush went the way of Dean's stomach problems—down the toilet. Still, she gave Clay a gloating smile.

He called, won, and was gentleman enough to say, "Nice try. But you shouldn't have tipped me off with that devilish grin. Gives an opponent away every time."

"I appreciate the tip... opponent."

"I'd rather be your ally. With that in mind, feel free to dredge up *the* deep, dark secret I'm just dying to know."

There he went again, tossing off the word *dying* like it was no big deal. It *was* a big deal, she wanted to yell at him, because she couldn't bear the thought of losing him that way. But she couldn't think about that now—not when he was ready to pounce with a question and she had to act cool.

"And just what would that deep, dark secret be?"

He leaned in and pressed a palm between her breasts, making her heart, her hormones and her nerves threaten to explode in tandem.

"Quite simply, I want to know what makes you—" he lightly flicked a covered nipple "—tick."

Clay withdrew, not trusting himself to linger. Was that a sigh of relief or a stifled groan of distress he heard? And had that sound come from him or her? Relief and distress—the two collided each time he touched her. He supposed it came from that horrible, wonderful sensation that felt like an electrical current put to an unbeating heart, jolting it to life while the resuscitated body jerked from the charge.

Mel was a charge. Most definitely a kick. So guileless, so gutsy, she was a mire of feminine contradictions and clear vision that saw past the tough guy to the sensitive soul who'd forgotten how to cry. He liked the hell out of her. More than liked; Clay had a bad feeling a certain four-letter word was in the making. And that was damn scary.

His Revenge Unlimited shingle could be in dire jeopardy of getting hit by a force more powerful than the law. And should Mel be the law? Then he couldn't discount the possibility she was acting on her conscience, maybe even considered him a pity case to save—albeit one she was attracted to—and once done, would leave.

And where would that leave him?

"What makes me tick?" She chewed her bottom lip, seeming thrown by the question. As for the one he'd put to himself, Clay pushed it aside for future thought.

Future. There it was again, that spark of wanting to reach for some promise and let the past go. Mel was doing this to him, and he resented her some for it. The urge was strong to ravage her mouth and prove what a bastard he could be. But she'd probably kiss him right back and turn him to mush. Damn her. Bless her.

"Hmm, that's a really good question. Actually, Clay, I'm not exactly sure what makes me tick. Is anyone?"

"Maybe not completely. But this is one inquiring mind that's itching to get into yours. Take your best shot."

"Okay." She chewed on her lip some more and just when he was ready to have at it himself, she chuckled.

"Maybe you can help me out. Why would a grown woman rather sleep with a teddy bear her daddy gave her than share pillow talk with a man?"

It was a turnaround question that told him more about Mel than any flip or philosophical answer could have provided.

"Maybe because a teddy bear listens and doesn't pass judgment and she knows he'll keep her secrets safe. Maybe because it's cuddly and cute, much less demanding than a man with needs that the woman creates and he wants her to satisfy. Maybe she's afraid to lay her heart out on a very real chest—one with a heart that beats for her." *Stop right there,* he told himself. "And maybe because . . ."

"Yes, Clay?" she asked expectantly.

"Maybe because your own heart's been on hold while you waited for a special someone who could make you feel as safe and loved as your teddy bear does." *Way to go, now you've done it. So what're you waiting for? Go ahead and kiss her.*

He did. But just a soft rub of his lips over hers, long enough to feel the buzz and short enough to get out while the getting was still good. "Does that help?"

"Much more help than that, and my teddy bear could be jockeying with you for position on my pillow."

The closeness they were sharing was more intimate than any pillow talk he'd had in a long, long time. And it wasn't enough; only made him want more.

He was wanting too much too soon. Clay drew away and into himself as best he could. "Your deal."

She dealt; he lost. And could only hope she didn't ask for an insight as revealing as what he'd won from her.

"My turn." Mel's calculating regard didn't bode well for the loser. "One deep, dark secret is deserving of another. So tell me, Clay Barker, what makes *you* tick?"

"Revenge Unlimited," he said in automatic defense.

She hooked an arm around his neck, sifted her free hand through his chest hair, curled it in...and yanked.

"Hey!"

"That's what you get for cheating. Now I'll ask you again— What...makes...you...*tick?*"

He stared at her, hard, as if he were going toe-to-toe with the Grim Reaper incarnate. And just maybe he was. Mel could indeed be the death of the business he'd come to live for—or the death of him, should he continue.

"What makes me tick?" Before he could stop himself, Clay vented his frustration and yearning on the one who had caused it. He pushed open the robe and possessively cupped her covered breasts. Cinching his hold, he pulled her to him, insistent but gentle with that tender weight he grasped, until their bodies touched.

"*This*. What this does to me. Thanks or maybe no thanks to a woman who makes me feel like I'm holding heaven in my hands. A woman who's hell on wheels and running roughshod over me every time she smiles, every time she looks as uncertain as she makes me feel—while making me ever more certain of one single, gut-churning fact: *you*. You are what's making me tick. Again."

His heart was pounding in time to her quick gasps for breath. Jesus, he wasn't just ticking. He was a friggin' time bomb set to go off and all it would take was a single, compulsive act. Make love to her once, just once, and he'd surely spill more than what was brewing now. Every hope, every shame, every dream and every nightmare bottled up inside him—he'd spill it into her mouth, into her ears, into her womb.

This was the need he'd warned Mel of, but the force of it was stunning even to him. The gathered momentum of seven years deprivation was rising with a vengeance. He wasn't just losing his edge, he was *on* the edge of an emotional suicide ride that was eating him up and sure to consume her if he didn't get some control over the thing.

With a nearly frantic push, Clay let go. "I think I'm out of secrets for the night."

"Me, too," she said unsteadily, looking as shaken as he felt inside. Her small laugh only accentuated the tension. "Maybe we should have bet for clothes instead."

"Yeah." Lord knew, he would have felt less naked with his clothes off than with his bare bones nearly exposed. The damage done, the best thing he could do was leave. He ordered himself to say goodbye, to get out, but his body refused to move and his throat choked on adieu.

"You...uh, want to?" She looked hopeful. And a little startled by her own suggestion.

Did he want to? He wanted it so much he could only pray she'd refuse his terms. "Winner take all."

His prayer went unanswered. He played aggressively and made sure he won with the smuggest smile he could manage against a locked jaw and gritted teeth. Mel laid down two pairs; he tossed four aces into her lap.

"I thought you said that kind of grin gave an opponent away every time."

Clay slowly shook his head. "Not when the opponent is counting on you believing such a thing. The robe?"

"But you—you tricked me and I demand a rematch." She reached for the cards, protesting, "What you did wasn't—"

"Fair?" He knocked the cards away with lightning speed. "You're right. But anyone who *really* plays to win isn't always fair. I won and winner takes all. Take it off."

He noticed her chin trembled slightly before she lifted it proudly and with jerky movements paid the price for gambling on his sense of fairness.

She flung the robe at him and began to work the buttons of the gown. Her fingers were shaking and she lowered her head. Two buttons were released when he gripped her wrist.

"Stop." His heartstrings already stretched tighter than piano wires, they nearly came undone when she looked up. He saw the threat of tears she was blinking back, this woman who slept with a teddy bear and would have the equivalent of a starving grizzly to ward off if she went any further.

"Why?" she asked haltingly. "Why stop, Clay? You won."

The hell. They were both in danger of losing this rare and unexpected something if he put greed before wisdom.

"A pauper's share. I'm ambitious." Ambitious enough to hold out for the keys to the kingdom.

"If you're suggesting more than clothes, I'm not up for another round."

"Neither am I. Not tonight."

She was suddenly beaming at him. "So you are fair, after all."

Hardly. But he'd let her think so; those tears she'd held at bay had only been part modesty. Mostly, he believed, she'd been deeply disappointed in him.

Clay felt a stab of guilt for letting Mel think better of him than he deserved, and lowered his gaze from hers. Which was a mistake, and one he couldn't force himself to immediately retract as her high, firm breasts beneath the thin cotton snared his vision. Her nipples beckoned like pearls beading from an oyster just waiting to be opened with the rake of his teeth.

It seemed that his "fairness" had managed what his lack thereof had not: Mel was aroused. So was he.

She was in over her head.

So was he.

Clay hardly recognized his own voice, so roughened it was raw with his quiet accusation: "You're not wearing a bra."

"No."

He'd already known that, of course, touching her as he had. He didn't dare touch her there now, much less elsewhere. That was torture enough, but he must be a glutton for punishment since he wanted to imagine what he denied himself from seeing.

"Panties? Are you wearing any?"

"Yes," she said in a throaty whisper.

"Describe them for me." His simmering gaze met hers and what he saw in her eyes was an awakening, one much different from his own. Mel was a very sensual woman but he could swear she was just realizing it herself.

"They're white. And silky. Everywhere, except for..." She glanced away, her color high. "Except for..."

"The crotch," he smoothly supplied.

"Yes." And then she looked at him as though in challenge—but one that seemed equally directed at herself, given the decisive way she stood and quickly asked, "Would you like to see them?"

Clay bit back the urge to ask "What the hell kind of question is *that?*" Would he like to see them? Not much, only enough to give up his every worldly possession to claim what those panties contained. And there she was, rushing out the offer and probably because she was afraid good sense would intrude, steal away her exciting discovery. She *knew* there was a wealth of sensual sizzle just waiting to be tapped, and surely ample with which to drown the tappee.

What she probably didn't yet realize was the kind of power that would give her over him. *She already had too much.*

Mel apparently took his silence as a "yes" and began to inch up her gown. Quick as deflecting a fatal blow, Clay leaped to his feet, jerked her gown back down and his own things on. He was almost to the door before she latched on to his arm and swung him around.

"Where do you think you're going?" she demanded.

"I'll be saying good-night now, Mel. Sleep tight, don't let the bed bugs or anything else get close enough to bite."

He went for the doorknob and she slapped his hand away. "I want a good-night kiss."

"Any kiss you get from me at the moment won't be anywhere near nice and I can promise you that it wouldn't end before daybreak. Or on your mouth."

"And I suppose that I owe you for this." Given her glare and disgusted little snort, he figured she was pissed.

"You do," he assured her. "Just so you know, I always collect on my debts."

"Just so you know, I always pay mine." Quick as a flash she reached under her gown, pulled down her panties and stuffed them into his pants pocket. "With interest."

"Careful, darlin'." He took out the panties. "I'm trouble, Mel. Trouble with a capital *T*." Just so she got the message, he fondled the crotch with a significant rub of his fingers. "Don't go asking for more than you've already got."

Chapter Ten

INSTEAD OF THANKING him for the chivalrous warning, she pulled him down by his haphazardly knotted tie, then plowed ten fingers through his hair, murmuring, "If you're trouble, I like it."

"And I like you." Talk about trouble, he was beginning to think he had nothing on Mel. Clay firmly set her away. "Which is why I am leaving and I'm leaving *now*."

Once safe on the other side of the door, he waited for the sound of the dead bolt, which coincided with her muted string of curses. *Whew.* He wiped his brow with her panties before pocketing them.

No sign of snoopers in the elevator or lobby, but after tipping the valet at his idling car, Clay looked directly at the sedan that had tailed him and was waiting for him to get in before following him...home? Or maybe to Sally's place, where he could watch a late movie while the fellas outside drank bad coffee from a thermos and traded locker-room talk about his sex life.

Nah. They had enough to talk about already with his rumpled clothes and the just-got-laid mess of his hair.

With an "Eat your hearts out, boys" grin, Clay adjusted his tie and waved. No one waved back, including the man on the passenger side, whom he thought might be Dean.

Clay knew of him, had been told by his source that Dean was in charge of this case. It was about all the inside information to be had, except that Dean had resisted the assignment and had a reputation for tough-minded fairness.

Clay admired him for both. Maybe that's why he almost felt sorry for Dean having to do this crummy job while he was rediscovering what it meant to hope, to feel, to need.

Was he on the mend? Maybe so, since he wanted to give as much as he took, make Mel need him in every way as a man....

A man who'd rather sleep with a pair of panties than ten mistresses in the big, lonely bed he ached to share with Mel.

"DAMN." MEL SWORE softly at the run in her new panty hose. A glance at her watch and she swore again.

Great, just great. Her first day at work and she was five minutes late. If she was lucky, she told herself, maybe Clay would fire her on the spot. At least then she wouldn't be privy to anything he might say or do worth reporting—and end up not reporting it, which would only make her more of a silent accessory than she already was.

Rushing through the store's front door, she blew in with a wave to Amanda, calling, "Sorry I'm late, but—"

"No buts about it," Clay growled. "I do *not* put up with tardiness from my employees, not for any reason."

Mel swung around and saw him lounging lazily against the magnificent grand piano. He was grinning.

She heard Amanda snicker.

"Well, Miss Lovelace, what are you waiting for?" He tapped a gleaming mahogany sidepiece. "The boss wants some compensation for your late arrival." With a glissando up the keys, Clay pulled out an ornate piano bench. "Have a seat."

After their high-voltage departure the night before, the last thing she'd expected was his discreet stroke of her arm as he led her to sit, his chest bending close to her back, and his warm whisper of, "How did you sleep?"

"Not good." She glanced at him. "You?"

His eyes veritably danced and Mel wondered how long it had been since he'd looked at anyone that way. She was pretty sure it had been seven years, and what happiness it gave her to think she'd brought him some joy.

"Sorry, but I fared better. Slept like a baby."

She hated herself for asking, but the question was out before she could stop it. "Alone?"

He looked a bit hurt for a moment, but if misery liked company, Clay succeeded. "No. No, I did not sleep alone."

"I see," she said quietly, her heart dropping to the keys she wanted to pound, then falling to her feet.

"I don't believe you do." He came around and sat beside her. "I'll clear it up—hopefully well enough that you won't be asking me such a thing again. While you were sleeping with a teddy bear I snuggled with my winnings. Sweeter than a lullaby, Mel." Leading her hands to the keys, he invited, "Play me one? Do us both a favor and soothe the breast of the savage beast."

More than anything she wished that she could; wished that she could pour all that was running rampant within her onto the keys. Unfortunately, wishing and doing weren't the same.

"I, uh, Clay, I don't—"

"Aw, c'mon," he cajoled. "I know you've been hankering to get your fingers on this grand dame since you first saw her." When Mel didn't deny what was true or begin to play, either, he grinned wickedly and reached for his pants pocket. "Need some incentive? I couldn't part with my winnings so I brought them to work. Want to see?"

"No!" Down her hands went, the ivory rich and smooth beneath the fingertips that had always longed to be deft and skilled, but had a dismal lack of talent. One year of lessons and the teacher had told her father he was wasting his money. "The truth is, Clay, I can play two songs. 'Heart and Soul.' And..." Why couldn't it be Brahms's "Lullaby"? What the hell, confession was good for the soul, but this was embarrassing!

"And...?"

"'Chopsticks,'" she muttered, feeling foolish.

"Oh, well," he said with a chuckle and put two fingers on two treble keys. "That's one more than I've got in my repertoire. I don't know 'Heart and Soul.' How about a duet of the one I do know?"

And with that, they played "Chopsticks," laughing all the while until she heard the door open.

"There's a customer!" she whispered.

"Uh-huh, now get your hands back here. You're still paying for being late. No clock to punch in my store, but the proprietor always gets his way. And I say, play!"

Moments later, Amanda tapped him on the shoulder and told him the customer had asked to speak to the owner. While she delivered the message, another customer arrived.

Mel cast an uneasy glance at the man.

He needed a haircut and had a desperate look about him. His jacket was outmoded; his pants had a patch at the knee. He wasn't dressed for this store any more than the other "customer" who wanted to speak to

Clay. A worse-than-horrible feeling swamped her and she prayed they weren't here to seek Revenge Unlimited's services.

"Be right back," Clay said with a wink. "Oh, and by the way, you play 'Chopsticks' almost as good as a geisha fed me with some last night."

On that note, he left.

Mel watched him go, frantic to intervene. Moving from the piano, she could only hope her presence would have some influence on Clay. But as she approached, she noticed both men glanced at her, then at each other, before the second of them accosted Amanda. Not exactly accosted, but he seemed to be moving in on her in a deliberate, positioning way, so that she was within his reach but clear of Clay's.

As for the man Clay was just now introducing himself to, he was agitated—an edgy kind of agitation that went beyond any malarkey about a damaged delivery his wife had received.

And then Mel realized. These weren't potential clients any more than they were customers. A holdup was about to go down and Amanda was insurance to force Clay's cooperation.

But these guys weren't concealing their identities and that meant there was a good chance they didn't plan on leaving any witnesses behind. And clearly, they hadn't planned on a third employee to deal with either, given their furtive scrutiny of where she was going, whom she would join.

Mel avoided eye contact, afraid they'd see her sure knowledge of their intent—and her equally determined intent to protect not only Amanda, but Clay. He was all-too-capable of tearing these men apart, and if anything happened to her or Amanda . . . She shuddered to think.

"Hi," Mel brightly greeted Amanda's "customer" while planting herself between them. "Amanda, why don't you go get this gentleman some of our complimentary cappuccino? I'll help him and try to earn a few more points with the boss to make up for coming in late." As if Amanda also sensed something was amiss, she excused herself and headed toward Clay's office with a briskness that serving coffee didn't justify.

Mel darted a glance at Clay and their gazes connected. Briefly, but long enough for her to see a cold glint mingle with a silent command to join Amanda. Mel pretended not to notice and returned her attention to the man who was sure to pull a gun any second.

She started chattering and Clay could feel himself shaking, shaking with fury. And fear. God, was he actually making his apologies to this scum instead of breaking his neck? *Damn Mel*, Clay silently seethed while his heart pounded with terror that she'd be hurt or worse. Damn her for tying his hands into impotent fists—he didn't dare strike a single blow, lest the next shot should come from a gun put to her head.

From the corner of his eye, he saw the other man reaching beneath his jacket, only vaguely aware that the one with him was doing the same. With a backward fling of his arm, Clay knocked his would-be assailant into a glass showcase filled with Fabergé eggs. Hurling himself like a flying piece of human artillery, Clay was in midair when he saw Mel jerk up her knee, deck the bastard, and whip him over her shoulder.

In disbelief, he watched her stamp a heel on the hand still clutching a gun. A scream of pain coincided with Mel's sudden shout, "Clay, behind you!"

Whirling around, he saw the other assailant, cut and bleeding, taking aim and preparing to shoot. Before the trigger was cocked, Clay leaped on him like a pack of mad dogs after raw meat.

"I'll kill you, kill you for this," he snarled. *Red. All he could see was red blood on the floor.* Only this time it could have been Mel's. "You filthy piece of garbage, nobody hurts what's mine." His fingers closed around the neck he deigned not to snap. Too quick and painless. Digging in, Clay heard a strangled wheeze and with a cold smile, asked in his most gracious tone, "So, are you hurtin' yet?"

"Stop it, Clay!" Mel cried over the shrill scream of approaching sirens. Her voice cut through his rage and he looked at her, hardly noticing she had the other gun trained on a squirming chest. All he could really see were her eyes, holding his and begging him not to do this. "If you don't stop, you'll be throwing yourself away for some little bit of vengeance.'' The gun shook slightly in her hand as she nodded toward his own, which clamped a convulsing throat. "One's personal, the other's not. Please, let the police deal with him. He's not worth taking personally, Clay.''

Yet Clay did take this personally, very personally. Mel could have been killed, just like Martha. But Mel was alive—and he silently gave thanks to God for that—unlike Martha, who was dead. So was her murderer.

But snuffing him hadn't brought Martha back. Neither had settling scores for others who'd been wronged. And if he killed this man, Martha would still be gone. But it was for Mel, not Martha, that he was risking everything for this no-good nobody. Revenge did have its limits and he'd almost overstepped the bounds he'd sworn never to cross again.

"She's right.'' Deeply disturbed by his near crime of passion, Clay removed his choking grip. "You're not worth it.''

He kicked the gun away and went to her while several police cars screeched to a halt outside. "You're shaking pretty hard. Want me to hold that piece?''

"That's okay, the police are about to come in.''

And it would look better if she was the one holding the gun. She didn't say it, but Clay knew Amanda would have thrust it at him before he'd even made the offer.

It seemed he had himself a guardian angel, saving him from himself and the boys in blue, too. They burst into the store just then and he greeted them with a wave.

"I'm afraid you're just a wee bit late, but we're glad to see you just the same." And then he called, "Amanda, you can come out now." She emerged from his office with an ashen face. "Good going, Amanda. But you should have hauled it out the back after calling for help."

She didn't seem bothered by his small chastisement, and probably because he would have said the same to his mother. As for Mel, he'd chastise her plenty—in private.

If the police thought it odd that the foiled heisters seemed almost glad to see them, they hid it behind their approval of how well the situation had been handled. And finally, with statements given, Amanda sent home and the store closed for the day, Clay and Mel were at last alone.

With a mess. She picked up what Fabergé eggs were still intact, then grabbed a broom and started sweeping. He watched her with an intensity to match her sweeping, then closed in, glass crunching beneath his boots.

When he stood in the way of the bristles, she went around him. His hand shot out and he yanked the broomstick from her grip.

"What do you think you're doing?" he wanted to know.

"What does it look like? I'm cleaning."

A contest with Hazel and Donna Reed for Sweeper of the Year was more like it.

Clay tossed the broom. "That's what I pay my cleaning crew for. Now..." he said slowly, noting her longing glance at the broom as if it were a life raft that might save her from a tidal wave. "Time for a little talk, Mel. No one to listen in, my office door is shut, so let's hear it."

"Hear what?" she asked with a breathlessness that his stroke to her flushed cheek may or may not have warranted.

"Lots of things, actually. But we'll start with why you weren't on Amanda's heels after you sent her to fetch that cappuccino. A very clever ruse. What tipped you off?"

Mel didn't deny that it had been a ruse, so he was inclined to give what she did say credence. "It was obvious they weren't your typical sort of customers— so at first I thought they might be here to ask you a favor. I was afraid you'd agree, so I meant to barge in and—and—"

"Yes?" he prompted, fighting a smile of pure pleasure over Mel's intent to assert her protective presence.

"I wasn't going to say anything, but I hoped you'd choose staying safe for me over helping them. Only when I saw them exchanging looks, and Amanda was getting cornered, I knew help wasn't what they were after."

Clay digested that and decided any astute observer could have drawn the same conclusion. "But since you knew, why didn't you make your excuses and go call the police yourself?"

"I couldn't have left Amanda there! She wouldn't have stood a chance against that hood."

Aha! Now they were getting to the meat of the matter. "As it turned out he didn't stand a chance against you," Clay said pointedly. "Where'd you learn that move?"

Her eyes met his with a levelness that matched her voice. "I took two years of self-defense at college."

"And did they also teach you how to handle a gun?"

"No." She sighed, a wistful sound. "My father had a collection and he used to take me target practicing. I'm a pretty good shot." As if anticipating his wonderment over why she'd have any need of his protection, Mel hastened to add, "But I really don't like guns, Clay. A lot of people get shot with their own weapons when they can't bring themselves to pull the trigger. I've never been put in that position and I'm not totally sure I could do it."

Clay wasn't sure if he believed her because he so wanted to—it would substantiate her coming to him—

or if he really did trust every word out of her beautiful mouth.

He kissed it. Hard. Possessively.

Drawing away, he gave her a small shake. "I can't tell you how furious I was when you didn't beat a path behind Amanda. Why'd you stay, Mel? *Why?*"

"The same reason I came after you in the first place," she said with a tenderness that made him ache. "I was afraid you'd end up doing something that we'd both pay for."

"I nearly did." He cringed inside, remembering how close he'd come to doing murder. "Thank God you stuck around and stopped me. I owe you for that."

"Not really." Her heart in her eyes, she cupped his cheek. "I did it for both of us, Clay. And besides, you're the one who made the ultimate decision. The right one."

"True. But that's some powerful influence you have." So damn powerful that he really had been glad to let the police take over. A sign, perhaps? Could it be that the more taste he acquired for the ease he found with Mel, the less taste he would have for the danger and the justice he'd thrived on?

He did *not* want to die. Clay suddenly realized that his death wish was dead.

But his thirst for justice?

"When there is crime in society, there is no justice," he somberly reflected. "That's what Plato thought. What do you think, Mel?" he asked, truly wanting to know.

"I think..." There she went, chewing that bottom lip again and making him want to do it for her. "I think that there will always be crime in society. And I think that justice will always be there to fight it. But because we don't live in a utopian world, crime and justice will always be at war—like the eternal fight between good and evil."

Clay looked at his hands, knowing too well what they were capable of. "Good people can do bad things. And even bad people can turn a good deed. It'd sure be a lot simpler if everyone wore either a black or a white hat all the time. But I guess that'll happen about as soon as there's no corruption in some justice and no justice in some crimes."

He waited for her to refute him with some great truth he had yet to grasp; hoped she might somehow dilute the importance of what he did and why.

Almost sadly, Mel nodded her head. "You're right, Clay. But I wish that you weren't."

"Me, too." With a weary sigh he pulled her to him, rested his cheek on her sweet-smelling hair, and whispered again, "Me, too."

Chapter Eleven

"SO, LOVELACE, HOW WAS your second day at work?" Dean looked up from a magazine in the motel room Mel was starting to hate. All the trappings were a reminder of why she was here and doing everything but her job. "Better than the first, I hope."

"It was." Not that the first had proved so bad. She'd made the most of it by praising Clay's restraint during the holdup to Dean. Her intercession hadn't borne mention.

"I'm all ears—just don't fill them up with more Barker accolades, okay? Much more of those and he should be a candidate for sainthood instead of hard time."

Squelching the big, dopey smile of a girl with an enormous crush on her new boss—who was far from a saint, unless a saint could kiss like the devil and make her hot as hell—Mel recounted her day. "Let's see.... I learned more than I never wanted to know about different grades of leather and what makes one manufacturer of armoires superior to another that specializes in—"

"Sounds even more boring than listening in on his conversations with his suppliers. I don't suppose you saw any customers that appeared to be in the market for something other than what's on the showroom floor?''

Mercifully, she hadn't. "Nary a one."

Dean hesitated before saying, "You look a bit tired. Reece told me he saw you come in late last night."

Taken unawares, she could only pray he didn't take her sudden attention to sorting the items in her suitcase as the nervous ploy it was.

"Uh-huh," she blandly replied. "I decided to check out a local hot spot and met a really cute guy." Forcing herself to meet Dean's gaze straight-on, she asked, "Nothing wrong with me spending my free time how I like, is there?"

"Uh...no."

"Good." Seizing the opportunity to avoid any future second-guessing as to her whereabouts, she let loose that big, dopey grin. "We really hit it off and I'm meeting him again tonight." Throwing a pair of panties and stockings on the bed, she noticed Dean had the decency to flush slightly. Her own color high with anticipation, she gave him the only clue he'd be getting from her on Clay Barker.

"Who knows? Maybe I'll decide Dallas has enough fatal appeal to stick around for more than a visit."

SEVERAL NIGHTS LATER, Mel stuffed the short auburn wig into her purse and finger-combed her own blond hair. A simple disguise, but a necessary precaution, as she once again approached the suite that had become both haven and hideout.

She lived for these stolen moments with Clay. But because they were stolen, she felt a constant urgency to make them count because they couldn't last. The wig only partially concealed what she was hiding from those she worked for. And what she was hiding from Clay was worse, much worse. Did she feel guilty? Only always. But deep as her guilt went, even it couldn't rob her of the joy she'd found with a man who made her feel like the rarest of jewels. Clay was rare. Unlike any man she'd ever met.

He made her laugh...and that made him laugh. They talked and shared easy silences. She had even made dinner in the microwave; he had raved despite the fact her culinary talents were on a par with her piano playing. They played "Chopsticks" each morning. They played footsies while watching movies at night.

They played no cards. But there was always a skirmish at parting time. Clay had drawn a hard line at kisses. He seemed to want her for everything *but* sex.

Definitely unlike any man she'd ever met.

She adored him. And Clay left no doubt he felt the same way about her. But once he learned her true identity, as he inevitably must, how would he feel then? It was a question that dogged her as tenaciously as the federal hounds sniffing his tracks.

Time. She didn't have much—a couple more weeks if she was lucky before she would be judged ineffectual and pulled off the case—and then she'd have no choice but to tell him. There would go her job. And if Clay didn't love her enough to forgive her for all her lies and willingly shut down Revenge Unlimited, her sacrifice would be for nothing.

But at least they had now. And now was too precious to let her troubles taint the evening. Mel blocked them out as best she could and let herself into the suite.

His coat was on the couch, along with his tie.

On the coffee table were his keys, wallet, and gun.

She heard the shower going in the private bath adjoining the bedroom. He was singing "The Yellow Rose of Texas" off-key. Clay might as well have issued her an engraved invitation to inspect his personal effects at her leisure.

Her hand hovered over his wallet. Even a curious girlfriend would be tempted; an agent wouldn't think twice about taking advantage of the opportunity.

Why had he done this? she wondered. Was it a test?

Or was it Clay's way of expressing his trust?

Either way, to even touch his wallet would be to prove she didn't trust him.

Mel wiped the offending palm on her skirt. She tossed her coat next to his and laid her purse beside his things on the coffee table. Nothing like greeting the lion in his den.

"Clay! Oh, honey, I'm ho-ome!"

Though he heard her, Clay continued singing while he quickly stepped into the running shower.

He'd barely gotten his hair wet when from the other side of the steamy glass came her offer: "Towel?"

He quit singing, but within he sang his supreme gratification that Mel had wasted no time in seeking him out. He slid open the shower door and was further gratified by her quick intake of breath as she tried not to look him over.

And failed miserably.

"Like what you see?" he asked with a grin.

"Too much," she admitted, flapping the white terry cloth to her rosy cheeks while she jerked her gaze up to his.

"If you didn't notice, I like what I see, too." His smile faded. "Put down the towel." It had yet to hit the floor when he gripped her arm and pulled her in.

"My clothes are getting wet!"

"Then I'll take them off." He peeled away the soaked clothing with a slowness reserved for unwrapping a package too special to tear into; by the time he was done she was hanging on to his shoulders for support. He pulled her like a second skin against him and simply held her.

"Clay," she murmured, nuzzling into his embrace as the water sealed them in liquid warmth. "Clay."

"It's what my feet are made of. But to hear you say my name, they feel less than bound to the earth. What are you doing to me, Mel?"

"I can only hope it's half of what you're doing to me."

Into her ear he seductively whispered, "Should I take it that your clothes aren't all that I managed to get wet?"

Her reply was a moan.

"Mercy, woman, but you are good for a man's ego. I haven't even kissed you yet. Makes me feel like a cock struttin' his stuff for a—" He stopped short as she slid her hand between them and gripped the "stuff" in question. Two sliding pumps and his hips jerked urgently forward. Clay grabbed her wrist.

"Let me," she softly demanded.

"I want to let you, God knows that I do." He sucked in a steadying breath. "Too much, Mel."

"No such thing," she insisted, making a small cry of distress when he pried her hand loose.

"But there is, darlin'. *There is.*" Muffling his own groan of distress in her palm, he held fast to the fringes of his control. Then, with a kiss to her fingertips, he pressed her palm to his chest and tried to explain. "You make my heart beat too fast, my mind unable to think past you—which is the only excuse I have for pulling you in here when I should have known better. I just wanted to be close, but I didn't expect to—" He shook his head, still disturbed by his reaction. "When you touched me I nearly lost it."

As if she considered that a compliment beyond measure, she smiled in delight and licked her lips. "Makes a woman wonder what a kiss might do."

"Don't even think about it." He gripped her wandering hand and stared at her, hard. "Listen to me and listen good. That kind of response just goes to show how hungry I am. Anyone deprived of nourishment too long, does not make for a healthy individual. It takes time to recover and thanks to you, I am. But I need more time, more healing to get to that place where I can give as much as I get."

"All right," she conceded even as she swept her breasts against his chest, tempting him to take her. "What can I do to help you get there?"

"Not that," he said raggedly. Lifting her streaming face to his, he let her see the barrenness of his soul, imploring those tender mercies she could bestow. "I need more of what you're already giving me, Mel. I need to take turns drying each other off and watch you put on a nightgown, then read the paper together in bed. I need you to sit on my lap and flip channels from the couch. I need to feel your back against my chest while we cuddle up like two spoons in a drawer."

"I'd love to give all that to you." She kissed him softly and arched against him. "But I want to give you more."

"You will." Close, he was so close to felling her right here on the tiles, pouncing on her like some frenzied animal. Mel deserved better and because she did, he pulled away. "Once I'm able to give you more of what you need."

"And just what do you think it is that I need?" she demanded, frustration evident in the simmer of her gaze.

"The same thing I need. An emotionally healthy relationship," he said, summing it up as best he could. "Please, try to take my refusal of what you're offering as a sign that, frankly, my dear, I *do* give a damn. In fact, I give so much of a damn, I want to see how much I can give you without taking for a change. Let me?" His eyes searching hers, he slid gentle hands over her breasts and traced the sweet-woman frame of her pelvis and belly. Then, ever so slowly he dipped—a single finger to her cleft, a single stroke—and he whispered, "Please, darlin'. *Let me....*"

Her low, endless moan, her clutch of his shoulders, Clay took as assent. It took all the willpower he had and then some to give without taking more than the sighs he drank from her lips as he delved.

"You feel like wet velvet," he whispered while pretending it was him—all of him, the best and the worst of him—that her body greedily accepted.

Greedy. Lord, he'd never felt so greedy for the cocoon of a woman's intimate hold. So tight yet so pliable, hot and sweet, wrapped around his finger as surely as she had him wrapped around hers. Then suddenly she was coming unraveled, coming in his hand and crying his name as she did.

And then she was just simply crying.

"Hey," he murmured, sipping at her tears. "What's this?"

"I'm sorry, it's just—just that—" She sniffled and began to laugh. Softly, soft as the arms she wrapped around him, soft as her raining kisses. "Thank you, Clay. That was the most wonderful lovemaking I've ever had with a man."

"And it was the most wonderful I've had with a woman since... never." And it was true. The intimacy he and Martha had shared had been satisfying and so very good. But he'd taken it for granted until it was gone. This he did not take for granted, for he prized it with the gratitude of a man who'd lost everything and would never again take for granted what he was blessed to have.

"For being such an empty well, Clay Barker, you're incredibly full of generosity."

"And selfish enough to hope that generosity keeps you coming back for more. Again and again and—"

"I think I'm in love with you Clay."

His heart leaped at those words, yet he wanted more. Pressing his forehead to hers, he told her, "I certainly hope so, because I know I'm falling in love with you. But..."

"But what?" she asked, as if falling in love was all it took to have a happy ending.

If only it were true. "Falling in love, Mel, that's one thing. But love, the kind that really lasts and won't go away no matter what life can throw at it, that's another thing altogether. It doesn't have room for division or doubts."

"Are you..." She paused, then rushed on. "Are you saying that you doubt me?"

"Do I doubt your sincerity or depth of feeling for me? No." An evasive answer, but an honest one. "As for myself, what I feel for you is...consuming. The kind of love that suffocates. What I want with you has no more room for that than my commitment to Revenge Unlimited. You're an all-or-nothing proposition, Mel. Be patient with me? I still have some mending to do before I'm capable of more than simply falling in love." Yet he did wonder if it already went beyond that. He'd taken such pleasure in satisfying Mel without regard to himself. Selflessness—definitely a good sign.

"Now," he said, smiling, "if you want to hurry that mending along, how about drying each other off?"

She gave him an impish grin. "Only if you read the paper in your underwear while I put on my nightgown. Then we could maybe, um, flip channels from the couch and cuddle up like two spoons in a drawer?"

Cherishing every minute of it, they did each and every. It was only after they were snuggled together on the couch that Clay felt some remorse for what he'd done.

He frowned at the wallet he'd planted false information in, should she take the opportunity he'd given her to search his things.

And because she hadn't, he took hope that the only thing standing between them were the ghosts of his past, growing ever more distant by the day.

TEN DAYS LATER, Clay decided he more than gave a damn.

Did he love Mel? he asked himself as he shuffled some paperwork on his desk. Yeah, boy and hot damn, he did. He loved her like crazy, this woman who moved like a poem of unstudied prose that made no sense when taken apart and all the sense in the world as a whole.

He felt whole.

Every need he'd spoken of, and even some he hadn't, she filled. She was a friend, a couch-potato pal who started popcorn fights. She was a surrogate wife, minus bedroom intimacies, who still shared intimacies aplenty. Like brushing their teeth together and seeing who could spit faster into the sink.

They were easy in their cohabitative skin, but he sensed her patience with their separate-beds arrangement was wearing thin. Lord knew, his own was. Domestic companionship by night and working side by side during the day were only whetting his appetite for more.

More than her kisses, which greeted him at the suite's door, along with that beloved ritual of, "Hi, honey, how was your day?" More than their mutually bad cooking in their borrowed nest's efficiency kitchen—but considering he could be there without the urge to heave, why, that said a lot.

A lot more than Mel was inclined to say about herself. It wasn't that she didn't share anecdotes about her past, but when he pressed for more recent details of her family and her life, there was an evasiveness about her that disturbed him.

Clay shoved aside the papers with a scowl.

He knew the feds were waxing impatient with this waiting game. So was he, despite the benefits he was reaping. Those benefits were a lot, but they weren't enough. Not nearly. And until this high-stakes game was over, the best he could manage was a draw.

He banged a fist on the desk, surged to his feet. Paced.

Was Mel an agent? If she was, then why didn't she tell him? If she loved him the way he knew he loved her, there should be no choice to make. It was as simple as telling him the truth and trusting him to understand she'd been caught between divided loyalties. It wasn't as if he couldn't empathize, given his own tug-of-war between her and Revenge Unlimited.

Pacing, pacing, debating. *Should he confront her?* That would get everything out into the open. It would also be the equivalent of saying he doubted her.

No, he decided, if there was anything between them on her end, it was up to Mel to expose it. He wasn't averse to giving her a nudge, however.

And if there was no reason for a nudge, then the time was ripe for the dominoes to fall anyway.

Decisively going to the door, he signaled Mel. As he watched her eager approach, saw the light of her smile, Clay knew he was playing for keeps and winning her was worth the risk he was taking.

The waiting game was over.

Chapter Twelve

"GOOD JOB, MEL," Clay said approvingly as he shut the door and proceeded to back her against his desk. The closer to the bug, the better to be overheard. "I tallied up your sales for yesterday. Ten thousand dollars. Not bad."

"I'll say—"

Her voice caught. Bearing down, he left no question that the wood against her spine had nothing on his condition—purposefully relayed with a slow bump and grind.

"Say you'll have dinner with me tonight." He kissed her quick and hard. While she was busy stifling a gasp, he pressed his advantage. "Just between us—" he tapped the desk for emphasis "—I consider you the most valuable salesperson I've ever had. The least I can do is show my appreciation for your outstanding services."

She looked cornered as she gave him a push—one he countered with the heavy weight of his chest to her breasts.

"That's—that's very nice of you to offer, but—"

"But I won't take no for an answer. Why, I do believe you could sell furnaces in the midst of a heat wave.'' He noticed moisture sheening her upper lip and it wasn't from his kiss. ''Is it just me or does it seem a bit overwarm in here to you?''

''Yes, it does,'' she said curtly, not sounding at all like a gracious employee and not acting like one either, as she stiffly accepted his invitation and gave another shove.

Having gotten his way, Clay released her.

Making haste to the door, she cast him an accusing glare. ''If you don't mind, I'd like some fresh air.''

''Oh, I don't mind. Don't mind at all. In fact, why don't you take the rest of the day off. As for dinner, I'll pick you up at, say, seven?''

''No! I mean, I'd rather just meet you.''

He regarded her with a steady, probing gaze that she met unflinchingly. Only after she chaffed her arms, despite the sweating she'd been doing moments before, did he grin.

It didn't reach his eyes.

''Fine by me. Since you're new to Dallas, might I suggest we hook up for dinner at Shogun? That is, if you like Oriental cuisine.''

Considering how much she liked such stuff, her appetite for it seemed to have disappeared, given her brusque agreement before putting the door between them.

Clay's smile vanished.

Yep, one hell of a poker game he was playing out, and the stakes were higher than high. But he didn't have to be a good bluffer to give the feds an earful of what they could have concluded themselves.

He gave a catcall whistle, followed by an observation to the bug: "My, oh my, what a saucy little dish. A mouth to die for and a great ass, too."

"WHERE HAVE YOU BEEN?" Dean demanded several hours later.

"What does it look like? Shopping." Mel tossed several bags on the bed she had come to truly loathe after returning from the luxury of The Mansion suite. Between losing some much-needed shut-eye and her frustration with Clay's limits on intimacy, she was getting cranky.

Hands on her hips, she managed not to snarl. "Have you got a problem with that? After all, I did make more money on commission today than I get paid in a week doing a shitty assignment like this."

"I'll say it's shitty," muttered fellow agent Reece, who was flipping channels. "This is the most boring case I've ever worked." He gave her a glance that was oddly assessing. "Except for all the action he gets with the ladies, that is. Man, he must be one helluva—"

"Reece, you're outta here." Dean hooked a thumb at the door. "Go spell Parks. He radioed in an hour ago to bitch about his butt being numb from sitting in the back of the van all day."

As for butts, Reece seemed to be taking a look at hers on the way out while he grumbled, "Yeah, great.

With any luck Barker'll lead me on another wild-goose chase.''

As soon as they were alone, Dean snorted in exasperation. "Shopping. Hell, the way things are perking along here, I should have gone with you. We've gotta speed this thing up, Lovelace. The powers-that-be are not impressed with our performance. As for yours in his office, I can only hope you're more convincing tonight. Damn!" He smacked a fist into his palm. "Damn, but unless my hearing needs checking, you actually tried to get out of having dinner with him.''

"Maybe I don't want to jeopardize my new job," she retorted. "After all, once the mission is accomplished, there goes my new boyfriend along with my mad money." *Mad.* God, she was mad. Mad at Dean, mad at Clay. But mostly she was mad with herself for lacking the guts to expose Melissa Lovelace as the fraud she was. Easy, right?

Easy as telling Dean that Clay was the boyfriend she was sneaking around to meet each night.

Easy as telling Clay the woman he thought to be beyond reproach was a fake who prayed he'd tell her that he loved her no matter what, loved her so much he would take away the never-ending terror that he might leave the suite only to pull a job she'd read about in the morning paper—along with his death notice.

Her own job as an agent might as well be over. She'd lost enough faith in the system to quit. The only thing holding her back was giving Clay a reason to rake in his winnings and her along with them. Hey, two weeks of bliss—she could surely convince him there was a lifetime more where these came from; that they had the kind of love that could withstand anything life might throw at it.

Easy? Yeah, right. A real piece of cake.

"Look," Dean said, "I don't like telling you this, but if you can't get something substantial accomplished in the next week I'll have to bring someone else in on this."

"No. No, Dean, you can't do that!"

His sigh was resigned, even sympathetic. "The problem is you're not trying, Lovelace. I can understand why, and because of that I'm willing to relieve you of your duties and assign you to another case. All you have to do is show up for dinner and tell Barker you got word that the bad guy who was after you died in an accident, that you're safe and much as you like your new job, it's time to go home. Since there's nothing personal going on between you two, he'll let it go at that."

Nothing personal? she wanted to shriek. The hell! And the hell if she was about to take Dean up on his offer.

"You're right. I haven't been trying," she agreed, suddenly realizing she was off the case already if she didn't do some fast talking. "I like the man and I've let that get in the way of doing my duty. It's a bad way to start off my career, and starting tonight you can count on me to make up for my mistakes. You won't need to bring anyone else in. I'll simply do whatever I have to do. Okay?"

He hesitated before giving a curt nod. Then he pulled out a wrinkled handkerchief and dabbed his brow, apparently sweating his decision already. "Okay, but I'm only giving you one week to turn this around. Understood?"

"Yes, sir." Thinking quickly, she added, "I get the feeling he'd like to get something going, if you know what I mean. I'll do whatever seems smart and the rest of you take a night off. That way you won't have to be privy to any details you'd rather not know about. Deal?"

Dean gave it a little thought—just enough to confirm that he was cutting her some slack and, despite his own duties, what slack he could for Clay Barker.

"You've got it."

"Thanks, boss. Now, if you don't mind, I need to get dressed for a dinner date. I'll take a cab so he'll have an excuse to offer me a ride."

"Poor sucker, between the hots he has for you and—no offense—apparently most anything female, he doesn't stand a chance."

Melissa bit her tongue trying not to come to Clay's defense. "So, what makes you think he has the hots for me?"

Dean tapped the receiver to the office bug. "After you left he whistled. Made a comment or two to himself."

"Such as?"

"'A saucy little dish with a mouth to die for,' I believe were his words."

Despite herself, she blushed. But with pleasure, not with the offense she commanded herself to display. "Why, that . . . ! Can't he look at a woman without reducing her to a sex object? Probably not. Did he say anything else?"

"Uh, yeah." Dean cleared his throat awkwardly as he went for the exit. "Seems he thinks you've got a great ass."

"GREAT DRESS," Clay said, giving Mel a head-to-toe once-over as she laid aside her coat and joined him at the bar. "I made the reservations for eight so we could talk first."

"Sure you wouldn't rather sneak out the back and pinch my behind instead?"

"Excuse me?" He stifled his demand how she'd gotten that idea and signaled the bartender for an extra glass of plum wine.

"Never mind." She fussed with the hem of her short silky red dress that looked like it had come off a China doll. Her lips were slicked with crimson lipstick and he fought the urge to kiss it right off. "Just hoping, I guess."

"Then hope no more." His own hope great that she was speaking the truth, Clay gave a possessive stroke to her back that he followed with a pinch to her derriere. If anyone was watching they'd surely gotten more jollies out of that than losing him in rush-hour traffic and missing out on the Revenge Unlimited meeting he'd kept. "I'll pick up where I left off after dinner since I prefer to pinch your butt in private."

Her plum wine arrived and she took an inordinate amount of time to savor a single sip.

"Why are we here?" she suddenly demanded.

"Because much as I'm enjoying our time together alone, I wanted to get out and make every man who sees you with me jealous as hell. And it did occur to me that it would be considerate on my part to give those who are doing their job a chance to write off a fabulous meal instead of drinking bad coffee in a van or a car while imagining what fun I must be having." He scanned the bar once more. "No takers. So far."

"How do you know?"

"Why, darlin', what with my expertise, I can spot the enemy before they can spot me. It's how I've stayed alive." When she didn't call him on his bluff, he clinked the rim of his glass to hers. "So far."

"Know what I think?"

"No. But I get the feeling you're about to tell me."

She shot him a quelling glance that was closer to a bullet between the eyes.

"I think you're too cocky. And if you don't practice more care than you did today, then your tomorrows are numbered and that must upset me more than it does you, since I'm very upset and you're cool as ice."

"Is that all?" He blew a warm breath into her ear, fully aware that he didn't feel cool in the least. There was a lot to be said on his part. But he wasn't saying it until he was certain Mel had no confessing of her own to do.

She jerked away, her eyes snapping fire. "Actually, no. I think that you used me in your office for your own sneaky purposes without my consent and I don't like it one damn bit."

"Sorry," he said contritely while not feeling sorry one damn bit himself. Sneaky his purposes were, but he deemed them worthy. "Call it a whim, but it seemed the thing to do at the time. I thought you wouldn't mind helping me along. I trusted my judgment as much as I do yours. Apparently I was wrong."

"Of course I want to help you," she was quick to assert. "I just don't want to help you get caught in a trap of your own making."

Clay studied her until she pulled at her too-short skirt and filled the charged silence with a thirsty sip.

He figured her throat must be awfully dry. And was it due to feeling the squeeze of a trap of *her* own making? If so, he was giving her every out he could.

"Everyone gets caught in a trap of their own making sooner or later, Mel," he said, trying to relay his understanding of the position she might be in. *Might.* The mights and the maybes were driving him crazy and he wanted them gone before the night was through. Drawing on what patience he could summon, Clay further extended his empathy. "It's not hard to do, hindsight being twenty-twenty vision. We'd all do some things differently if we could foresee the consequences and outcomes. But since we can't, we're like justice and society, muddling our way through the muck."

"You're right," she agreed. "And sometimes a person gets sucked in so fast and so deep they can't find a way out, no matter how much they regret what they've done."

Now they were getting somewhere!

"Sounds like a situation you're acquainted with."

"I am." Picking up a discarded cocktail umbrella, she twirled it. After a deep breath, she said, "It's one of those skeletons in my closet that I've kept hidden from you. I even try to hide it from myself, but it's there, always there."

"Go on," he urged. "You can tell me anything and I'll keep your secrets as safe as a teddy bear."

Despite his assurance, Mel hesitated.

And began to tear at the fragile paper held together by flimsy wood sticks. It reminded her of the way her life had so easily been ripped from what she'd believed to be sound. Maybe that was why she was so terrified to expose the truth to Clay. No one had loved her more than her father, but even he had deserted her in the end.

"My father was a good man but he made some bad mistakes he couldn't undo." God this was painful. But maybe, maybe Clay would better understand where she was coming from once their borrowed time ran out. Her heart beating in time to that too-fast clock, she forced herself to go on. "What you said that day of the holdup really hit home. You see, Daddy traded in his white hat for a black one and committed a crime to pay for my tuition at Brown."

Was it her imagination that Clay frowned in disapproval? Or was it disappointment? Neither, she decided, when he patted her hand and nodded in sympathy.

"That must have been really tough for you. It's awfully hard to see someone you believe in fall from grace."

He was hitting home again, but so much closer. Mel cringed inside, knowing she would soon be falling from grace in Clay's eyes. Would he resent her as she had her father? Would it make any difference that she resented herself enough for them both? Daddy had; but she had hurt him by nursing her own hurt and closing him out when he'd needed her the most. If Clay did the same, she would be in no position to cast blame.

"I did take it hard," she said, then confessed what she'd never be able to forgive herself for: "But I was so wrapped up in myself that I was blind to what it was doing to him. My mother died in an accident when I was five and he'd devoted his life to making mine the best it could be. And how did I repay him? I was all he had for support but instead of holding him up, I shamed him for what he had done. That was a worse punishment than anything the law ever could have dished out."

Clay squeezed her hand. "Did he go to jail?"

"I'm sure he would have, but since it wasn't a violent crime, he was released on bail and his own recognizance." Downing the remains of her plum wine, she wished it could numb her from the chill gripping her within. "He never served time because he killed himself before the case made it to court."

"I'm so sorry. I wish I could have been there for you."

"Well, it certainly would have been more than Daddy got from me."

When she lifted a finger for another glass, Clay zeroed in on the reason why. "Surely you don't hold yourself responsible, do you?"

"I do." Making no pretense of politeness, she tossed down half the glass. "If I had stood behind him, I really believe that Daddy would be alive today. Not that anything I do can bring him back, but I keep trying to atone for my sins against him. It's as if...if I can make him proud of me, then maybe I can be proud of myself again." There it was, the heart of her quest to restore the family name. For Daddy, she'd believed. But the truth was, Mel suddenly realized, it was mostly for her.

"I have three things to say to all this," Clay replied, his voice gentle but stern. "First, you have to get rid of the notion you're to blame for what happened. That kind of thinking will eat you alive, Mel. It was his decision, not yours, and you have no way of knowing if anything you could have done would have changed the outcome. All you can change is this penance of guilt you're paying. Quit beating yourself up and let it go."

"That's good advice, Clay. But you of all people should know that's a lot easier said than done."

"Touché," he conceded. "Something to work on together." There was a pause and he continued. "Now secondly, having been a father myself, I can assure you that any parent would be proud of a daughter as fine as you. Any disappointment your father might feel would be in your thinking that you have to prove yourself worthy of what a father freely gives. By doubting yourself, you're projecting that doubt onto his fatherly love."

Mel considered that and decided Clay was right. But again, easier said than done when it came to the mess she was squarely in. Why was she hiding behind the tenuous protection of time? Simple. She doubted her hold over Clay enough to project that doubt onto what love he might bear the woman he believed her to be.

"Point well-taken," she said, fighting the impulse to declare herself an imposter and get this awful burden off her shoulders. Weary from the weight, she wanted to slump onto the bar instead of squaring her shoulders and lifting the glass to her lips that lied even now by omission. "Last point?"

"More an observation." He slid his fingers over hers and claimed the glass. "At the rate you're going with that stuff on an empty stomach, you could be tossing your cookies before anything lands on your plate."

She laughed a little at that. Clay had a special knack for making her laugh even when she wanted to cry. Only one of the reasons she loved him. And if only she didn't love him so much, how much easier it would be to clear her conscience and not care whether or not she fell from grace. She'd simply be doing what was right; that would be reason enough to be proud of herself, consequences be damned.

"Thanks, Clay. You saved me from myself."

"Hey, turnabout's fair play. You've been doing much the same for me. Maybe too good a job."

"How's that?"

Before he could answer, a call came for "Barker, party of two."

"We'll pick up where we left off later." Clay paid the tab and got up, quickly—as though he had sudden reservations about whatever he'd meant to say. "Hungry?"

"Actually, no. I seem to have lost my appetite."

"Even for me?" he asked, tracing her bottom lip and stopping her in midnibble.

"Never that." Mel nipped the tip of his finger. "If it's all the same to you, could we forget dinner here and go to the suite? It's the closest thing to home and that's where I'd rather be. Home. With you."

"I like that idea." He was quiet for a moment, then said decisively, "We'll go home. But not to the suite."

"You mean . . . your home?"

"That's the one. I've never taken a woman there before." Draping her coat over her shoulders, he gave her a quick, tender kiss. "Does that tell you anything?"

"It does." She took his arm and looked up at him with a fierce affection as they made their way outside. "But I'd like you to tell me anyway."

"I care for you. Deeply. And I trust you more than anyone I know. Trust has become a rare commodity for me—but Mel, I'd trust you with my very life." The smile he gave her was warm but his words cut at her heart. And once in the car he heaped guilt upon guilt as he fastened her seat belt, saying, "I've got a lot riding on you, darlin'. I'll drive safer than usual since I'm carting some precious cargo."

"Clay, I—" *Just tell him. Tell him you're a fed and he's a felon and please to not quit trusting you just because you made him believe you're someone you're not. Tell him, damn it!*

"Yes?" he asked expectantly. When she darted her gaze to the parking lot and didn't readily reply, he said, "If you're worried about your car we can pick it up later."

"The car's not here. I took a cab tonight."

"If you've got car problems I'll be glad to loan you—"

"No need, the car's fine. I took a cab because..." Her stomach rolled over and her throat locked. She hated herself for her cowardice, for the sheer selfishness of coveting what time they had, before her confession put their relationship to a trial-by-fire test. Somehow, she managed a convincing smile. "Because I wanted to ride together for a change."

"Certainly suits me fine." As he gunned the engine, Clay slid a palm over her knee. "You're shaking a bit. Cold?" At her nod, he flipped on the heater—although between her coat and the agreeable weather, he had to wonder at the source of her chill. "I'll concentrate on driving if you'll watch for anyone following us."

As they rode, Kenny G. filled the silence. Mel seemed to be somewhere else, preoccupied. Was she thinking of her father? Or was she doing battle with those maybes he was carefully probing for while giving her every vote of confidence he could?

He did trust Mel—despite any other secrets she might have—and that included watching their backs.

She didn't spot the tail that stayed two cars behind.

A fed should have picked that up. Then again, if she was looking for a familiar vehicle, this wasn't it.

They had new company. Which meant all those maybes were quite possibly a resounding not.

Clay suddenly wished she was an agent. Far better that than Mel, *his* Mel, being endangered by a stalker come to town.

For if there was a stalker, he was going down. And Clay Barker would be the one who sent him straight to hell.

Chapter Thirteen

CLAY WATCHED HER. Here, in his private sanctum, he watched her even more closely than he had the red Corvette that had driven on as the iron gates closed behind them.

His heart had been closed just as iron tight before Mel had done a neat bit of emotional surgery. He wondered if she made emergency calls. There was a rending sensation going on in his chest, so sharp he felt close to bleeding all over the place.

She was holding a silver frame containing a picture of a once-happy family that had resided in a big happy home.

This was not that home. Nor was it happy.

"Your wife and little girls are beautiful, Clay."

"Were," he corrected. He felt very odd at that moment, disturbed and yet strangely consoled when she touched each of their faces before gently replacing the photo on the desk.

Mel looked directly at him. No smile.

"You moved, didn't you?"

"Stuck it out a year but there were too many ghosts. Just curious, but how did you know?"

She gestured to the impeccable surroundings that were an echo of the other rooms he'd shown her.

"This is a house, Clay. An exquisite house. But it's not a home. Your wife has Earth Mother written all over her and she would have seen to the grace notes. Vintage-warm, not museum-stiff."

"That's okay, you can say it: cold. Because that's what it is, a cold and lonely showroom that's not half as warm as my snooty store." He opened his arms and Mel was in them, just like that. "This house could use more of your presence, Mel. Just being here, you make me feel like there's a fire in the hearth and—"

She kissed him. A tenderly consuming kiss that had the effect of salve to a wound. It was the most honest and truly caring touch, and he knew he couldn't live without it.

He also might not live because of it. Clay gripped her to him—too tightly, but he couldn't help the protectiveness surging against the threat that could have doubled back and parked outside.

He had sworn never to kill again, but he knew he would to protect this woman he loved more than life itself. The FBI would have little trouble linking him to the crime, given his ties with Mel and hers with the potentially deceased. Those who wanted him dead in a prison cell wouldn't care if the evidence was circumstantial—they might even fabricate something that would stick.

Or worse, try get to him through Mel. All they had to do was threaten to charge her for putting out a contract and he'd agree to anything to spare her that injustice.

Justice. What kind of justice would make them both suffer for his need to protect a loved one? Society thought itself so progressed, and yet it lacked the justice a past civilization had had a right to. More than ever, he felt as if he belonged in another time, with a gun riding his hip, a horse beneath him and a home he'd built from logs on the horizon.

And Mel greeting him at the door.

Kissing her, holding her, he loved her too much.

Strong as his lust for bad blood was, the cost of personal vengeance was too high. The price for his brand of justice wouldn't be his alone. He couldn't do that to Mel; couldn't rob them of the future they deserved.

What could he do?

Pay a visit to the local law tomorrow and call in his favors? Not nearly as satisfying as taking care of his own, but the benefits would be more than worth it: From the station he'd proceed to buy the biggest, gaudiest diamond he could find. Next, he'd carry Mel out of the store and right there on the sidewalk—in clear view of everyone, including those in the government van—he would propose on bended knee.

Mel would never know he'd suspected her of being an agent sent to entrap him, only for them both to get caught by a four-letter word. That Corvette had gone a long way in convincing him she was clean as driven snow.

And if by some fluke she wasn't? He wouldn't love her any less.

But he would be pissed. Mad as hell, to be exact, that she hadn't trusted his trust in her. Even madder for putting him through this grinding concern over her safety.

Lifting his mouth from hers, Clay wondered how safe she'd be from him once he took her to bed. The time had come. There was no question of his love for Mel or suspicions to be appeased. All decisions of where his absolute loyalty lay had been made.

"I want to make love to you, Mel," he murmured.

"Want no more, Clay. Make love to me. Here. *Now.*" Wrapping herself around him, she all but pulled him to the floor, pleading, "Make love to me and make the world go away. Hold me like you'll never let me go."

Sweeping her into his arms, he made haste from the room. His voice was thick with desire, hoarse with emotion he made no effort to disguise. "I want to take this bed. The one I've imagined you sharing with me every night I return to an empty house that's crying to be a home." *Marry me, Mel. With you by my side, anywhere is home.* He kissed her all the way up the stairs to keep from saying the words.

Tomorrow, he promised himself, he'd propose properly, ring in hand. As for tonight, he would bind her to him with lovemaking and more.

And yet, by the time they fell on his bed, Mel jerking off his clothes while he tore at hers, Clay had reason to fear his lovemaking would be rough. Whole as he felt, he still wanted to consume her—but with passion, not the kind of love that didn't allow room to breathe.

Breathing in the sweet smell of her, feeling her softness while he was half out of his mind wanting to drive into her with a ravaging force, Clay knew his love was right and good. It had to be, for him to fling himself off her and silently vow to hold her until he had more control than a rutting dog after a bitch in heat.

"Please," she whimpered, urgently trying to pull him back.

"You don't know what you're asking for," he rasped. "I don't trust myself, Mel. I'm— I don't want to hurt you. I want to protect you and—" Protection. Sweet Jesus, he *was* half out of his mind. He didn't even have a friggin' condom here, the only times he'd used one being with the woman he'd ended a monogamously sterile affair with. Six months advance rent paid, a handshake, that was it.

"I trust you," Mel was saying. "And if you do hurt me, it can't hurt any more than wanting you so much and not having you. *Take me,*" she demanded.

With a tortured groan, he tried to soothe them both by pressing her head to his chest and stroking her hair. "I'm afraid we have a problem, darlin'," he explained as calmly as he was able. "Like I said, you're the first woman I've brought here. I've had no reason to keep such things as we're currently in need of around." Not trusting himself to linger lest he say "The hell with it, we'll take our chances," Clay gave her a quick hug, then forced himself off the bed. "I'll be back as soon as I—"

"You're not going anywhere," she asserted with a ferocity to match her staying grip of his hips. Her head lowered and she nuzzled his pubis, making his legs almost give way.

Although they held, Mel proceeded to so stun him that she could have knocked him over with a feather.

"I'm twenty-four, Clay. At my age it's embarrassing to admit that my experience is...limited. Old-fashioned as it sounds, I was waiting for the right man to, uh, you know. So I'm afraid I'm not very accomplished at this. Just tell me what you want and—and I've always been an overachiever. A few pointers and a little practice and I'm sure I'll be up to the standards you're accustomed to."

Holy—! Mel was a virgin? He actually had himself an old-fashioned girl who'd held out for Mr. Right? Well, Clay decided, then he could indulge his own old-fashioned whims. He'd marry Mel first, then give her a wedding night worthy of the woman he was taking for his wife. They could make do until then with everything but "you know." The "everything but" would not only satisfy Mel, it would enable him to make love with the TLC he felt but his body presently lacked the ability to express.

Thank God for those nonexistent rubbers. Given the state he'd been in, he could have torn her apart. To hurt Mel, his Mel, like that—why, he never would have forgiven himself.

Relief and anticipation mingling, Clay smiled down at her with all the love and joy she'd brought him—and he sent back to her in his elated gaze. "The standards I've become accustomed to fall far beneath yours. As for being embarrassed about your limited experience, for the life of me I can't understand why. To be the man you held the others at bay for...what a priceless privilege. I'm humbled."

She cast an assessing glance at what she was holding. "For being so humbled you're standing incredibly tall." Her glance became a wary stare. "And big."

Her candid observation he took as earthy praise. And yet here he was, laughing and fighting a lump in his throat all at once.

"You make me feel like a virgin again, Mel. No need to be an overachiever with me, you're the best just as you are."

"Only the best for the best, Clay Barker." She gave him a most intimate kiss. "And so, about those pointers...?"

"Like this, darlin'..." By word and gently coaxing deed, he guided her in learning his preferences and responses—yet he felt as though he were just discovering them himself.

All bodies were as unique as the people who inhabited them. And it was Mel's own uniqueness, her special touch, that embraced his heart and seized his groin more surely than any expertise could have done.

By the time she was finished, he was a goner for sure. All but collapsing to the floor, he was flat on his back. What strength he had left was put to hauling her down atop him.

With a glow on her face and fever in her eyes, she asked hopefully, "Was it as good for you as it was for me?"

He didn't have to think twice about that and immediately assured her, "Darlin', in all my intimate encounters, not a one could compete with you. In fact, I feel so completely satisfied I could die happy just like this."

"But I don't want you to die," she whispered fervently, stroking his chest. "Not now. Not ever."

"I know." He wanted to tell her he had no intention of doing such a thing when they had a lifetime of loving ahead of them. But he'd save that little speech for tomorrow to go along with the ring. For now, he decided, he'd quell her immediate fears and give her a hint of what he had in store. "Keep killing me softly,

the way that you do, and I could yet have every reason to die of old age along with you.''

A LOT HAPPENED that night as she gave him enough
reasons to justify a felon's innocence, and he gave her
just as many to declare herself an innocent no more.

When she pressed him to make a fast trip to the
store, he convinced her, most persuasively, that he
couldn't tear himself away that long. Not only was he
set on his plans, no way was he about to leave Mel
alone in case a stalker was watching. Clay kept that to
himself, as well; the night was too wonderful to spoil
with the problem he'd take of tomorrow.

Yes, how wonderful it was to make a meal of
Campbell's best, crackers and cheese, and feed each
other picnic-style on the bed. What a delight as Mel
washed the bowls and he dried, then together they
popped bubbles in the sink. And with each bubble
popped, each nuzzle of his chest to her back, Clay
gave thanks to heaven, exulted in these simple riches
that were blessings beyond measure.

Come the midmorning light, not a wink of sleep
between them, he served Mel a bracing espresso with
a wink.

''Drink up, darlin'. We were due at work an hour
ago. But something tells me that the boss won't be
docking your salary for showing up late.''

''But I don't want to go to work,'' she protested
while he threw on his clothes and she eyed her own

discarded remains with a wrinkle of her nose. "Can I at least take a shower first?"

Rather than remind her that they'd both greatly enjoyed themselves in the shower a few hours prior, he said, "Anything for you, darlin'. Anything for you."

Clay watched her go and silently willed her to make it quick. As it was, he was so eager to get this show on the road he felt like an engine with the accelerator to the floor and the transmission in Park.

It wouldn't be easy but he'd wait until lunch to run all his personal errands. He'd ask Mel and Amanda to hold down the fort in his absence—which would probably be a little bit. But Mel would be safe even without him there, since stalkers hunted in private.

As for a certain gentleman who would return with a ring in his pocket and a proposal on his lips, he preferred to go public. Fact was, he wanted to shout to the world his intentions to marry the finest woman alive.

But since his voice couldn't carry that far, the sidewalk and a rock the size of Texas itself would just have to do.

Chapter Fourteen

"MAY I HELP YOU?" Mel asked politely while trying not to yawn. Thirty more minutes to lunch and a nap on the sofa in Clay's office. She didn't think he was likely to arm-wrestle her for it since he seemed closer to adrenaline high than exhausted.

The woman glanced around uneasily. "I was hoping I might be able to see the owner. A Mr. Barker, I believe. Is he in?"

Mel snapped fully awake, suddenly aware that the customer wringing her hands wasn't after a store purchase. An urge seized Mel to tell her that Mr. Barker was not only *not* in, he would not be in *ever* for the reason that she was here.

"Just a moment, please, and I'll check." Knowing the best she could hope for was a word in private with Clay first, she went directly to his office and signaled him to the door.

"What's up?" he asked conversationally before whispering in her ear, "Besides me, that is. Wanna neck?"

"Like crazy," she whispered back. "After you tell me that you're not available to see the customer who just walked in and asked for you. She's not here to shop, Clay." Gripping his hand, she pleaded, "Please. *Please,* don't even talk to her."

His regard was thoughtful. "I'm sorry, Mel, but that wouldn't be right. Surely you realize anyone who comes to see me is in dire straits. The least I can do is lend an ear."

A thought came to her then—one that was as jarring as the possibility his compassion might induce him to take the woman's case.

"How do you know that?" she quietly demanded. "Has it occurred to you that she could be part of a setup to catch you in an illegal act?"

Clay seemed to find some humor in that, which she didn't. He was chuckling. "Actually, the thought did cross my mind." He winked. "All the more reason to speak to her and find out for myself if she's up to no good." That said, he got his suit coat and pecked Mel's cheek on the way out.

Heart in her throat, she grabbed his arm. "Wait."

"Yes?" he drawled. "Something you want to tell me that can't wait till I'm back?"

Tell him, she ordered herself. *Tell him she could be a replacement that'll get the job done I couldn't in a lifetime, and Dean knows it.*

But what if the prospective client was just that? Would Clay take the case? Or did he love her enough to keep himself safe for her sake as well as his? If not, no amount of sacrifice on her part would a future together make.

His decision. It was out of her hands.

His hand, she kissed. "I love you."

"I know," he said simply. "And I love you, too."

As if that settled it and she was supposed to be content, he left her there at his office door while he went straight to the woman. They had a brief word and he offered his arm before off they went.

Unable to bear simply standing there and doing nothing, Mel didn't waste time grabbing a jacket before calling to Amanda, "I have to run an errand. Be back soon."

She was gone faster than Amanda could reply. Following the direction she'd seen them take, she was soon close behind them, given their leisurely stroll.

The sidewalk was crowded enough for her to blend in and note the nod of Clay's head as he listened to the lady who seemed to be talking a mile a minute. In her own head was the sound of a silent scream.

She also had a very strange feeling. Her neck prickled as if someone's cold breath was on it. Mel stopped. Glanced around.

To the ordinary observer, nothing was amiss. She was not the ordinary observer. He had an old army jacket on, ratty blue jeans, a once-handsome face.

Someone had recently altered the latter.

His gaze connected briefly with hers. He paused and lit a cigarette. She scanned the crowd for Clay and saw he was about to cross the street.

Hurrying on, Mel didn't need to look behind her again to know that she was being followed.

Or was it Clay the plainclothes fed was trailing?

Chances were, they were both under surveillance.

HE RETURNED TO THE STORE alone. Mel's cheeks were flushed as she met him, and Clay didn't have to touch them to know they were chapped from the cold. Much as he'd wanted to see directly to his plans, he knew she'd been worried enough to follow him and he wanted to set her mind at ease before taking off on the pretext of lunch.

"We have to talk," she said without preamble.

"Sounds important, Mel. Is something wrong?"

"Extremely wrong, Clay. I went after you."

"So I noticed. And to tell the truth, it made me feel good that you did." Heedless of several customers, he kissed her a good one right in the middle of the showroom floor. "Does that put your mind at ease? I sure hope so, since I really have to go. There's some important business that I—"

"Nothing's as important as this." She gripped his arms and pressed her face to his chest, close and intense, lingering so that she seemed to be memorizing his heartbeat. When she spoke, her voice trembled. "Someone was on my heels. It was—"

"I know who it was, damn it," he gritted out, wanting to go hunt the bastard down instead of getting to the police station pronto. "Don't worry, Mel. That stalker of yours is about to—"

"The only one who's being stalked is you, Clay."

She forced herself to look directly at him. "He's a fed. And so am I."

The silence was absolute. It was all Mel could hear except for what sounded like the grind of Clay's teeth. A muscle ticked in his cheek.

And his eyes—oh, God, they were like coals simmering with the fury he was just scarcely banking.

But worst of all was his controlled, even whisper: "I am going to clear the store. While I do, go to my office. We will tend to our business there. If you do not wish for your associates to listen in, I suggest that you get rid of the bug. I'm sure you know where it is."

He removed her clenching grip from his arms with a firm but light touch. Mel had the distinct feeling he was exercising immense restraint to keep from shaking her until her teeth chattered—although they already were as he swiftly distanced himself and went directly to Amanda.

Without so much as a glance back her way, he then went on to politely approach a customer. Amanda followed suit, surely giving the same message that they were closing, with apologies and a good-day.

Realizing she was still rooted to the spot and the store would soon be empty—except for her and a very scary Clay—Mel rushed into his office, fighting the urge to heave.

The bug went directly into Clay's cup of leftover coffee.

No sooner had it landed with a plunk than Clay entered the room. He shut the door, softly. Slowly, each step like the roll of a drum announcing an execution about to commence, he closed the distance.

The tips of his shoes nipped hers. Down went his arm to the desk in a single, vicious swipe. She flinched as papers flew, thuds and shatters sounding from the floor.

Before she could suck in a nonexistent breath, Clay pushed her onto the desk and covered her mouth with his.

His lips were on hers, but she couldn't call it a kiss. It was more a punishment—angry thrusts of his tongue and stinging little bites that far exceeded passionate nibbles. Never had she imagined so much fury could be poured into an act that lovers made an art of.

And yet, she didn't fight him. Her arms were around him, holding on for dear life, and her mouth was greedy even for this raw expression of livid emotion. Clay was honest in his anger. And she was honestly grateful to have it. No one could be so furious and not love a person just as much. Resentment, coldness, indifference—those were the things to truly fear. But not this anger that was spending itself, tempering to a firm chastisement of his lips rubbing over hers, then ending with the gentle rebuke of her bottom lip drawn between the light rake of his teeth.

"Do you know what that was for?" he whispered, his breathing hard while her own came in panting gasps.

"For—for me lying to you, deceiving you. Clay, I'm sorry, so sorry. Please forgive me, but—"

He cut her off with a palm over her mouth. "No. That's not the problem here, Mel," he informed her curtly. "You think I blame you for conning me when that was your job? Hell, no. Give me more credit than that. The same way I gave you credit for being worthy of my trust even when I was wondering if you were a fed—which was up until last night. I gave you every opportunity I could to tell me the truth, but you didn't take me up on a one. Why?" He lifted his hand. "Spit it out, Mel. I'm waiting."

"Be-because I was afraid if I told you that you wouldn't trust me anymore. And—and I didn't want to hurt you by telling you I didn't deserve—"

"There you go. *That's* the problem. If you had trusted me and believed as strongly as I do in what we've got, you never would have had a second's doubt about my faith in you. It's unshakable, the same as my love. Hurt me? You have. How could you have so little confidence in me, in yourself, in *us?*" He searched her eyes for an answer she couldn't bring herself to speak. But she let him see the little girl within whose self-doubts compelled her to prove herself again and again, afraid that failure would call her unworthy of what a parent, a true love, freely gave.

Slowly, he shook his head. "No one, Mel, no one could be more deserving of everything I have to give, than you. My commitment, my devotion, my ring that I still fully intend to buy today. But don't you dare say yes unless you're ready to promise you'll never spout such rubbish again. Like I told you last night, you're the best, the absolute best, just as you are. And don't you *ever* forget it."

Her head was spinning—or was it the room and she really was on solid ground while her heart soared to the sky?

"Is . . . is this some kind of marriage proposal?"

"To have and to hold, till death do us part," he assured her, then growled, "And you can count on that being a very long time—minus natural causes such as a heart attack due to worrying myself sick over your safety. God, am I mad at you for putting me through that! Here I was on my way to the police to hand all your information over so they could nail that stalker and—"

"The police? You were going to the police?"

"Well, where else?" He snorted. "Hell, no place else to go. Especially since Mr. Revenge Unlimited himself called a meeting with his associates yesterday and officially closed shop. I've made my contribution, now it's up to justice and society to slug it out without me."

In reply to her reaction, he said, "You could catch flies with a jaw dropped like that. Close your mouth, darlin'. And don't open it again until you're ready to say, 'Yes, Clay, I'll marry you because you are a wonderful, just man who is absolutely crazy about me. *And* I will never insult you again by doubting that we've got anything less than the stuff that lasts no matter what life can throw at it.' Tough love, Mel.

Now quit your crying long enough to give me my answer."

She couldn't quit crying, but she did give him that answer. Verbatim.

They sealed the sweetest justice Mel was sure they'd ever claim with an endless kiss. One as lusty as it was loving, so full and complete that she thought her heart might break from trying to contain the abundance of rapture within.

And then it did break, such was his aching tenderness as Clay dried the last traces of wetness on her cheeks.

With a handkerchief—freshly starched and snowy white. She couldn't help but think that Dean could use a few like it.

Dean! Mel could just see him mopping his brow and guzzling from a Maalox bottle. He would have contacted the van as soon as the bug was snuffed and the lookout would have been watching for any unusual activity.

All the customers had been sent away. Clay had locked up after them. Mel could only hope Dean had surmised that Clay was having his randy way with Agent Lovelace, who hadn't reported back by daybreak.

"Well, Mrs. Barker—soon-to-be, that is, and the sooner the better—where to from here?" Clay kissed the handkerchief, then pocketed it with the panties he'd brought along to work. Took them with him everywhere, he'd told her, having won them from a geisha who was his lucky charm and had him eating out of her hand. "Personally, I've got my sights set on a jewelry store. You can choose the ring—just make it big enough for anyone within a mile to see. From there, your pick. A farewell rendezvous at The Mansion suite? Or my house? Whichever, count on lots more kissing and making up between discussing what kind of wedding you want."

"Your house that's about to become a home," she replied without pause. "But first, I want to get my things and give notice to my boss."

"Something tells me Dean had better have a case of antacid handy. He's gonna catch enough hell for you both after this." At her stunned gape, Clay chuckled. "We have common friends but we've never been formally introduced. I'd very much like to meet him and personally invite him to our wedding. Why, I'll even let him kiss the bride."

HER STOMACH WAS REELING along with her head by the time they arrived at the motel—minus the van Clay had lost as he wove in and out of traffic faster than a carnival ride.

Still, she had that sensation again. Although a scan of the lobby didn't reveal the man who had followed them before, Mel shuddered.

"Something's not right, Clay. I can feel it like a clammy palm on my shoulder. Maybe we should leave and I'll handle this later by myself."

"Absolutely not. We face Dean together, Mel, and from this day forward everything else, as well." He punched the elevator button, then pinched her butt. "Besides, what could possibly be wrong? It's not like I'm walking into a room without being fully aware of who I'm with and that every word, every motion will be recorded. Given that, let's be sure to give them a show to remember—or rather, one they'd give anything to forget."

She tried to match his playful mood but the closer they came to the room where Dean would be taken unawares—all the paraphernalia in plain sight and the sting exposed to he who had escaped being stung—the more certain she was that something was about to go down.

"This isn't a good idea," she said with the force of her instincts insisting it was worse than bad. "Tell me why they wanted you. I wasn't given that information."

Briefly, he explained. "So there you have it. And now that you've surpassed all expectations, including mine, and reformed me, there's no revenge on their part to be had."

Revenge. There it was, that palm on her shoulder. Suddenly it was moving closer to her throat.

"You, of all people, should realize that some grudges just won't die. The agent who's responsible for all this, what does he look like?"

"Now? Probably not too pretty." The description he then gave her confirmed her suspicions.

"That's him. He's the one who was following you. Maybe us both." She jammed the key into the lock and said heatedly, "I'll confront Dean with this. That guy's after blood and whoever assigned him knows this is a personal vendetta and one that doesn't have a damn thing to do with justice."

Two of a kind, Clay thought with satisfaction as Mel threw wide the door. Justice was the code of honor he would always revere and if there were more law enforcers like Mel, then justice would be better served.

"Lovelace! He killed the bug and—" Dean looked from her to Clay in disbelief. "And *what* are you doing here with—"

"Clay Barker," he supplied, extending his hand. Dean stared at it; then gave a wipe to his brow and offered a brief grip. "Such a pleasure to meet you. Special Agent Dean, I believe."

"Yeah," he confirmed, scowling. But there was a twitch in his lips that looked awfully close to a grudging smile. "I don't suppose you're here to turn yourself in?"

"Turn myself in? For what? might I ask." Since they had nothing on him that would stand up in court, Clay couldn't resist a grin. "Unless it's a crime to fall in love with one's employee and have plans to get hitched, then I'm afraid you're speaking to the wrong man. I am, after all, a law-abiding citi—"

He stopped as he registered a shift in the air. Without turning, he knew company had just arrived at the door Mel had yet to shut.

"Out, Dean," the company demanded, slinking in like the snake he was. A viper disguised by what had been pretty-boy looks. Clay knew that a little plastic surgery could remedy that eye-for-an-eye damage. But it wouldn't change what he really was. Pure poison that tainted the legal system he abused with his lording of power over others.

"What are you doing here, Evans? And just what the hell is the big idea of waving that gun?"

"You didn't see it, Dean. And you didn't see me."

"You're crazy! Get out of here before I—" The cock of a trigger cut him off.

Clay kept his back turned and from his peripheral vision saw Mel edging toward a nearby chair with an open suitcase on it. *She was going for her gun.* He wanted to yell at her to get out and fast, but he didn't dare do anything that would set the crazy off. Crazy, he had to be. Crazy enough to go on a shooting spree and plead temporary insanity to a sympathetic judge who likely played golf with his top-dog uncle.

"Stop! Move another inch and I'll blow your head off so you can join your father. A bad seed, just like you." Evans barked an ugly laugh. "Sleeping with the enemy. Shame, shame on you. You're supposed to screw them, not the other way around, bitch."

"Watch it," Clay warned in a lethal growl. "That's no way to talk to a lady."

"Oh yeah? Are you going to teach me another lesson, Barker? Go ahead, just try." Cold steel tapped his nape. "I might be a slow learner but you won't be learning much of anything with your brains spilled on the floor.''

"Listen, Evans," Dean said reasonably, "we can work this out. All you have to do is put down the gun and—"

"And I said *get out*. You can go. The bitch stays and watches. But you'd better leave now before I change my mind."

Rage flared and swept Clay with a consuming fury. It was as instantaneous as his crystalline certainty that he'd willingly die on the spot to give Mel the chance to escape.

Faster than light, he whirled. *Boom!* The blast shattered the air and then all he could hear was silence, feel himself staggering back and see the room tilt while all about him the horrific scene unfolded in slow motion.

The maniac raising the gun and pointing it at Mel. Mel, whose mouth was open in a huge screaming O while she lurched toward the suitcase, overturned it as blood spurted from her shoulder, then rolled and rolled and came up on her knees.

Gun in her grip. Taking aim. Jerk. Jerk. Jerk. Unloading the pistol. Crawling to him. Dean pulling at his shirt. Grabbing for the phone.

Mel. Sweet, darlin' Mel. Her face filling his vision, her mouth moving. He could hear her crying his name. Crying. Crying. Tears falling from her face and onto his.

"Don't...cry, darlin'," he rasped. His voice seemed to be coming from a great distance and it seemed miles before he reached her cheek with his fingers—numb, so numb.

"Don't you dare die on me, Clay Barker," she sobbed.

"I'm too—too ornery to die." He coughed and a searing pain spread through his chest. "Killed the...the...bastard didn't...you?"

"He deserved it. And I'll kill him all over again if—"

"Once is...enough." He tried to smile but that only made her cry harder. "He'll get what...we all get in...the end. Judgment Day. Hope mine goes...better than...his."

The sound of sirens competed with Mel's pleas for him to hang on, just hang on and love her enough not to die. The blood streaming from her shoulder mingled with his as she bent over him and covered his face, his wounded chest, with kisses.

"The blood of the lamb," he wheezed, patting her head. And then peace, such peace he felt, as he succumbed to a lethargic darkness.

His last coherent thought was that he was a lucky man indeed, for he was well and truly loved by a good woman who had been willing to give her life to save him.

Chapter Fifteen

"HOW IS HE TODAY?" Mel asked the scowling nurse just leaving Clay's hospital room. The door was jerked not quite shut and Mel was sure she'd get an earful to her question from Nurse Richardson.

"Crankier than hell and making us all glad that he's getting his way and checking out a day early," she said loudly enough for Clay to hear.

"Mel?" came his yell from the room. "Is that you out there talking to Miss Priss?"

"That's Miss Richardson to you, *Mister* Barker," the nurse retorted. "Miss Priss," Clay called her, but Melissa thought "Admiral" would be more apt. Steel gray hair and eyes the same color, she liked to run a tight ship—which wasn't easy with the mutiny Clay had been waging. As if anticipating he was on the verge of another uprising, she ordered, "Get back in bed and stay there until you're released! If I have to come in again, I'm bringing an enema with me."

"I'm not talking to you." His growl coincided with the squeak of bedsprings. "Mel, I know that's you out there. Hurry your sweet little butt in here and come lay one on me before Miss Priss has a fit for me taking it upon myself to prove that I am perfectly capable of walking my way to freedom without the damn wheelchair I'm supposed to leave in!''

"Good riddance," the nurse muttered before adding, "And good luck getting married to a man like that. I've had some ornery patients before, but this one takes the cake.''

Mel laughed with pure joy as she thought of the cake the best caterers in Dallas would be baking for their wedding day. Another week. That was, if Clay didn't make good on his threat to hog-tie her down if he had to and jet to Vegas the second he was out of this "damn hellhole of a prison."

Where he'd gotten the idea to elope first and then marry her properly in a church for good measure, she didn't know, but something told her he'd thought it up between bitching about the lousy food and yelling at his "wardens" in the two months he'd been confined to the hospital.

"Sounds as if you've been a bad boy today," she said brightly while wagging her finger his way.

"Shut the door," he ordered, flipping aside the bedcovers and swinging his feet to the floor. "Dare I hope those are my clothes in that bag?"

"Yes, you dare," she assured him. Given all his threats to up and leave, the doctor had requested she take away his street clothes.

"How are you feeling?" She wrapped her arms around his neck and nuzzled against the steady beat of his heart. The heart a bullet had come frighteningly close to ravaging.

"Meaner than a pit bull and friskier than a pup."
He bumped his hips forward. "I am also horny as hell
and champing at the bit for a past-due wedding
night."

"From the sound of that, I could be the one laid up
for months." She knuckled his jaw. "Dare I hope?"

"You dare." He kissed her completely, fiercely.
Cupping his face, she traced the proud set of his lips
that moved beneath her fingertip to impart the ritual
greeting that was theirs, all theirs: "Now that you've
put me in a better frame of mind, let's start over. Hi,
darlin'."

"Hi, honey." She hugged him like she'd never let
him go and Mel knew that never, ever, would she. A
kiss to each cheek and she asked, "How was your
day?"

HARLEQUIN®

Temptation®

Secret Fantasies

Do you have a secret fantasy?

Researcher Eva Campbell does. She's an expert on
virtual reality and in her computer she's created the
perfect man. Except her fantasy lover is much more
real than she could ever imagine.... Experience
love with the ideal man in Mallory Rush's #558
KISS OF THE BEAST, available in October.

Everybody has a secret fantasy. And you'll find them
all in Temptation's exciting new yearlong miniseries,
Secret Fantasies. Throughout 1995 one book each
month focuses on the hero or heroine's innermost
romantic desires....

Take 4 bestselling love stories FREE

Plus get a FREE surprise gift!

Special Limited-time Offer

Mail to Silhouette Reader Service™

3010 Walden Avenue
P.O. Box 1867
Buffalo, N.Y. 14269-1867

YES! Please send me 4 free Silhouette Desire® novels and my free surprise gift. Then send me 6 brand-new novels every month, which I will receive months before they appear in bookstores. Bill me at the low price of $2.66 each plus 25¢ delivery and applicable sales tax, if any.* That's the complete price and a savings of over 10% off the cover prices—quite a bargain! I understand that accepting the books and gift places me under no obligation ever to buy any books. I can always return a shipment and cancel at any time. Even if I never buy another book from Silhouette, the 4 free books and the surprise gift are mine to keep forever.

225 BPA AWPN

Name	(PLEASE PRINT)
Address	Apt. No.
City	State	Zip

This offer is limited to one order per household and not valid to present Silhouette Desire® subscribers. *Terms and prices are subject to change without notice.
Sales tax applicable in N.Y.

Become a Privileged Woman,
You'll be entitled to all these Free Benefits. And Free Gifts, too.

To thank you for buying our books, we've designed an exclusive FREE program called *PAGES & PRIVILEGES™*. You can enroll with just one Proof of Purchase, and get the kind of luxuries that, until now, you could only read about.

BIG HOTEL DISCOUNTS

A privileged woman stays in the finest hotels. And so can you—at up to 60% off! Imagine standing in a hotel check-in line and watching as the guest in front of you pays $150 for the same room that's only costing you $60. Your *Pages & Privileges* discounts are good at Sheraton, Marriott, Best Western, Hyatt and thousands of other fine hotels all over the U.S., Canada and Europe.

FREE DISCOUNT TRAVEL SERVICE

A privileged woman is always jetting to romantic places.

When <u>you</u> fly, just make one phone call for the lowest published airfare at time of booking— <u>or double the difference back!</u>

PLUS—you'll get a $25 voucher to use the first time you book a flight AND <u>5% cash back on every ticket you buy thereafter through the travel service!</u>

"Richly imbued with steamy passion, deftly spiced with dangerous intrigue, and neatly tempered with just the right amount of tart wit."

—Booklist

A HELLION IN HER BED

"A lively plot blending equal measures of steamy passion and sharp wit. . . ."

—Booklist (starred review)

"Jeffries's sense of humor and delightfully delicious sensuality spice things up!"

—RT Book Reviews (4½ stars)

"Jeffries's addictive series satisfies."

—Library Journal

THE TRUTH ABOUT LORD STONEVILLE

"Jeffries combines her hallmark humor, poignancy, and sensuality to perfection."

—RT Book Reviews

"Lively repartee, fast action, luscious sensuality, and an abundance of humor."

—Library Journal (starred review)

"Captivating . . . [with] delectably witty dialogue and scorching sexual chemistry."

—Booklist

Sabrina Jeffries

'Twas the Night After Christmas

POCKET BOOKS

New York   London   Toronto   Sydney   New Delhi

Pocket Books
A Division of Simon & Schuster, Inc.
1230 Avenue of the Americas
New York, NY 10020

This book is a work of fiction. Any references to historical events, real people, or real places are used fictitiously. Other names, characters, places, and events are products of the author's imagination, and any resemblance to actual events or places or persons, living or dead, is entirely coincidental.

First Pocket Books paperback edition November 2013

POCKET and colophon are registered trademarks of Simon & Schuster, Inc.

For information about special discounts for bulk purchases, please contact Simon & Schuster Special Sales at 1-866-506-1949 or business@simonandschuster.com.

The Simon & Schuster Speakers Bureau can bring authors to your live event. For more information or to book an event contact the Simon & Schuster Speakers Bureau at 1-866-248-3049 or visit our website at www.simonspeakers.com.

Manufactured in the United States of America

10 9 8 7 6 5 4 3 2 1

ISBN 978-1-4767-0822-5
ISBN 978-1-4516-4250-6 (ebook)

To the Biaggi Bunch—thanks for always having faith in me!

And to the love of my life, who lost his parents at a young age.
This one's for you, babe.

Acknowledgments

First, to my critique partners, Rexanne Becnel and Deb Marlowe, thank you for always knowing what's wrong even when I can't put my finger on it. And Deb, thank you for finding the secret door even when I painted myself into a plot corner!

Thank you, Becky Timblin and Kim Ham, for keeping me sane during the months and months of insanity.

This book wouldn't even have been conceived without my agent, Pamela Ahearn, who has always encouraged me to push beyond my comfort zone.

And I can't do anything without my wonderful editor, Micki Nuding, who didn't even blink when I said

I needed another month to finish. Thanks, Micki, for understanding that sometimes characters need time to come into fruition.

Most of all, thanks to Rene for enduring all the chaos with stoic grace. You're the best!

'Twas the Night After Christmas

Prologue

No one had called for him yet.

Eight-year-old Pierce Waverly, heir to the Earl of Devonmont, sat on his bed in the upper hall of the Headmaster's House at Harrow, where he'd lived for three months with sixty other boys.

Today marked the beginning of his first holiday from Harrow; most of the other boys had already been fetched by their families. His trunk was packed. He was ready.

But what if no one came? Would he have to stay at Harrow, alone in the Headmaster's House?

Mother and Father would come. Of *course* they would come. Why wouldn't they?

Because Father thinks you're a sickly weakling. That's why he packed you off to school—to "toughen you up."

His chin quivered. He couldn't help that he had asthma. He couldn't help that he liked it when Mother showed him how to play the pianoforte, which Father called "dandyish." And if he sometimes hid when Father wanted to take him riding, it was only because Father always berated him for not doing it right. Then Pierce would get so mad that he would say things Father called "insolent." Or worse, he'd start having trouble breathing and get panicky. Then Mother would have to come and help him catch his breath, and Father *hated* that.

He scowled. All right, so perhaps Father *would* leave him to rot at school, but Mother wouldn't. She missed him—he knew she did, even if she didn't write very often. And he missed her, too. A lot. She always knew just what to do when the wheezing started. *She* didn't think playing music was dandyish, and *she* said he was clever, not insolent. She made him laugh, even in her infrequent letters. And if she didn't come for him . . .

Tears welled in his eyes. Casting a furtive glance about him, he brushed them away with his gloved fist.

"What a mollycoddle you are, crying for your parents," sneered a voice behind him.

Devil take it. It was his sworn enemy, George Manton, heir to the Viscount Rathmoor. Manton was five years older than Pierce. Nearly *all* the boys were older. And bigger. And stronger.

"I'm not crying," Pierce said sullenly. "It's dusty in here, is all."

Manton snorted. "I suppose you'll have one of your 'attacks' now. Don't think I'll fall for that nonsense. If you start wheezing with *me,* I'll kick the breath out of you. You're a poor excuse for a Harrovian."

At least I can spell the word. You couldn't spell arse *if it were engraved on your forehead.*

Pierce knew better than to say that. The last time he'd spoken his mind, Manton had knocked him flat.

"Well?" Manton said. "Have you nothing to say for yourself, you little pisser?"

You're an overgrown chawbacon who picks on lads half your size because your brain is half size.

Couldn't say that one, either. "Looks like your servant's here." Pierce nodded at the door. "Shouldn't keep him waiting."

Manton glanced to where the footman wearing Rathmoor livery stoically pretended not to notice anything. "I'll keep him waiting as long as I damned well please. I'm the heir—I can do whatever I want."

"I'm the heir, too, you know." Pierce thrust out his chest. "And your father is just a viscount; *mine's* an earl."

When Manton narrowed his gaze, Pierce cursed his quick tongue. He knew better than to poke the bear, but Manton made him so angry.

"A fat lot of good that did you," Manton shot back. "You're a pitiful excuse for an earl's son. That's what comes of mixing foreign stock with good English stock. I daresay your father now wishes he hadn't been taken in by your mother."

"He wasn't!" Pierce cried, jumping to his feet. The glint of satisfaction in Manton's eyes told Pierce he shouldn't have reacted. Manton always pounced when he smelled blood. But Pierce didn't care. "And she's only half foreign. Grandfather Gilchrist was a peer!"

"A penniless one," Manton taunted. "I don't know what your father saw in a poor baron's daughter, though I guess we both know what she saw in *him*—all that money and the chance to be a countess. She latched onto that quick enough."

Pierce shoved him hard. "You shut up about my mother! You don't know anything! Shut up, shut up, shut—"

Manton boxed Pierce's ears hard enough to make *him* shut up. Pierce stood there, stunned, trying to catch his bearings. Before he could launch himself at Manton again, the servant intervened.

"Perhaps we should go, sir," the footman said nervously. "The headmaster is coming."

That was apparently enough to give Manton pause. And Pierce, too. He stood there breathing hard, itching to fight, but if he got into trouble with the headmaster, Father would never forgive him.

"Aren't you lucky?" Manton drawled. "We'll have to continue this upon our return."

"I can't wait!" Pierce spat as the servant ushered Manton from the room.

He would probably regret that after the holiday, but for now he was glad he'd stood up to Manton. How dare the bloody bastard say such nasty things about Mother? They weren't true! Mother wasn't like that.

The headmaster appeared in the doorway accompanied by a house servant. "Master Waverly, your cousin is here for you. Come along."

With no more explanation than that, the headmaster hurried out, leaving the servant to heft Pierce's trunk and head off.

Pierce followed the servant down the stairs in a daze. Cousin? What cousin? He had cousins, to be sure, but he never saw them.

Father himself had no brothers or sisters; indeed, no parents since Grandmother died. He did have an uncle who was a general in the cavalry, but Great-Uncle Isaac Waverly was still fighting abroad.

Mother's parents had been dead for a few years, and she had no siblings, either. Pierce had met her second cousin at Grandfather Gilchrist's funeral, but Father had been so mean to the man one time at Montcliff— the Waverly family estate—that he'd left in a huff. Father didn't seem to like Mother's family much. So the cousin who was here probably wasn't one of Mother's.

Pierce was still puzzling out who it could be when he caught sight of a man at least as old as Father. Oh. Great-Uncle Isaac's son. Pierce vaguely remembered having met Mr. Titus Waverly last year at Grandmother's funeral.

"Where's Mother?" Pierce demanded. "Where's Father?"

Mr. Waverly cast him a kind smile. "I'll explain in the carriage," he said, then herded Pierce out the door. A servant was already lifting Pierce's trunk onto the top and lashing it down with rope.

Pierce's stomach sank. That didn't sound good. Why would Mother and Father send a relation to pick him up at school? Had something awful happened?

As soon as they were headed off in the carriage, Mr. Waverly said, "Would you like something to eat? Mrs. Waverly sent along a nice damson tart for you."

Pierce liked damson tarts, but he had to figure out what was going on. "Why did you come to fetch me home? Is something wrong?"

"No, nothing like that." Mr. Waverly's smile became forced. "But we're not going to Montcliff."

A slow panic built in his chest. "Then where are we going?"

"To Waverly Farm." He spoke in that determinedly cheery voice adults always used when preparing you for something you wouldn't like. "You're to spend your holiday with us. Isn't that grand? You'll have a fine time riding our horses, I promise you."

His panic intensified. "You mean, my whole family is visiting at Waverly Farm, right?"

The sudden softness in his cousin's eyes felt like pity. "I'm afraid not. Your father . . . thinks it best that you stay with us this holiday. Your mother agrees, as do I." His gaze chilled. "From what I gather, you'll have a better time at Waverly Farm than at Montcliff, anyway."

"Only because Father is a cold and heartless arse," Pierce mumbled.

Oh, God, he shouldn't have said that aloud, not to Father's own cousin.

He braced for a lecture, but Mr. Waverly merely laughed. "Indeed. I'm afraid it often goes along with the title."

The frank remark drew Pierce's reluctant admiration. He preferred honesty when he could get it, especially from adults. So he settled back against the seat and took the time to examine the cousin he barely knew.

Titus Waverly looked nothing like Father, who was dark-haired and sharp-featured and aristocratic. Mr. Waverly was blond and round-faced, with a muscular, robust look to him, as if he spent lots of time in the sun. Pierce remembered now that his cousin owned a big stud farm with racing stock.

Most boys would be thrilled to spend their holiday in such a place, but Pierce's asthma made him less than eager. Or perhaps Manton was right, and he really was a mollycoddle.

"So I'm to stay with you and Mrs. Waverly for the whole holiday?" Pierce asked.

The man nodded. "I have a little boy of my own. Roger is five. You can play together."

With difficulty, Pierce contained a snort. Five was practically still a baby. "Are Mother and Father not coming to visit *at all*?" He wanted to be clear on that.

"No, lad. I'm afraid not."

Pierce swallowed hard. He was trying to be strong, but he hadn't really expected not to see them. It made no sense. Unless . . . "Is it because of something I did when I was still at home?"

"Certainly not! Your father merely thinks it will be good for you to be at the farm right now."

That made a horrible sort of sense. "He wants me to be more like the chaps at school," Pierce said glumly, "good at riding and shooting and things like that." He slanted an uncertain glance up at his cousin. "Is that what he wants you to do? Toughen me up?"

His cousin blinked, then laughed. "Your mother did say you were forthright."

Yes, and it had probably gotten him banished from Montcliff. Perhaps it would get him banished from Waverly Farm, too, and then his cousin would *have* to send him home. "Well, I don't like horses, and I don't like little children, and I don't want to go to Waverly Farm."

"I see." Mr. Waverly softened his tone. "I can't change the arrangement now, so I'm afraid you'll have to make the best of it. Tell me what you *do* like. Fishing? Playing cards?"

Pierce crossed his arms over his chest. "I like being at home."

Settling back against the seat, Mr. Waverly cast him an assessing glance. "I'm sorry, you can't right now."

He fought the uncontrollable quiver in his chin. "Because Father hates me."

"Oh, lad, I'm sure he doesn't," his cousin said with that awful look of pity on his face.

"You can tell me the truth. I already know he does." Tears clogged Pierce's throat, and he choked them down. "What about Mother? D-doesn't she want to see me at all?"

Something like sadness flickered in Mr. Waverly's eyes before he forced a smile. "I'm sure she does. Very much. But your father can't spare her right now."

"He can never spare her." He stared blindly out the window, then added in a wistful voice, "Sometimes I wish Mother and I could just go live in one of Father's other houses." Brightening, he looked back at his cousin. "Perhaps in London! You could ask her—"

"That will never happen, lad, so put that out of your mind." Mr. Waverly's tone was quite firm. "Her place is with your father."

More than with her son?

Manton's nasty words leached into his thoughts: *I guess we both know what she saw in* him—*all that money and the chance to be a countess. She latched onto that quick enough.*

It wasn't true. Was it?

His cousin would know—he had to know something about Mother and Father, or he wouldn't have said what he did. And he had a friendly look about him. Like he could be trusted to tell the truth.

"Is . . . that is . . . did Mother marry Father for his money?"

"Who told you that?" his cousin asked sharply.

"A boy at school." When a sigh escaped Mr. Waverly, Pierce swallowed hard. "It's true, isn't it?"

Moving over to sit beside Pierce, Mr. Waverly patted him on the shoulder. "Whether it is or no, it has nothing to do with how your mother feels about *you*. In fact, she gave me this letter for you."

As he fished it out of his pocket and handed it over, the tightness in Pierce's chest eased a little. Eagerly, he broke the seal and opened it to read:

My dearest Pierce,
    Your father and I think that staying at Waverly Farm will prove a grand adventure for you, and you do enjoy a grand adventure, don't you? I miss you, but I'm sure you will

*learn all sorts of fine things there. Don't forget
to write and tell me what fun you have!*

*Do be a good boy for your cousins, and keep
your chin up. I know you will make us proud.*

*And always remember, I love you very, very
much.*

> *With many kisses,*
> *Mother*

Relief surged through him. She *did* love him! She
did!

He read it again, this time paying closer attention,
and his heart sank a little. It had the same determined
cheer as Mr. Waverly.

And then there was the line: *I know you will make
us proud.*

He sighed. She loved him, but she had still let Father send him away. And why? *You will learn all sorts of
fine things there.* Just like Father, she wanted to see him
toughen up.

Tears filled his eyes, but he ruthlessly willed them
back. Very well, then. No more crying, and no more
behaving like a milksop and a mollycoddle. He had to
get big and strong, to learn to ride and to fight like the
other boys.

Because clearly neither Father nor Mother would
let him come home until he did.

1

December 1826

Thirty-one-year-old Pierce Waverly, Earl of Devonmont, sat at the desk in the study of his London town house, going through the mail as he waited for his current mistress to arrive, when one letter came to the top, addressed in a familiar hand. An equally familiar pain squeezed his chest, reminding him of that other letter years ago.

What a naive fool he'd been. Even though he *had* grown bigger and stronger, even though he'd become the kind of son Father had always claimed to want, he'd never been allowed home again. He'd spent every school holiday—Christmas, Easter, and summer—at Waverly Farm.

And after Titus Waverly and his wife had died unexpectedly in a boating accident when Pierce was thirteen, Titus's father, General Isaac Waverly, had returned from the war to take over Waverly Farm and Titus's orphaned children.

Even though Pierce hadn't received a single letter from his parents in five years, he'd still been certain that he would finally be sent home—but no. Whatever arrangement Titus had made with Pierce's parents was apparently preserved with Pierce's great-uncle, for the general had fallen right into the role of substitute parent.

Despite all that, it had taken Pierce until he was eighteen, when neither of his parents had appeared at his matriculation from Harrow, to acknowledge the truth. Not only did his father hate him, but his mother had no use for him, either. Apparently she'd endured his presence until he was old enough to pack off to school and relations, and after that she'd decided she was done with him. She was too busy enjoying Father's fortune and influence to bother with her own son.

Pain had exploded into rage for a time, until he'd reached his majority, at twenty-one, and had traveled home to confront them both . . .

No, he couldn't bear to remember *that* fiasco. The

humiliation of that particular rejection still sent pain screaming through him. Eventually he would silence that, too; then perhaps he'd find some peace at last.

That is, if Mother would let him. He stared down at the letter, and his fingers tightened into fists. But she wouldn't. She'd poisoned his childhood, and now that Father was dead and Pierce had inherited everything, she thought to make it all go away.

She'd been trying ever since the funeral, two years ago. When she'd mentioned his coming "home," he'd asked her why it had taken his father's death for her to allow it. He'd expected a litany of patently false excuses, but she'd only said that the past was the past. She wanted to start anew with him.

He snorted. Of course she did. It was the only way to get her hands on more of Father's money than what had been left to her.

Well, to hell with her. She may have decided she wanted to play the role of mother again, but he no longer wanted to play her son. Years of yearning for a mother who was never there, for whom he would have fought dragons as a boy, had frozen his heart. Since his father's death, it hadn't warmed one degree.

Except that every time he saw one of her letters—

Choking back a bitter curse, he tossed the unopened letter to his secretary, Mr. Boyd. One thing he'd learned from the last letter she'd written him, when he was a boy, was that words meant nothing. Less than nothing.

And the word *love* in particular was just a word. "Put that with the others," he told Boyd.

"Yes, my lord." There was no hint of condemnation, no hint of reproach in the man's voice.

Good man, Boyd. He knew better.

Yet Pierce felt the same twinge of guilt as always.

Damn it, he had done right by his mother, for all that she had never done right by *him*. Her inheritance from Father was entirely under his control. He could have deprived her if he'd wished—another man might have—but instead he'd set her up in the estate's dower house with plenty of servants and enough pin money to make her comfortable. Not enough to live extravagantly—he couldn't bring himself to give her *that*—but enough that she couldn't accuse him of neglect.

He'd even hired a companion for her, who by all accounts had proved perfect for the position. Not that he would know for himself, since he'd never seen the indomitable Mrs. Camilla Stuart in action, never seen her with his mother. He never saw Mother at all. He'd laid down the law from the first. She was free to roam Montcliff, his estate in Hertfordshire, as she pleased when he wasn't in residence, but when he was there to take care of estate affairs, she was to stay at the dower house and well away from *him*. So far she'd held to that agreement.

But the letters came anyway, one a week, as they had ever since Father's death. Two years of letters, piled in a box now overflowing. All unopened. Because why should he read hers, when she'd never answered a single one of his as a boy?

Besides, they were probably filled with wheedling requests for more money now that he held the purse strings. He wouldn't give in to those, damn it.

"My lord, Mrs. Swanton has arrived," his butler announced from the doorway.

The words jerked him from his oppressive thoughts. "You may send her in."

Boyd slid a document onto Pierce's desk, then left, passing Mrs. Swanton as he went out. The door closed behind him, leaving Pierce alone with his current mistress.

Blond and blue-eyed, Eugenia Swanton had the elegant features of a fine lady and the eloquent body of a fine whore. The combination had made her one of the most sought-after mistresses in London, despite her humble beginnings as a rag-mannered chit from Spitalfields.

When he'd snagged her three years ago it had been quite a coup, since she'd had dukes and princes vying for her favors. But the triumph had paled somewhat in recent months. Even she hadn't been able to calm his restlessness.

And now she was scanning him with a practiced eye, clearly taking note of his elaborate evening attire as her smile showed her appreciation. Slowly, sensually, she drew off her gloves in a maneuver that signaled she was eager to do whatever he wished. Last year, that would have had him bending her over his desk and taking her in a most lascivious manner.

Tonight, it merely left him cold.

"You summoned me, my lord?" she said in that smooth, cultured voice that had kept him intrigued with her longer than with his other mistresses. She had several appealing qualities, including her quick wit.

And yet . . .

Bracing himself for the theatrics sure to come, he rose and rounded the desk to press a kiss to her lightly rouged cheek. "Do sit down, Eugenia," he murmured, gesturing to a chair.

She froze, then arched one carefully manicured eyebrow. "No need. I can receive my congé just as easily standing."

He muttered a curse. "How did you—"

"I'm no fool, you know," she drawled. "I didn't get where I am by not noticing when a man has begun to lose interest."

Her expression held a hint of disappointment, but no sign of trouble brewing, which surprised him. He was used to temper tantrums from departing mistresses.

His respect for Eugenia rose a notch. "Very well." Picking up the document on the desk, he handed it to her.

She scanned it with a businesswoman's keen eye,

her gaze widening at the last page. "You're very generous, my lord."

"You've served me well," he said with a shrug, now impatient to be done. "Why shouldn't I be generous?"

"Indeed." She slid the document into her reticule. "Thank you, then."

Pleased that she was taking her dismissal so well, he went to open the door for her. "It's been a pleasure doing business with you, Eugenia."

The words halted her. She stared at him with an intent gaze that made him uncomfortable. "That's the trouble with you, my lord. Our association has always been one of business. *Intimate* business, I'll grant you, but business all the same. And business doesn't keep a body warm on a cold winter's night."

"On the contrary," he said with a thin smile. "I believe I succeeded very well at keeping you warm."

"I speak of you, not myself." She glided up to him with a courtesan's practiced walk. "I like you, my lord, so let me give you some advice. You believe that our attraction has cooled because you're tired of me. But I suspect that the next occupant of your bed will be equally unable to warm you . . . unless she provides you with something more than a business arrangement."

He bristled. "Are you suggesting that I marry?"

Eugenia pulled on her gloves. "I'm suggesting that you let someone inside that empty room you call a heart. Whether you make her your wife or your mistress, a man's bed is decidedly warmer if there's a fire burning in something other than his cock."

He repressed an oath. So much for this being easy. "I never guessed you were such a romantic."

"Me? Never." She patted her reticule. "This is as romantic as I get. Which is precisely why I can offer such advice. When we met, I thought we were both the sort who live only for pleasure, with no need for emotional connections." Her voice softened. "But I was wrong about you. You're not that sort at all. You just haven't realized it yet."

Then with a smile and a swish of her skirts, she swept out the door.

He stared bitterly after her. Sadly, he *did* realize it. Leave it to a woman of the world to recognize a fraud.

Matrons might panic when he spoke to their innocent daughters, and his exploits might appear so regularly in the press that his Waverly cousins kept clippings for their own amusement, but his seemingly aimless pursuit of pleasure had never been about pleasure. It had been about using the only weapon he had—the family reputation—to embarrass the family who'd abandoned him.

Leaving his study, he strode to the drawing room, where sat his pianoforte, his private defiance of his father. He sat down and began to play a somber Bach piece, one that often allowed him to vent the darker emotions that never saw the light of day in public, where he was a gadabout and a rebel.

Or he had been until Father's death. Since then his petty rebellions had begun to seem more and more pointless. There'd been no deathbed reconciliation, but also no attempt to keep him from his rightful inheritance. And no explanation of why he'd been abandoned. None of it made sense.

The fact that he *wanted* it to make sense annoyed him. He was done with trying to understand it. The only thing that mattered was that he'd triumphed in the end. He'd gained the estate while he was still young enough to make something of it, and clearly that was the most he could hope for.

Of course, now that he was the earl, people expected him to change his life. To marry. But how could he? Once married, a man had to endure the whims of his wife and children. He'd grown up suffering beneath the whims of his parents; he wasn't about to exchange one prison for another.

He pounded the keys. So for now, everything would stay the same. He would go to the opera this evening to seek out a new mistress, and life would go on much as before. Surely his restlessness would end in time.

Leaving the pianoforte, he was walking out of the drawing room when the sight of Boyd heading toward him with a look of grim purpose arrested him.

"An express has come for you, my lord, from Mont-cliff."

He tensed. His estate manager, Miles Fowler, never sent expresses, so it must be something urgent.

To his surprise, the letter Boyd handed him hadn't come from Fowler but from Mother's companion. Since Mrs. Stuart hadn't written him in the entire six months she'd been working for him, the fact that she'd sent an express brought alarm crashing through him.

His heart pounded as he tore open the letter to read:

Dear Sir,

Forgive me for my impertinence, but I feel I should inform you that your mother is very ill. If you wish to see her before it is too late, you should come at once.

Sincerely,
Mrs. Camilla Stuart

The terse message chilled him. Based on Mrs. Stuart's recommendation letters and references, not to mention the glowing accolades heaped on her by Fowler, Pierce had formed a certain impression of the widow. She was practical and forthright, the sort of independent female who would rather eat glass than admit she couldn't handle any domestic situation.

She was decidedly *not* a woman given to dramatic pronouncements. So if she said his mother was very ill, then Mother was at death's door. And no matter what had passed between them, he couldn't ignore such a dire summons.

"Boyd, have my bags packed and sent on to the estate. I'm leaving for Montcliff at once."

"Is everything all right, my lord?" Boyd asked.

"I don't believe it is. Apparently my mother has fallen ill. I'll let you know more as soon as I assess the situation."

"What should I tell your uncle?"

Damn. The Waverlys were expecting him in a few days; he still spent most holidays with them. "Tell Uncle Isaac I'll do my best to be there for Christmas, but I can't promise anything right now."

"Very good, my lord."

As far as Pierce was concerned, the Waverlys—his great-uncle Isaac and his second cousin Virginia—were his true family. Mother was merely the woman who'd brought him into the world.

He ought to abandon her in death, the way she'd abandoned him in life. But he still owed her for nurturing him in those early years, before he was old enough to be fobbed off on relatives. He still owed her for giving birth to him. So he would do his duty by her.

But no more. She'd relinquished the right to his love long ago.

2

In a cozy sitting room of the dower house on the Montcliff estate, Camilla mended a petticoat while keeping a furtive watch on her six-year-old son, Jasper. With his blue eyes wide, he sat in Lady Devonmont's lap, waiting for her to read him a story.

"What shall we read?" Lady Devonmont asked him. "*Cinderella*?"

"That one's stupid," Jasper said airily. "Princes don't marry servant girls."

Camilla bit back a smile as she pushed up her spectacles. Lady Devonmont had a fondness for German fairy tales because of her late mother being German, but Jasper had no such bias. He also didn't like girls in his fairy tales. Not surprising for a boy his age.

"Why wouldn't a prince marry a servant?" her ladyship asked.

"He has to marry a princess. That's the rule. Everybody knows that. I never saw a servant marry a prince."

Her ladyship shot Camilla a rueful glance. "Clearly he spends far too much time in the servant hall."

"Better there than at his uncle's," Camilla said softly.

After Camilla's husband, Kenneth, had died unexpectedly, leaving her and Jasper destitute, she'd had no choice but to go to work, and most employers frowned on having children around who distracted their mothers. So until she had come to work for the countess, she'd always been forced to leave her son with Kenneth's brother, a somber Scot with a dour wife and three children of his own.

But when Lady Devonmont learned of Jasper through the servants, she'd insisted on having him brought to the dower house to live. For that kindness alone, Camilla adored her ladyship.

Of course, neither the earl nor the estate manager knew about Jasper. Nor must they ever. Mr. Fowler, who'd hired her, had been adamant that she be unencumbered with children—he'd said the dictum had come straight from the earl himself. So she and Lady Devonmont had agreed that Jasper's presence had to be kept a secret.

"Read the poem about Christmas again," Jasper said. "I like that one."

The countess's American cousin had sent her a newspaper clipping of a poem that was becoming very popular in America during the season, called "A Visit from St. Nicholas." Camilla had thought it perfectly lovely the first three times she'd heard it, but its magic had begun to fade now that they were up to the fifteenth reading.

Lady Devonmont laughed. "Aren't you sick of it by now, lad?"

"I like to hear about the reindeer. Will there be reindeer at the fair in Stocking Pelham next week? I want to see one." He turned a sly glance up at the countess. "Mama says we can't go, but I really want to."

Camilla tensed. "Jasper, you mustn't—"

"Of course we can go," Lady Devonmont put in. "We have to. I'm in charge of a booth there."

"Forgive me, my lady," Camilla said, "but we can't risk Jasper being seen with us in town by Mr. Fowler."

The countess sighed. "Oh. I didn't think of that. I suppose that *would* be unwise." Her tone turned wistful. "It's a pity, though. I used to take my own boy when he was only a bit older than Jasper."

"And now he's a fine earl," Jasper said.

"Yes, a fine earl," Lady Devonmont echoed.

Camilla nearly stabbed her finger trying not to react to *that*. "Fine earls" did not abandon their mothers.

Still, she probably shouldn't have sent his lordship that misleading letter. But she'd had to do something. How could the wretch not even plan to visit his own mother for Christmas? It was unfathomable.

Besides, he would no doubt ignore the summons. Mr. Fowler might praise the earl for his handling of the estate, but that was clearly his lordship's only virtue. And it wasn't much of a virtue at that—any man who neglected his property was a fool, and apparently the earl was no fool. But according to London gossip, the man was also a selfish scoundrel who spent most of his time in an empty pursuit of pleasure. If he didn't come, it would at least prove what she'd known all along—he might have brains, but he had no heart.

Then Camilla could reveal to her ladyship what she'd done, and the woman would recognize once and for all that her son wasn't worthy of all the pining she wasted on him every day.

Of course, if he did appear . . .

She swallowed. She would cross that bridge when she came to it.

"And anyway, I don't think there will be any reindeer at the fair," Lady Devonmont said, stroking Jasper's wild, red-brown curls. "Just a lot of boring cattle and horses."

"What about St. Nicholas? Will he be there?"

"I doubt that," Camilla said with a laugh.

"Do you even know who St. Nicholas is?" her ladyship asked.

"He's a 'jolly old elf.'" Jasper slipped off her lap, impatient with being petted. "His belly shakes like a 'bowlful of jelly.' And he comes down the chimney. Do you think he'll come down *our* chimney?"

"Perhaps," the countess said. "My cousin tells me that Americans believe St. Nicholas brings gifts to children on Christmas Eve."

Jasper stared at her in wide-eyed wonder. "Will he bring *me* a gift?"

"I'm sure he will," her ladyship said, her twinkling gaze meeting Camilla's over his head. "Why should he only bring presents to American boys, after all?"

Camilla stifled a smile. The woman spoiled Jasper shamelessly and encouraged all of his wild imaginings, but Camilla didn't mind. She wanted him to have a better childhood than her own. There'd been no gifts in St. Joseph's Home for Orphans. And no fairy tales or stories of St. Nicholas to dream on, nothing but Bible readings and moral stories of children who got into trouble whenever they disobeyed. Perhaps that's why she'd developed such a perverse tendency to disobey as an adult.

Suddenly a great noise rose up beneath them, of voices calling and footmen and maids rushing about.

"Good Lord, what has happened?" Lady Devonmont said.

Mrs. Beasley, the housekeeper, rushed into the room, uncharacteristically panicked. "Begging your pardon, my lady, but his lordship has sent a man ahead to say he will arrive here in a matter of minutes!"

Lady Devonmont tensed. "I don't see how that affects *us*. I'm sure he'll be staying at Montcliff Manor as usual."

"No, my lady—here! He's coming *here*, to the dower house. He asked that we prepare the Red Room for him and everything!"

"Oh, my word!" The countess leaped to her feet. "But I'm not dressed. . . . I look a fright!" She cast Camilla a look of such joy that it cut her to the heart. "My son is coming to visit, my dear!" She hurried toward the door leading into her bedchamber. "I must change my gown at the very least. And perhaps freshen my hair." She ran into the other room, crying for her lady's maid.

Mrs. Beasley turned for the door to the hall, but Camilla called out to stop her. "Please, madam, would you take Jasper upstairs to Maisie?"

The housekeeper blinked. "Oh, yes, of course. I forgot about the lad." She made an impatient movement with her hand. "Come, boy, come. You must spend your day with Maisie, do you hear?"

Lady Devonmont had hired a maid to look after Jasper whenever Camilla couldn't. Maisie, a sweet little Scottish girl of about seventeen, also served as a sort of lady's maid to Camilla.

Though Jasper was fond of Maisie, at the moment he was obviously more excited about the arrival of the master of the estate. "I want to see the great earl!" he protested.

Camilla knelt to catch his hands, aware of Mrs. Beasley's impatience to be off attending to her duties. "Listen, muffin, do you remember what I told you about the earl's being too important to have little boys underfoot?"

With a hard swallow, Jasper nodded. "But I just want to—"

"You can't. If you wish to continue to stay here with me and her ladyship, and not be sent back to live at your uncle's, then you must do as I say. Go with Mrs. Beasley. I'll see you tonight when I come to tuck you in, all right?"

Though he cast his eyes down, he thrust out his chin like a little man and mumbled, "Yes, Mama." Then he let Mrs. Beasley take his hand and lead him from the room.

Only after Camilla heard their footsteps dying away on the stairs did she let out a breath. It wouldn't do to have his lordship discover both her deception regarding his mother *and* Jasper's presence.

My, but he had come quickly. Since the earl never answered his mother's letters, Camilla had assumed it would take him a while to get around to reading the express. And that even then he might not care.

Clearly she'd made a disastrous assumption.

But what was she supposed to have done when she'd found the countess sobbing on the evening of her fiftieth birthday? Lady Devonmont had spent the entire day hiding her feelings about her son's absence, but once alone, she'd apparently been unable to do so.

When Camilla, in trying to comfort her, had said that she was sure he would come for Christmas, the countess had dismissed the very possibility. She admitted that she hadn't seen him at Christmas in some years. Then she'd mumbled something about having only herself to blame for that. But Camilla had scarcely heard that.

Not see his own mother at Christmas? How could he? Camilla might not have had a family growing up, but she knew how one ought to work. The parents loved and supported their children, and in return the children did the same, even as adults. What sort of man trampled over a mother's love without a thought?

Obviously, a man who needed reminding of what he owed the woman who had raised him. So Camilla had fired off her letter without considering the consequences.

Well, she was considering them now. He might very well dismiss her for her deception. Although really, it wasn't *that* much of a deception—his mother *had* been feeling poorly, and Camilla was almost certain it was all for lack of him. So it did seem—

"Who the devil are you?"

Startled, Camilla spun around to find a finely dressed gentleman standing in the sitting room doorway. Heaven save her. His lordship had come.

She curtsied deeply. "I am Mrs. Stuart, my lord. That is, I assume you are—"

"Yes, yes, of course," he said impatiently. "I'm your employer." He scanned her with a narrowed gaze as he entered the room. "And *you*, madam, are not what I was expecting."

Nor was he. His mother had spoken of an asthmatic child with a slim build and slight frame, so Camilla had imagined the earl as a fashionable coxcomb with extravagant manners and dress, a perfumed handkerchief eternally pressed to his nose.

Fashionable he might be, but this was no coxcomb. The Earl of Devonmont was an imposing fellow indeed. She'd once seen a portrait of his father in Montcliff Manor, and they were very like. Both were lean and tall, with eyes the color of mahogany and hair a shade darker, and both had the same brooding stare.

The present earl was less formally dressed, but he wore his clothes better. His exquisitely tailored frock coat of brown cashmere skimmed broad shoulders, while his buff trousers and striped waistcoat showed the rest of his figure to good effect. His snowy cravat emphasized his strong jaw, and he had a high brow somewhat altered by a frown fierce enough to frighten small children. Not to mention paid companions who had vastly overstepped their bounds.

"How's my mother?" he asked, his voice hoarse and his hands seeming to shake as he removed his gloves and tossed them onto a writing table.

Or was she imagining his distress? Oh, Lord, she hoped so. Because if he was as upset as he seemed, then she *really* had gone too far when she'd sent that letter. Although it did mean he might care for his mother more than she'd realized.

"Well, sir," she began, nervously pushing up her spectacles. "I believe I should probably explain . . ."

"Pierce!" Lady Devonmont cried from the doorway. "It's wonderful to see you, my boy."

He couldn't have looked more shocked if a ghost had risen from the grave to speak to him. Relief seemed to flicker briefly in his eyes, but it was swiftly supplanted by anger as he realized the deception that had been played on him.

Casting Camilla a hard glance that made her shiver, he faced his mother with an unreadable expression. "You're looking well," he said civilly, though he made no move to approach her.

Her smile faltered. "So are you."

"I was told . . ." His voice cracked a little before he got control of it. "I was under the impression that you've been very ill."

The countess paled. "I've been a little under the

weather, but nothing of any consequence. I told you that in my last letter."

Her mention of letters made his jaw go taut. "So you are not near to death, as I was led to believe."

Lady Devonmont lifted her chin. "I'm sure you can tell that I am not. I don't know who would lie to you about such a thing."

Camilla froze, waiting for the accusation that was sure to come.

His gaze didn't so much as flick to her. "It's of no matter. A misunderstanding, I'm sure." He jerked up his gloves, his motions oddly mechanical. "So I'll be returning to London in the morning. It's too late to set off tonight."

"Of course." With a forced smile, his mother pretended not to care.

Only Camilla noticed how her shoulders shook.

Or perhaps not only Camilla, for his lordship turned for the door quickly, as if he couldn't bear to look at his mother one moment more. "Have Mrs. Beasley send dinner to my room," he ordered. "The footmen have already put my bags in the Red Room, so I might as well remain here for the night instead of at the manor."

"Certainly, Pierce," the countess said in a voice tinged with bitterness. "Whatever you wish."

Something in her tone must have pricked his conscience, for he paused at the door. Then he stiffened and walked out without a backward glance.

Camilla could only gape after him, then turn to gape at his mother. "I can't believe it! That is the most despicable behavior I've ever witnessed!"

"Do not blame him, my dear. He has his reasons." She watched after him, her gaze thoughtful. "At least he came when he thought I was ill. That's something, isn't it?" Ignoring Camilla's lack of a response, she added, "And I got to see him for a bit, too. He's very handsome, don't you think? He grew up to be so strong and tall. He was such a sickly child that I never expected—"

"How can you ignore his abominable treatment of you?" Camilla broke in.

"On the contrary, he treats me better than I can expect, given . . ." She managed another determined smile. "You don't understand, my dear. Better to leave it alone."

"How can I? He tucks you away here in the country—"

"Because I prefer the country to town, and always have."

"That's not the point! He acts as if you don't even exist!"

"Ah, but there you're wrong. He acts very much as if I exist," she said acidly. "Or he wouldn't demand that I stay out of his way whenever he's here."

"And that's another thing. When he came this summer, I didn't know you well enough to say anything about his avoidance of you, but now—"

"Good Lord," her ladyship said, whirling on Camilla. "*You're* the one who told him I was near to death." When Camilla looked guilty, the countess scowled at her. "Are you mad? Do you realize what you've done?"

The reproach, coming from the generally mild-mannered lady, took Camilla by surprise. "I-I suppose I shouldn't have presumed, but—"

"You certainly shouldn't have. You could lose your position over it." At Camilla's stricken expression, Lady Devonmont added hastily, "Not that *I* would dismiss you, my dear. Surely you realize I can't do without you." Her ladyship began to pace. "But my son could very well send you packing."

"I know," Camilla said, letting out a relieved breath. She could deal with his lordship's temper as long as Lady Devonmont didn't hate her.

The countess rounded on Camilla with her shoulders set. "Well, I shan't let him. He has every right to be angry at me, but you're an innocent bystander, and I won't let him punish you for your ill-considered actions."

"They were *not* ill-considered! And I'll tell him so myself, if it comes down to it."

Lady Devonmont flashed her an impatient glance. "You will do nothing of the kind. You have your boy to think of." She mused a moment, a sudden look of calculation on her face. "But since Pierce didn't mention that you were the one to write him, perhaps he's not so very angry about it, after all. So we'll leave it alone, make no more mention of it." She paced before the fire. "Yes, that's how to handle it. And if he tries to dismiss you, I'll hire you myself, using my pin money. He gives me enough for that."

Guilt attacked Camilla with a vengeance. "My lady, I don't want—"

"Nonsense, that's the only thing to do." Lady Devonmont pressed her hand to her forehead. "I have a bit of a headache, so I think I shall lie down for a while before dinner."

Camilla sighed. That was one thing about Lady Devonmont; she always made it perfectly clear when she wanted to end a discussion. "Of course. I'd be happy to read to you, if you like."

"No need for that." She glanced at Camilla. "Though if you don't mind telling Mrs. Beasley about his lordship wanting a tray in his room . . ."

"Certainly." She was being sent off. Miraculously, her ladyship had overlooked her impertinence.

Unfortunately, his lordship probably wouldn't. And despite everything she'd said to Lady Devonmont, the woman was right. Camilla had risked much with her deception. She deserved to lose her position over it.

But she hadn't dreamed he would have such a visceral reaction after the way he'd been behaving, never answering his mother's letters, never coming to see her. Camilla had expected him to flit in, say a few words to his mother, pretend to be relieved that she was well, and flit out. And if seeing his mother coaxed him into staying for a bit, all the better.

Not in a million years had Camilla expected him to be alarmed at the possibility of his mother dying. And then angry that he'd been deceived.

Indeed, the more Camilla thought about that as she headed for the kitchen, the angrier *she* became. What could Lady Devonmont possibly have done to deserve such behavior? How could any man resent a woman of such grace and kindness? It was unfathomable.

Her ladyship thought she should leave it alone, but she just couldn't. If not for the countess, Camilla might be working for some condescending matron who insisted that Jasper be left at his uncle's. So as long as Lady Devonmont was on her side, she would fight for the woman, even against the earl. Her ladyship was the closest thing to a family that Camilla had ever had.

She entered the kitchen, where Mrs. Beasley was whipping the servants into a frenzy with preparations for dinner.

"Is Mr. Fowler going to be here for dinner, too?" Cook asked the housekeeper as she basted a pork loin. "He don't like pork, y'know."

"I don't think he's coming," Mrs. Beasley said. "I hope not, anyway. With his lordship here, he's sure to put on airs."

"I doubt that," Camilla interjected. "Mr. Fowler never puts on airs."

Mrs. Beasley eyed her askance. "That's only because he's sweet on you."

"Oh, please, not that again," Camilla murmured. "Mr. Fowler is nearly old enough to be my father."

"That don't mean nothing," said Cook, who saw romance blooming everywhere she looked. "And he's always asking how you're getting on with her ladyship, always wanting to know what you two are up to. He's got his eye on you—I'm sure of it."

Camilla did think he had his eye on *someone,* but not her. Of course, if her suspicions were correct and he was sweet on the countess, she could never tell the servants such a thing. They would be appalled.

It was fruitless anyway—Lady Devonmont always said she didn't mean to marry again, and in any case, the social gulf between Mr. Fowler and her was nigh unto impassable. Especially when her ladyship might not even share his feelings.

"Like most widowers," Camilla said, "Mr. Fowler is merely desperate for another woman to look after him."

"True, true." Cook cast her a considering glance as she tucked back a gray curl. "Though it would be a good situation for you, given Master Jasper and all."

Camilla sighed. *Any* marriage would solve her problem of what to do with her son as he got older. But she'd married for practical reasons once, and except for Jasper, that had proved oddly unsatisfying. If she ever remarried it would be for love, and she felt nothing like that for Mr. Fowler.

"Did his lordship *say* anything about Mr. Fowler's coming to dinner?" Mrs. Beasley asked. "It'll be a trial for Cook to do a large meal on such short notice. She's got her hands full preparing the plum pudding for Christmas so it can sit a couple of weeks."

"No trial at all," Cook retorted. "I've already got the pudding steaming, which it has to do for a few hours. So I can cook whatever dinner you want."

"Actually," Camilla said, "his lordship is only staying the night, and he doesn't intend to come down to dinner. He wants a tray sent up."

Cook gaped at her. "Well, don't that just beat all? Waltz in here with no warning and then not even have the decency to join his mother for dinner." She sniffed. "I suppose he thinks to get a better meal up there at the manor, with that foreigner cooking the food and that snooty Mrs. Perkins running the place."

"That foreigner" was his lordship's French cook, and Mrs. Perkins was the manor housekeeper. The two cooks were archrivals, as were the two housekeepers. Mr. Fowler had hired both sets of servants upon the earl's inheriting the estate and inexplicably pensioning off the old ones. Apparently Lord Devonmont had wanted to install his own, who now took on airs because they served the earl. They were fiercely loyal to him.

Meanwhile, the dower house servants were equally loyal to her ladyship. So with the countess and her son estranged, neither group mixed with the other to any great degree.

It left poor Mr. Fowler somewhat in the middle.

"I'll put together a tray that will have his lordship tossing the 'monsieur' out on his ear," Cook said almost militantly. "The earl will be begging to stay here a week, just see if he won't. And if we could keep him here until Christmas, I've got the biggest goose picked out—"

"I wish we could," Camilla said with a sigh. "But I fear that's impossible."

Mrs. Beasley set her hands on her hips. "Now I've got to spare Sally to go bring up the tray, just when I need her."

An idea leaped into Camilla's head. "Actually, he wants *me* to bring up the tray." Why not? It would give her an excuse to have it out with him.

"You?" Mrs. Beasley exclaimed, then exchanged a veiled glance with Cook.

"Is something wrong with that?" Camilla asked, perplexed.

Cook made a clucking noise. "The master does have a reputation, m'dear."

"Wouldn't be the first time a man took a fancy to

someone in his employ, if you know what I mean." Mrs. Beasley turned to fetch a tray. "And if he's asking you in particular to carry up his meal . . ."

"It's nothing like that," Camilla said hastily, wishing she'd considered how the servants would regard her claim. Her eyes went wide as something else occurred to her. "Surely you're not saying that the female servants at the manor . . . That is, there've been no complaints of—"

"No, indeed," Cook said firmly.

"Not yet, anyway," Mrs. Beasley said in her usual voice of doom. "But plenty of gentlemen do toy with their servants, and your being so young and handsome—"

Camilla burst into laughter. "I don't think you need worry about that. I'm not all that young."

And "handsome" was what people called a woman between plain and pretty. "Handsome" was merely acceptable. Not that she minded being thought of that way. If every woman was a beauty, the word would mean nothing. But "handsome" would never be good enough for the sophisticated earl. Even if he wasn't on the verge of dismissing her from her post, he would never set his lecherous sights on a short, slightly plump widow with spectacles, reddish hair, and freckles. Not when he could have any blond goddess in London.

She had nothing to fear on *that* score.

3

Pierce paced the bedchamber, badly shaken by the sight of his mother. Great God, but she'd aged. When had she gone gray? She hadn't been that way at the funeral two years ago.

Actually, back then she'd worn a hat and veil that covered her hair and her face, and he'd barely spared her a glance anyway. If he'd stayed to see her without them, would he have noticed the gray? Or the crow's-feet around her eyes and the thin lines around her lips? Because he'd noticed them today, and they'd unsettled him. She was getting older. He should have expected it, but he hadn't.

And he certainly hadn't expected her face to light

up when she saw him. It brought the past sharply into his mind. All those years of nothing, no word, no hint that she cared . . . Why, he couldn't even remember the last time she'd looked on him so kindly.

How dared she do it *now*? Where had she been all those damned years at Harrow, when Manton was knocking him around? When the boys had taunted him for his asthma, before he'd grown out of it and begun standing up for himself?

How many Christmases had he lain in bed praying that this would be the one when she came sweeping in to kiss him on the forehead and make it all better? As mothers ought to do. As the other boys' mothers routinely did.

He loosened his cravat, trying to catch his breath. It wasn't a return of his asthma that plagued him but the weight of the past on his chest. The literal *smell* of the past.

The dower house had actually been his first home. Father began building the grand mansion that was now Montcliff Manor when Pierce was fourteen, so Pierce hadn't even been inside it until after his father's death. *This* was his childhood home—that's why he had put Mother here, so he would never have to stay in it himself and suffer reminders of all that he'd lost at age eight.

One of those reminders was the smell of Mother's favorite plum pudding being steamed. She'd always specified that certain spices be used, and that's why the house now reeked of cloves and lemon peel. It would choke him for certain. He should never have come.

He *wouldn't* have come if not for the impudent Mrs. Stuart. The audacity of the woman to lie to him! And to Mother, too, apparently, since Mother had looked perplexed by his assumption that she was dying. Meanwhile, her companion, the conniving baggage, had looked guilty.

But even if Mother hadn't known of Mrs. Stuart's letter to him, she somehow had to be complicit. Probably she'd spun enough tales about her son's poor treatment of her to make Mrs. Stuart take it upon herself to right the wrong. Clearly Mother had done an excellent job of hiding her true nature around Mrs. Stuart, who seemed willing to risk losing her livelihood just to make her scheming charge happy. And she *ought* to lose her livelihood—he should have her dismissed at once for her impertinence.

Yet in his mind he kept seeing the shock on her face when he'd entered. Apparently, he hadn't done a very good job of hiding his panic over the idea of Mother dying. What had the damned woman thought—that he was some monster with no soul?

Probably. After he'd announced he was leaving, she'd certainly glared at him as if he were. Insolent chit! No telling what his mother had said to secure the young widow's sympathies.

Whatever it was, it wouldn't be the truth—that

once he'd turned old enough to be passed off to some relative, Mother had deliberately cut him out of her life. And now that he had inherited everything, she was suddenly eager to pay attention to the son she'd ignored for *years*.

To hell with that! He was *not* going to yield, no matter how gray Mother looked, and no matter what some officious companion with a penchant for meddling—

A knock at the door interrupted his pacing. "What?" he barked.

"I have your tray, my lord," a muted voice said from beyond the door.

He'd forgotten entirely about that. "Set it down and go away!"

A moment of silence ensued. Then the same voice said, "I can't."

"Oh, for the love of God . . ." He strode to the door and swung it open, then halted.

There before him stood the very woman who'd brought him here under false pretenses. "It's *you*," he spat.

Though she blinked at the venom in his voice, she stood her ground. "May I please come in, my lord?"

He considered slamming the door in her face, but a deeply ingrained sense of gentlemanly behavior prevented him. Besides, he wanted to hear what she had to say for herself.

With a curt nod, he stood aside to let her pass, taking the opportunity to get a good look at her. He still couldn't believe she was so young. She couldn't be more than twenty-five, far too young to be a widow *or* a paid companion.

And far too attractive, though he hated that he noticed. Despite what everyone thought of him, he did not run after every creature in petticoats. He'd gained his reputation as a rogue in the years when he was determinedly embarrassing his family, and those days were waning.

But the rogue in him wasn't dead, and it noticed that she had the sort of voluptuous figure he found attractive. She was a bit short for his taste but her evocative features and the red curls she wore scraped into a bun made up for that. Even with her spectacles on, she had the look of a fresh-faced country girl—eyes of a fathomless blue, a broad, sensual mouth, and a smattering of freckles across ivory skin. The odd mix of bluestocking and dairymaid appealed to him.

She dressed well, too. Her gown of green Terry velvet was out of fashion and too sumptuous for her station, so since servants' clothes generally were castoffs from their employers' wardrobes, it must once have been Mother's. Given that it fit her like a glove, she was obviously good with a needle.

That would serve her well in her *next* post, he

thought sourly, though he still hadn't decided if he would dismiss her.

As she set the tray down on a small table by the fire, he snapped, "I suppose you've come to beg my pardon."

She faced him with a steady gaze. "Actually, no."

"What?" he said, incredulous. "You brought me racing here from London by lying about my mother's illness—"

"I did not lie," she protested, though her cheeks grew ruddy. "Granted, she isn't ill in the conventional sense—"

"Do enlighten me about the *un*conventional way to be ill. I must have missed that lesson in school."

At his sarcasm, she tipped up her chin. "Anyone can see that she has been ill with missing you, her only family."

He let out a harsh laugh. "Has she indeed? I suppose she's been shedding crocodile tears and weaving a sad story about how I fail to do my duty by her."

Mrs. Stuart's pretty blue eyes snapped beneath her spectacles. "On the contrary, whenever we discuss you, she excuses your refusal to visit or answer her letters, not to mention your wanton disregard for—"

"Her well-being? Does she complain of how I treat her?"

The fractious female cast him a mutinous glare. "No."

That surprised him, though he wasn't about to let on. "Then there you have it." He turned toward the writing desk, where sat a decanter of brandy and a glass.

"But I'm not blind," the woman went on, to his astonishment. "I see how your lack of attention wounds her, and I hear her crying when she thinks no one is near. As your mother, she deserves at least a modicum of attention from you, yet you leave her to pine."

"My mother doesn't know the meaning of the word *pine*." He fought to ignore the image of his mother crying all alone. "And if *she* has sent you—"

"She doesn't know I'm here. She didn't know I wrote that letter. Actually, she, too, says I should stay out of it."

Despite his determination to hold firm against his mother's tactics, that shook him. "You should listen to her."

"I can't." The plaintive words tugged at something he'd buried for countless years. "I wouldn't be doing my duty to her if I let her suffer pain, whether at the hands of a stranger or those of her own son." She strode up behind him, her voice heavy with concern. "You can't expect me to keep quiet when I should do right by her."

He whirled to fix the woman with a cold glance, but he couldn't escape her logic. Her loyalty was to his mother, and *should* be, even though he had hired her. After all, what good was hiring a companion his mother couldn't trust?

Still, that didn't mean he had to let her manipulate him. "Doing right by her doesn't include lying to her family. You said she was dying."

"No, I said you should come before it was too late." She pushed her spectacles up. "I'm sorry if you interpreted the words as meaning she might die any moment—"

"Right," he said dryly. "How could I have made such a leap?"

"But I meant them." Concern furrowed her lightly freckled brow. "She needs you, and if you put off mending your relationship with her, you will eventually regret it."

Bloody hell, the woman was stubborn. "That isn't for you to decide, madam." Crossing his arms over his chest, he stared her down. "Whatever you expected to accomplish with this stunt hasn't come to pass, so you should quit trying while you still have a post. I can easily dismiss you for your presumption."

"I'm aware of that."

Yet she held her chin firm and her shoulders squared. He'd been right to term her "indomitable" without even having met her. She was one determined woman.

"But some things are worth risking all for," she added.

"My *mother*? A woman who didn't even care that her son was alive until two years ago, when my father died and she could no longer depend on *his* largesse?"

That seemed to shake her. "You think that this is about *money*?"

"Of course! She married Father for money, and now that it's all under *my* control, she suddenly 'needs' me desperately."

Her gaze locked with his. "If her feelings are as false as you think, why does she have a chest full of your school drawings and papers? Why does she read to me your childhood letters, pointing out your witty turns of phrase and clever observations?" She stepped nearer. "Why does she keep a miniature of you by her bed?"

Her descriptions beat at the stone wall he'd built against his mother. But he couldn't believe them. He *wouldn't* believe them. He wouldn't let Mother hurt him again.

Clearly Mother had fashioned Mrs. Stuart as a weapon to get what she wanted. The young widow might not even know she was being used, but that didn't change a damned thing.

He moved close enough to intimidate. "She's trying to enlist you as an ally in her scheme. And she knows it won't work unless she can convince you that she is slighted and put upon."

Mrs. Stuart blinked. Obviously, it was the first time she'd considered the possibility that she was being taken in. "You're wrong," she whispered, though she didn't seem quite so certain. "She's not like that."

"You've known her for six months," he ground out.

"I've known her my entire life. Or at least the part of my life that she—"

He broke off before he could reveal the mortifying truth—that his parents thought so little of him they'd cut him out of their lives. It was none of her affair, no matter what she thought. He didn't have to explain himself to some paid companion, damn it!

Besides, as meddlesome as Mrs. Stuart had proven to be, she clearly had Mother's best interests at heart. He didn't want to dismiss the woman, and he saw no reason to poison her against his mother. He just wanted her to stop making trouble.

He forced some calmness into his tone. "By now you've probably gathered that matters between me and my mother aren't as clear as you think. So I will forget how far you've overstepped your bounds, if you'll agree to keep your opinions to yourself and stay out of my relationship with her in future."

Though she swallowed hard, she continued to meet his gaze. "I don't know if I can do that, my lord."

"Oh, for God's sake . . ." He dragged his hand over his face. He was tired and hungry and annoyed. The bloody woman was a plague! "What do you want from me, damn it, short of attaching my mother to my side with a tether?"

The image made her start, then give a little smile. It took him by surprise. Until that moment, she'd lived up to his impression of a self-righteous bluestocking, but a sense of humor lurked inside the indomitable Mrs. Stuart. And somehow he'd tickled it.

"You needn't go to such an extreme," she said, her eyes twinkling beneath the spectacles. Then she turned earnest again. "But if you could stay here with your mother until Christmas—"

"No." He remembered only too well his last Christmas at home. The one that he hadn't realized was to *be* his last Christmas at home. "That's impossible."

He turned away. Perhaps he *should* dismiss the woman.

But she followed him as he headed for the brandy. "You wouldn't have to spend much time with her, just have the occasional meal with her. The slightest attention from you would make her happy."

"You think so, do you?" Pouring himself a healthy portion of brandy, he downed it in one swallow. If ever a woman could drive a man to drink, it was Mrs. Stuart.

"I am sure of it. You could stay at Montcliff Manor as you always do, but even if you merely came to dinner with us every night—"

"You're not going to let this go, are you?" He set down the glass and faced her with a scowl. "You'll keep plaguing me until I do as you ask or you force me to send you packing."

That seemed to give her pause, but only for a moment. "I would of course prefer that you *not* send me packing. But I must speak what I know to be true, sir."

Her voice softened. "And now that I've met you, I believe that you have more of a heart than you let on."

He snorted. "Do you, indeed?"

Then perhaps it was time he dispelled that ridiculous notion. And in doing so, perhaps he could dissuade her from meddling and tormenting him to death, without his having to dismiss her and go to the trouble of hiring another, who might not be as reliable.

He stalked forward, deliberately crowding her space, forcing her to either back up or stand her ground. Not surprisingly, she did the latter, which put him toe to toe with her, looming over her.

"I tell you what, Mrs. Stuart," he drawled. "I'm already staying here at the dower house until tomorrow. So I'll attend dinner tonight with you and my mother and try to be civil. But in exchange, I'll expect some compensation after she retires."

Her gaze turned wary. "What sort of compensation?"

"Entertainment. The kind I would normally receive in London." He let his gaze trail leisurely down her body in a way that should illustrate exactly what he was pretending to demand of her. "And I will expect *you* to provide it."

4

Camilla's cheeks heated as she gaped at the earl. What a despicable, wicked—

Then her brain caught up with her moral outrage. The earl wore a calculating expression, as if he knew exactly what her reaction would be.

That devil was making this up as he went along. He wanted her so insulted by his proposition that she would stop bothering him about his mother. That made far more sense than believing he actually meant it. She wasn't the sort of woman whom notorious rakehells tried to seduce.

She made herself look bewildered. "I'm afraid I

don't understand, my lord. How could I possibly entertain a worldly man like you?"

His sudden black frown strengthened her supposition that his bargain was a humbug. "You know perfectly well how. After dinner is over, you and I will have our own party. Here. In my bedchamber, where you can slip in and out without being noticed. If I must spend dinner with her, then you must spend the night with *me*."

"Entertaining you," she said primly, buying time to figure out what answer would best gain her what she wanted. "Yes, I understand that part. I'm just not sure what kind of entertainment you want."

He gritted his teeth. "Oh, for the love of God, you know precisely what kind of entertainment a 'worldly man' like me wants."

Now that she had caught on to his game, it was all she could do not to laugh at him. He was so transparent. What was wrong with all those women in London, that they didn't see right through him?

"On the contrary," she said blithely. "I don't know you well enough to know what you enjoy. Perhaps you would prefer me to sing for you or dance or read you a good play. I understand there is quite an extensive library at Montcliff Manor. Your mother says you bought most of the books yourself. I'm sure there is some volume of—"

"I'm not talking about your reading to me!" he practically shouted.

When she merely gazed at him with a feigned expression of innocence, he changed his demeanor. His eyes turned sultry, and a sensual smile crossed his lips. "I mean the kind of entertainment most widows prefer."

My, my, no wonder London ladies were rumored to jump into his bed. When he looked that way at a woman and spoke in that decidedly seductive voice, the average female probably melted into a puddle at his feet.

It was a good thing she was *not* an average female. In her other posts, she'd seen plenty of rakehells seducing their way through halls and balls. So even though they'd never tried their skills on her, she had a good idea how to handle such scoundrels.

This was a trickier situation, however. If she was not an average female, he was definitely not an average scoundrel.

She pretended to muse a moment. "Entertainment that widows prefer . . . Works of charity? Taking care of their families? No, those are not actually entertaining, though they do pass the time." She cocked her head. "I confess, my lord, that you have me at a complete loss."

Uh-oh, that was probably doing it up too brown, for understanding suddenly shone in his face. "Ah, I see you are deliberately provoking me. Well, then, let me spell it out for you. You'll spend the night in my bed. Is that clear enough?"

He said it in such a peeved manner that she couldn't help but laugh. "Clear indeed, though preposterous."

His gaze narrowed on her. "How so?"

Time to let him know she had caught on to his game. "I'm aware of your reputation, sir. I'm not the sort of woman you take to bed."

Something that looked remarkably like admiration glinted in his eyes. "I thought you said you didn't know me all that well," he drawled.

"I know what kind of women you are most often seen with. By all accounts, they are tall, blowsy blondes with porcelain skin and clever hands."

He looked startled. "You *do* know my reputation."

She shrugged. "I read the papers. And your mother insists upon hearing all the stories of you, even the salacious ones."

Mention of his mother made his gaze harden. "Then you should know that men like me aren't that discriminating."

"Oh, but I'm sure you're discriminating enough not to wish to bed a short, mousy, freckled servant when there are any number of beautiful, blond actresses and opera singers awaiting you in London," she said coolly.

Crossing his arms over his chest, he dragged his gaze down her again, then circled her in a slow, careful assessment that made her nervous. A pity he wasn't a perfumed dandy; she could have handled one of those easily enough. But this sharp-witted, secretive rakehell was unpredictable.

Camilla had never liked the unpredictable.

"And what if I say that I really *am* that indiscriminate? Would you then share my bed in exchange for my dining with my mother tonight?"

She swallowed. Why did he persist in bamming her when he knew she'd caught on to him?

Well, two could play his game. "Why not? You *are* rumored to be quite good at that sort of thing, and I *have* been married." She couldn't keep the edge from her voice. "Besides, the likelihood of my ever again having the chance to be seduced by such a notorious fellow as yourself is slim."

Her frank statement made him halt, then shake his head. "Great God, Mrs. Stuart, remind me never to play cards with you. I daresay you're a terror at the gaming tables."

She bit back a smile. "I've won a hand or two at piquet in my life."

"More than a hand or two, I'd wager." He let out a long breath. "All right, then, let me propose a bargain that we could both actually adhere to. I'll do as you wish—I'll dine with you and Mother. Afterward, you will come here to join me in one of your more innocuous entertainments."

She let out a breath. She'd won! "I am happy to attempt to entertain you, my lord, if you will just give your mother a little time with you. That's all I ask."

"I'm not finished." He gazed steadily at her. "In exchange for my doing so, you must agree never again to try forcing my hand in the matter of my mother."

When she drew a breath as if to speak, he added more firmly, "One night of watching me and Mother together should demonstrate to you why you have no business involving yourself in our relationship. But even if it doesn't, tomorrow must mark the end of your meddling on that point. Or I *will* dismiss you, without a qualm. Am I understood?"

She hesitated, but really, what choice did she have? "Yes, my lord." The dratted devil was tying her hands. She'd have only one night to attempt some repair to his relationship with his mother. But it was better than she'd had before.

A heavy sigh escaped him. "I must be out of my mind to be letting you off so easily, after what you did."

"Easily?" she said tartly. "Did you forget that I will have to entertain you this evening?"

"Ah, yes, such a trial," he said with heavy sarcasm. "And I'll expect rousing entertainment, too. At the very least, you must show me your reputed ability at piquet, so I can trounce you." He stared her down. "Now that you've brought me here to endure this house, it's only fair that you join me in my suffering."

The bitter remark gave her pause. Hadn't Lady Devonmont said that this was the original manor house on the estate? The one where he'd grown up?

As if realizing he'd revealed more than he'd meant to, he flashed her a bland smile. "It won't be that difficult. I can be charming when I want to."

"No doubt," she said dryly.

"Then we're agreed. I'll see you here this evening after Mother has retired."

And after Camilla had put Jasper to bed, though she couldn't say that.

"But you *will* come down to dinner first, sir?"

His face turned rigid. "That's the bargain, isn't it?"

She let out a breath. "I was just making sure."

"Whatever else you may think of me," he said sharply, "I do honor my promises."

"Of course, my lord."

She turned for the door, relief overwhelming her. She'd braved the lion's den and survived. She'd even won a small concession. It wasn't much, but it might be enough to soothe the countess's hurt feelings. Spending a night "entertaining" his lordship would be no sacrifice at all, compared to that.

"One more thing, Mrs. Stuart," he said as she reached the door.

She paused to look back at him.

"You were right when you said I'm discriminating in my choice of bed partners. But you aren't remotely mousy." His gaze scoured her with a heat that didn't seem the least bit feigned.

Could he really mean it?

Oh, she hoped not. Because the last thing she needed in her life right now was a lover—not with Jasper to take care of.

Only when he had her thoroughly agitated did he lower his voice to a husky drawl. "Fortunately for you, I'm not in the habit of abusing the trust of those in my employ, whether chaste maidens or experienced widows. So as long as you want me to play the respectable gentleman, I will do so."

He fixed her with a smoldering look. "But let this be a warning to you. Give me an inch, and I will take two miles. If you offer more, I will be only too happy to take you into my bed."

"Then I shall have to take care not to offer more, shan't I?" And with that, she slipped from the room.

But as she made her way down the hall, her knees shaking and her hands clammy, she had to acknowledge that this bargain might not be quite so easy to keep. Because insane as it might be, she found the idea of being in the earl's bed rather intriguing.

Oh, what was wrong with her? He didn't mean a thing he said—clearly he'd issued his dire "warning" just to vex her. Why, the man was seen every week with some fine beauty at the opera or the theater or balls where he scandalized everyone with his flirtations.

Yes, exactly! He was an awful man with a terrible reputation. Being attracted to such a fellow was utterly unlike her. Even if he *was* so very handsome. And more clever than she'd expected. And full of secrets that intrigued her.

She scowled. They did *not* intrigue her. They all centered around his clear lack of concern for his mother's feelings.

Well, perhaps not entirely clear.

She married Father for money, and now that it's all under my control, she suddenly "needs" me desperately.

Camilla shook off a chill. Pausing only to tell a passing maid that his lordship's plans had changed again, she headed for the countess's bedchamber. He was utterly wrong about his mother. She was almost sure of it, and she knew her ladyship better than anyone. Didn't she?

A woman who didn't even care that her son was alive until two years ago, when my father died and she could no longer depend on his largesse?

Why would he say that? Though come to think of it, the countess only spoke of her son as a boy and as a grown man. She said nothing about his school years.

Then again, he would have been away during his school years. But he would have come home for holidays. He would have gotten into scrapes and adventures; even a sickly boy would have done *that*.

And why did the countess never speak of the previous earl? Camilla assumed that their marriage had been a formal one, since the woman rarely mentioned him, but now she had to wonder . . . Could Lady Devonmont really have married the man just for his money?

If only some of the old servants were still employed who could say what the countess's husband had been like and if he'd played a part in the estrangement between mother and son.

Since Camilla had secrets of her own, she had a firm rule against prying into her employers' private affairs. But she was sorely tempted to break her rule in this case. Dealing with the prickly earl would be much easier if she knew more about him and his mother.

She found the countess already up from her rest. "I have some good news, my lady. His lordship has decided to join us for dinner this evening."

Lady Devonmont faced her warily. "I don't understand."

Camilla forced a cheery smile to her lips. "He's had a change of heart. You see? He *does* care."

As joy lit the countess's face, she seized Camilla's hand. "You did this. I know you did. But how? What did you say to convince him?"

"Nothing of importance. I merely appealed to his sense of decency." Not for anything would she tell the countess of the bargain she'd made. The woman would leap to the wrong conclusion, and that could only worsen matters.

Unless the countess had *wanted* Camilla to do something to keep him here?

She's trying to enlist you as an ally in her scheme. And she knows it won't work unless she can convince you that she is slighted and put upon.

Ridiculous.

He was right about one thing, though—there was more to the situation than met the eye. And given his mother's words earlier, she knew his lordship wasn't the only one who didn't wish to discuss the past.

Very well. She'd have to be more creative in uncovering this tangle. Lady Devonmont had made Camilla and Jasper part of her family, and families helped each other. So the least Camilla could do was try to restore the rest of the countess's family to her. No matter what it took.

5

Dinner was pure misery.

Not that Pierce was surprised. How could it be anything else? He was sitting in the very chair his father had always used, staring at the lofty portrait of a grandfather he'd never known, and listening to the achingly familiar voice of his mother prattling on about nothing while Mrs. Stuart shot him furtive glances.

The damned woman didn't understand—he couldn't act as if the past twenty-three years hadn't happened. Mrs. Stuart expected him to make witty conversation with his *mother*. Might as well ask him to give a sermon in hell.

Especially with bitter memories resurrecting themselves every moment he sat here. As a boy, he'd taken his meals in the nursery, but he'd been allowed to join his parents for dinner at Christmas and special occasions. Those nights invariably deteriorated as Father berated him for being weak and sickly, until he retorted with some bit of insolence that got him banished from the table. The memory made his stomach churn.

He forced a spoonful of soup between his lips and swallowed, barely tasting it. Mother had always tried to mediate but had rarely been successful. It was as if Father *wanted* to drive Pierce off, so he could have Mother all to himself.

Well, if that had been Father's aim, he'd gotten exactly what he wanted, hadn't he? And Mother hadn't protested it.

Glancing over at her, he looked for signs of the heartless creature he knew her to be. But aside from her ornate gown and fine jewelry, which reminded him that what she really wanted was more of Father's fortune, he could see nothing other than the mother he'd adored as a boy.

Except a far older one. He couldn't get over how much she'd aged. Seeing it made something in his chest twist.

When that became too painful to endure, he turned his gaze to Mrs. Stuart. Instantly, the aching turned to annoyance. The woman was a bloody meddler, presumptuous and self-righteous, and so blindly loyal to his mother that it made him want to . . . to . . .

To respect her. He sighed. That was mad. Blind loyalty shouldn't be an admirable quality. But somehow, in Mrs. Stuart it was. Perhaps because she was loyal for the most naive reasons. She considered it the right thing, the caring thing, to champion his mother.

It was the caring part that stymied him. How could she care about a woman who'd abandoned her own son? Of course, the young widow didn't seem to know that, and he wasn't ready to tell her. Not until he had a better sense of what the situation was.

"Do you not agree, my lord?" Mrs. Stuart's pleasant voice intruded.

Damn, his long stares had made her think he had an opinion on whatever nonsense she and Mother were discussing. "I suppose," he said noncommittally.

"You didn't hear a word, did you?" Mrs. Stuart said.

The woman certainly liked to speak her mind. "Listening appeared unnecessary. Once the conversation turned to decorations for Christmas, I knew any points I made would be ignored."

"Not at all," she protested. "Why would you think so?"

Feeling Mother's gaze on him, he shrugged. "I'm a man, and we're generally thought incompetent to advise in that area."

"That doesn't mean you are," his mother said earnestly. "Mr. Fowler says you've made many improvements on the estate—better roofs for the tenant cottages, a new fishery, modern additions to the dairy—"

"Those are my purview. Decorations for Christmas are not."

"They could be." A hopeful look crossed her face. "Perhaps this year you could even join us for the season."

A hard knot formed in his chest. "Impossible. I'm expected at the Waverlys'." He cast her a meaningful glance. "As usual." When his mother flinched, it soured his temper further, which made him glare at the pretty young widow who'd brought this about in the first place. "I wouldn't even be here, if not for the interference of certain individuals."

She calmly continued to eat her soup, though her cheeks reddened considerably. "As I recall, I apologized for misleading you about your mother's health, sir."

Since Mother didn't look shocked by her comment, Mrs. Stuart must have confessed all to her. That was a surprise. "Apparently I missed your apology during all the chiding and lecturing."

"You just now admitted to a certain laxness in listening," Mrs. Stuart said pertly. "Perhaps your attention wandered during my apology, too."

Perversely, that made him want to smile. The widow's impudent streak caught him unawares sometimes. "Then I'll have to pay better attention in future," he said, struggling to sound stern.

It was hard to be stern with her. He wasn't sure why. She just had this way of bringing him out of himself when he least expected it.

Suddenly he felt his mother's gaze on him. He looked over to see her eyes dart from him to Mrs. Stuart and back, and his bad mood returned. Best not to give her any ideas, or she'd be priming Mrs. Stuart to be even more of an ally.

He frowned at them both. "So what do you want my opinion on, anyway?"

"We have to decide whether to have a Christmas tree like those that your mother had in her youth," Mrs. Stuart said gamely.

"And in Pierce's youth, too." Mother cut her roast beef. "I always made sure we had at least a small one, hung round with candles and toys and such, though Pierce's father thought it a foolish waste of good timber."

He tensed. Mother was still following that peculiar German custom? Great God. In his childhood, the scent of cut fir had permeated the house every Christmas. Even now, whenever he smelled firs he thought of that strange little tree with its sparkling baubles and little bags of nuts . . . and he ached with the bittersweet memory of his last Christmas at home.

Oblivious to his reaction, Mrs. Stuart generously buttered a slice of bread. "We'll have to find one ourselves, with your supervision, my lady. The servants won't know what sort of tree to choose. And once they cut it down and bring it in, you'll have to show us how to decorate it and affix candles to it."

"Excellent," he grumbled. "Might as well show you how to set fire to the whole damned house, while you're at it."

When they turned startled looks on him, he forced the frown from his face. Not for the world would he let them know how their talk of Christmas trees stabbed him through with sharp memories. "Candles on a tree are dangerous."

"Not if the tree is green," his mother put in. "And it will only stay up for a day or two." She busied herself with sopping up gravy with her bread. "No point in keeping it up until Twelfth Night if you're not even going to be here for Christmas."

If she thought her unsubtle hints that he should stay would work on *him*, she was mad. "True," he said firmly. "Then it will be fine for so short a period."

"Good," his mother said with a hint of belligerence. "Because I think a tree would make the holiday truly lovely."

Casting him a shuttered glance, Mrs. Stuart sipped some wine. "I agree. It sounds like a perfectly charming custom."

"And an expensive one, given its short duration." Which was probably the point. He faced his mother. "How much will this cost me, anyway? You'll need baubles and candles for your precious tree, not to mention—"

"Don't be ridiculous, Pierce. I have all that already. The baubles, as you call them, are the same ones I store in the attic every year."

That caught him entirely off guard. He'd expected her to disguise a request for funds by saying it was for her precious tree. "You want *nothing* purchased for this tree?" he persisted, ignoring Mrs. Stuart's smug smile.

"Certainly not. The point is to perpetuate the traditions of one's family. My glass ornaments come from your grandmother, and the other decorations are fruit and nuts, all of which can be found here on the estate, even the candles." She brightened. "Oh, and paper cut-outs! We must do those. Don't you remember, Pierce? We used to cut tiny little angels—"

"I remember," he said bitterly. "Trust me, I remember only too well." When the two women lapsed into an awkward silence, he added, "But in case you haven't noticed, Mother, I've grown too big for angels. Devils are more my style."

"Ah, but I don't think devils are a good idea for a Christmas tree," Mrs. Stuart put in, as if to draw his fire.

He turned toward her with a challenging glance. "And why is that?"

She didn't waver. "Well, for one thing, pitchforks are exceedingly difficult to cut out."

He blinked, then gave a rueful laugh. Damn the

woman, but she made it hard to stay annoyed. And when she stared at him with a silent plea in her eyes, he relented for the moment.

Relaxing back against his chair, he took a sip of wine. "You'd feel differently if you'd ever tried cutting out a tiny halo, Mrs. Stuart. Or stars, for that matter. Mine always ended up round, which goes against every rule of star artistry." He leaned close to say in a confiding tone, "Apparently, they're expected to have points."

"Are they?" she said brightly. "Then clearly I shall have to stick to moons. Those are allowed to be round."

"Ah, but would you put a moon on a Christmas tree?" he asked. "The three wise men following the moon doesn't have quite the same effect."

"And it's not in the Bible besides," she said, clearly struggling not to smile.

"I wouldn't know," he drawled. "That's not a book I'm terribly familiar with."

"A fact that you regularly demonstrate to the world," his mother said archly.

He stiffened. He'd almost managed to forget she was there. "Yes. I do." He stared her down. "Every chance I get."

He was on the verge of pointing out that if she'd wanted some say in his behavior, she should have stayed to see him grow up, when Mrs. Stuart broke in. "In any case, since his lordship won't be here to join us in decorating the tree, I will be eager to assist you, my lady."

"That would be lovely," Mother said.

"And then perhaps his lordship could come back for a day or two to see it when it's all done," Mrs. Stuart said in that managing voice females sometimes used. The one that didn't work on him.

"As I said before, that's impossible."

His mother looked crestfallen. "You used to enjoy the season."

It was on the tip of his tongue to point out that she'd put an end to all that by making holidays synonymous with being unwanted. But he wouldn't give her the satisfaction.

"Do whatever you wish with your tree," he muttered, now thoroughly annoyed again. He drenched a chunk of beef in gravy and devoured it. "Just leave me out of it. My days of relishing such mundane pleasures are long past."

"That's a pity," Mother said. "Mundane pleasures are about the only kind we have here in the country."

With a meaningful glance at Mrs. Stuart, he waited for his mother to ask for some new toy to keep them amused, or perhaps a costly trip to Italy, where she could indulge her love of expensive things to her heart's content.

Then she went on, "But we do enjoy them." She smiled at Mrs. Stuart. "We sing and play and act charades and have our own sort of fun. Camilla is very good at reading aloud—very dramatic."

He was still stunned by his mother's prosaic idea of "fun" when the door opened and a footman came in bearing some confection.

"And we have an excellent cook," Mrs. Stuart said cheerily as her portion was placed before her. "There's nothing mundane about *that* pleasure." She took a bite and her face lit up. "Her almond blancmange is sheer heaven."

He arched one eyebrow. "I take it that you share Mother's love of sweets."

"I do, indeed," Mrs. Stuart said, dabbing a bit of custard from the corner of her mouth. "Dessert was rare at the orphanage, I'm afraid, and now that I can have it whenever I please, I never seem to tire of it."

He'd forgotten that she was raised an orphan. For a moment, he flashed on a little girl coveting every pastry she saw in the London bakeries, and his chest tightened inexplicably at the thought of her having something so simple routinely denied to her.

"Don't you like sweets yourself, my lord?" she asked, jerking him from his dark thoughts.

"He never did," Mother answered. "Pierce was a most unusual child—he would rather have fruit and cheese for dessert." She cast Pierce a tentative smile. "That's why I had Cook prepare some of that, too."

And with a little flourish, the footman placed a plate of apple slices and a selection of cheeses before him.

Mrs. Stuart's earlier words clamored in his brain: *If her feelings are as false as you think, why does she have a chest full of your school drawings and papers? Why does she read to me your childhood letters, pointing out your witty turns of phrase and clever observations? Why does she keep a miniature of you by her bed?*

He could feel himself weakening, feel the barricades crumbling a little, and it sparked his temper. Damn it, she could not just whisk away years of neglect with a plate of fruit and cheese and a few remarks about his childhood! He'd had as much of this as he could stand.

He forced a nonchalant smile to his lips. "I've grown up now, Mother. What I like best for dessert these days is a good cigar." He rose. "And since that's the case, I'll step outside to indulge in one now that the meal is done." He bowed stiffly in her direction. "Good night."

Then he leveled a hard gaze on Mrs. Stuart. "Au revoir, madam."

She blushed at his oblique reminder that her evening with him wasn't yet at an end, but she managed a smile. "Au revoir, my lord."

He strode out of the dining room, relieved that he was done. Mrs. Stuart had made better use of his bargain with her than he'd expected. She and his mother had obviously decided to plague him at dinner with talk of Christmas trees and prettied-up tales of his childhood until he turned to putty in their hands.

Well, he wasn't without defenses of his own. If Mrs.

Stuart insisted on making him uncomfortable at dinner, then he would damned well return the favor. Since he couldn't seduce her, he'd have to consider other possibilities. Cards wouldn't serve his purpose, and so far she'd proved herself adept at parrying his barbs in conversation. As for reading to him . . .

His eyes narrowed. She had a penchant for reading aloud dramatically, didn't she? Good. Then he would give her something damned interesting to read.

6

Though his lordship had used a flimsy excuse to absent himself from the meal, Camilla couldn't fault him for it. Dinner had been far tenser than she'd expected, and not just on his side, either. Lady Devonmont had seemed determined to provoke him. Perhaps this hadn't been such a good idea after all.

But as the dessert plates were carried away, Lady Devonmont smiled broadly at her. "Thank you."

"For what?"

"For making him join us for dinner."

"You don't know your son very well if you think anyone could *make* him do anything he doesn't want to," Camilla said dryly.

"I know him better than you think," the countess said enigmatically. "You must have said something to convince him to dine with us. He would never have done so just to please me."

"You're wrong," she lied. "He may be gruff, but I'm sure he loves you in his own way."

What else could she tell the woman without breaking her heart? She would walk through fire before she would see her ladyship hurt.

The countess sighed. "Perhaps." She seemed to brood a moment, then shook it off and rose from the table. "Shall we go say good night to our boy?"

"Certainly." It had become a nightly ritual for them to tuck Jasper in before they settled down with needlework or books or whatever their choice of amusement was for the evening.

Her mind wandered as they headed up the stairs. What had his lordship meant, he'd be spending his Christmas at the Waverlys' "as usual"? Camilla knew he had cousins near London, but why would he prefer to spend Christmas with them over his mother? She was tempted to ask the countess, but she hated to spoil her ladyship's happiness at having him here, however briefly.

Camilla and Jasper's room was on the third floor, next to what used to be the nursery. The earl's tutor had originally occupied their room, but it had been years since anyone had lived in it, so her ladyship had suggested it would be perfect for Camilla. Once Jasper had come to live here, too, the countess had ordered the tutor's bed changed out for a trundle bed so mother and son could be together.

It was the perfect arrangement to keep Jasper safe from discovery. Mr. Fowler was often in the servants' quarters, but he would find it highly inappropriate to invade the floor where supposedly only Camilla lived. And the room was still close enough to her ladyship's for Camilla's purposes.

As they entered, Maisie was trying futilely to get Jasper to settle down. He practically bounced in his trundle bed. "Mrs. Beasley said his lordship is very big and scary," he pronounced. "Is that true?"

"Only with young boys who don't do what they're told," Camilla said. It was a bit of a falsehood, but she couldn't take any chance that the earl would see Jasper and banish him from Montcliff. It would break her heart. "So behave yourself."

Her ladyship sat down on the bed and chucked Jasper under the chin. "But he'll be gone tomorrow. Just stay with Maisie, all right? And if the earl should happen to see you and ask who you are, tell him your mother is a servant. Don't say her name."

"But Mama *isn't* a servant," he protested.

"Actually—" Camilla began.

"Your mother is a special kind of servant very important to me," Lady Devonmont said. "And you're important to me, too. So if you'll be a good boy and stay out of his lordship's sight until he leaves tomorrow, I'll let you keep one of those tin soldiers that you like to play with so much."

As Jasper's face lit up, Camilla's heart caught in her throat. The countess was always doing such lovely things for Jasper. Her ladyship had rapidly become the closest thing to a grandmother that he would ever have.

But her ladyship didn't have to buy Jasper's love—she had it already, whether or not she realized it. "You needn't give him anything," Camilla murmured. "I know he'll be good just for your sake."

"Even so, he deserves a prize for it. And there are a hundred in the set—one won't be missed. Let me spoil the lad a bit." Her tone grew wistful. "I didn't get to spoil my own boy near enough."

Camilla burned with curiosity to ask why not, but now wasn't the time.

Lady Devonmont kissed Jasper on the forehead, then headed for the door. "I believe I shall retire early this evening. This has been a very long day."

"Would you like me to read to you?"

She shook her head. "I suspect I'll fall asleep as soon as my head hits the pillow. In any case, you deserve an evening to yourself once in a while."

"Thank you." That would certainly make it easier for her to see his lordship alone later.

How Camilla wished she could ask her ladyship

more about the stormy relationship with her son. But her ladyship had refused time and again to speak about her son's neglect. That wasn't liable to change just because he'd had dinner with her. Besides, it might be easier to startle the truth out of him, given how readily he got provoked when the subject involved his mother.

Camilla crooned Jasper's favorite lullaby until he fell asleep, then motioned to Maisie to join her outside the door. She considered lying to the girl, but she needed one person to know the true situation. And she trusted Maisie, who adored Jasper as if he were her own.

Quickly she explained the bargain made between her and his lordship, making it very clear that their assignation was *not* of the intimate kind. "I would prefer, however, that you not mention this to *anyone,* even the other servants, and especially not to her ladyship. Her feelings would be hurt if she learned of it."

"I'll be silent as the grave, I swear," Maisie murmured.

The girl probably would, too. She had immediately taken to Camilla because of Camilla's Scottish surname, even knowing that it only came from her late husband. No, she would never reveal Camilla's secrets, at least not to all the English running about the estate.

"I won't be in his chambers too late, I promise," Camilla said, "but with the way her ladyship has been pining for him, I just couldn't refuse to meet his terms."

"I understand, truly I do. I know you wouldn't do anything unseemly."

"If Jasper should happen to wake and need me . . ."

"I'll take care of it. We don't want his lordship guessing that he's here, and we don't want those gossips in the kitchen thinking the wrong thing, either, do we?"

Camilla beamed at the girl. "Exactly." She glanced at the case clock in the hall. It was already later than she'd have liked. "I have to go."

Maisie caught her arm. "Be careful. With a man like that—"

"I'll be on my guard, don't you worry." Then she hurried down to the second floor, where the family rooms were.

As she approached his bedchamber, her hands grew clammy. She honestly didn't know what to make of him.

After their earlier encounter, when he'd railed at her and tried to cow her, she'd expected him to be officious and cold to her at dinner. He was an earl, for pity's sake. Her previous two employers, of far lower rank, had never treated her with anything but condescension. But although he'd been stiff with his mother, there'd been that moment when he'd joked with Camilla about the angel cutouts. . . .

She shook her head at her softening toward him. It hardly made up for the fact that he was denying his mother his presence for the Christmas season. No matter how attractive he was, with his London sophistication and his dry wit, he was still behaving quite heartlessly to the countess.

And her ladyship deserved better. That was one thing Camilla meant to do this evening—make sure that he knew it.

She reached his bedchamber and tapped on the door, and when he swung it open, her heart practically failed her. Despite the chill in the room, he was dressed only in shirtsleeves and trousers, with nary a waistcoat, coat, or cravat to be seen. The sight of him so casually attired threw her off balance and stirred feelings she'd thought long dead.

She had a hard time not noticing the impressive chest well-displayed by his thin lawn shirt. And the broad shoulders. Not to mention the muscular forearms laid bare, since his shirtsleeves were rolled up to the elbows.

Oh, how could she pay attention to such things? Why did she care that his shirt was open at the throat? Why couldn't she tear her gaze from the patch of skin so tantalizingly revealed?

Because it had been a long time since she'd spent time with a man so informally dressed. That's all.

With some effort, she forced her gaze up to his face. He held a glass of brandy, which he sipped from before stepping back just enough to let her enter. "I began to wonder if you forgot our bargain," he groused.

She slid past him, acutely aware of how his eyes

followed her and how his body loomed over hers. He smelled of spirits and smoke. She wasn't used to that, for Kenneth had neither smoked nor drank strong liquor. It should have repulsed her.

But it was so . . . indescribably male. And for a woman who'd spent most of her time in the last few months with an older woman, a young maid, and a small child, it was a rather refreshing change. A little *too* refreshing for her sanity.

She moved to put some distance between them. "Perhaps *you* forgot I have other duties in the evening. Surely you didn't want me to tell your mother that I had to leave her in order to come to your bedchamber."

"Of course not." He strode over to stoke the fire. "She keeps you up this late every night?"

"It's barely ten o'clock. We often stay up later than this. And I enjoy keeping your mother company, no matter how late." She cast him an arch glance, determined to provoke him into revealing more about his estrangement from the countess. "Just because you find your mother irksome doesn't mean that *I* do."

"It's not that I find Mother irksome," he snapped. "It's—" He caught himself. "Never mind. It's of no matter."

Stifling a sigh, she tried another tack. "At dinner, I couldn't help but notice that she confounded your expectations about her need for money."

"No doubt you warned her of my suspicions."

"As a matter of fact, I did not," she said stiffly. "Though I do think you ought to give her the chance to—"

"Let us be clear on one thing." He bore down on her with a fierce scowl. "Talking about my mother is not entertaining. So if you intend to spend the evening trying to soften me toward her, you'd better readjust your plans. I will not discuss her with you."

"But—"

"Not one word. Not if you want to keep working here. Understood?"

She huffed out a frustrated breath. The man was maddening! How was she supposed to find out anything when he and his mother were so bent on being stubborn? Clearly, she would have to be more subtle.

When she didn't answer, he glowered at her. "Do we understand each other, Mrs. Stuart?"

"I'm not hard of hearing," she grumbled. "Nor am I lacking in comprehension."

His glower faded, and he cast her a thin smile. "We'll see about that."

"I'm sure we will, my lord."

"No need to be so formal when we're alone," he drawled, dropping into one of two well-upholstered chairs by the fire and taking another sip of his brandy. "You could call me Devonmont, as my friends do. Or 'darling.'"

She rolled her eyes. "We've already settled that we're not to have that sort of . . . friendship, sir."

"Yes." He let his gaze trail down her with an exaggerated heat clearly meant to provoke. "What a pity."

"Tell me, do women generally respond to your transparent attempts to get beneath their skirts?"

"Probably about as often as gentlemen flee your transparent attempts to reform them."

A smile tugged at her lips. She'd never tried reforming an employer before. Something in him must bring out the devil in her. "*You* don't flee."

"No need—I'm not the reforming type, so you don't frighten me." He lifted his glass in a pantomime of a toast. "And *you* aren't responding to my attempts to get beneath your skirts. So that makes us even."

Only because he wasn't *seriously* trying to get beneath her skirts. And thank heaven, too. If he ever did, she might have trouble resisting him.

She glanced about the room, which had been closed up until today. As with many such rooms in country houses, "Red Room" was a misnomer—there wasn't anything red in it. Probably it had been red a hundred years ago, and the name had stuck long after it was refurbished. Now the curtains and linens were an azure print, and the walls were painted a similar blue.

It was furnished with an imposing canopy bed and the two armchairs by the fire, separated by a little table. The only other piece of furniture was a bookcase of walnut that sat against the wall, next to a surprisingly large window that looked out over the lawn.

"Was this your room when you lived here?" If so, he'd left it utterly barren of anything that might have been his as a schoolboy—no globes or telescopes or even old racing journals. Only a few books were there, which was odd, given his rumored obsession with increasing Montcliff Manor's library.

"No," he said tersely. "The nursery was my room."

"Well, of course, until you were older, but after you went off to school, you must have had—"

"I've decided what entertainment I wish for tonight," he said bluntly.

Shrugging off his lack of interest in discussing his room, she walked toward him. "All right. And what might that be?"

With a sudden, suspect gleam in his eye, he reached for a book on the table next to him. "Since Mother said you were an excellent reader, I thought you might read aloud to me."

His manner reminded her of Jasper when he thought to play some trick on her.

Warily, she sat down in the chair opposite him and took the volume he offered. Then she pushed up her spectacles so she could better view the cover. *Fanny Hill: Memoirs of a Woman of Pleasure.*

A woman of pleasure? Oh, dear.

She felt the earl's gaze on her, felt him waiting for

her to make some expression of horrified dismay. The desire to thwart his expectation was too overwhelming to resist.

Opening the book, she read the title aloud in a resounding voice that surprised her almost as much as it seemed to surprise him. Then she turned the page and began to read the text:

> *Madam,*
> *I sit down to give you an undeniable proof of my considering your desires as indispensable orders. Ungracious then as the task may be, I shall recall to view those scandalous stages of my life—*

"You're actually going to read it," he interrupted.

Biting back a smile, she lifted her gaze. "That *is* what you asked of me, isn't it?"

His gaze hardened. "Of course. Do go on."

So she did. It was the account of a country girl who set off to make her fortune in the city, only to be taken in by a suspiciously friendly older woman. Camilla instantly recognized the older character as a bawd in disguise. Not for nothing had she helped her vicar husband with his work in Spitalfields. She knew how easily naive girls were deceived.

But the narrator, relating the beginnings of her own

downfall, didn't seem overly bothered by it. Indeed, she had no sense of shame at all.

Camilla found that fascinating. She was becoming quite intrigued by the book when his lordship said, "You can stop now if you wish."

She glanced up to find him looking nervous. "Don't be ridiculous. I've only read ten pages."

"But I doubt you'll like where it goes from here."

He seemed so uncomfortable with the idea of her going on that she couldn't resist provoking him. "Nonsense. This happens to be a book I read often," she lied blithely. "I'm enjoying revisiting it."

Perhaps she had done it up a bit too brown, for he eyed her with rank skepticism. "Are you indeed?" He leaned back in his chair. "What's your favorite part?"

She gauged the length of the book and took a guess. "Page ninety-six."

He lifted an eyebrow. "Then by all means, do read that aloud."

"All right." So far there hadn't been anything terribly shocking, so she thumbed through to it without a qualm.

But page 96 did not contain text. Instead, there was only a crudely drawn illustration so appalling it took her breath away.

A woman lay on a bed, naked from the waist down, with her legs parted as she prepared to receive a man whose overly large appendage, also quite naked and rendered in some detail, jutted out from his breeches. The female actually had her hand on it, as if to . . . to assess its dimensions.

Nothing in Camilla's experience had prepared her for such a blatant display of carnality.

"Well, read on," the earl taunted when she hesitated.

A blush rose on her cheeks. "I can't." She lifted her stunned gaze to his. "There are no words. Just a . . . picture."

The color drained from his face. Reaching over, he snatched the book from her and stared at it, then shot her a horrified look. "Oh, holy hell. It has pictures."

7

If Camilla hadn't been so mortified, she would have laughed. "Surely you knew that."

"Not exactly." When she eyed him skeptically, he shut the book and set it down. "I recently acquired this edition as part of a lot of fifty books I won at auction. I hadn't looked at it since I bought it. My other edition, in London, is not . . . er . . . illustrated."

"You have *two* editions of that?"

His eyes narrowed. "You shouldn't be surprised. You read it 'often,' remember?"

The jig was clearly up. "You know perfectly well I've never read that book." She stared him down. "And if that's what the illustrations are like, I shudder to think what's in the text."

"You have no idea." He released an exasperated breath. "You, madam, are the most stubborn female I've ever met. If not for that picture, I wonder how far you'd have read before throwing the book at my head."

"I'd never throw it at your head, sir." She tilted up her chin. "Just into the fire."

"I would have *your* head if you did. It's damned difficult to obtain a copy of it. There are only a few hundred."

"Yes, I can see why," she said dryly. "The illustrations are very poorly rendered."

He laughed full out. "They are indeed. Perhaps we should choose some other book." His eyes gleamed at her. "One with art of a higher quality."

"Or *writing* of a higher quality," she countered. "Poetry, for example." When he groaned, she added, "Lord Byron's *Don Juan* ought to be just your cup of tea. Or perhaps some of Lord Rochester's poems. I believe he used a great many naughty words."

"I believe he did." He picked up his glass to down some brandy. "But alas, there are no pictures."

She forced a stern expression onto her face. "You, sir, are nothing more than an overgrown child."

"Indeed I am," he said without a trace of remorse. "That's what happens when a man has no real childhood to speak of. He has to make up for it later."

Even as she caught her breath to hear him reveal something about his past, he realized what he'd said and added, "But how the devil does a sheltered female like you know of *Don Juan*? Or Lord Rochester's poems?"

"I'm not so sheltered as all that. As you well know, I was raised in a London orphanage."

"Where they fed you on risqué poetry?" he quipped.

"Well, no. I found out about Lord Byron's scandalous *Don Juan* from the newspaper."

"Ah. So you haven't actually read the poem."

"I don't believe I've had the pleasure, no," she said primly.

He lifted one eyebrow. "Trust me, you'd know if you had."

"I suppose *you've* read it."

"I have my own copy. But I don't have Lord Rochester's poems. So how did *you* get them?"

Heat rose in her cheeks. "I didn't. Not exactly. When I served as paid companion to an elderly lady with a bachelor grandson, he gave me free access to his library, which contained a few . . . questionable books of verse."

"That you decided to read?"

She scowled at him. "I didn't *know* they were questionable until I read them, now, did I? And I happen to like verse. I'd read some of Lord Rochester's more respectable poems, and I never guessed—"

"That he was such a naughty boy?"

"Exactly." Her tone turned arch. "Apparently you're not the only lord out there who's a naughty boy."

"We do get around." He took another sip of brandy, then eyed her seriously over the rim of his glass. "And speaking of that—did this bachelor with the vulgar library ever behave as a naughty boy to *you*?"

"No more than you have."

"I've been a perfect gentleman to you. For me, anyway."

"Trying to blackmail me into your bed and then asking me to read naughty literature to you is not gentlemanly."

"But it's certainly entertaining," he pointed out.

She rolled her eyes. "To answer your question, the bachelor grandson never laid a hand on me. For one thing, he lived in terror that his grandmother, my employer, would cut him off. For another, he had no time for me. He spent it all courting women with large fortunes."

"Ah. Why did you leave?"

"His grandmother died." Camilla had been torn between dismay and relief. She hadn't wanted to look for a new post, but neither had she wanted to continue with the miserly and highly critical Lady Stirling. "He wasn't nearly as bad as the man who employed me next, as companion to his widowed sister. *He* wanted her to marry a rich marquess twice her age in order to gain him an entrée into White's and further his political career."

"And did he succeed?"

She smirked at him. "She ran off with his best friend. And he couldn't blame *me* for it, since he was the one who'd thrown them together." Her smile faded. "Unfortunately, he also no longer had any need for my services, which is how I ended up here."

He drank more brandy. "I keep forgetting this isn't your first post. Indeed, that's why I was so surprised to see how young you are."

"I'm not all *that* young. I'm nearly twenty-eight."

"A greatly advanced age indeed," he said sarcastically.

"Only three years younger than you," she pointed out.

One corner of his mouth quirked up. "True. But it's different for a man. We see more of the world in thirty-one years than a woman sees in a lifetime."

"Trust me, I've seen plenty enough of the world at my age."

He fell silent, his brow pursed in thought. "Twenty-seven. And you had two posts before this. You must have married very young."

That observation put her on her guard. "I was old enough."

"How old?"

"Why do you care?"

"You work for me. I have a right to know more about your circumstances." When she bristled, he softened his tone a fraction. "Besides, why should your age at marrying be such a secret? Were you ten and sold off from the orphanage to a ninety-year-old fellow with gout?"

"Don't be ridiculous. I was nineteen. And the orphanage was perfectly respectable. Indeed, I stayed there to work until I married."

"Ah. So you met your husband there."

"Yes," she said warily, not sure she wanted to talk about Kenneth with *him*. "He used to perform religious services for the children, and I would help him."

"And he fell in love." His voice was almost snide. When she hesitated a bit too long in answering, he added, "Or not."

Uncomfortable with his probing, she rose and went to the bookcase. "Perhaps you'd like me to read another book."

Setting down his glass, he rose, too. "You don't wish to talk about your marriage. I wonder why."

She faced him with a frown. "Probably for the same reason you don't wish to talk about your relationship with your mother. Because it's private."

He ignored that. "Did your husband mistreat you?" he asked in a hard voice. "Is that why you don't wish to discuss him?"

"Certainly not!" she said, appalled at the very thought. "You always assume the worst of people, don't you? He was a vicar, for pity's sake."

"That means nothing," he said evenly. "Men who mistreat women exist in every corner of society, trust me."

"Well, my husband didn't mistreat anyone. He was a crusader for the poor and the sick."

"Yet not in love with you?" Before she could answer, he added, "Let me guess. He saw you at the orphanage and determined that you would be the perfect helpmeet for him in his work."

She shot him a startled glance. "How did you know?"

He shrugged. "The average crusader tends to see women only as an extension of his mission."

"That's a most astute comment for an overgrown child."

He walked over to lean against a bedpost. "Children often pay better attention to their surroundings than adults give them credit for."

"Another astute observation," she said.

"I have my moments." He crossed his arms over his chest. "So how did you end up married to this crusading vicar? You seem the kind of woman who would marry only for love." His eyes glittered obsidian in the candlelight. "Did he tell you that he didn't love you? Or did he pretend to be enamored of you until after he got you leg-shackled for life?"

"You're very nosy, aren't you?"

"If you have nothing to hide, why should you care?"

Since she preferred to keep her most important

secrets from him, she should probably fob him off with inconsequential ones. "If you must know, he never pretended anything. We'd been friends a few years when he made his proposal. He pointed out that he needed a woman of my skills, and I could use a home and a family. So he suggested—" She caught herself with a scowl. "I don't know why I should tell you this. I haven't even told your mother. Then again, she was never so rude as to pry."

"No, Mother isn't much interested in anyone's situation but her own."

She glared at him. "That's not true! She's kind and thoughtful and—"

"Don't change the subject," he bit out. "You were saying that your vicar gave you a most practical proposal. Go on. Didn't he spout *any* romantic drivel to get you to accept him?"

A pox on him. He was going to push her until he knew it all, wasn't he? And if she refused to tell him, she risked having him delve deeper into her past, which she couldn't afford.

"Kenneth wasn't the romantic sort," she said tersely. "If he felt anything deeper than friendly affection for me, he didn't say. For him, our marriage was more of a fair trade in services."

"That sounds cold-blooded even to me, and I'm definitely not the 'romantic sort.'"

"What a surprise," she muttered.

"So, was it? A fair trade, I mean."

She pushed up her spectacles. "Fair enough . . . until his heart failed him three years after we married, and he left me a widow."

"Ah, now I understand. You married him because he was older, more mature—"

"I married him because he offered," she said blandly, annoyed that he presumed to know so much when he knew so little. "And he was only a few years older than you. The doctor told me that it happens like that sometimes, even to young men in good health. One day Kenneth was well; the next he was gone." Leaving her alone with an infant, very little money, and her grief.

Some of her distress must have showed on her face, for he said, "You loved him."

The earl had misunderstood entirely, but she wasn't about to explain how complicated even a loveless marriage became when there was a child involved. She'd sought to build a family; instead she'd gained a dissatisfying union with a man she barely knew. Turning on her heel, she headed for the bookcase again. "If we're to do any more reading tonight, then you'll have to choose another bo—"

"You were in love with your husband," he persisted, pushing away from the bedpost to follow her. "It might have been a marriage of convenience for your vicar, but it wasn't for you, was it?"

Determined to ignore him, she ran her fingers over the books in the case. "There's a novel by Henry Fielding here that I understand is very good," she said firmly.

"Admit it!" He caught her arm and pulled her around to face him. "You loved your husband."

"No, I did not!" She wrenched her arm free as he stood there gaping at her. "I grieved for him, yes. But I did not love him." That was the most embarrassing thing of all to admit. "I wanted to love him. I thought that once we were married, I would feel something, but I never . . . I couldn't . . ."

His gaze on her was intent, penetrating. "Don't blame yourself for that. Romantic love isn't for everyone."

For some reason that sparked her temper even more. "You mean a woman like me is incapable of love."

He scowled. "I didn't say that."

"You think that a woman with no resources is *always* on the hunt for a man with money," she went on hotly.

He looked as if she'd punched him. "I don't think any such thing!"

"Don't you? I married to escape the orphanage and a future as a spinster." To gain a family, though to say so would make her sound even more pitiful. "You said your mother married your father for money. Neither of us married for love. So I'm not much different from her."

"That's not true," he gritted out. "You didn't marry

a man of means and rank whom you *knew* could aim higher. You came to a mutual agreement with a fellow who didn't profess to love you—"

"How do you know that she didn't do the same?" When he merely glowered at her, she thrust her face up in his. "You don't know *what* she did, do you? You don't even know the full circumstances of her situation, yet you pass judgment on her."

She must have hit a nerve, for his face closed up. "I won't talk about my mother."

"Of course not. You might learn that you don't know her as well as you think. That you might be wrong about—"

"Quiet!" he growled. "I won't discuss her with *you!*"

"You're ready to defend *me,* whom you barely know," she persisted, heedless of how reckless she was being to provoke him, "yet you refuse to defend your own mother, who bore you and raised you."

"She did not—" He caught himself. "You don't know anything about it, damn you!"

"No, I don't! So *tell* me! How else can I learn if you don't?"

"If you don't stop talking about her, I'll—"

"What?" she pressed him. "You'll dismiss me? Run back to London, where it's safe? Except that it isn't safe, is it? Because even I, a complete stranger, can see the noose that is choking you more and more with every day that you—"

"Damn you!" He grabbed her by the shoulders as if he meant to shake her. "Damn you to hell!"

She stared him down, daring him to do his worst.

Then he kissed her. Hard. Fiercely. On the lips.

It startled her so much that she jerked back to gape at him. "What in creation was that for?"

"To shut you up," he said, eyes ablaze. Then his gaze dropped to her mouth, and the blaze became smoldering coals. He removed her spectacles and tossed them onto the nearby bed. "But this one, my dear, is for me."

His second kiss was a revelation. The fact that he was kissing her at *all* was a revelation. Men just didn't kiss her.

Of course Kenneth had done so whenever he'd come to her bed, but his kisses had always been brisk and no-nonsense, as if he was trying to get right to the point.

There was nothing brisk and no-nonsense about the *earl's* kiss. It invaded and persuaded, inflamed and invigorated. His brandied breath intoxicated her, made her want to drink him up even as he was fogging her good sense. She could hardly think, with his hands sliding into her hair and his mouth possessing hers.

And when he deepened the kiss, delving between her lips with his tongue, she couldn't prevent the moan that rose in her throat. She'd forgotten how good it felt to be held by a man, kissed by a man, even one who didn't love her. But this was so much more even than that. It was heady, thrilling . . . magical.

She caught herself. Of course it was magical. Rogues built their reputations on magical kisses. Magical *seductions*.

The thought made her tear her mouth from his. "You probably shouldn't . . ."

"Damned right I shouldn't." He clasped her head in his hands, his eyes dark and fathomless as he gazed into hers. "Even I know better. But it doesn't stop me from wanting to. Or you from wanting me to."

How had he guessed?

Probably because she'd just let him repeatedly thrust his tongue inside her mouth. And her hands now gripped his waist like those of a woman drowning.

She forced her hands to release him. "My lord—"

"Don't call me that." He bent his head, stopping his lips a breath away from hers. "In this room, we're Pierce and Camilla, understood?"

For no reason she could explain, she nodded, and that was all the invitation he required. With a sharp intake of breath, he took her mouth again.

8

Pierce knew what he was doing was unwise. He might be a scoundrel and a thousand other vile things, but he didn't attack women in his employ. He didn't pinch the maids or sneak a fondle from the housekeeper. And he did *not* kiss his mother's paid companion.

Except that he *was*. And he couldn't seem to stop.

It didn't help that she was kissing him back. It didn't help that he knew she was a widow, that he knew she hadn't loved her husband, that he found her enticing and clever and all those things that made him desire a woman.

He certainly desired this one. Her fierce soul made

him ache to lay her down on the bed and take her with slow, hot intent until she cried out her pleasure beneath him. She smelled of honey water and tasted of cinnamon, and he'd have liked nothing more than to eat her up.

She broke the kiss again to stare up at him with that clear-eyed gaze that seemed to see deeper than she let on. "Is this how you always silence a woman?"

He brushed kisses over her cheek. "Never needed to before," he murmured in her ear.

"So I'm the only woman who plagues you?" she asked skeptically, then gasped when he nipped her earlobe.

She was certainly the only one who'd ever plagued him about Mother. But then, he'd never let anyone else close enough to even know he *had* a mother.

"The only one I couldn't silence with a few words," he murmured as he kissed her neck. "Or with a threat to cut off their tidy allowances."

Her breath came in staccato bursts against his brow. "Then you must know some . . . very weak-willed women."

"Or very avaricious ones," he said dryly. Then he kissed her again to prevent her from pointing out the obvious—that perhaps he had different rules for women when it came to money. The first time she'd pointed it out had made him angry enough.

Besides, he wanted to keep kissing her. She kissed like a woman who didn't know her own sensual power.

Most women did—even the virginal ones. The fact that she didn't made him want to show it to her.

Graphically. Thoroughly. Over and over, until she realized what he'd known from the moment she first stood up to him—that she was one of those rare women who understood how the game was played . . . and then played it by her own rules.

He just wanted to break all the rules, even his own. With her. Now. In his bed.

So he covered her breast with his hand and kneaded it, exulting to feel her nipple harden through the fabric. For a brief, hot moment, she leaned into his caress, making him want to tear her gown off so he could tongue the sweet, ample softness of her breasts until she gasped her enjoyment.

But when he tugged at the fastenings of her gown in back, she froze and shoved him away. "Don't." Devoid of their spectacles, her eyes glittered a perfect cobalt blue in the firelight. Her lips were swollen and flushed from his kisses, and her chest rose and fell with her quickened breath. "That is not . . . part of our agreement."

No, it wasn't, and he knew it. He just couldn't make himself care. "It could be," he rasped, his body hard with need, and his blood running molten through his veins.

Her expression grew wary as she moved to the bed to snatch up her spectacles and don them once more. "I won't let you seduce me just to prove that you can."

The words sparked his temper. "Is that what you think this is?"

"You want a woman, and I am near to hand."

"Not near enough to hand," he said testily, and reached for her once more. But this time she darted across the room and put a chair between them.

Oh, for the love of God . . . He'd be damned before he took to chasing a woman about the furniture. Bad enough that he'd put her on her guard just by kissing her and giving her one little caress.

One delicious, intoxicating little caress that made him want more, made him want—

Devil take it all. He mustn't do this.

As he stood there, breathing hard, fighting for control, he began to come to his senses. What was he thinking? She was in his employ. He did *not* attempt to seduce servants. She wasn't even his preferred type! He liked his women tall and blond and self-involved so they didn't peer too deeply into his secrets.

She was none of that, yet he couldn't remember the last time he'd wanted a woman so much. Even now, looking at her lush mouth and even lusher body made him ache. . . .

Bloody hell, what was wrong with him?

He was bored and alone and randy. That's all. And he wasn't about to let his uncharacteristic desire for some plague of a female make him do anything he'd regret.

Leaning back against the bookcase, he crossed his arms over his chest and forced his breathing to slow. Then he donned his rakehell facade. Because that was the safest one. The only one that felt comfortable.

"Fine," he drawled. "We'll do it your way." He skimmed his gaze down her with deliberate heat. "Though I can't say I'm happy about it."

"It wouldn't be wise for us to—"

"I'm aware of that." He cast her a humorless smile. "I merely got caught up in the moment. It won't happen again."

Her wide, beautiful eyes looked uncertain. "You said that if I gave you an inch, you would take two miles. At the time, I didn't think you meant it, but—"

"I believe we just established that I meant it." Pushing away from the bedpost, he noted how she tensed as if to flee, and he halted. "But I'm in full control of my urges now, I assure you."

She gave him a tight nod. "Then I suppose I should choose another book to read to you."

"No, you may go," he said in a dismissive tone. At her look of surprise, he added, "I traveled long and hard today, and even a wicked fellow like me gets tired occasionally."

But that wasn't why he was ending their evening. Nor was it because he couldn't have her in his bed. The truth was, the longer she stared at him with that deeply probing gaze, the more uncomfortable he grew.

If she guessed it, she didn't show it. Relief was the only emotion on her face. "Thank you, Pierce. I'm rather tired myself."

Her use of his Christian name unsettled his insides. No one except his family called him Pierce. Even his mistresses had always called him Devonmont or "my lord." He almost wished he hadn't asked her to go against that long-standing rule; it made him feel oddly vulnerable. But he wasn't about to take it back and have her guess why.

"You're welcome," he said tightly. When she headed for the door, seemingly eager to flee his presence, he added, "Tomorrow evening we'll play piquet."

Damn it, why had he said that?

She faced him with a wary gaze. "I thought you were returning to London in the morning."

He'd planned to. Until she'd looked so bloody glad to leave him, so bloody scared that he might toss her into his bed and ravish her. Which was only marginally worse than her looking at him as if she understood things she couldn't possibly understand.

You'll dismiss me? Run back to London, where it's safe? Except that it isn't safe, is it? Because even I, a complete stranger, can see the noose that is choking you more and more with every day . . .

She could see no such thing, devil take her! He'd fought hard to bring himself to the point where he didn't care one whit *what* Mother did. But if he left for

London now, Camilla would think he did care, and that galled him.

"I need to consult with Fowler before I go, and that always ends up taking longer than I expect. Since I'll be on the estate anyway . . ." He shrugged.

Tipping up her chin, she stared at him with those penetrating blue eyes. "Does that mean you'll dine with me and your mother again, too?"

Damn. She'd misunderstood him. She thought he wanted to repeat tonight's bargain.

At his silence, she blushed and went on hastily, "Because otherwise I don't think it would be appropriate for you and me to—"

"Same bargain as before," he heard himself say as if through a fog. "I dine with the two of you, and you come here afterward."

Idiot. Yet he could hardly compel her to show up in his bedchamber again, unless he wanted to be one of those loathsome employers who forced their servants into their beds. And what would one more dinner with Mother matter, anyway? He knew her game. He could remain immune to it. Indeed, he would show Mrs. I-Can-See-Your-Darkest-Secrets Stuart that he wasn't letting any damned "noose" choke him.

Camilla's gaze softened, making him regret he'd even suggested staying another night. "All right. Same bargain as before. Though I think we should avoid the naughty books."

"Indeed." Just the thought of her reading more of *Fanny Hill* aloud to him in her sultry voice made his cock harden again. "No naughty books."

"And no more kisses," she said firmly.

It rubbed him raw that she thought him incapable of controlling himself. He was known for his control. "Of course." When she looked skeptical, he managed a bored expression. "Don't worry, Camilla. As I said this afternoon, I don't make a practice of abusing the trust of those in my employ. We'll merely play piquet. Or rather, I'll trounce you at piquet."

"If you can," she said lightly.

He snorted. "I've spent a good portion of my life in gaming hells. I think I can beat a woman whose only experience at the game is with little old ladies and orphans."

"I take it you don't remember the name of that little old lady I served as companion to." When he frowned, trying to recall the contents of her reference letters, she added, "Lady Stirling. And she taught me everything she knew about piquet."

Which was plenty. The late viscountess had been one of the best piquet players in England. "Then it's a good thing I beat her twice during my salad days."

Her face fell. "You're bamming me."

"You'll find out tomorrow night, won't you?"

"I suppose so," she said with a nod, and swept out the door.

A pity he would have to run the gauntlet of dinner with Mother again before he got a few hours with Camilla, who still had no idea what her meddling had wrought.

So tell me! How else can I learn if you don't?

He scowled. He ought to do just that—tell her everything and let her see just how heartless was the woman she apparently adored.

But she wouldn't believe him. Mother had spent the last six months persuading Camilla that everything was *his* fault. He wasn't going to overturn that just by giving her a few facts. And that rankled. Because Camilla seemed to be a sensible woman who ought not to be taken in by such machinations. It bothered him that she was. That he might be missing something in all this.

Missing something? Not bloody likely.

No, Camilla was naive, that's all. Charming and pretty, but a babe in the woods when it came to the sort of manipulative woman Mother was. Given a bit more time seeing him and Mother together, she would recognize the truth. That she'd been wrong about him and Mother and his blame in all this.

Then there would be no more reckless letters summoning him to Montcliff.

In the hall, Camilla leaned against the wall to catch her breath and steady her racing pulse. He was staying for another day, another dinner with her and the countess.

Earlier, she would have exulted at a second chance to convince him that his mother deserved his attention.

Now she wasn't so sure. Because the way he'd kissed her . . .

Oh, heavens, the man knew exactly how to kiss. There was no hesitation or awkwardness. He just seized a woman and ravished her mouth like a marauding Viking. Thoroughly. Repeatedly. With great enthusiasm.

But he'd promised not to do it again. Could she trust that? She'd never had a man desire her so intently before. And his attraction to her had *not* been feigned. She'd felt his arousal when he'd held her.

Sadly, she shared the attraction. She wasn't sure why. Yes, he had an interesting face and brooding eyes and a mouth that could turn any woman wanton, but he was also childish and arrogant. Such men generally annoyed her.

It was just that he seemed so very . . . lost. Tonight, his nonchalant mask had slipped long enough to reveal the bravado beneath. He was like the orphan boys who told everyone they didn't *need* parents, so they could hide how very desperately they did.

But *he* had a mother who loved him. Somehow Camilla had to make him see how precious that was. For the good of everyone.

Right. Selfless altruism is your only motive.

She pushed away from the wall. All right, so there was more to it than that. She wanted not to be at odds with him. She wanted another chance at feeling that warm mouth on hers and those knowing hands kneading her flesh . . .

Sweet heaven, she must be losing her mind! The last thing she needed was to make a lover out of her employer. Once an affair with him ended—and it always did with men like him—she'd lose both a lover *and* a good position. She couldn't afford that.

Especially when she and Jasper had finally found a family for the first time in their lives. Kenneth had been exactly as Pierce described him. He'd spent all his time in Spitalfields helping the poor, sick, and wicked. She'd run herself ragged to help him with his work and make a home for him and Jasper, and she'd rarely received thanks for her trouble. Their home together had been mostly a prison for her. Whereas here . . .

She sighed. Montcliff was a haven. Here she got not only thanks but warmth and kindness and the closest thing she'd ever had to a mother. Here Jasper was flourishing. And she wouldn't ruin that.

Thoughts of her son made her quicken her steps. She paused outside his room to check her reflection in the glass of the case clock and groaned. She looked disheveled and unsettled. Wanton. She couldn't let Maisie see her like this.

Swiftly, she repaired her hair and straightened her bodice, hoping she didn't look as if she'd just been thoroughly kissed by her employer. Her handsome, incredibly virile employer, who'd asked her to read a naughty book and then been horrified to realize it had pictures.

The thought made her smile, then curse herself for being so charmed by it.

Heading resolutely to her room, she entered to find Jasper sound asleep with Maisie dozing beside him. The girl roused as soon as Camilla neared the bed.

"Oh! You're back, are you?" Maisie rubbed sleep from her eyes and rose to help Camilla undress. If she noticed anything untoward, she didn't mention it.

But Camilla couldn't relax until the girl had left for the maids' rooms, upstairs. Even then it took her a while to get to sleep. She kept remembering his lordship's husky voice: *Even I know better. But it doesn't stop me from wanting to. Or you from wanting me to.*

That was the worst of it—she really *had* wanted him to kiss her. To keep kissing her. And to do even more.

She'd never been kissed with such passion. How alarming to discover that she would very much like it to happen again. Like delicious desserts, kisses provoked cravings for more at odd hours. And she'd never been good at resisting dessert . . .

Oh, she'd have to watch herself around him until she and the countess settled back into their normal life.

But that wasn't what Camilla wanted, either. Clearly, her ladyship and Pierce were both miserable in their present state. If she could just figure out what had torn them apart, then perhaps she could . . . could . . .

What? Knit them back together? She sighed. She hadn't even been able to turn her marriage of convenience into something solid. Why on earth did she think she could mend this very broken relationship?

Especially when she had only one more night in which to do it.

9

To Camilla's shock, it turned out to be more than one night, and for the most unlikely of reasons. His lordship's whim.

The night she'd gone to play piquet with him, he had indeed trounced her. Then he'd stated offhandedly that he had more work to do concerning the estate, so he was staying another day. He might as well have dinner with her and his mother again. If Camilla would agree—again—to come to his bedchamber to "entertain" him afterward.

So she had. And he'd stayed another day.

Then another. And another. Then three more. Each

time, he'd claimed that some matter of estate business kept him at Montcliff.

She would have believed him, except that it wasn't estate business that had him staying at the dower house instead of the manor. Or dining with her and the countess every evening. Or demanding that she come to his room afterward. She didn't know what to make of it.

She didn't know what to make of *him*. As far as she could tell, nothing had changed between him and his mother. Their dinners were still awkward. The earl was largely quiet during dinner, unless Camilla drew him into a conversation that interested him. She found herself making a game of figuring out what would engage him enough to keep him from bolting his dinner and running off to have his cigar.

Meanwhile, the countess seemed grateful for every halfway polite word he bestowed on her. It made Camilla want to slap him. And given how congenial he could be when her ladyship wasn't around, his behavior was perplexing, too.

Especially since his mother refused to talk about him, no matter how much Camilla hinted and cajoled and finally asked outright for answers. It sometimes astonished her that neither saw how much alike they were—both of them maddeningly obstinate.

Most disturbing was how he changed when Camilla was alone with him in the evenings. He turned into the clever, entertaining, and utterly false creature whom she'd begun to call Devil May Care Devonmont. Oh, she didn't think he lied to her, but that was only because he didn't discuss anything worth lying about. He hid his true opinions, his real self, beneath layers of wit.

They played chess and cards, they read books, and last night she'd told him amusing stories about her years as a lady's companion. But it was all very superficial. And he hadn't once tried to kiss her. Of course, that was a relief—or so she told herself every time she saw Jasper.

But sometimes, in those moments at the end of the evenings with him, while she was holding her breath and wondering if this would be the last time she saw him, she found herself wanting so fiercely for him to kiss her that she had to crush the urge to throw herself at him. Because it maddened her that he hid himself from her. It made her want to force him out of his facade.

And she was *still* no closer to finding out why he and his mother were at odds, *still* no closer to mending the breach between them. It was enough to make a sane woman run mad through the estate.

Now, as she sat in the drawing room with the countess and Jasper, she wondered yet again how to convince the countess to confide in her. Camilla could sense his lordship's growing impatience to be away, feel his building irritation with the situation. She might not have much more time to uncover the truth.

Unfortunately, today wasn't ideal for raising the

subject. Since Pierce was at Montcliff Manor handling estate affairs and wouldn't return until dinner, she and Lady Devonmont were spending the afternoon with Jasper. And Jasper's presence made it awfully difficult to have a deep discussion with the countess.

Lady Devonmont glanced up from the stocking she was embroidering. "That looks lovely. The net bags were an excellent idea."

Camilla wrapped another circle of net about a few walnuts, then tied it with a ribbon so it could be hung on the tree. "How many do you think we should make?"

"Lots and lots!" Jasper said from his seat at the table. "Then my soldiers can have some nuts to eat, too."

After Pierce had begun extending his stay, her ladyship had told Jasper that he would get a tin soldier for every day he stayed out of his lordship's way. He was up to six now, and for the past twenty minutes he'd been keeping the little fellows engaged in a lively battle. That was ten minutes longer than he could usually keep his mind on one thing.

"What makes you think these nuts are for *you*, muffin?" Camilla teased.

He shot her an alarmed frown. "Won't I get any of them?"

"Of course you will," Lady Devonmont said soothingly. "We'll give you some now if you like."

"Not before dinner," Camilla cautioned.

"Oh, a few won't hurt him." The countess put aside

her embroidery to crack open several nuts and hand the meats to Jasper. "There, my boy."

"What do you say?" Camilla asked.

"Thank you, my lady." He downed them in a flash, then asked, "Can I have the shells, too?"

Looking perplexed, the countess handed them over. Jasper turned them into pieces of the battle landscape and continued with his explosions and attacks as Camilla and her ladyship laughed.

After a while, however, he grew bored with that and glanced over to where the countess was embroidering. "Is that a stocking like in the poem? The ones that are 'hung by the chimney with care'?"

"That's the idea," Lady Devonmont said. "We're hoping to start a new tradition in Stocking Pelham. Given the name of our town, why not? We could make Stocking Pelham famous for stockings. And at the same time make some money for the church by selling them at the fair."

"So everyone can hang them by their chimneys 'in hopes that St. Nicholas soon would be there.'"

Camilla eyed him in surprise. "You remember that."

He nodded. "I know the whole poem by heart."

She and her ladyship exchanged a skeptical glance.

"I do! I really do. After the part about the stockings, it says, 'The children were nestled all snug in their beds, / While visions of sugar-plums danced in their heads.'"

"Very good," the countess said.

"I *like* sugarplums," Jasper announced slyly.

"So do I," said her ladyship with a grin. "We'll have to get some."

Camilla rolled her eyes. Either the countess was oblivious to how deft Jasper was at extracting treats from her, or she didn't care. Camilla suspected it was the latter.

"Then the next part says:

And Mama in her 'kerchief, and I in my cap,
Had just settled our brains for a long winter's nap—

When out on the lawn there arose such a clatter,
I sprung from the bed to see what was the matter . . ."

He cast Camilla a knowing glance. "It was St. Nicholas, you see."

"Aren't you getting ahead of the story?" the countess asked with a soft smile.

But Jasper had apparently given up on a word-for-word recitation and had settled for paraphrasing. "He's on the sleigh with the tiny reindeer and—" He halted. "What's a sleigh?"

"It's like a sled, only big," Camilla said.

"Or like a carriage for driving on snow," her ladyship said.

"And for flying, right?"

Lady Devonmont glanced at Camilla, amusement in her gaze. "Well, I've never seen one that flies."

"But St. Nicholas has one. That's how he gets up to the roof to come down the chimney."

"The reindeer pull him up there," her ladyship reminded him.

"Right." He ticked them off on his fingers. "Dasher and Dancer and Prancer and Vixen and Comet and Cupid and Dunder and Blixem."

"You know all their names?" Camilla said, rather surprised. He really did have the poem memorized. Or mostly, anyway.

He held up his toy soldiers. "That's what I named the fellows. Well, six of them. I don't have Dunder and Blixem yet."

Camilla swallowed. Her ladyship would have to invent a reason to give him Dunder and Blixem if his lordship didn't stay.

"What will you do when you have all eight?" the countess asked him.

"Why, make them pull a sleigh, of course. They're soldiers, so they're very strong." He frowned. "That's why I need to know what a sleigh is. So I can get them one."

"Ah," her ladyship said.

"Do you think they might have one at the fair that I could look at?"

Camilla sighed. No matter what she told him, he couldn't give up the idea of attending the fair. "I told you before, dearest, we can't go."

He looked crestfallen. "I could pretend to be your groom."

"Aside from the fact that you're too young, everyone in town knows that I don't ride," Camilla said gently.

She'd never learned. Indeed, she'd hoped when she took this post that she might get to do so, for she could imagine nothing more enticing than racing along a road on horseback.

But alas, her ladyship had a bad hip that made riding painful, so the possibility never arose. "And since her ladyship doesn't, either, no one would believe that you're our groom."

"You know what?" the countess put in. "I think there just might be a picture of a sleigh over there in one of the books on the bookcase. It's the one about travels in America and Canada. Do you think you could find it?"

"Yes, my lady!" He grabbed up his soldiers and carried them off to the bookcase.

"That's all he's been talking about for the past week," Camilla said in an undertone. "Going to the fair."

The countess cast her a rueful smile. "Earlier he told me he wanted to go so he could buy you a present. When I asked him how he would pay for it, he thought a bit, then said he would sell the soldiers I'd given him."

"Oh, dear." Camilla's throat tightened. How sweet that was.

"You're so lucky," Lady Devonmont said wistfully as she watched him hunt through the books. "To have a son who would do anything for you, even sell his own toys."

Camilla caught her breath. Now was her chance to bring up the subject of her ladyship's relationship with Pierce. "Yes. I'm lucky to have a son who doesn't begrudge me a few 'baubles.'"

The countess stiffened, then leveled a dark gaze on her. "What do you mean by that?"

Camilla chose her words carefully. "Didn't you hear his lordship at dinner his first night? Haven't you noticed how he keeps attempting to provoke you into asking for money?"

Lady Devonmont frowned. "Well, yes, but I just figured he's like most men—worried about finances."

"Actually . . ." She debated, but decided it would be better for the countess to hear it from her than from the earl one night when he was in a black mood. "The earl thinks that you . . . He seems to be laboring under a misapprehension that . . . well . . you want him here so you can ask him for more funds."

Any fears she might have had that his lordship was right were instantly put to rest by his mother's astonished expression. "The devil you say!"

"He thinks you married his father only for his money, and now that your husband is gone . . ."

"Ah." Lady Devonmont visibly withdrew. "I see that my son has ignored what I said in my letters, preferring to listen to old gossip."

"Which is clearly lies," Camilla said.

The countess forced a smile. "I'm afraid not. I mean, the idea that I want more money from Pierce is absurd, but . . ."

When she paused, Camilla drew in a ragged breath. "But?"

"I did marry Pierce's father for his fortune." Her gaze grew distant. "My late husband made sure of that."

Camilla frowned. "What do you mean?"

Just then Maisie burst into the drawing room. "His lordship is coming up the front steps!"

"So soon?" Camilla jumped up.

"He must have finished his business early," her ladyship murmured. "He probably won't come in here, but just in case—"

Camilla was already rushing over to Jasper. "You must go with Maisie now, dear. The earl is coming."

"But I just found the book!" he complained.

"Take it with you, and Maisie will show you the picture." Swiftly Camilla grabbed the tin soldiers sitting on the top of the case and thrust them into his hand.

They heard boot steps in the hall as Lady Devonmont scanned the room, looking for anything else that might give Jasper away. Grabbing up Jasper and the book, Maisie darted to the servants' door.

She slipped through it right before the boot steps paused outside the drawing room. Camilla hurriedly took a seat at the table, as did the countess, although it was highly unlikely Pierce would come in. He avoided them except at dinner, and he already knew that they spent most of their afternoons in the drawing room.

So she was quite surprised when the door opened and he stepped inside.

Trying to quell her pounding heart, she looked up and forced a smile. "Good afternoon, my lord."

"Good afternoon, ladies." He glanced about the room and then frowned. "I could have sworn I heard a child's voice coming from in here."

Camilla swallowed hard. What on earth was she to say to *that*?

10

Pierce was surprised that Camilla looked panicked by his appearance.

"A child?" his mother said with a brittle laugh. "You must have heard us talking, that's all."

"Probably." His remark had merely been an excuse for entering the drawing room. He knew this old house well; sounds could travel and change within it. He didn't really care what he'd heard. He'd just seized on a chance to talk to Camilla.

He was tiring of seeing her only during their stiff dinners with his mother and their slightly less stiff encounters after. He wanted to see her during the day, to catch her unawares in her natural environment, when she wasn't on her guard against him—as she was in his bedchamber, thanks to his unwise kisses that first night. She showed her carefree side only to his mother, never to *him*.

That was one reason he was still here after a week. At first he'd stayed to prove to her—and himself—that he was in complete control of his emotions when it came to Mother. That he was no longer bound to the pain of the past. But that soon changed into a determination to figure out why a woman as astute as Camilla continued to champion a woman like his mother.

He couldn't understand her, and it nagged at him. So he had come in here, hoping that Mother might be upstairs napping and he could chat alone with Camilla in a place where she didn't feel threatened.

No such luck.

He chided himself for the keen disappointment that shot through him. Apparently this idiotic behavior was what happened when he denied himself a woman he desired, something that had never occurred before. That would explain why he was reacting like some besotted arse.

Yet he couldn't bring himself to leave the room.

Something was going on. He could feel it. Camilla's hands shook as she fiddled with some piece of fabric. And for the first time since his arrival a week ago,

Mother wasn't pretending to be happy to see him. Her mouth was set in a thin line, and she was stabbing her needle with sharp strokes into her embroidery.

"You're back early, aren't you, my lord?" Camilla said.

He focused on her. "It started to snow, so I came back in case it got too deep for riding."

"It's snowing?" Camilla said. "Oh, dear, I hope that doesn't ruin things for the day after tomorrow."

"What's happening then?" he asked.

"The fair that's held in Stocking Pelham twice a year," Camilla explained. "I suppose you haven't been to one in a while."

"A long while." Pierce shot his mother a veiled glance, wondering if she remembered. "I was about eight the last time. In fact, I believe it was the same one—right before Christmas."

Mother had the good grace to color. "Yes, that was the one."

When silence stretched out between them, Camilla sought to smooth over the awkwardness. "Your mother and I are running a booth to raise money for repairs to the church's organ. It's in bad need of refurbishment."

"Ah."

Feeling like an intruder, he scanned the room he'd avoided heretofore. He'd forgotten how cozy it was, with its large hearth, its faded but thick carpet, and the pianoforte his fingers itched to play.

Odd that Mother had done nothing to make the room more fashionable. It had the same peeling red wallpaper with a large pomegranate design, the same mahogany Pembroke table with its matching chairs upholstered in red velvet, and the same marble pedestal displaying a bronze bust of the first Earl of Devonmont. It even had the same cold draft coming from the window.

It all felt terribly familiar. He'd spent many an hour here as a boy, playing at Mother's feet or sitting beside her on the bench as he learned to play the pianoforte.

Shoving that disquieting memory from his mind, he wandered over to the table and noted the walnuts, net, and festive ribbon. "What's all this? Something for the booth?"

"Bags of nuts for our Christmas tree," Camilla said.

That damned tree again. "You're eating as many as you bag, apparently," he quipped as he swept some shells to the side. Beneath the pile, he found a tin soldier.

He froze, recognizing it as one of his. He'd played with an entire set of them as a boy. His father had given them to him, no doubt to encourage him in warlike pursuits, but he'd pretended the tiny figures were all explorers and had sent them off on great adventures.

He'd wanted to take them with him to Harrow, but the rules hadn't allowed it. Little had he known that it would be the last time he would see them.

"Are you planning to hang tin soldiers on the tree as

well?" he asked hoarsely, unable to look at his mother as he turned the toy round in his hand.

"Why not?" Mother said with an edge in her voice. "There are plenty of them. They'd make an original 'bauble,' don't you think?"

He lifted a bitter gaze to her. "They certainly make an inexpensive one. I'm surprised you don't want something more costly, though."

"I can't imagine why you're surprised by that," his mother said sharply. "I've never cared about it before."

"My lord, perhaps you would like—" Camilla began.

"Oh, don't pretend with me, Mother," Pierce snapped. He was tired of waiting for Mother to show her true self. It was time to force her into it. "We both know that you care a great deal about money. For once in your life, be honest and admit that this entire farce is about your wanting to get your hands on Father's fortune."

She paled. "Camilla, dear, if you would leave me and Pierce alone to have a private word . . ."

When Camilla rose, Pierce stayed her with a glance. "What my mother doesn't want you to know is that my maternal grandfather, the baron, liked to live a bit too well for his income. Mother grew up in luxury, but by the time she was old enough to marry, Grandfather Gilchrist had been forced to economize, which I gather he wasn't very good at. That's why Mother cast her net for

Father, so she could return to the wealth and prestige of her girlhood."

He smiled coolly at his mother. Let her deny it to his face, damn her.

But her gaze on him was steady and unabashed. "Since you seem determined to air our family affairs before Camilla, pray do not mince words. As you know perfectly well, my papa wasn't ruined by high living but by gambling. He amassed so many debts that he was in danger of going to debtors' prison."

That took Pierce completely aback.

Mother shifted her gaze to Camilla. "Pierce's father bought up all of Papa's vowels and offered to forgive them entirely in exchange for my hand in marriage. So yes, I married him. It seemed the best course of action at the time." She rose abruptly, her color high. "Now, if you'll excuse me, I'll get someone to bring us some tea."

Pierce stared, thunderstruck, as his mother swept from the room. What the hell was she talking about?

"You didn't know," Camilla said in a hushed tone.

He glared at her. "She's lying."

"Why would she? That would mean telling the sort of secret about her family that no woman could want known. And telling it before me, who isn't part of your family."

Her logic beat at his defenses. "Then why is this the first time I'm hearing it?" Shoving the tin soldier into his coat pocket, he paced beside the table. "My cousins told me she married Father for his fortune. And it took a great deal of wheedling for me to find out the little I know—that Grandfather was practically penniless when Mother married Father. There was no mention of gambling debts."

Abruptly he realized why. Who would have told him? Father's last solicitor had been hired well into the marriage. The Waverlys were from Father's side of the family; they would know only what they'd been told. And Father would have been too proud to let it be known how he'd acquired his wife.

Consumed by a need to hear it all, Pierce strode out the door, with Camilla following. They both stopped short when they found the countess standing there, breathing hard, clearly trying to regain her composure.

"Father *bought* you?" he demanded.

Setting her shoulders, Mother faced him. "Don't be so dramatic. He courted me like any other gentleman. He just made sure that his suit would be received more favorably than most. I could have refused him. No one forced me to accept, not even your grandfather." She tipped up her chin. "I made my own choice."

He stared at her. Perhaps. But somehow it didn't seem quite as mercenary as before. "I didn't know," he rasped. "I never knew any of this."

She looked perplexed. "But I explained it in my letters."

Pierce felt the familiar guilt like a punch to his gut.

She must have read it in his face, for she paled. "You didn't read them." When he let out a low curse and turned away, she murmured, "I thought you just . . . couldn't forgive me for . . . I understood that, considering. But you didn't . . . you haven't even . . ."

Releasing a low moan, she turned for the stairs. "Pray excuse me. I feel a sudden headache coming on."

Camilla watched as his mother fled, then whirled on him with eyes flashing. "You didn't read them? *Any* of them? I thought you might just have been ignoring what they said, but not to read them at all . . ."

The outrage in her voice roused his own temper. "Don't condemn me without knowing the entirety of the case." He nodded jerkily toward the stairs. "Didn't you hear her speak of my not being able to forgive her? Don't you wonder what it is I can't forgive her for?"

"Oh, I'm sure you blame her for all sorts of silly things."

"Silly thi—" He choked out a laugh. "Ask her about my matriculation from Harrow, about every school holiday." He scowled at her. "Ask her what happened when I came into my majority. I daresay she won't answer you. And until she does, you have no right to judge me."

"Why not tell me yourself?" she demanded.

"You're not going to believe any of it unless you hear it from her. That has become perfectly clear."

Besides, before he destroyed Camilla's faith in his mother, he needed to know more of the truth. He was obviously missing a few pieces.

Wheeling around, he walked away and headed toward his father's old study, the one place where he might find answers. But when he reached it, he halted at the door. He couldn't bring himself to go in there—not after the last time.

In any case, if Father had left documentation, it would be at Montcliff Manor, not here, since he and Mother moved into the manor when Pierce was twenty-two. And after Pierce inherited, he went through every inch of the place, looked over all his father's papers for some indication of the truth. He found nothing.

Perhaps you should have read her letters.

Mother's expression when she realized he hadn't swam into his mind. She'd looked wounded. Shocked. Betrayed.

The eight-year-old inside him wanted to shout, "Good! Now you know what it's like to be ignored and abandoned!"

But the mature man felt shame—then anger at himself for even feeling shame. Why was he letting her affect him? For all he knew, she was inventing this to suit her needs. Had she given any proof in her letters? Referred him to anyone who might confirm her tale?

Damn it, he should have read them, if only to be prepared for whatever she threw at him. That would have put him ahead of the game when he came here. Now he had to muddle through this as best he could.

Had she really written to him about Grandfather's gambling? She must have—she'd assumed he'd read the letters, so there'd be no point now in her lying about *that*. What else might she have told him? Something to explain her complete lack of interest in him until two years ago?

No, at Father's funeral, she'd refused outright to give him answers. There was no reason to think she had put them in a letter, especially given her reticence to talk about the past since he'd been here. But the fact that he'd so thoroughly misunderstood the nature of his parents' marriage made him wonder what else he'd misunderstood.

He threaded his fingers through his hair. If Grandfather had sold her to Father, if it really hadn't been a love match, then perhaps Father had been behind her refusal to see her son. Might he have threatened her with something to keep her by his side and away from Pierce?

That made no sense. Why would Father essentially abandon his only heir? Why would he demand that she do the same? Besides, that day when he'd come here at twenty-one, she had been just as cruel as, if not more so than, Father when—

He spat an oath. It made far more sense to believe that Mother had thrown in her lot with the man who could give her everything, and Pierce had been an inconvenience. When he was in school, he always read of Lord and Lady Devonmont flitting to this dinner or that ball in Bath or York or London. They'd seemed to be going incessantly to house parties with the loftiest members of society.

At the same time, it was getting harder and harder to see Mother as some . . . frivolous, money-grubbing female who'd snagged an earl to move up in society.

His throat tightened. This was why he hadn't wanted to come here, damn it! There were no answers here, just more questions, more opening of wounds he thought he'd sewn shut with steel thread.

Damn her! *And* her meddling companion.

That thought swirled in his brain the rest of the afternoon, fortifying him for dinner. He would demand to know what was in the letters. Then he would demand to know what exactly she wanted from him after so many years of neglect. And if she wouldn't tell him, he would lay out for Camilla why he'd been estranged from his parents.

Yes, that's what he would do.

But when he came down to dinner, fully prepared for a confrontation, no one was there. On his plate was a folded sheet of paper addressed to "Lord Devonmont" in what must be Camilla's hand, since it certainly wasn't his mother's.

He gritted his teeth. God, but he was sick of missives. Letters were what people resorted to when they didn't want to lie to your face. When they wanted to pretend they weren't ripping your heart out.

With an oath, he opened it to read:

Your Lordship,
Your mother has a fierce headache and will not
be coming down to dinner. With your permission,
I shall stay with her this evening.

Sincerely,
Mrs. Stuart

Balling it up, he tossed it into the fire. With his permission—right. As if he had any say in the matter.

He could read between the lines. No dinner with Mother, so no evening with Camilla. He was being punished—for speaking the truth, for not reading Mother's letters. Punished for not opening Camilla's eyes to what his mother really was.

Except he wasn't sure anymore what his mother really was. *Who* she was. He couldn't even be sure anymore what he meant to her.

And that was driving him insane.

11

Camilla paced the countess's sitting room, praying that she would emerge soon. The lady's maid insisted that her ladyship had asked not to be disturbed because of her headache.

Camilla sighed. More likely, the woman's heart had been cleaved in two by her unfeeling son.

Ask her what happened when I came into my majority. I daresay she won't answer you. And until she does, you have no right to judge me.

All right, so perhaps he wasn't so much unfeeling as wounded. But why? And how? As a paid companion, she'd seen plenty of families torn apart over foolish nonsense—a father embarrassing his son in public, a daughter who turned down a marriage proposal. Families were difficult to fathom.

But she began to think it wasn't something small that had torn this family apart. The rift seemed deeper and wider than she'd assumed.

Perhaps Pierce was right. Perhaps she should *not* have meddled. Certainly she'd brought more pain to Lady Devonmont in the process. Still, how could he not have read his own mother's letters? It didn't seem worthy of him.

Then again, she didn't really know him, despite having spent a week of evenings with him. He was entertaining—witty, clever, and even charming when he wanted to be. She'd poked at his mask, lifted it a bit, tried to peek beneath it, but whenever she got a good glimpse of his real self, he jerked the mask back into place.

It was maddening.

The door to the bedroom opened, and the countess walked out. At once Camilla's heart dropped into her stomach. Her ladyship's eyes and nose were red, her features drawn.

She looked startled to see Camilla. "I thought you'd be at dinner."

"I'm not about to abandon you when you're upset."

The countess forced a smile. "I'm not upset. I'm just a bit . . ." Her face began to crumple, and she turned away to hide it.

"You *are* upset, and you have every right to be so." Camilla hurried over to put her arm about the woman's shoulders. "It was cruel of him to ignore your letters."

"He had his reasons," she choked out.

"You keep saying that. But what could they possibly be?" When the countess just shook her head and pulled free to walk back toward her bedchamber, Camilla steadied her nerve and added, "He told me to ask you about his holidays from school."

Lady Devonmont froze.

"He didn't tell me why I should ask, and he wouldn't tell me why he mentioned it. He left that to you. Why? What happened during his holidays?"

The countess stood there a long moment, as if debating something. Then she sighed. "Nothing happened. That's the trouble."

"If nothing happened, then why—"

"I wasn't around for his holidays. *That's* what he wants you to know."

Camilla blinked, sure that she had misunderstood. No feeling mother was absent for her child's holidays from school. "None of them? No Christmases, no Easters?"

"Not a one," she whispered.

Shock coursed through her. Even when she'd been forced to leave Jasper with her husband's family, she'd always made an effort to be with him for important occasions. She couldn't imagine not seeing Jasper for Christmas, for pity's sake.

The rest of Pierce's words leaped into her mind. "And his matriculation ceremony? He said I should ask about that, too. Don't tell me you weren't there for that, either."

The countess faced her with a shattered expression. "He spent every school holiday from the time he was eight with his cousins at Waverly Farm. They were the ones, along with his great-uncle, to attend his matriculation ceremony. I couldn't go. I wasn't allowed."

"What do you mean?"

Lady Devonmont's eyes, the same warm brown as Pierce's, darkened, and she released a long, tortured breath. "Pierce's father wouldn't allow it."

"The earl?"

"Yes, of course the earl," she snapped. "Who else?"

"Right, sorry," Camilla mumbled. Her mind reeled at the very idea of Pierce being left to relations when he had two perfectly good parents. "I don't understand."

"Of course you don't. Neither does Pierce."

No, how could he? It must have driven a stake through his heart to essentially lose his parents so young. He'd been only two years older than Jasper!

Her ladyship began to pace. "That's why I've never told him that his father was the reason for my absence. Because it would only raise more questions that I can't answer."

"So you don't know why the earl kept you from your son?" she said incredulously.

"I do know why." The countess's face closed up. "But I shan't discuss it. I can't. Some things must remain private."

"Private? The reason your son was abandoned is something you consider *private*?" Camilla cried. "I daresay he deserves to know why."

"He does, but I can't . . ." Her voice broke. "I won't speak of it. I begged his forgiveness in my letters for not being a mother to him all those years, and I understand if he can't forgive me. But as I told him, I had good reasons for agreeing to let others raise him. I did what I had to. He will simply have to accept it."

Camilla gaped at her. "Don't you see why he can't, not without knowing why?"

The countess shot her a warning glance. "Stay out of this, my dear."

"How can I, when I see how it pains you both?"

"Curse it, why can't you both just leave the past be? Why can't we just start anew and forget—"

"Because you can't! Not if you want to repair your relationship with your son."

Her ladyship let out a low moan but wouldn't say more.

"Why wouldn't the earl let you see him?"

The countess just shook her head.

Drat it, the woman was as stubborn as Pierce! And what did she mean, some things were private?

Oh. Camilla could think of only one reason the

countess might feel a need for privacy in such a situation. And it would explain why her ladyship had snapped at Camilla for unwittingly implying that Pierce wasn't the earl's son.

Perhaps Pierce really *wasn't* the earl's son.

It would explain so much—why the countess didn't want to talk about it, why Pierce didn't want to talk about it. If he were another man's son . . .

The thought brought her up short. She'd seen a portrait of the late earl. Pierce was the very image of his father. Anyone with eyes could tell *that*.

Besides which, he'd been born well on the right side of the blanket, for the countess often said she'd had him ten months after her marriage at eighteen. And while Camilla could almost imagine the countess giving herself to one man, and then being forced to marry another after she found herself with a babe in her belly, Camilla had trouble imagining her ladyship as an adulteress. Especially married to a man as rigid as the earl.

Nor did Pierce seem to think such a thing. Surely he would have hinted at it if he'd known. But perhaps he didn't know. *If* there was even anything to know, which she began to doubt. He *did* look amazingly like his father.

Which meant something else was at work here.

Remembering other things Pierce said, Camilla added, "At least tell me what happened when he reached his majority. He said you would never say."

The color drained from Lady Devonmont's face. "He's right."

"But why?"

"Because . . . because you would hate me if I told you." Her throat moved convulsively. "And I just can't . . . bear to have you hating me, too."

Camilla couldn't imagine anything her ladyship could have done that would be as awful as all that. "I would never hate you, my lady. If you'd only explain—"

"Enough, curse it!" The countess drew into herself, putting on her own mask—a cold, uncaring one that didn't hide a thing, for her eyes blazed bright within it.

Then she turned on her heel and headed for her bedchamber. "I'm retiring for the evening. We will not speak of this again."

"But, my lady—"

"No!" She halted just short of the door, her shoulders trembling as if she fought to contain tears. Then she seemed to steady herself. "I never asked you to interfere in this, Camilla, and if you continue . . ." She left the words hanging, but the implication was clear.

Camilla choked down the sudden raw pain in her throat. Her ladyship would never dismiss her. Would she? No, Camilla couldn't believe it. But the fact that she would even threaten such a thing showed how desperate she was.

It also showed that Camilla had gone as far as she dared. It was one thing to defy the earl. But defying the woman who'd been good enough to bring Jasper here would be madness. She couldn't afford to behave irrationally; she had her son to think of.

"As you wish," Camilla said quietly. "We won't speak of it again."

But that didn't mean she would stop trying to learn more another way.

As soon as the countess gave a tight nod and disappeared into her bedchamber, Camilla turned on her heel and headed for the earl's room. She was tired of seeing two people she'd begun to care about hitting their heads against the brick wall of the past.

Part of her understood. There were things about her own past that she'd rather not have revealed. But this was carrying "privacy" too far. At least when *she* had briefly given her son over to relatives to be raised, she'd told him why. He'd never doubted that his mother loved him.

Clearly Pierce doubted that very deeply. Something inside her chest twisted at the thought. She hadn't known her own parents, which was why she realized how precious it was to have ones you could trust and believe in.

She knocked on the door. His voice bade her enter. Drumming up her courage, she opened the door, only to find the room completely dark. The fire had burned out, and there were no candles lit except the one in her hand.

Sweet heaven, he must already have retired for the night.

"I beg your pardon," she mumbled, and began to ease the door shut.

"Don't go," he said, his voice low but commanding. It certainly wasn't the voice of someone just roused from sleep.

She hesitated. "I think I must."

"I'm not in bed. I'm just sitting here in the dark." A hint of sarcasm laced his tone. "I'm fully dressed, and I promise not to pounce." When she still stood uncertain, he said, more softly, "Please come in and keep me company awhile."

Please. It was a word he rarely used—a word that men of his rank had no need to use. But something in the tenor of his voice, in the way he asked for her company so humbly, made tears start in her eyes. No doubt he'd asked for his mother's company many times in his childhood and never got it.

She slipped inside, shutting the door behind her. As her eyes adjusted to the dim room, she saw him in his favorite armchair, which he'd apparently dragged over to face the window. "Do you often sit in the dark?" she asked as she headed toward him.

"Only when there's a full moon and snow on the ground." He gestured before him. "Look at that."

She had to blow out the candle to be able to see beyond her reflection in the glass, but when she did, she was treated to a rapturous view. Spread out below them was the snow-draped lawn, turned magical by moonlight. The bushes were like frosted cakes served up on a blanket of marzipan, and footsteps in the snow looked like almonds dotting the pastry of a tart. Only the black, leafless beeches skirting the edge of the gardens struck a somber note.

"I used to love this view." His voice was a rumble in the dark. "During the day, you can see the dairy, the trout stream, even a few tenants' cottages. When I sat here as a boy, I imagined what it would be like once I inherited. I had grand plans for the estate. I was going to be the benevolent ruler of all from this very room, even though it wasn't the master bedchamber."

A choked laugh escaped him. "Of course, Father, in his infinite idiocy, decided to build a bigger, grander palace next door. He never liked this house. He said it was too dilapidated to be worthy of an earl. So now when I come to Hertfordshire, I spend my days in a soulless mausoleum that doesn't have one tenth of the charm and beauty of this old place."

He shook his head. "Meanwhile, Mother lives in the place I love. And all because I thought to punish her. I assumed she hated it as much as Father did. That she must have been the one to press him into building Montcliff Manor." His voice turned distant. "Instead, she settled in here and made it her own, as cozy and warm as I remember from my childhood. I thought my fond memories of that time were an illusion. Now I just don't know."

Her heart leaped into her throat. So that was why he'd said this was his favorite room. And why he'd said that first day that it wasn't *his*. If the countess were to be believed, he'd never had a room in this house, except the nursery.

But he'd mentioned something that had happened when he reached his majority. Had he lived here briefly? She had to find out.

"I asked your mother those questions you told me to," she ventured.

When she heard his sharp intake of breath, she wondered if she should have left the subject alone. But he had started this, and surely he had expected a report once she'd done as he commanded.

A long moment passed before he rasped, "Did she answer you?"

"Somewhat. From what she said, I gather that you left home to go to school at eight and weren't brought back here for years. You spent holidays with your cousins?"

He gave a terse nod.

"Did anyone ever say why?"

"The Waverlys gave different reasons each time." His voice grew taut, thick. "They told me my parents were in Brighton or they'd gone to a house party in York. Or they were in London for the season." He fisted his hands in his lap. "There was always some excuse. But it all came down to one thing—Mother and Father were flitting about the country to anywhere that *I* wasn't."

"Oh, Pierce," she murmured, trying to imagine what that must have been like. It seemed almost worse to have parents who willfully abandoned you than to have no parents at all.

She wanted to tell him what his mother had said about not being *allowed* to see him, but he seemed willing to speak of the past here in the dark. She was loath to say anything that might stop the flow of words— *genuine* words—about himself and his childhood.

"At first I wrote to Mother," he went on. "Once a week, faithfully. But she didn't write back, and after a couple of years I stopped. By then the Waverlys had also stopped making excuses for why my parents—" He muttered a curse under his breath, then went on in a harder tone. "Why they didn't want to see me anymore. My cousins simply adopted me into their family."

"That was very laudable." She might not like Kenneth's brother very much, but he'd been kind to add Jasper to his responsibilities.

She considered telling Pierce about Jasper. It had begun to feel wrong somehow to hide her son from him, but she simply couldn't risk it without being sure how he would react. "Anyone who takes in someone else's child to raise has a core of good in them."

"Yes. They're good people, the Waverlys." He gazed out the window. "They did their best to hide the painful truth from me, but when my parents didn't even bother to show up for my matriculation, I figured out that Mother and Father really didn't want anything to do with me. That they never intended to bring me home."

His voice had grown more choked by the moment, and it made her heart lurch in her chest. "It sounds awful," she whispered.

With a shrug that looked forced, he shot her a quick glance. "Not as awful as growing up in an orphanage, I'd imagine."

"It's not the same, but no less awful. I never knew my parents, so I didn't feel I'd had them snatched from me, the way you must have. The orphanage was all I ever knew."

"Your parents must have died very young then," he said.

They hadn't spoken of her parents before. She'd managed to avoid the subject whenever their conversation headed in that direction. But she couldn't avoid it now.

So she searched for a way not to lie to him. "I went to the orphanage as an infant." That was the truth. But she'd left out so much. "Fortunately, it was a good place—not one of those dreadful ones where they mistreat the children."

He gave a self-deprecating laugh. "You must think me spoiled, to be complaining about not having my parents around when I had so many more advantages than you. I went to Harrow and spent my holidays with fine people like the Waverlys. I even had a sort of parent. My great-uncle Isaac was—still is—like a father to me."

His attempt to put a good face on things made her heart break for him even more. "Not spoiled in the least," she said softly. "It must have been very painful, not knowing why your parents didn't . . ."

"Want me?" he clipped out. "Yes, that was the hardest part. I was always a difficult child, but if they would have told me what I'd done to deserve such banishment—"

"You did nothing to deserve it!" she said hotly. "No child deserves that."

"Then why did they do it?"

She sighed. "Your mother said that your father wouldn't allow her to see you."

He dragged in a heavy breath. "And do you believe her?"

"I do. She was very upset over it." She stared down at his dark head, wishing she dared to stroke his silky hair, to soothe him somehow. "Would your father have done such a thing? She never speaks of him, and none of the servants seem to know what kind of man he was."

"He was an arse most of the time. He never liked having me around. So yes, it's possible."

"Even though you were his heir?"

"That never seemed to matter to him. I honestly don't know what did." After a moment's hesitation, his tone turned speculative. "Although now that I think of it, he was always very possessive of Mother. If he cared about anything, it was her." He glanced up at Camilla. "Did Mother happen to say *why* he kept her from me? Or is that something she put in those letters I didn't read?"

"No." She debated telling him the rest of it, but it might hurt him more to hear that his mother knew the truth and still wouldn't tell him. "I . . . I . . . we did not talk long. She said she would prefer that I . . . stayed out of the matter."

He uttered a harsh laugh. "Clearly she doesn't know you very well."

"I'm sorry," she whispered. "I had no idea when I summoned you here—"

"I realize that you meant well," he said coolly.

"Honestly, I didn't expect all of this." When he said nothing, she realized that she still hadn't gotten answers to some of her questions. And as long as he was in a talkative mood . . . "So you were away from home for ten years? You didn't see them in all that time?"

"More like thirteen years. Until I reached my majority." He glanced up at her again, the moonlight glinting off his dark eyes. "Did she tell you about that, too?"

"No. That was one question she refused to answer. She said I'd hate her if she did, and she couldn't bear to have us both hating her." Camilla hesitated, then laid her hand on his shoulder. "So you will have to be the one to tell me what happened."

He stiffened. Then, to her disappointment, he shrugged off her hand and rose to pad across the room in his stocking feet to the hearth. He bent to start the fire.

When he still didn't say anything, she imagined all sorts of awful scenarios. "Your father didn't . . . I mean, he wasn't the sort of man to knock you around or anything, was he?"

"No, nothing like that," he ground out.

Thank heaven. If his father had abused him somehow, Pierce and his mother might both be reluctant to speak of it. And she supposed that even at twenty-one, Pierce could still have been thrashed by his father.

Or even by— "And . . . what about your mother? She didn't . . . I mean, I can't imagine that she would, but—"

"Neither of them ever laid a hand on me," he assured her. He continued to feed kindling into the burgeoning flame. Then he let out a ragged breath. "But she's right, you know. If you heard the whole story, you might very well hate her. You might even tender your resignation. And I can't have that."

"Why not?"

He rose to face her, his eyes glittering in the firelight. "Because I don't want you to leave."

Her heart thumped madly in her chest. The very air

changed, sparking with meaning. His gaze locked with hers—intense, fathomless . . . hungry.

Then his usual mask shuttered his face, and he shrugged. "After all, I can't afford to lose a good companion for my mother. She needs *someone* to keep her occupied so she won't meddle in estate business. And you seem to do that admirably."

She stood there, stunned, as he strode for the brandy decanter. Once more, Devil May Care Devonmont had reappeared, and it hurt. His words, so casually spoken, hurt.

Then her common sense reasserted itself. Sweet heaven, she had quite the imagination. Had she thought that he might actually care about her? That he might even miss her if she left?

She was losing all sense of proportion. They'd had a handful of kisses one night, which probably meant nothing to a rogue like him. He may have confided in her, but that was only because she was handy. And no matter how many evenings they spent together, he was still an earl, and she still had no connections. Earls did not develop deep feelings for penniless vicars' widows of no consequence. If he wanted her here at all, it was for his mother.

Shoving up her spectacles, she said with determined cheer, "If you are to have any entertainment from me tonight, I suppose we ought to begin. What are you in the mood for?"

He concentrated on pouring brandy and didn't look at her. "Since I didn't dine with Mother, you don't need to stay."

His dismissive tone made it clear that he preferred to be alone. "Of course." She fought to keep the disappointment out of her voice. She'd begun to look forward to their evenings together, but she would die before she let him know it. No doubt he was already growing bored with them.

"Besides," he added, his voice softening, "you haven't had any dinner, I expect. Bad enough that you're having to play the arbiter between me and my mother. Our nonsense shouldn't be the cause of your wasting away."

"I hardly think I'm going to waste away from missing one dinner," she said dryly. "But I do appreciate your concern. And I am a bit hungry, now that you mention it."

Feeling only slightly less disappointed, she headed for the door.

"Camilla," he called out as she reached it.

"Yes?" She turned to look at him.

"Thank you for asking her those questions." He stared down into his glass. "And thank you for giving me the benefit of the doubt after you found out I hadn't read her letters. I suppose I should have, but—"

"I understand. You were justifiably angry. Sometimes anger provokes a person to do things they might not otherwise. If it makes you feel any better, I don't think she revealed anything of consequence in them."

"What makes you say that?"

"If she won't talk to you about it, and she won't say anything to me, I can't imagine she would put it in a letter." She measured her words, not wanting to wound him more. "Besides, she acted as if she . . . er . . . wasn't ready to talk about it."

He sipped his brandy. "All the same, I'd like to read them, find out what's in them."

"That's probably a good idea."

"And just so you won't think me a complete arse, in the past I did demand answers of her. At Father's funeral, I asked her why the two of them sent me away. She wouldn't say. She just told me she wanted to keep the past in the past."

"She said much the same to me tonight. I told her that it wouldn't work—that she couldn't leave you wondering like that." She shook her head. "She ordered me to stay out of it, so I'm afraid I didn't do much good."

"You did enough," he said enigmatically. He gulped the rest of his brandy, and when he spoke again, he was back to being Devil May Care Devonmont. "Now go have your dinner, before I drag out some naughty books for you to read."

She wanted to ask if he meant to stay, but she had *some* pride, after all. So she left, wishing she hadn't learned so much about him tonight. Before that, she'd been able to keep from caring too deeply for him by reminding herself of how awful he'd been to his mother.

But now, with everything a muddle and her ladyship's hands seeming dirtier by the moment, she was finding it far more difficult to protect her heart.

12

After Camilla left, Pierce poured another glass of brandy. He didn't know what to think. He could see Father wanting to keep Mother to himself, but why had Mother gone along with it? She'd always stood up to Father before. What had changed when Pierce turned eight?

Perhaps she really had just been waiting until he was old enough to be packed off to school. But if she hadn't wanted to send him away, why not write to him? Why not try to see him? By that point, Mother's parents had long been dead, so what hold could Father have possibly had over her that would keep her from a son she truly loved?

Unless she didn't truly love you, came the insidious voice that had plagued him ever since that day at Harrow. *Unless she's just working on you another way, for her own ends.*

He gulped down some brandy, wishing it could wash away his suspicions. But too much had happened between him and Mother; too many questions were left unanswered. Father was dead—she had no reason to keep his secrets anymore. So why was she?

Damn it all!

He threw the glass into the fireplace, feeling only a cursory satisfaction from the sound of it shattering and the sight of the brandy flaring as it caught fire. This madness of incessant questions and uncertainties was precisely what he'd been trying to avoid. He had been better off in London, believing that Mother hated him, believing she merely wanted more of Father's money.

But then you wouldn't have met Camilla.

He stared blindly into the fire. Ah, yes. That was the rub.

Though why he cared about meeting some widow with a warm smile and a generous heart was beyond him.

She understands your pain.

She did. She saw right to the bone of it. Perhaps because she was an orphan, she knew what it was like to yearn for parents. That must be what drew him to her, along with her stubbornness and her loyalty to her charge and the way she made him want and want and . . .

Damn it all to hell! This was mad. He was imagining some intimate connection that simply didn't exist.

Imagination isn't what made you practically beg her not to leave.

Even as he'd said the words, he'd known they were unwise. She would assume they meant something, when he'd only been clutching at the sympathy she offered.

Right, that's all. And that's why you've never told any other woman the things you told her tonight. That's why you're letting her get under your skin. Because she offers you sympathy.

He swore under his breath. All right, so perhaps there was a bit more to it than that, but only because of this situation with Mother. And all the talk of Christmas. And his painful memories of that day in the study—

No, damn it—he wasn't going to let this affect him! He certainly wasn't going to let *Camilla* affect him. Just because she turned that soulful gaze of hers on him didn't mean he had to spill out all his hurts.

It was time he put her out of his mind. He was a rogue, damn it! He didn't care about anything or anyone. He would go back to London tomorrow.

Taking up another glass, he filled it to the brim with brandy. Tonight he was going to get drunk and forget he'd ever come to this cursed place, forget he'd ever met the meddling Camilla. Then tomorrow morning, he'd be able to see everything with clearer eyes.

So he began to drink. And drink. And drink some more. He carried out his plan with such ruthless determination that by the time he went to bed, he was well and thoroughly sloshed.

Unfortunately, when he awoke midmorning, he was not only incapable of seeing everything with clearer eyes, he was incapable of seeing much of anything without wanting to retch.

Clearly his plan had gone awry. Especially since he belatedly remembered that he'd promised to meet with Fowler this morning to discuss the servant gifts for Boxing Day. The man would await his leisure, of course, but Pierce never liked to keep his people waiting. Father had always done that, and though people said Pierce looked like his father, he didn't want to resemble him in character, not if he could help it.

So Pierce rang for the footman acting as his valet at the dower house and then dragged himself out of bed to call for coffee. It took three cups to still the churning in his belly so he could be dressed. It took another three to steady him for the ride over to Montcliff Manor.

By the time he arrived there, it was nearly noon. So he wasn't surprised to find Fowler hard at work in the study where Pierce did most of the estate business.

When Pierce entered, the man jumped up. "I hope you don't mind, my lord, but I went ahead and started making a list. I thought if I laid everything—"

"It's fine," Pierce gritted out, wishing the man didn't have to speak *quite* so loudly. "I meant to be here sooner."

"No doubt it's hard to sleep comfortably at the dower house," Fowler said politely.

That was an understatement. "You know how it is—an unfamiliar bed and such. Takes some getting used to." As did being around his mother, although being around Camilla took no getting used to at all. He'd never met a woman so easy to converse with.

No, he wasn't going to think about her anymore, remember?

Frowning at his unruly tendency to let her invade his thoughts, Pierce took his seat behind the desk. Fowler moved around to the front and sat down.

Nearly fifty, Miles Fowler was an interesting fellow. Born a bricklayer's son, he'd won a spot as a poor scholar at Harrow. He'd excelled in all his subjects and had so impressed his school chum the Viscount Rathmoor that the man had hired him as his estate manager.

But then Rathmoor died some years ago, leaving his son, Pierce's schoolboy nemesis George Manton, to inherit everything. Typical of the arse, Manton apparently alienated so many of his servants that several sought other positions, including Fowler.

Pierce never regretted stealing the man out from under Manton's nose. Fowler was a damned good estate manager. Nothing got by him, and he had an impenetrable code of honor.

Unfortunately, he was also very diligent, and today Pierce wasn't in the mood for diligence. His brain still felt like mush as he stared down at the documents and tried to focus.

"I do hope your lordship is finding the rest of the dower house comfortable," Fowler ventured when Pierce remained silent a long while.

It would be infinitely more comfortable if there were no people in it, he wanted to say. Except that wasn't true. He liked having Camilla there.

Damn it, there he went again, thinking about her. "It's fine."

"Good. Because there's something of great importance regarding your stay there that I wish to discuss."

The strain in Fowler's voice came through clearly, forcing Pierce to pay attention. He sat back in his chair to stare at the older man. "Go on."

"I was shocked to receive a letter from Boyd this morning expressing his concern for her ladyship and wanting more particulars about her condition. Imagine my surprise to hear that you came here last week because of a message from Mrs. Stuart informing you that the countess is deathly ill."

Uh-oh. He should have sent a note of reassurance

off to Boyd at once, but in the midst of everything, he'd forgotten that he'd told anyone about Mother's supposed illness. And he hadn't intended to stay here so long.

Fowler was watching him with consternation. "Since you haven't mentioned it and the servants here have heard nothing of it, I can only assume that either your mother never *was* deathly ill or she had a miraculous recovery between the time you left London and the time you arrived here. The servants at the dower house can be very closemouthed about her ladyship, but I doubt that even they would keep such a situation quiet for long."

"You're right," Pierce said smoothly. "My mother is fine." If that term could *ever* be used in connection with her. "It was merely a misunderstanding."

Sadly, Fowler was too sharp a fellow to let Pierce slide that one past. "If you don't mind my asking, sir, what exactly was the nature of the misunderstanding? I thought when I hired Mrs. Stuart that she was a forthright woman. I can't imagine why she would alarm your lordship by inventing some tale about her ladyship being deathly ill."

Inwardly cursing Fowler for being so perceptive, Pierce debated what to tell the man that wouldn't have him marching over to chastise Camilla.

"Because if I'd dreamed that the woman had any propensity to lie," Fowler went on, "I would never—"

"It wasn't Mrs. Stuart's fault," Pierce said firmly. "It was Mother's. She actually had been ill, and she gave Mrs. Stuart to understand that she was more ill than she was."

That was sort of true; Mother supposedly had been pining for him. And if Camilla was to be believed, she really had been.

Fowler's face cleared. "Ah. I see. So Mrs. Stuart was overly hasty in informing you?"

"Exactly. You know the sort of careful woman she is. And once I realized that matters weren't as bad as I'd feared, I was so relieved that I decided to stay on a few days." When Fowler looked perplexed by that, he added, "In case Mother has another bout of illness, you see."

The man nodded, though it was clear that he still found the situation odd and was simply too discreet to say so.

Although Fowler knew that Pierce and his mother were estranged, he didn't know the reasons for it. Pierce hadn't wanted his own feelings to be reflected in how Fowler treated the residents of the dower house.

"But you *are* pleased with Mrs. Stuart," Fowler persisted. "She hasn't done anything to . . . concern you?"

Clearly the man was worried about how Camilla's behavior might reflect on him, as the one who'd hired her.

"Of course I'm pleased with her. Mother seems to like her a great deal."

Relief spread over Fowler's hawkish features. "That's good. Very good." Fowler glanced away. "I thought her ladyship might enjoy having someone young and lively about her. Mrs. Stuart has such a cheery nature that it would be hard *not* to like her."

The man had written similar things about Camilla before, but hearing him speak them gave Pierce pause. "And the lady is quite pretty, too," he ventured as he kept a keen eye on Fowler's face, "which is always an added advantage."

Fowler's startled gaze swung back to Pierce. "Is she? I hadn't noticed."

That was a feigned response if Pierce had ever seen one. "I noticed at once," he said, then added dryly, "but then, I'm considered quite the rogue, and we rogues always notice such things."

An uneasy laugh escaped Fowler. "You'd be wise not to let her ladyship see you 'notice' Mrs. Stuart. Your mother wouldn't approve."

Interesting. "Why not?"

"Lady Devonmont thinks the world of the young widow. She's very protective of her and would be most upset if she thought that you . . . that is, that anyone might try to take advantage of the lady." He added hastily, "Not that you would do such a thing, of course, but your mother might . . . interpret any friendliness toward Mrs. Stuart in that way."

Pierce gave the man a hard stare. Was Fowler trying to warn him off Camilla? And how did he know so much about the relationship between Mother and Camilla anyway?

"You sound as if you spend a great deal of time with my mother and Mrs. Stuart."

"Not a great deal, no." He tugged nervously at his cravat. "But when they invite me to dinner, I generally accept."

"Do they invite you often?"

"Once every couple of weeks. They're amiable ladies, and I sometimes crave a bit of female companionship."

As did every man. But a widower might crave it more than most. And Fowler wasn't too old or ugly to attract a woman, either. Indeed, most women would probably consider him well-favored. His position as estate manager to a wealthy earl would also open the door of many a female heart.

Camilla's? Would she be attracted to Fowler?

A ridiculous thought. Why, the man must be twenty years her senior!

Father was nearly twenty years Mother's senior, and it didn't stop him . . . or her.

"Female companionship can be useful," Pierce said blandly, determined to ferret out the truth.

"It certainly can." Fowler sighed. "With Mrs. Stuart's past experience working at an orphanage, she is always full of sound advice about how to deal with the various servants at the two houses. She has this way of getting right to the heart of the problem—"

"I know exactly what you mean. She's very astute."

"And sensible and eager to help without being overly pushy, as some women are. Between her and her ladyship—" He broke off, coloring a bit, as if realizing how he was gushing about Camilla. "Well, anyway, they are both very informative."

"I see." Oh, yes, he saw a great deal. Fowler had his eye on Camilla. And why wouldn't he? She had an open heart, a sweet manner, and a great deal of common sense. And all of that came in a body that was most appealing. Any man with eyes would want to bed her.

Or court her.

He scowled. Yes, Fowler would aim for that, wouldn't he? He was a respectable widower, probably eager for a second wife. He had no children, so he would want a son.

But did Camilla welcome his attentions? She'd never mentioned the man, but then, she wouldn't. Most employers didn't approve of their servants courting each other.

Was it possible she'd nurtured some secret tendre for Fowler all this time? That Fowler nurtured some secret tendre for her?

There was a very easy way to find out. "Well, then, you should come to dinner this evening," he said, priding himself on the fact that he sounded nonchalant.

Never mind that he'd sworn to return to London today. He didn't feel much like traveling right now anyway, not with this devil of a headache. Besides, it was past noon already, not the best time to start a trip. And what difference would one more night make?

"Come to dinner," he repeated. "It's the least I can do to make up for interrupting a long-standing tradition."

"Oh, no, it hasn't been anything so settled as that, my lord," Fowler said hastily, his cheeks now scarlet. "I wouldn't dream of intruding on your time with your mother."

"Nonsense. It will be nice to have an ally at the table," he said tightly. "The two ladies are wearing me out with all their talk of Christmas preparations."

Fowler relaxed a fraction. "Ah, I can well imagine that."

"If it makes you feel any better, we can discuss business. You have no idea how much that would please me."

That garnered a chuckle from the man. "Believe me, my lord, I'm well aware of how women can go on about such matters."

"So you'll come save me?"

"When you put it that way, how can I refuse?"

"Excellent," Pierce said. "You won't get the fine French fare you'd receive from my table here, but as you've probably noticed, the cook at the dower house is surprisingly good. I'll send word to Mrs. Beasley that you're coming."

Tonight he would watch Fowler and Camilla to figure out just how intimate their connection was. After all, he couldn't have his servants sneaking around behind his back, having assignations, and—

Hypocrite.

He could practically hear Camilla say it. And she'd be right, too. He'd never before cared a fig if any of his servants were courting. What they did in their free time was their own business. As long as it didn't interfere with their work, they were free to hang from the trees like monkeys, as far as he was concerned.

Yet the thought of Camilla keeping secrets from him . . . Damn it, he had to know. He couldn't stand being left in the dark.

And if she *did* fancy Fowler?

Pierce snorted. It wasn't as if he had a claim on her. Just because she had a way of spreading balm over the pain that continually crushed his chest didn't mean anything. Nor did the fact that she looked up at him with those soft, understanding eyes that made him feel as if someone *did* care if he lived or died. And just because she soothed his temper and—

What an idiot he was.

It might be better for him if she *did* have a tendre for Fowler. Because then he could put his obsession with the pretty widow to rest once and for all, before he made a complete bloody fool of himself.

13

Camilla generally didn't mind having Mr. Fowler join them for dinner, but tonight she wished he hadn't come. Especially since his lordship hadn't returned to London. It was silly of her, she knew, but after she and Pierce had talked so intensely last night, she'd hoped . . .

Oh, she didn't know *what* she'd hoped. That they might continue their intimate discussions this evening? That she could play mediator between him and his mother this time, and it might actually work?

That was foolish. Her ladyship hadn't said one word today about last night's events. Meanwhile, the servants said his lordship had slept until noon, and there'd been whispers about how he'd drunk himself into a stupor last night. Clearly neither he nor his mother was ready to be honest with each other.

It was driving Camilla mad. And Mr. Fowler's presence merely confused the matter. Perhaps that was why Pierce had invited the man—to escape discussion about anything weightier than the weather. Avoiding things did seem to be his favorite way of handling them.

She cast him a furtive glance from beneath her spectacles. Tonight he was playing Devil May Care Devonmont. He'd dressed more formally, in a tailcoat of black superfine, a waistcoat of white figured velvet, and silk breeches, looking fiendishly handsome as always. No sign of the conflicts that must have been raging within him showed in his faintly bored expression.

Her ladyship thrust her fork into a stewed cockle. "How lovely it is to have you here with us again, Mr. Fowler. It's been a couple of weeks, hasn't it?"

Mr. Fowler was finely dressed as well, though he looked nervous. That was understandable, given that he was dining with an earl and a dowager countess. "Yes, my lady, I believe so."

"And how are things at the manor house?" Camilla asked, to put him more at ease. "Did Mrs. Perkins get over her nasty cold?"

"She did indeed." He shot the countess a quick glance. "And she said she would send some of the maids to help the two of you with the booth at the fair tomorrow, if you need them."

"That's very kind of her," Lady Devonmont said, then added, under her breath, "and rather unexpected."

"Why unexpected?" Pierce asked in that low rumble of a voice that never failed to strum Camilla's senses.

Lady Devonmont stiffened but doggedly kept eating her cockles.

Since this wasn't the time or place to explain that the estrangement between her ladyship and his lordship was effectively carried on between the servants of the two houses, Camilla said hastily, "Because they're so much busier over there than we are here. The manor house is quite a bit larger, after all." She smiled at Mr. Fowler. "That's why it's so lovely of Mrs. Perkins to offer her help for the booth."

Mr. Fowler served himself some ham. "I confess that until she said it, I didn't even know that you ladies were having a booth. But I suppose I shouldn't be surprised. The fair has become quite a big undertaking this year. All the females in town are quite aflutter over it. Apparently some woman read a poem by an American fellow about hanging up stockings by the chimney for St. Nicholas. Now the ladies have all got it into their heads to make ornamental stockings for sale there."

Camilla blinked at him. Did he not realize the "woman" was his employer's mother? Oh, dear.

"This woman has got them convinced that hanging Christmas stockings will become all the rage," he went on in a faintly condescending tone. "An absurd notion that will never catch on."

Her ladyship's eyes narrowed on him. "How can you be so sure?"

"Because it's silly." Mr. Fowler cut his ham. "If people start hanging stockings, what will we have next—handkerchiefs hung by the staircase? Caps hung by the windows?"

"Mr. Fowler—" Camilla began.

Her ladyship cut her off. "It's no more silly than hanging dead tree branches in a hall, or dangling mistletoe from a ribbon and expecting people to kiss each other when they pass under it."

The oblivious Mr. Fowler lifted an eyebrow. "On the contrary, my lady, those are all time-honored ways to celebrate the season. But hanging a stocking is just doing laundry. Hardly festive, I should think."

Lady Devonmont blinked, then gave a rueful laugh. "You do have a point, Mr. Fowler. Though in truth, if you read the poem yourself, you might understand what a charming idea it is." Her eyes gleamed at him. "And why the woman in question is producing such stockings to raise money for refurbishing the church's organ."

"Wait, I thought that's what your booth—" Though he paled a little as the truth dawned on him, he fixed her with a steady gaze. "Forgive me, my lady. I see that I have inadvertently insulted you."

Her ladyship flushed at his gentlemanly apology. "On the contrary, sir. I confess to having a bit of fun at your expense, and it was very wrong of me." She flashed him a tentative smile. "But truly, I should read the poem for you later. You might find the custom of hanging stockings not quite so silly after hearing it described properly."

Beneath the warmth of her smile, he relaxed. "While that sounds enticing, I should much rather hear you play the pianoforte. You do it so well."

This time when the countess flushed, it was with pleasure. Camilla narrowed her gaze on Mr. Fowler. He'd asked her ladyship to play the last time he'd been here, too. And the time before. Her suspicions about how the man felt toward the countess grew stronger by the minute.

"I'm not the only one who plays the pianoforte," the countess pointed out.

"My playing is wretched and you know it," Camilla put in.

"Actually, I was speaking of Pierce. He used to play as a boy."

Pierce stiffened. "That was a long time ago, Mother. I'm sure we would all rather hear *you* play."

Lady Devonmont gazed softly at him. "You used to enjoy hearing the Sussex Waltz."

"I'd forgotten about that." Pierce sipped some wine.

"And as I recall, you played a livelier version of it than most."

"Your mother plays a livelier version of everything," Mr. Fowler put in. "She likes lively music. As do I."

"Is that why you always request that she play?" Camilla asked.

After a furtive glance at her ladyship, Mr. Fowler met Camilla's question with a smile. "I request that she play because then I know I will get to hear *you* sing, Mrs. Stuart."

"Oh, yes," Lady Devonmont chimed in. "You must sing, my dear."

"You must indeed." Mr. Fowler turned to Pierce. "You may not have discovered this yet, my lord, but Mrs. Stuart has the voice of a nightingale."

Pierce pinned her with his dark gaze. "I had no idea. Then we should definitely have a performance later."

Camilla stared at him, perplexed by the edge in his voice. "I'm always happy to entertain you, my lord. And Mr. Fowler, too, of course."

"Of course," Pierce echoed, his eyes boring into her. "I'm merely surprised I hadn't heard of this talent of yours before. But perhaps you save it for special guests, like Mr. Fowler."

What was *that* supposed to mean? "I save it for when I have accompaniment. You're always in such a hurry to leave us for your cigars in the evening that I never have the chance to offer."

"Well, then, I'll have to put off my cigar smoking tonight," he said tersely. "I don't want to miss hearing you sing."

"Oh, and Mr. Fowler, you must sing, too!" the countess exclaimed. She cast Pierce a bright smile. "Your estate manager is quite the fine tenor."

"Is he, indeed?" Pierce said, shooting Camilla another of those shuttered glances he kept throwing her way.

"He certainly is," his mother went on blithely. "When he and Camilla do duets, you'd think you were listening to paid opera singers in London."

"You would certainly know, Mother," Pierce snapped. "You went to opera houses plenty enough when I was in school. I was always reading about it in the papers."

As the countess paled, Camilla tensed, wondering if he was going to drag poor Mr. Fowler into his fight with his mother now. Then Pierce forced a smile and added, "My parents used to be such gadabouts, Mr. Fowler. I never knew when their escapades would turn up in the *Times*."

"I didn't have to worry about that with my parents," Mr. Fowler said amiably. "My mother was best known for her figgy pudding. It's hardly something to make the papers."

"Depends on what she did with her figgy pudding," Pierce said dryly. "If she shot it out of a cannon, I can guarantee it would make the papers."

They all laughed, breaking the tension. From there, the conversation drifted to a discussion of what was worthy of being mentioned in the papers.

With a relieved sigh, Camilla turned her attention to her dinner, hoping there would be no more crises. It was hard enough playing arbiter of the dispute between the countess and Pierce. She didn't think she could handle it if the estate manager jumped in, too.

Once again, Pierce felt like an intruder. Clearly Camilla, Mother, and Fowler had spent plenty of time in one another's company. They shared jokes he didn't understand, told tales about the servants that he'd never heard, and seemed quite at ease together. In the midst of so much camaraderie, how was he supposed to tell exactly how Camilla felt for Fowler?

She'd certainly dressed sumptuously for the man. Her dinner gown of rose satin was bedecked with puffy things around the skirt, and it had smaller puffy things at the bodice that drew attention to her ample bosom. So did the necklace of paste gems nestled between her lightly freckled breasts. She'd never worn that before. Or the gown, for that matter. Had she been saving it for Fowler?

If so, she'd made a good choice. Pierce couldn't stop looking at her, wondering what it would be like to lick his way down the smooth hollow between her breasts to find one taut nipple with his mouth—

Bloody hell. This was maddening.

He cast a furtive glance at Fowler, but the man was too polite to stare at Camilla's bosom. Fowler did glance at her a great deal, but he glanced at Mother a great deal, too. That proved nothing except that he was enjoying their "female companionship."

As for Camilla, Pierce could tell that she liked Fowler. She'd obviously tried to head the man off when he was blundering into insulting Mother. But was that just the act of a kind woman? Or a woman taking the side of a man she hoped to marry one day? She didn't seem to smile at Fowler with any particular regard, but could he trust that?

After all, Camilla was good at hiding her feelings. She had never once let on to Mother that she and Pierce were spending time together in secret every night.

So Camilla might be madly in love with Fowler and just being discreet. Though it was odd that she would choose discretion for something like that when she was never discreet about other things. Like her championing of Mother.

"What do you think, my lord?" Fowler asked, breaking into his tangled thoughts. "Shall we forget about our brandy and cigars for one night, and go right to the music?"

"Certainly," Pierce said.

He rose to help Camilla from her chair, but Fowler beat him there, damn his eyes. Pierce watched her face—she didn't blush as Fowler offered her his arm, but she did flash the man a soft glance as she clasped it. Something very disquieting settled in Pierce's chest.

Then belatedly he realized that he'd been left to accompany Mother into the drawing room. Bloody hell.

With a tightness in his throat, he offered her his arm. Only after she took it did he remember the last time he'd done so—at Father's funeral. With so many eyes on him, he'd been unable to avoid it. He'd been angry about it, since the last thing he'd wanted was to escort the woman who'd abandoned him.

But now that his heart had thawed a little toward her, he realized how hard it must have been for her to lose her husband of nearly thirty years. Had she cried at the funeral? He didn't know. He hadn't been able to see beneath her veil.

She'd trembled, though. He remembered that. And she was trembling now, too, her small hand gripping his arm as if she never wanted to let go.

Trying to ignore the childhood memories that her touch roused, he stared ahead to Fowler and Camilla, who was laughing at something Fowler said, her pretty face animated as she stared up at him.

Pierce scowled. "Is Mrs. Stuart sweet on Fowler?" he asked Mother in a low voice, unable to help himself. She was the only person who might know.

"Not to my knowledge," Mother said. "Why?"

He swiftly invented a reason. "Because if she marries him, he'll expect her to bear him a passel of children, which means she won't be around to keep you company anymore."

"I don't care about that," she surprised him by saying. "I want her to be happy. I'd be thrilled to see her find a man who loves her and wants to marry her. She deserves better than to be sitting around playing cards with a middle-aged woman."

She did; he just didn't want it to be Fowler. Because then he would have to see her on the man's arm at social affairs and be forced to endure them cooing at each other.

He snorted. Since he came here only when necessary, he would never see Fowler at social affairs. And somehow he couldn't imagine either of them "cooing." Though that didn't make the thought of Fowler with her any less disturbing.

Mother narrowed her eyes on the pair as they walked into the drawing room ahead of them. "But I think Mr. Fowler would be wrong for her."

So did Pierce, though he doubted his reasons would match Mother's. "Why? Because he's too old?"

She eyed him askance. "He's not too old—he's younger than I am."

Not by much. No, he'd better not say that.

"He's too cautious," she continued. "Not that Camilla is reckless, mind you, but she doesn't always follow society's dictates."

That was certainly an understatement.

She went on. "Mr. Fowler would hate that. He's always so circumspect."

"Not always," Pierce pointed out. "You certainly had him going there for a while tonight."

To his surprise, Mother looked ashamed. "I know. It was very bad of me. I just get annoyed when men are so firm in their opinions."

"I remember," he said softly, thinking of the fierce arguments between her and his father.

Her gaze darted to him, then returned to Camilla and Fowler. "But Mr. Fowler deserves better from me. He's generally a nice man." Mother's voice grew curiously taut. "Even if he is overly aware of what's appropriate for his station."

They'd reached the drawing room. It was only after Mother left Pierce's side to go to the pianoforte that he realized he'd just had a fairly normal conversation with her without Camilla acting as a guide and buffer.

How had that happened?

"All right," Mother said to Fowler as she sat down before the instrument and took out a piece of music. "I know how you scoff at it, sir, but the two of you *must* sing 'The Gallant Hussar.' Otherwise, I shall be very disappointed."

Camilla laughed, then released Fowler's arm to begin hunting through the music atop the pianoforte. "You'll have your wish, madam, but only if I get mine.

We must sing a few Christmas carols." She smiled at Pierce. "That way his lordship can join in."

"Not me." Pierce dropped into a chair. "I make a better audience than I do performer."

"Come now, my lord." Camilla shoved up her spectacles. "It doesn't matter how well you sing. It's all in good fun."

Fowler shot Pierce a quick, apologetic glance. "I think his lordship isn't fond of Christmas carols."

"Oh," Camilla said, awareness dawning on her face. Obviously she was remembering that he'd spent all his holidays without his parents. "Well, then, in that case—"

"It's fine," Pierce ground out, chafing at being the object of her pity. "I enjoy hearing a carol as well as the next person. I just don't want to sing any." He glanced at Mother. "Besides, it's been a while since I heard Mother play, and I can't enjoy it if I'm up there caterwauling."

Surprisingly, he really was looking forward to it. Now that he knew he'd misread so much of his parents' relationship, he was finding a sort of pleasurable pain in reliving the past and trying to make out what he might have misunderstood. And part of that past had included Mother playing carols on the pianoforte.

Once the music started, however, it wasn't Mother's playing that he noticed but Camilla's singing. Fowler had been wrong. She wasn't a nightingale at all, a comparison often used for those preening sopranos at the opera house. No, Camilla was a siren . . . with a contralto so rich and sultry that it made those sopranos' voices sound like screeching.

And expressive! She swept him up in the tale of a woman who begs her soldier love to let her go off to war with him. Fowler took the part of the Hussar and Camilla took the part of Jane, the maiden, and for the length of the song, Pierce could easily believe they were lovers.

Too easily. When Fowler gazed down into Camilla's face as he sang of "her beautiful features," Pierce wanted to throttle him. Nor did the song end tragically, as so many of the broadside ballads did—this one had Jane and her gallant Hussar heading off to the war "united forever."

It was churlish, but he wished Jane and her Hussar to the devil, especially when Camilla and Fowler blended their voices so splendidly for the final verse that anyone, even a man as jaded as himself, would want to weep from the beauty of it. Despite Mother's opinion, it appeared to him that Fowler and Camilla made a perfect pair, damn them.

As the last notes died, he forced himself to applaud. They deserved it, even if he resented the fact that Fowler had gained so much enjoyment from joining his voice to hers.

Then Camilla smiled warmly at Pierce in response,

and somehow that calmed his agitation. For the moment, anyway.

"So tell me, Fowler," Pierce said, "why does my mother say you scoff at this particular song?"

"I don't scoff at it," Fowler protested. "I just think any soldier who contemplates taking his true love off to war with him is a fool. Don't you agree?"

Pierce shrugged. "Depends on which war. If they're just going to be marching up and down some Belgian town, he might do well having a woman to cook and clean for him."

As Fowler laughed, Camilla frowned at Pierce. "Is that the only thing you think a woman is good for—cooking and cleaning?"

"And providing entertainment," he drawled, thinking ahead to when she would come to his room later. *If* she would come, with Fowler hanging about. When she blushed, he added, in a tone of pure innocence, "As you're doing here . . . with the singing."

Camilla eyed him askance. "And where does love come in? Can't the Hussar just want Jane with him because he loves her?"

Pierce snorted. "Love is for children and fools. No grown man with an ounce of sense makes monumental decisions based on some half-baked sentiment he read on a St. Valentine's Day card." He certainly didn't give up everything for it.

"*I'm* a grown man," Fowler put in solemnly. "And I spent many happy years in love with my wife." He cast a furtive glance over to where Camilla stood beside Mother. "That's why I would do almost anything for another chance at love."

The bottom dropped out of Pierce's stomach. At least now he had his answer from Fowler. "What about you, Mrs. Stuart?" he asked, fighting to ignore his visceral reaction. "You were married. Do *you* want another chance at love?"

Though she flinched at his veiled reference to her loveless marriage, she answered with great gravity. "Of course, my lord. A life without love is like a voice without a tune to sing. No grown *woman* with an ounce of sense wants to go on without love. Not if she can help it . . . not if she can catch that elusive tune. Sadly, not everyone can."

Silence fell on the room as every eye turned to Pierce. But for once, he was at a loss for a snappy rejoinder.

To his surprise, it was Mother who jumped in to save him. "Are we going to sing Christmas carols, or not? I believe we should start with 'The Cherry Tree Carol.' Don't you agree, Pierce?"

He demurred but didn't hear the rest of the discussion, his mind whirling around Camilla's words. A life without love. He'd had that, and he'd once thought himself fortunate to escape the emotional dramatics that plagued a life *with* love.

Now he wasn't so sure. And the fact that she made him doubt it irked him.

So did the possibility that she hoped to find love with Fowler. She didn't belong with Fowler. It would be a mistake. And it was high time he made her see that.

14

Her ladyship had retired at last, so Camilla went up to kiss the sleeping Jasper before heading for Pierce's room. It was later than usual, so she wasn't even sure that Pierce would want her there this evening. But she had to make sure, in case their bargain from the previous nights held firm.

She snorted. Right. Their bargain was why she couldn't wait to see him alone, why she couldn't breathe for the thought of being with him. What a fool she was. But she couldn't help it. He'd looked so unsure of himself when they'd spoken of love; it broke her heart.

She quickened her steps, but as she reached the floor where the bedchambers were she heard a faint sound wafting up from the drawing room. It was the pianoforte.

Had the countess roused again in the brief time Camilla had darted up to kiss Jasper? Was she unable to sleep? If so, Camilla dared not go to Pierce. She couldn't take the chance of her ladyship wanting her and not being able to find her.

She hurried down to the drawing room to investigate, then halted abruptly as she entered. The earl himself was playing the instrument. And doing it extremely well, too.

"I assume that Mother has gone to bed," Pierce said without looking up from the music.

"Yes." She closed the door. "Aren't you worried she'll hear you?"

"Not likely. This house is sturdy, and the master bedchambers are at the other end. When I was a boy, Mother used to play sometimes while Father was sleeping. He never heard."

"Is that when you learned to play? While your father slept?"

His jaw went taut. "Occasionally."

When he kept on playing, she edged behind the pianoforte so she could watch his fingering. "You're very good."

He shrugged. "It's what I do to relax. I have an excellent instrument in my London town house."

"Does this mean you're planning to provide tonight's entertainment?" she said lightly. "Or are we going upstairs?"

"Neither." He stopped playing to stare up at her intently. "I want you to sing for me."

That startled her. "Your mother will surely hear *that*."

"If she does, she'll figure that you're playing and singing for yourself."

"Or she'll come to see why I'm still up and find us here together."

"And what if she does?" A faint smile touched his lips. "Surely we can be allowed to entertain ourselves in the drawing room after she's in bed."

"Is there some reason you suddenly don't mind if she finds us alone together?"

He stared steadily at her. "Is there some reason you suddenly *do* mind singing for me?"

"No. Why would there be?"

A shadow crossed his face, and his voice turned bitter. "Perhaps it's something you only save for when Fowler is around."

She blinked. He'd made a similar remark at dinner. At the time, she hadn't thought much of it, but now . . . "Don't be absurd. Why would I do that?"

"I don't know." Pushing the bench out, he rose to stand near her, his expression stormy. "Why did you never once offer to sing to me for our evenings together?"

"For obvious reasons." She gazed up into his glittering

eyes. "If I sang to you upstairs, your mother would definitely hear. Her room is near enough to yours for that."

Her logic seemed to catch him off guard. Then he leaned against the pianoforte with a scowl. "Perhaps, but why didn't you ever even mention that you could sing? That you could do it so well?"

Pleasure that he liked her singing warred with confusion over this peculiar conversation. "It never came up. Why didn't *you* ever mention that you play the pianoforte?"

He crossed his arms over his chest. "It's not the sort of thing a man admits. It's not the sort of thing a man *does*."

"Nonsense. Men play instruments all the time." When he glanced away, a muscle ticking in his jaw, she added, "Ah, but not earls, I suppose. Not often, anyway."

His gaze shot back to her. "No, not often. Not when their fathers think it's *dandyish*."

Her heart caught in her throat. "I'm beginning to hate your father."

"You wouldn't be the only one." Narrowing his gaze on her, he added, "So your refusal to sing for me has nothing to do with Fowler." He bent close and lowered his voice to a hiss. "Nothing to do with how he looks at you. How he speaks of you."

Confused by the anger in his voice, she stared up into his finely etched features. "How *does* he look at me?"

"As if you're the answer to all his loneliness."

And that's when it hit her. "You think Mr. Fowler . . . and I . . ." She laughed. "You're quite mad, you know. He's twenty years older than I, at least."

Apparently he didn't share her amusement, for all he did was glare at her. "Some women like older men. And I can see why the attentions of a man like him would be appealing to—"

"A mere lady's companion?" Her temper flared. "An orphan?"

"A widow from a loveless marriage who wants to, as you put it, 'catch that elusive tune.' He practically said he's in search of love, so I can see how you might fancy yourself in love with him, too."

"Oh, you can, can you?" she said tartly.

"But it would be wrong, the two of you."

She stared at him, not sure what to make of his new concern that she might "fancy" herself "in love" with Mr. Fowler. She could think of only two reasons he might feel that way—one was insulting, the other intriguing. She was almost afraid to find out which.

But she had to know. "Are you worried that I might leave your employ to marry Mr. Fowler, forcing you to find another companion for her ladyship?"

"No!" he said, the look of outrage on his face relieving her. "I'm speaking to you as a friend, that's all."

"A friend," she echoed. "Are we friends?"

That took him aback. "I thought we were."

"I see. So you, as my *friend,* think me and Mr. Fowler wrong for each other."

"Exactly."

"Do you have any particular reason for feeling so? Since you think his age isn't a problem?"

Glancing away, he threaded his fingers through his hair. "I didn't say it wasn't a problem—just that you might not consider it so yourself."

"If I'm not bothered by it, then I don't see why it should concern *you.*"

"It's not just his age," he grumbled. "The two of you wouldn't suit. He's too straitlaced. And you're too . . . too . . ."

"Wild?" she said archly.

"Of course not," he snapped. "But you have life and vitality. He would crush it in his attempt to make you respectable."

"How odd—I thought I was already respectable," she said, beginning to enjoy his discomfiture.

He let out a low oath. "I didn't mean it like that. I meant—"

"That I shouldn't have a life beyond being companion to your mother."

"Damn it, no!" When she couldn't resist a laugh, he frowned at her. "You're enjoying this."

"I certainly am. So far you haven't given one sensible reason that I should *not* marry Mr. Fowler."

His frown deepened to a glower. "You're considering it?"

"You seem to think I am."

"Tell me the truth—do you and Mr. Fowler have an understanding?"

"If we do, why do you care?" she countered. If her suspicions were correct and he was actually jealous of the man, she wanted to hear him admit it. And without this nonsense about his concern for her "as a friend."

But she could tell from the sudden chill in his expression that he was withdrawing. "I wouldn't want to see you make a mistake."

"Because you're so selfless."

He flinched. "Because he's wrong for you."

"So you say." She turned for the door. "I suppose that means I shouldn't invite you to the wedding."

He caught her by the arm and tugged her back around to face him. "Don't marry Fowler, damn it!"

She thrust her face up to his. "Give me one good reason—one *genuine* reason—why I shouldn't."

Something dark and feral flickered in his gaze. Then he said, in a low, guttural voice, "Because I don't want you to."

And while she was still reeling from that incredible admission, he brought his mouth down on hers.

Her heart soared as he kissed her in a fever of need that mirrored her own. Even though she knew how mad it was to let this go so far, she couldn't help but respond. They'd spent the last week dancing around their attraction to each other, trying to shove it into a closet. But it kept creeping out when they least expected it, and she was tired of it.

She wanted him. Some part of him clearly wanted her. And for once, she was going to let herself enjoy being desired by a man.

His kisses were so hot, so deep . . . so lovely that she let them carry her where they would. He took her mouth with what felt like possessiveness, even though she knew he wasn't the possessive sort. But apparently he could be jealous, which astonished her. She hadn't thought he cared even that much.

After several long, mesmerizing kisses, he tore his mouth free to growl, "Promise me you won't marry Fowler."

She drew back to stare at him, amazed. He was serious. Even after the way she'd let him kiss her, he still thought . . . He really was so oblivious sometimes. She wanted to laugh, but the part of her that ached for him settled for teasing him.

"Convince me not to," she said.

He dragged in a harsh breath. Then without warning, he grabbed her by the waist and lifted her atop the pianoforte so forcefully that her spectacles fell off. Music skittered to the floor but she didn't even notice, for he was kissing her again, pressing his body into hers, parting her legs until he was plastered so close against her she could feel his arousal.

A thrill shot through her. She slid her hands inside his coat, wanting to be closer to him, and when the silk of his waistcoat thwarted her, she slipped her hands up beneath it. Feeling his muscles flex and tighten through his shirt, she explored them shamelessly. His mouth grew almost savage.

He kissed gloriously . . . ravenously, as if he couldn't sate his need. He covered her breasts through her gown, kneading, rubbing, teasing her mercilessly. It wasn't nearly enough, so when he brought one hand behind her to loosen her gown, she didn't protest.

He tore his lips free to rake kisses down the arch of her throat. She knew where he was headed. And she couldn't wait for him to get there.

Just as her gown came free, she lifted her bosom to him. With a groan that showed he knew what she wanted, he dragged the fabric down so he could get to her corset cups and chemise and pull them below her breasts.

"Pierce . . ." she whispered. "Sweet heaven, Pierce . . ."

"I've wanted to do this all night," he murmured as he drank in the sight of her bosom bared to him. His dark eyes were alight, hungry. "Every time you drew breath to sing, I wanted to put my mouth right here." He pressed his lips to the top of one breast. "And here." He kissed his way down the slope. "And here."

At last, he closed his mouth over her nipple and sucked.

It was wonderful. *Wonderful.* She clasped his head close, burying her fingers in his silky hair as he tongued her nipples, first one, then the other, playing with them so deliciously that she thought she might lose her mind. Kenneth had never spent time on her breasts. She'd had no idea they could provide such a feast of sensation.

Drawing back to stare at her, he murmured, "Have I convinced you now?"

"Perhaps a little," she teased.

A storm spread over his brow as he caught her at the waist and pulled her against him. "If you think I shall stand by and watch while Fowler—"

She began to laugh. She couldn't help it. "He doesn't . . . he doesn't even *want* me . . . you fool," she managed to gasp between laughs.

"You're wrong. You may not want him, but he definitely wants you. It was you he wanted to hear sing. It was you he was looking down at when he spoke so feelingly of love."

"Think, Pierce," she said as she stroked his hair. "Who was sitting right next to me on that bench?"

He blinked. "Mother?" Shock filled his face. "Oh, God."

"He's nearly her age. He always asks her to play when he comes here, and he always worries about her. *She's* the one he's sweet on."

With his hands still on her waist, Pierce glanced away, a frown knitting his brow. "But he's an estate manager and she's—"

"A countess, yes. Why do you think he keeps his feelings so close to his chest? I don't even know if she returns them. But I suspect that won't stop him from wanting her."

"Wait a minute." Pierce swung his narrowing gaze to her. "You knew all along he felt that way."

She caught her breath. Uh-oh. She'd been found out. "I might have . . . guessed, yes."

"Yet you let me go on and on about his wanting to marry you." He scowled. "I never took you for a coquette."

"That's because I've never been one before." She felt giddy. Who could have dreamed it would be so delightful to tease a man? "I never took you for the jealous sort."

"I'm not." At her raised eyebrow, he admitted sullenly, "Or at least I haven't been until now."

She eyed him skeptically. "Never?"

"Never. There was no need." He drew himself up. "I'm considered something of a catch."

"I am well aware of that," she said dryly. "You forget that I've read all about you in the papers."

That seemed to bring him up short. "I'm not as bad as they make me out to be."

"Says the man who already has me half naked in a drawing room."

His gaze drifted down to her breasts and grew heated once more. "Do you mind?" He reached for her hem with both hands and began dragging her gown up her legs.

Her silly pulse jumped. "No." She shivered as his fingers passed her garters to brush naked flesh. "I should. But I don't."

"I did warn you that if you gave me an inch . . ."

"Yes, you did," she rasped, looping her arms about his neck. "So now you may take a mile or two if you like."

That was all the encouragement he seemed to need to slide his hands up her thighs until he found the damp, aching center of her. He rubbed her there, his thumb working magic on the very sensitive spot Kenneth had always ignored.

But when he slipped two fingers inside her, she gasped, taken by surprise.

"God, dearling," he choked out, "you're so warm and tight."

"It's been a long time," she admitted.

Her eyes slid closed as he fondled her with a fervor she'd never known from her late husband. Oh, what an amazing feeling . . . She'd had no idea.

Pierce bent to whisper hoarsely in her ear, "I want to see you come. I want to see you break apart in my hands, right here in this drawing room. And then I want to take you upstairs to my bed and have my wicked way with you."

"What if I . . . don't wish to go?" she asked, though she did. Rather fervently.

"Then I'll have to convince you, won't I?" he said, his breath coming heavier now.

So was hers. She couldn't find it, couldn't catch it. A slow heat was building between her legs that made her squirm and ache, made her press herself harder against his hand.

He responded by increasing the pressure of his caresses, quickening the rhythm until she was writhing atop the pianoforte, shamelessly riding his hand. It began like ripples on water, sensation building on sensation until suddenly it erupted like the hot springs at Bath. She gripped him to her with a little cry that he silenced with his mouth.

It was like nothing she'd ever known. Was that what he'd meant by wanting to see her "break apart"? Because if so, he'd gotten his wish. She felt broken open, exposed to him in the most intimate way a woman could be.

His mouth on hers was intense, eager, even as her own desire ebbed a little. He tore his lips free to murmur, "Come to my bed, Camilla. I can't bear it anymore. And I want privacy for all the things I want to do to you. With you."

"All right," she whispered, still insensible of anything but how perfect it felt to be in his arms.

He tugged her off the pianoforte and began to

help her repair her clothes. She couldn't believe she was doing this, preparing to go to his bed, but she was tired of fighting her own urges, tired of being near him yet not *with* him.

It didn't even matter anymore that they would only be lovers. If she could have him for a brief while . . . "Do I look presentable enough?" she asked as she tucked a strand of hair back into her coiffure.

He bent to pick up her spectacles, which had landed on the floor. "I doubt we'll come across anyone this late," he murmured as he settled them on her nose. "Besides, I'm just going to tear your clothes off as soon as we're in the room."

The excitement that bolted through her leveled all her doubts. She'd never had a man desire her so fiercely—it was incredibly enticing.

They headed for the door and were a short distance from it when it opened.

To her horror, a small voice said, "You didn't put me to bed, Mama, and then I got up to use the chamber pot and Maisie was asleep and you were gone and . . ."

Jasper trailed off as he saw Pierce. "Oh no," he whispered, his eyes wide. "I woke up the great earl."

15

Pierce just stood there, shocked. A small, brown-haired, blue-eyed boy was standing in his drawing room, wearing a nightshirt and clutching something in both fists. And he was looking at Pierce as if he'd just seen the devil himself.

Then he began to cry. "M-Mama!" he blubbered. "I–I don't want to be s-sent away!"

Camilla hurried to his side and caught him up in her arms. "It's all right," she said soothingly as she pressed his head to her shoulder. "I'm sure it will be fine, muffin, just fine."

She wouldn't meet Pierce's eyes. She just kept cradling the boy, whose little frame shook from the force of his fear.

"Your son, I take it," Pierce managed to croak.

Oh, God, she had a child whom she'd hidden from him. And here he'd been thinking that he meant something to her, that they meant something to each other, when all the while . . .

"Don't let the g-great earl send me away!" the boy wailed, and Pierce got ahold of himself. At the moment this concerned a child, and only a child.

A child who was Camilla's *son*, for God's sake.

"No one will send you away, lad," Pierce said hoarsely.

The boy stopped crying to peer at him through red-rimmed eyes. "But . . . but her l-ladyship said I h-had to keep out of s-sight or—"

"Mother knew?" Pierce asked Camilla, his chest tightening painfully. "You've both been keeping this from me?"

Camilla's gaze shot to him at last, a look of pure panic in her eyes. "Please, you have to understand." Hitching the boy higher on one hip, she clutched him close as if he might be snatched from her at any moment. "I needed to work to support Jasper, and my employers expected me to be unencumbered, so I always told them I was. Then I sent Jasper to live with Kenneth's brother and his wife."

"They don't like me," the boy muttered.

"That's not true, Jasper," Camilla chided gently. She met Pierce's gaze. "They're very Scottish, you see, and very religious. And they already had three young children of their own." She stroked the lad's curls. "But even so, I wouldn't have brought him here if your mother hadn't found out about him and asked me to."

"*Mother* asked you to bring a child here?" he echoed, incredulous. She wouldn't keep her own son, but she'd had some stranger's boy brought to Montcliff?

"Yes," Camilla said warily, no doubt guessing the source of his incredulity. "Why do you think it was so hard for me to believe that she could ever have been cruel to you? She's been very kind to me and Jasper."

He took a step toward them, and the lad squealed and grabbed his mother. "It's all right, lad. I won't hurt you." He glared at Camilla. "What the devil have you been telling him about me?"

"You're the g-great earl," Jasper whispered, his eyes wide with fright. "I'm not s-supposed to let the great earl see me, or I'll be s-sent away."

"You won't be sent away," Pierce bit out. When the boy flinched, he modulated his tone. "No one will send you away from your mother, boy, least of all me." He cast Camilla a hard look. "I can't imagine why you would tell him such a thing."

She lifted her chin. "Mr. Fowler was very clear

in my interview—he said that you required that I be childless," she said defensively. "I needed the position. I wasn't about to tell him I had a little boy."

"Well, I don't know why he would think—" He groaned. "Damn. It must have been the day we talked about children. I let it slip that I didn't intend to have any. Since I didn't want to elaborate on why, I told him some nonsense about not liking them."

When Jasper looked horrified at the thought, Pierce caught the boy's gaze and said firmly, "But I never meant that last part." He shifted his gaze back to Camilla. "And I never gave Fowler any specific rule about not having children on the estate, either, I swear. He came to that conclusion on his own."

Great God, they must have been keeping it secret from Fowler, too. From the beginning? How had they managed it?

Then something else occurred to him. "It was Jasper I heard yesterday in the drawing room."

Swallowing hard, Camilla nodded. "We had to send him off with Maisie in a bit of a hurry. You gave us quite a fright coming home early."

The thought of the two women living in fear that he might send the lad off made his heart wrench in his chest. "Do *all* the servants know?"

"Just the ones here. We dared not tell anyone else, for fear that Mr. Fowler would find out. And as you may have noticed, there's a bit of rivalry between the manor servants and the dower house servants, so the latter were more than happy to keep the secret."

He hadn't noticed any rivalry. Bloody hell, he was oblivious. He'd been thinking he had a firm grasp on everything regarding his estate, not to mention his life and his relationship with Mother, when the truth was, he didn't know a damned thing.

Even Camilla was a stranger to him again. But despite the betrayal he felt over the secret she'd been keeping from him, he couldn't blame her. At least she fought for her son. It was more than he could say for his own mother.

Except that Mother had fought for *this* boy. Pierce didn't know whether to resent her or respect her for that.

The boy was staring at him less fearfully now. "So you're not . . . going to send me away?"

"No," he managed to say past the lump in his throat. Memories of that day in the carriage with Titus swamped him. Jasper couldn't be much younger than he'd been, and he remembered only too well how much it had ached to be separated from his parents. "You're safe here, Jasper. It is Jasper, right?"

The lad bobbed his head.

"How old are you, lad?"

Jasper glanced to his mother, and she nodded encouragement. His eyes still held a hint of wariness as he stared up at Pierce. "I'm six and three-quarters."

Pierce bit back a smile. "As old as all that, are you?" He ventured nearer, relieved when Jasper didn't recoil from him. He kept his voice soft and unthreatening. "What's that in your hands?"

Jasper eyed him a long moment before opening them to show three tin soldiers in each. "Her ladyship said that for every day I kept out of sight, I could have one. I've got seven now." He frowned. "Well, six. I lost one yesterday."

The lump in Pierce's throat thickened. "Here in the drawing room." It took all his effort not to react to the fact that his mother had been giving this lad *his* soldiers. It wasn't as if he needed them anymore.

Camilla's gaze on him softened, became apologetic. "She said there were a lot. I hope you don't mind."

"Of course I don't mind." Somehow he forced humor into his voice. "I'm a bit old for them now, don't you think?"

Jasper hesitantly held out a hand. "If you want, you can have one of mine. I can share."

The peace offering from a reluctant six-year-old was nearly more than he could take. "You keep them," he rasped. "You've been a brave lad, and you deserve them."

That actually got a smile out of the cherub. And he really was a cherub, with reddish-brown curls and sky-blue eyes that saw too much. Rather like his mother's.

"What do you say?" Camilla prompted.

"Thank you, sir," he mumbled.

"You call him 'my lord,' dearest," she corrected him.

"'Sir' is fine," Pierce interjected.

Jasper gave a big yawn, and Camilla looked at Pierce. "I should probably put him back in bed."

Pierce nodded. My God, what a nightmare it would have been if the lad had wandered in while they were in the midst of . . . "You should stay with him," he said gruffly, even as his body still ached for her. "He needs you right now."

The grateful look in her eyes cut him to the soul. "Thank you."

She had already started for the door when the boy said, "Wait! I got to ask the great earl something."

Pierce went up to them. "What is it, lad?"

"You're more important than Mr. Fowler, right?"

Pierce stifled a smile. "You could say that."

Jasper tipped up his chin in an unconscious imitation of his mother's usual gesture of defiance. "So if Mother and me and her ladyship wanted to go to the fair tomorrow, you could tell Mr. Fowler it was all right, and we could go."

Camilla sighed. "Jasper heard me tell your mother that we couldn't take him there because Mr. Fowler might see."

"But her ladyship *said* we could go, before Mother said we couldn't," Jasper went on in a rush, "and I really, really *want* to go, in case they have a sleigh there. I want to see a sleigh, and the fair is tomorrow, and—"

"I'll tell Mr. Fowler myself that you're allowed to go anywhere you wish. You needn't worry about that."

The beaming smile that spread over Jasper's face made Pierce's heart tighten. It was so easy to please a child. And yet so easy to bring his world crashing down around his ears, too.

"Are *you* going, my lord?" When Pierce stiffened, Jasper added hastily, "Because if *you* went, Mr. Fowler couldn't do anything to stop it. And none of the boys would bother me or Mother."

"What boys are bothering you and your mother?" Pierce asked, more fiercely than he'd intended.

"He's thinking of London," Camilla explained. "You know how it can be in the city for a woman and a boy alone—just the usual nonsense. But nothing has happened here. Jasper hasn't even been to town yet, because I didn't dare risk his being seen by Mr. Fowler. I'm sure everyone in Stocking Pelham will be perfectly polite."

"Especially if *you* went with us," Jasper persisted.

"Jasper!" his mother chided. "His lordship has more important things to do than to squire you to a fair."

"Do you want me to go?" Pierce heard himself ask.

The boy's eyes lit up. "That would *grand*."

"Really, you don't have to," Camilla put in hastily, her voice low. "It's kind enough of you to overlook the fact that—"

"It's not kind of me," he clipped out. "It's the right thing."

She dropped her gaze. "Of course."

He hated seeing her so cautious around him, so worried that he would somehow send her boy away from her. *Him,* of all people. She ought to know better.

"We'll all go, Jasper," he said, though it also meant spending the day in Mother's company. "We'll leave first thing in the morning—you, me, your mother, and her ladyship."

"And Maisie, too?" Jasper asked, rubbing his sleepy eyes.

"Jasper!" her mother said, obviously exasperated.

Pierce couldn't help laughing. The lad was certainly adept at getting what he wanted. "Maisie, too."

"I'm so sorry, my lord," Camilla said. "I swear, I don't know what's gotten into him."

"Don't apologize," he said, hating how formal she was being with him, but understanding why. "He's a good lad and deserves a reward."

Even if it meant that Pierce spent a day in hell.

"Thank you," she said softly. "You have no idea what it means to me. And to him."

He stared at her. "I have some idea, believe me."

She flushed. "Forgive me for not trusting you with the truth. You deserved better."

"It's all right—I understand. When a child is involved, nothing can be left to chance."

A sweet smile, the very twin to her son's, spread over her face. When she glanced down at Jasper, who'd fallen asleep on her shoulder, her expression grew pensive. "My lord, I think perhaps it would be better if after this we did not . . ."

"I know." She had come to her senses, realized how unwise it would be for her to share his bed when she had her son to consider. Not that he relished the idea of making love to her, knowing that she'd be doing it out of gratitude for his not sending her son away. But he still wanted . . . still yearned . . .

It didn't matter what he wanted. The boy was what mattered at the moment. "Besides," Pierce added with a forced smile, "you have an early day ahead of you tomorrow. I believe Mother mentioned that the two of you had to be at the fair with the servants to help set up the booth."

"Yes, we do. Thank you for understanding."

But as she left the room with her lad in her arms, he realized he didn't care if she had a son. He didn't care that it meant she might be looking for a husband, something he didn't intend to be to *anyone,* even her. Nor did he care that getting intimately involved with a woman in her situation was unwise at best and dangerous at worst.

Like the devil that he was, he still wanted her in his bed.

The question was, what the bloody hell was he going to do about it?

16

At seven the next morning, Camilla hurried a very excited Jasper down the stairs. She was already late—her ladyship had risen at six and was hoping to leave by seven thirty. But wrangling a six-year-old into his first skeleton suit took some doing, even for a woman who'd done it countless times with young lads in the orphanage. And Maisie hadn't been able to help, because she was busy helping her ladyship.

The countess met them at the bottom, a look of worry on her face.

Camilla immediately launched into an apology. "I know we're running late. Do Jasper and I have time for breakfast?"

"Of course, my dear. It's going to be a long day, so he definitely needs fortification." She took his other hand as they started for the breakfast room. "But are you sure you understood Pierce correctly? He doesn't mind about Jasper?"

This morning, Camilla had given her ladyship a highly edited version of the previous night's events, leaving out all the parts about Pierce's jealousy of Mr. Fowler and . . . other things.

"His lordship agreed to take us to town for the fair," Camilla said. "I'd say that's a strong indication that he doesn't mind."

And that still surprised her. Pierce had been so good, so kind to her son. Given his look of shock and betrayal when Jasper first appeared in the drawing room, Pierce's behavior was nothing short of astonishing. How she wished she'd confided in him sooner. But then, until last night she hadn't realized that he cared for her even a little. Or that she would have learned to care for him, too. That she might consider doing something as reckless as going to his bed.

A blush heated her cheeks. For pity's sake, Jasper had nearly found them together! That would have been horrible.

At least the near miss had brought her to her senses. Or as much of her senses as weren't still aching for him. He made her blood sing, and that had never happened to her before. The part of her that yearned for more in her life was desperate for the next time they could be alone together.

I want to see you come. I want to see you break apart in my hands, right here in this drawing room. And then I want to take you upstairs to my bed and have my wicked way with you.

She shivered every time she thought of it. Every time she thought of *him*. How he'd touched her. How he'd stoked a fire that Kenneth had never even acknowledged was there.

But she couldn't take a lover, not with Jasper to think about. What if she found herself pregnant again? It didn't bear thinking on.

They entered the breakfast room to find Pierce standing by the sideboard. As he turned to smile at her, her heart gave a ridiculous leap. He'd never joined them for breakfast before—he'd either had a tray brought to his room or waited to eat until he'd gone over to the manor house to handle estate business. Was this all for her and Jasper's benefit?

If so, it made her absurdly happy, especially when he trailed his admiring gaze down her lavender-blue morning dress. She was so glad she'd taken extra care with her appearance this morning, even adding a few sprigs of holly to her hair.

And he looked rather fine himself, in a morning suit of bottle-green cashmere with a striped waistcoat and Hessian boots polished to a high sheen. She hoped the snow had melted enough so he wouldn't ruin them, for they looked costly.

The moment Jasper spotted the earl, he let out a cry of surprise and went running up to the man as if they were grand friends. "Good morning, sir!"

Pierce ruffled Jasper's hair. "Good morning, lad. You're looking very well."

"Mama said I had to wear my new clothes." He pouted as he scratched one leg. "They itch."

Camilla sighed. Jasper had only just gotten too old for skirts, and he wasn't fond of being buttoned up tight.

"I wore a skeleton suit, too, when I was your age," Pierce said confidentially. "You'll get used to it. And only big boys wear breeches, so when they see you in your new clothes in town, they'll be impressed by how old you are."

"I hadn't thought of that." Jasper glanced at Pierce's Hessians. "They'd really be impressed if I wore boots like you, sir. And I'd be ever so much *taller.*"

"You would indeed," Pierce said with a chuckle. "Although you'd be even taller if I did this." And without warning he hoisted Jasper up onto his shoulders.

Jasper squealed with delight as he grabbed the earl's head. "Look, Mama, at how tall I am!"

"Yes, very tall indeed," Camilla managed through the lump in her throat as Pierce marched about the room with him. Pierce looked as carefree as she'd ever seen him, his eyes twinkling and his face wreathed in smiles as he hefted Jasper off his shoulders and into a chair at the table.

"Oh, Lord," Camilla murmured to her ladyship. "I believe we've opened a Pandora's box by introducing them to each other."

"I don't know," Lady Devonmont said softly. "Pierce hasn't looked this happy since he was a boy. Perhaps it will be good for him."

Perhaps so, but it could be very difficult for Jasper. Pierce might not even stay at the dower house beyond today. And if Jasper grew attached to him—

"You do have a winter coat, don't you?" Pierce bent to ask Jasper.

"Oh, yes, my lord," Jasper said as a footman placed a full plate of food in front of him. "Her ladyship bought it for me. It has fur on the inside and everything."

"That sounds warm enough," Pierce said, slanting an enigmatic glance at his mother. "I hope she bought a hat and gloves for you, too."

Annoyed that he might think she and Jasper had been taking advantage of his mother, Camilla stepped in. "Her ladyship has been very kind, but I supplied those items myself. I do look after my son."

"Of course," Pierce said.

"Good morning, everyone," said a deep voice from the doorway.

Camilla's stomach clenched. What was Mr. Fowler doing here?

"Ah, Fowler, there you are!" Pierce said, keeping one hand on Jasper's shoulder. Jasper's eyes widened in alarm, but before he could say a word, Pierce added, "Let me introduce you to my young friend, Jasper Stuart. Master Jasper, this is Mr. Fowler, my estate manager."

As Jasper mumbled a greeting, with his small brow creased in a frown, Camilla watched Fowler. Oddly, he betrayed no surprise. "Good morning, Master Jasper. His lordship was telling me all about you earlier."

Pierce had risen that early? Heavens.

"It seems I've been remiss in welcoming you to Montcliff," the man went on, his cool, remote tone belying his genial words. Camilla tensed. No doubt Pierce had lectured him about his stringent rules. She had better tread carefully.

"Of course," Mr. Fowler continued, "if I'd known of your presence here, I wouldn't have been so remiss." But it wasn't Camilla he glanced darkly at. It was her ladyship. "Apparently, I wasn't to be trusted with such a valuable secret."

Lady Devonmont flushed. "I've learned through the years to be careful whom I trust with valuable secrets, sir. So has Camilla. And you mustn't blame her. It was my idea to bring the boy here and my idea to keep him to ourselves."

Anger flared briefly in Mr. Fowler's features before he masked it. "I don't blame Mrs. Stuart." He tore his gaze from the countess. "I don't blame anyone. I was merely making an observation."

Into the heightened tension came Jasper's small voice. "We're going to the fair today, Mr. Fowler. Are you going, too?"

Mr. Fowler drew himself up with a sort of stiff pride. "I wouldn't wish to intrude."

"Nonsense," her ladyship said, her color deepening. "It's no intrusion. We'd be quite pleased if you would join us. Wouldn't we, Camilla?"

"Of course. Do come with us, sir."

He tipped his head at Camilla, carefully avoiding her ladyship's gaze. "Very well. Given such a cordial invitation, I can hardly refuse."

Camilla sighed as Pierce invited the man to fill a plate at the sideboard. Mr. Fowler was clearly wounded by the lack of trust she and her ladyship had placed in him. But given his firm stance on children, he could hardly be surprised.

It *was* surprising, however, that her ladyship had invited him to join them. Camilla lowered her voice to murmur, "Mr. Fowler took that very well."

The countess gazed at the man's broad back. "He'll take it even better once he gets to know the boy."

"That depends entirely on how well Jasper behaves, I fear," Camilla said. "Look at him—he's about to burst out of his chair from excitement."

"If Mr. Fowler gives you any grief about Jasper,

you let me know," her ladyship said with a sniff. "I may not be mistress of this estate, but I can still set a man straight if I'm pressed to it."

Camilla watched as the countess headed over to coddle Jasper, which as usual had him beaming with pleasure. More and more, the woman presented a conundrum. Clearly she had *not* stood up to her husband on behalf of her own son. Was that why she was so protective of Jasper?

Watching her with the boy must pain Pierce. Though if it did, he gave no evidence of it as they ate a quick breakfast and headed out the front door to find both her ladyship's barouche box and a massive coach-and-four awaiting them.

"Would you like to ride with me?" Pierce asked Jasper.

"Can Mama come, too? And Maisie? And her ladyship?"

Pierce looked amused. "Do the three of them go everywhere with you?"

"Well . . ." Jasper thought a moment. "Mostly. When I don't have to stay with Maisie on account of nobody wanting me seen by—" He shot Mr. Fowler a furtive glance, then added in a whisper, "By You Know Who."

Fortunately, Mr. Fowler was engrossed in helping the countess determine which items were to be loaded onto the top of the coach-and-four.

"You needn't worry about that anymore," Pierce said in a confidential voice. "You can be seen by anyone you please. And if we can fit everyone inside the coach, they're welcome to ride with us."

In the end, the servants were put into the barouche, leaving the six of them to be crammed inside the coach.

As they set off, with Camilla, Maisie, and her ladyship on one side and the two gentlemen and Jasper on the other, Pierce turned to Mr. Fowler. "Are there usually many people at this fair?"

"I don't know," the estate manager answered. "I've never been."

They both looked at her ladyship. "There's generally a few hundred at least," she said.

"The Christmas one is the most popular," Maisie put in, then reddened as she realized she shouldn't speak among such lofty personages.

Pierce smiled encouragingly at her. "Is it because of the horses? As I recall from my childhood, a great deal of horse selling went on during this particular fair."

Feeling Lady Devonmont stiffen beside her, Camilla shot her a quick glance but could tell nothing from the woman's smooth expression.

"Oh, yes, my lord, they still sell a great many horses," Maisie said. "And cattle and cheese, too."

"And reindeer?" Jasper asked hopefully.

"Reindeer?" Pierce echoed in obvious bewilderment.

"It's in the poem, you know," Jasper said, "the one about St. Nicholas."

Pierce glanced at Camilla. "Is this the famous poem that has enraptured the females of Stocking Pelham?"

Camilla smiled ruefully. "I'm afraid so. He's quite taken with it."

"I know it by heart," Jasper said. "I can say it if you like."

"Oh, by all means, let us hear the blasted thing," Mr. Fowler mumbled.

Taking him at his word, Jasper cheerily began to recite it, and Camilla didn't have the heart to stop him. Besides, she was having fun watching Mr. Fowler look so stoic about the matter.

When Jasper got to the part about the "eight tiny reindeer," Pierce interrupted. "I'm afraid I can't show you any of those, lad, but we can have a look at some regular deer, if you want."

Jasper's eyes went wide. "I guess they don't *have* to have reins on them."

Camilla stifled a laugh. Until now, she hadn't realized what Jasper thought reindeer were.

Pierce said very soberly, "Well, they only need reins when they're pulling a sleigh, but in this case, the deer are just lying about and eating. Would you like to see them?"

"Oh, yes, sir, very much!"

"I don't know if we have time," Camilla put in.

"It will only take a few minutes. It's not much out of our way." Pierce looked at his mother for the first time since they'd entered the coach. "If that's all right with you."

"It's fine. Tell the servants to go on to Stocking Pelham, and they can start helping set up the booth without me. Other ladies will be there, after all."

Pierce opened the panel at the front and called up some orders to the coachman, then settled back into his seat.

"I assume you're talking about the deer in the park?" Camilla asked, wondering how he could produce wild deer for Jasper's benefit, especially in a two-hundred-and-fifty-acre park.

"Actually," Mr. Fowler said, "his lordship keeps some for winter."

Lady Devonmont said, "What do you mean, 'keeps some'?"

"I got the idea from the Earl of Clarendon," Pierce explained. "He weeds out those deer among the herd that would never make it through the winter on their own. Then he pens them, coddles them, and fattens them up, so that by spring, his estate has venison without having to slaughter the strong breeders of his herd."

"Thanks to his lordship," Mr. Fowler put in, "we've been doing it for the past two years and we find that the herd has swelled admirably. It only takes a bit of feed and the gamekeeper's occasional attention to take care of the ones we pen. We sometimes have so much venison, we have to sell the meat."

"And there they are now," Pierce said as he hauled Jasper onto his lap so he could see out the window better. "Look, lad—all the deer you could want."

"Ohhhh, look at them!" Jasper exclaimed. "They're bigger than I thought they would be. I'll bet they could pull a *big* sleigh!"

They really were healthy-looking. Camilla shoved her spectacles up as she gazed out the window. She'd never been on this part of the estate, since she rarely left the dower house and couldn't ride. So she hadn't before seen the large pen, with a lean-to at one end to help protect the animals from the weather, hay strewn across the ground, and troughs that must contain feed.

Pierce's industrious use of the estate's resources astounded her. She would never have thought him that sort of owner—willing to try improvements, interested in new ideas. She would have thought him the sort to leave everything to his estate manager.

"Perhaps later, on our way home," Pierce said, "we'll stop and you can look at them up close."

"Oh, that would be *grand*!" Jasper said, his eyes huge as he watched out the window.

They drove slowly past the pen, and Camilla noticed something odd. "Why is the pen covered with netting?"

Jasper eyed her askance. "To keep the deer from

flying away, Mama," he said, as if anyone would have known that.

When Pierce shot her a questioning glance, Camilla laughed. "If you had let him keep reciting the poem, you would have discovered that the reindeer in it actually fly. So since my son is a city boy and doesn't know about such things, he assumes that all deer fly."

"No kind of deer flies, boy," Mr. Fowler said firmly.

Jasper glanced darkly at him. "Reindeer do."

"Only because the poem is about magical deer," her ladyship put in gently. "They're distant cousins to regular deer. I'm afraid that regular deer don't fly."

"Oh," Jasper said, nodding at her as if that explained everything. "I have cousins in London. They don't fly, either."

They all laughed, which apparently hurt Jasper's feelings, for he settled into a sulk.

Pierce shifted him on his lap and said kindly, "I have cousins in London, too. Or rather, not far from London. They own a stud farm with lots of horses. I spend every Christmas with them."

Jasper gazed up into his face. "But not this Christmas. You're going to spend it here at Montcliff. Right?"

Pierce stiffened, his smile growing forced. "I don't think so, Jasper," he said tightly. "My uncle is expecting me."

Before Camilla could jump in to smooth over the moment, Lady Devonmont surprised her by saying, "His lordship is a very busy man, lad, with a great many duties. He can't spend all his time in the country with us."

Pierce's gaze shot to his mother. "Good of you to understand."

Despair swept over Camilla. Her ladyship might make excuses for her son, but she very obviously did *not* understand. The countess really thought that Pierce could just leave everything in the past and start anew.

Little did she know her son. Pierce and her ladyship might be able to be civil and even spend time together now without too much strain, but they still had a large past lying between them like some immovable boulder, and it became clearer by the day that no amount of pushing was going to roll it away.

So it was time for Camilla to be sensible. He soon would be leaving for London or Waverly Farm, and when that happened, she would have to go on without him, no matter what she was beginning to feel for him.

Because once he was gone, she doubted he would ever return to the dower house.

17

Memories swamped Pierce the minute he disembarked at the fair. Just as it had been twenty-three years ago, the village green was packed with canvas tents and booths, and the snow-crusted ground had already been trampled by man and beast alike. The smell of hot beef pasties mingled with the scent of the festive greens that were twined about a few booths as decoration.

For a moment he stood frozen, lost in his childhood. Then the others swung into action under his mother's commands, and he forced himself out of his trance and into service carrying items to the church's booth, alongside Mr. Fowler, Camilla, and the dower house servants.

His mother took charge of little Jasper, holding the lad's hand as they all swept through the fair toward her booth. When she pointed out various sights that might interest the boy, Pierce shot right back to the day when she'd done the same with him.

That's when it finally dawned on him—the reason Camilla championed his mother. It was because of Jasper. Because Mother had brought the boy to live at Montcliff, when apparently none of Camilla's other employers had cared if the child lived or died. Because Mother treated the lad kindly.

Because Mother treated Jasper like a son.

Pierce choked down the bitterness rising in his throat. It spoke well of Mother that she'd behaved so graciously to Camilla and her child. And Pierce refused to envy a six-year-old boy for his hold on Mother's affections.

When they arrived at Mother's booth and were surrounded by the village church's ladies' committee, something else dawned on him. Young Jasper was a surprise to more than just him.

He should have expected that, given what Camilla had said last night about the secrecy they'd deemed necessary. But Pierce hadn't considered the ramifications—that until now no one had known that the child even existed. So there had to be explanations and introductions, not to mention a great deal of fuss from the six women running the booth.

Pierce hung back to watch. He knew better than to launch himself into a gaggle of hens fawning over a little boy.

"He's your son, Mrs. Stuart?" one lady exclaimed. "How delightful! Isn't he just adorable?" She ruffled Jasper's curls, which the boy seemed to take offense at, pulling closer to his mother.

"He looks cold," another lady said, and promptly wrapped a scarf tightly about his neck. "He should go stand by the brazier, where it's warm."

As Jasper tugged at the scarf, yet a third lady thrust out a plate of what looked from a distance like burned cakes. "Have a treat, my dear. I'm sure you're hungry."

"No, thank you," Jasper mumbled, clearly wary.

At least he was polite. Pierce wasn't sure *he* would have been at six. And Camilla was doing nothing to stop the ladies, obviously worried about offending them.

"Look at those chapped lips," said yet another female. "What you need, child, is my balm of juniper oil and honey water." She removed a vial from her reticule and, after pouring a bit of the contents onto her handkerchief, leaned toward Jasper's mouth with her hand outstretched. The poor lad started back in alarm.

"Excuse me," Pierce broke in, stepping up to place his arm about the boy's shoulders, "but Master Jasper and I were just heading off to take a look at the horses for sale."

Every female eye turned to him. And that's when

something else dawned on him: None of them knew who he was. It wasn't surprising, given that he hadn't attended church in Stocking Pelham since he was eight, but it was unnerving.

"Ladies," Mother said into the curiosity-laden silence, "you may remember my son, the Earl of Devonmont. Though it's been some years since he has visited Stocking Pelham, he was kind enough to help us transport items for the booth in his coach-and-four this morning."

The ladies gaped at him, obviously unsure what to think. They must have heard he was estranged from his family. But what had his parents said about it, if anything? Generally the heir to a title and a great house was known at least a little in the local village. They must think him quite full of himself, that he hadn't come to town in twenty-three years.

While he was still wondering about that, Mother said, "Pierce, I'm sure you remember . . ." and rattled off a list of names.

To his shock, he recognized a few. "Mrs. Townsend," he said, bowing to the chubby-cheeked lady with the balm. "I do hope your husband is feeling better." Townsend was one of Montcliff's most successful tenants. Pierce had spoken to the farmer several times, though he'd never met the wife.

Mrs. Townsend brightened. "Indeed, he is, my lord, thank you for asking. He was laid low for nearly a week, but yesterday he began to feel better and managed to get out of bed to come today. My son is helping him oversee the sale of our two sows."

"With any luck, they'll fetch a good price." Pierce turned to the gray-haired woman with the plate of treats. "Mrs. Wallace, please tell me those are your famous gingerbread nuts. Mr. Fowler brought me some once, and I've been craving another taste ever since."

Beaming at him, she held out the same plate she'd offered to Jasper. "That's exactly what they are, sir, and you're quite welcome to have some."

He took one of the round, dark brown treats for himself, then handed one to Jasper. "Here you go, lad. I promise you'll find them delicious."

Jasper skeptically took a bite, then his face lit up. "They're as good as sugarplums!" he announced.

As Jasper accepted another gingerbread nut from the plate, Pierce fielded a flurry of questions about the estate that soon turned to queries about how long he meant to stay in Hertfordshire and what the news was from London. He answered as best he could, reminded of what village life was like and how much of it centered around news, gossip, and the local landowners' lives.

Then, of course, he had to endure a tour of the booth. At every table, the ladies had placed a handwritten copy of the poem that Jasper was so enamored of, so that potential buyers understood the purpose of what the women were selling. Next to it was a pretty display of ornamental stockings. Apparently the ladies had each made several, which were flounced and furbelowed to excess.

Great God, how many would he be expected to buy? And how could he purchase only a few without insulting those ladies whose stockings didn't meet with his favor?

He knew how this worked. Whatever choice he made, they would talk for weeks about whose stockings his lordship had bought and whose he had ignored. There was only one safe avenue—to buy a stocking from each of the ladies. Perhaps he could use them as gifts, though even he didn't have that many female friends. Not respectable ones, anyway.

Still, it was for a good cause, he supposed.

By the time he'd made his purchases, he was ready to escape the cacophony of chatter. Since Jasper had been following him about the whole time, Pierce used the lad as his excuse.

"Forgive me, ladies, I hate to abandon you, but Jasper and I must get a look at the horses before the good ones all sell. I'm sure you understand."

The ladies were quite effusive about how well they understood, but not so much that he didn't notice Camilla in conversation with a sly-faced young buck who'd just entered and was examining the stockings at her table.

Pierce's eyes narrowed. Judging from the fellow's smiles and smooth compliments, he was shopping for something other than Christmas stockings.

"Mrs. Stuart!" Pierce called above the din. "I was hoping you would join me and young Jasper on our tour of the fair."

The booth went completely quiet. Camilla colored and darted a glance at his mother from beneath her bonnet. "I promised I would work here, my lord. But if you need someone to help you with Jasper, I'm sure Maisie will go."

He didn't need anyone to help him with Jasper, and he sure as hell didn't want Maisie to come. He wanted Camilla. Or rather, he wanted to save Camilla from being bothered by every country bumpkin who fancied a taste of the pretty London widow.

He thought it rather admirable of him, to be so concerned, too. It wasn't a mark of jealousy at all. Merely consideration of her position as a member of his staff.

"Let Maisie help here, and you can come with us," he said, unable to keep a peremptory note from his voice.

"You don't need Camilla *or* Maisie," his mother broke in, her voice oddly steely. "Jasper is a good boy. He won't give you any trouble. And if you don't think you can manage him, leave him here."

Pierce was already bristling at his mother's interference when Jasper chimed in. "I want to go with his lordship! And I want Mama to go, too!"

That seemed to startle Mother, then worry her. "Well, then, I suppose . . ."

"I'll go," Camilla said tightly, setting down the stocking she'd been showing to the bumpkin. She glanced at his mother. "That is, if you're sure you'll be all right without me."

"We'll be fine for an hour or two. We have plenty of ladies to help."

"And I'm happy to be of service where I can, too," Fowler put in. He shot Mother a soft glance that reminded Pierce of Camilla's suspicions about the man.

Poor arse. Mother had married an earl for money; she wasn't likely to marry an estate manager without it.

Then with a jolt Pierce remembered what he'd learned about the circumstances of his parents' marriage. He would have to start thinking of Mother in different terms. Unfortunately, he still wasn't sure what those terms were.

"Go on, enjoy the fair with your son," Mother told Camilla.

With a nod, Camilla came toward him, but she wasn't smiling, which put him on his guard.

As soon as they had left the booth, he offered her his arm, and she laid her gloved hand on it so lightly that he could tell at once she was angry. "What's wrong?"

"Nothing, my lord."

The "my lord" made him bristle. "For God's sake, I thought you'd be happy to get away from the old ladies for a while and enjoy yourself."

"You do realize what those 'old ladies' are thinking now, don't you?" She stared straight out to where Jasper was skipping along ahead of them.

"I don't give a damn what they're thinking," he snapped, irritated by her reproving tone.

Her gaze shot to his. "Exactly. Because you spend one day out of twenty at Montcliff and don't venture into the town even then. You don't buy ribbon at the shop on the green, or attend the church, or stroll past the farmers in the fields. *I* do."

Two spots of color appeared on her cheeks as she shifted her eyes forward. "And given the difference in our stations, not to mention your well-known reputation and the fact that I'm a widow with a child, everyone will assume the worst about your intentions toward me."

"That's quite a leap," he bit out, even as the sinking feeling in his gut told him she was right. Village gossip was a vastly different animal than London gossip. It didn't take much to start the wheels turning. And by singling her out, he might as well have placed a brand on her forehead.

What the devil was wrong with him? He knew better.

"I hope it's a leap," she said mournfully. "I already gave the ladies one shock by turning up with a son they didn't know about. Let's hope this doesn't convince them to start speculating about who Jasper's father might really be."

The words set him back on his arse. Great God, he hadn't even thought of that. And he hadn't helped matters any by paying such marked attention to both her and Jasper. No wonder Mother had tried to stop him.

What had Fowler said in the study that day? *Lady Devonmont thinks the world of the young widow. She's very protective of her and would be most upset if she thought that you . . . that is, that anyone might try to take advantage of the lady.*

Bloody hell. "Surely my long absences would squelch any such speculation. You've been here for months, while I've been in London."

"You were here this summer," she pointed out in a dull voice, as if she'd now resigned herself to her fate. "And for all they know, before that I'd been living under your protection until you hired me as companion to your mother."

"That's absurd," he said, though his stomach knotted at the idea that it might *not* be so absurd. With a glance at Jasper, he lowered his voice. "They couldn't possibly think I'd insult my mother by parading a mistress in front of her and her friends."

"No, why should they?" she said bitterly. "You've

only been estranged from her for years, which everyone in the county is aware of, even if they don't know the reason. They only know you by what they read about you in the paper."

He flinched as her barb hit home. Though his record as a good landlord would give him some credit with the townspeople, it could easily be overshadowed by his more spectacular record as a London rakehell. Especially since the latter was much longer than the former. This was the stodgy country, not sophisticated London.

Besides, even if his neighbors didn't construe his actions as unfavorably as *she* feared, they could still think he was starting up with her now. That would be little better. Once he returned to London, she'd have to endure the gossip. And the scandal.

"What a selfish arse I am," he muttered.

He hadn't realized he'd said it aloud until she said primly, "Well, I wouldn't go quite that far."

Glancing over, he noted that the tightness around her mouth had eased. "An oblivious clodpate?" he offered.

"Somewhere between arse and clodpate, I should think," she said with less temper, though he still hadn't managed to wipe the frown from her brow.

"An arse-pate, then."

That startled a laugh from her, which she instantly stifled. "More like a complication."

"Ah, yes. A complication. I'm used to being *that*." He slanted a glance at her. "I can't undo what I did, but is there any way to mitigate the damage?"

She sighed, her breath making small puffs of frost in the air. "The gossip will die down when you leave, especially if you're gone for months again and I'm still here with your mother."

"Of course." It would die down . . . as long as she lived an exemplary life.

As long as he stayed away from her and her tart opinions. And her attempts to smooth over every difficulty between him and Mother. And her bright smile and sympathetic ear . . . and the sweetest mouth he'd ever tasted.

The thought depressed him.

"Is that a sleigh?" Jasper asked, running back to them to point it out. "It looks like the one in the picture."

Pierce followed his gaze. "Afraid not, lad. That's a sledge used for harvesting rapeseed."

As Jasper ran up to get a better look at it, Camilla eyed Pierce closely. "How do you know about farming equipment?"

He cast her a sardonic smile. "What do you think I do all day in that study at Montcliff Manor? Read naughty books?"

She flushed. "No, but I just assumed . . . that is . . ."

"That I twiddle my thumbs and take naps," he

quipped. "Sorry to disappoint you, but I only do that every other day."

"Pierce," she chided, "be serious."

He searched her face, then let out a breath. "All right. Once I came of age, I started reading up on husbandry and planting and anything that might pertain to estate management. I figured I ought to know something about my inheritance for when I gained it, even if I didn't get to have any part in running it for a while."

"For a while? You never visited Montcliff as an adult, either?"

He'd forgotten that he hadn't told her about that awful confrontation years ago. "That should have been obvious from the ladies' reactions earlier."

"Yes, but you said you returned to Montcliff when you came into your majority."

"Briefly." Not wanting to dredge up that painful part of his past, he pulled away from her and strode over to where Jasper was attempting to climb onto the sledge. "Now, now, lad, that's a good way to break your head."

He dragged the wriggling boy off it and set him down in front of his mother, catching the boy's hat as it fell off. After Jasper clapped his hat back on, he raced off to look at a pen of cows.

Pierce shook his head. "That's one busy lad you have there."

"He's been cooped up in a house for weeks, remember?" she pointed out, though her tone had softened.

"Right." Out of fear that Pierce might send him away. The thought of it still sent a punch to his gut. "A lad like that needs the outdoors and plenty of space to run."

"True." She stared up at him with a gentler gaze than before. "Thanks to you, he'll have it now."

He offered her his arm again, and this time she curled her fingers about it with far more intimacy. It made his blood race. Apparently he'd been forgiven for his blunder with the ladies' committee.

Good. He would make the most of that while he had her to himself.

18

They wandered leisurely toward the end of the fair where the horses were kept. A month ago, Pierce would have found a country fair boring. But it was hard to be bored when a little pistol like Jasper was dragging you from here to yon, his face rapt at first one wonder, then another. Almost an hour had passed, and they still hadn't reached the horses.

"Maisie said they sell cheese here, right?" Camilla removed her spectacles and cleaned them with her handkerchief. "I want to buy a wheel of cheddar for Mrs. Beasley for Christmas. It's her favorite."

"That area over there seems to hold the food booths."

She called out, "Jasper, come here! We're going to get some cheese!"

Jasper frowned as he skipped back to them. "I don't like cheese."

"That's a good thing, muffin," she said as she took his hand, "since it's not for you."

"They have roasted chestnuts," Pierce pointed out. "Do you like those?"

"I *love* chestnuts!" Jasper cried.

"Ah," Pierce said as something dawned on him. "You must have been the one eating all the nuts in the drawing room the other day."

Jasper nodded solemnly. "When I lost my tin soldier."

"I almost forgot." Pierce drew the one he'd found out of his coat. "Is this your missing man?"

"Prancer!" Jasper cried as he took it. "You found Prancer!"

"Strange name for a soldier," Pierce muttered to Camilla.

"He's named after one of the reindeer in the poem," she explained. "They all have strange names."

"The only one I'm missing now is Blixem," Jasper said. "Then I'll have eight to pull St. Nicholas's sleigh."

Pierce couldn't help smiling. The boy's enthusiasm was infectious. "I tell you what. Tonight, when we get home, I'll give you one to serve as Blixem."

"Yay!"

"But first we have to find a good round of cheddar for Mrs. Beasley and some chestnuts for you. And perhaps some ribbons for your mother so she won't have to go buy them at the shop on the green."

As Camilla blushed, Jasper said, "Or we could get her a 'kerchief. Like in the poem."

"There's 'kerchiefs in the poem, too?" he asked as they headed for the food booths.

"Don't you remember?" Jasper said in that condescending tone boys used when they were impatient with grown-ups. "I recited that part. 'And Mama in her 'kerchief and I in my cap—'"

"Right, I forgot. That's where the reindeer came in." He stared down at Jasper. "What else is in this poem?"

"St. Nicholas comes down the chimney."

"Great God, that sounds dangerous," Pierce said. "I am going to have to read this thing for myself. Between the stockings and the 'kerchiefs and the flying reindeer, it sounds like something straight out of a fairy tale."

"Except there's no girls in it," Jasper said cheerily. "That's the best part."

"I beg your pardon?" Camilla said, feigning a deeply wounded tone. "*I'm* a girl."

"No, you're not. You're a lady. Girls are silly." He lowered his voice confidentially. "One of my cousins is a girl. She's *very* silly."

"She's only three, Jasper," his mother said.

Pierce chuckled. "I think you'll find her less silly as

she gets older. Trust me on this—girls make life more interesting." He cast Camilla a meaningful glance. "We would miss them if they weren't around."

As a shy smile lit her face, it hit him like a bolt from heaven—he would miss *her*. And there was no solution for that. He couldn't stay here, being the "complication" in her life. He wouldn't want to.

Would he?

They found the booth selling cheeses and took their time selecting one for Mrs. Beasley before stopping at a booth that sold roasted chestnuts. The one next to it sold cherry tarts, so while he purchased bags of nuts for him and Jasper, Camilla went to buy a tart.

As he watched her making friendly small talk with the booth owner, an idea occurred to him. If the ladies were going to make a scandal out of her association with him anyway, why not give them something to be scandalized about? Camilla could come to London. With Jasper. Pierce could put them up in a house somewhere, make her his mistress. . . .

He groaned. Was he mad? Aside from the fact that she would never agree to it, she was decidedly *not* the kind of woman he chose for a mistress. She knew too much about him already, saw too deeply. She was the kind of woman who would demand everything from him. And he couldn't give it to her.

Yet the idea continued to tantalize him as he watched her eat the cherry tart. Her blue eyes lit up, and her mouth—her rich, full mouth—was stained with cherry juice as she savored every morsel of the sweet treat.

He wondered if she would wear that same expression when he took her to bed in a neat little town house he'd pay for in London. Jasper would be off with a nanny whom Pierce would hire—perhaps Maisie, since she already knew the boy well—and . . .

No, impossible. Hadn't he already realized that?

But Camilla had a tiny smear of cherry at the corner of her lips, and he wanted desperately to lick it off, then lick a path down the soft silk of her skin to—

"When are we going to see the horses?" Jasper asked, pure trust shining in his gaze as he looked up at Pierce.

It jerked him back to the real world, the one where he had to keep his hands off the lad's mother. Pierce stifled an oath. He had to get control of himself. "Horses," Pierce choked out as he wrestled his urges into submission. "Certainly. If I remember correctly, they're this way."

At every step, Pierce was aware of her soft hand curled about his arm and her faint scent of cinnamon and honey water. But as they approached the paddock and saw a man putting a horse through its paces for a prospective buyer, a memory stirred that drew his attention from Camilla.

This felt familiar—the paddock, the horses, even the horse trader.

Then he recognized the man. Ah, *that's* why it felt familiar. "I bought a mare from this fellow last year." They came up to the paddock's makeshift fence, and Pierce hoisted Jasper up onto it so the lad could see everything. "It was a wedding gift for my cousin Virginia, who married into the infamous Sharpe family."

"Oh, yes, I remember reading about that," Camilla said lightly as she gazed up at him. "They're the ones people call the Hellions of Halstead Hall, right?"

Pierce arched an eyebrow. "There's not much hellion left in them these days. Marriage seems to have knocked it right out."

Her smile looked forced as she returned her gaze to the horses. "Marriage has a way of doing that to some people."

"True. That's why I've never married."

"You don't want to give up reading naughty books and drinking until dawn," she said dryly.

"Exactly." He wasn't about to give up control over his life to someone else ever again. "I like my fun." Except that his life wasn't much fun anymore. Not that he would ever admit that to *her*.

"But you'll have to marry one day," she pointed out.

"Why? So I can bear an heir to continue my cursed family line? No, thank you. It can die with me, as far as I'm concerned."

She gave him a sad look. "I see. You're not marrying because you want to punish her."

"I don't want to punish anyone," he snapped. He didn't need to ask who "her" was.

"Don't you? It's the only way to strike back at her for what she did. If you don't marry and don't have children, then she has no grandchildren to look after her in her old age."

"Given how little of my life she took part in, I wouldn't think she'd *want* grandchildren."

That was partly true. But what Camilla said made a certain sense, too. *Was* that the real reason he'd balked at marriage? To keep from giving Mother grandchildren?

No, the idea was absurd. He couldn't be that petty, surely.

Thrusting the lowering picture of himself from his mind, he leaned toward where Jasper was drinking up every sight in the paddock from his perch on the fence. The same sense of familiarity hit Pierce again, but he ignored it. There must be hundreds of these paddocks in fairs across England.

"Which of the horses do you like best, lad?" he asked Jasper. "The black gelding perhaps? Or the gray stallion?"

"I like the little brown one over there," Jasper said, pointing to a Shetland.

"Ah, the pony. I have a Welsh pony in my stables at Montcliff. You should ride it sometime."

"He doesn't know how," Camilla said.

"Why don't you teach him?"

"Because I don't know how, either."

Pierce gaped at her. "You don't know how to *ride?*"

She eyed him askance. "Until six months ago, I lived in London all my life. I didn't need to ride there. Mostly I walked. If my destination was too far away, there was always some equipage to take me long distances."

"But when you were a child, surely—" He broke off, cursing himself for being oblivious. "No, I don't suppose there are many mounts for children in an orphanage."

"None, actually," she said with clearly pretend nonchalance.

He always forgot how different her life had been from his. And suddenly it seemed a damned shame. "You should ride at Montcliff."

"Someone would have to teach me. Besides, I spend my days with your mother, and she has difficulty riding." Her tone turned wistful. "No, I think riding isn't destined to be one of my abilities."

"The hell it isn't. *I'll* show you how to ride."

She uttered a sharp laugh. "You're returning to London soon, remember?"

And you'll be going with me.

He'd nearly said it aloud. Damn it, but he couldn't let go of the idea of making her his mistress. It tantalized and intoxicated him. Ah, the things he could teach her, introduce to her . . . do with her.

And the first thing would be to buy her whatever damned horse she desired. She'd be a glorious rider; he was sure of it. He could easily imagine her riding to hounds, her hair streaming out behind her and her cheeks flushing with pleasure.

But first he had to convince her to go with him, and that would take some doing.

"Mama can't ride—her spectacles would fall off," Jasper announced. "But *I* want to learn."

"Of course you do," Pierce said, biting back a smile. "And you shall. I'll speak to Fowler about it." He cast her a long glance. "About both of you learning."

"Pierce—" she began in a low voice.

"Good morning, my lord, and welcome!" cried the horse trader, who'd finished with his customer and had now spotted Pierce. The man hurried up to them. "Looking for another horse to buy?"

"Perhaps, Whitley," he said with a smile. "My cousin was quite pleased with the purchase I made for her. So was her new husband."

"Good, good. That bay mare was an excellent choice. Glad she went to a good home."

Pierce laid his hand on Jasper's shoulder. "We're here because my young friend Master Jasper wanted to see your stock."

"Did you, now, lad?" Whitley said with a toothy smile. "And are you fond of horses?"

Jasper's eyes were huge. "I like that pony over there."

"I see," Whitley said with a covert glance at Pierce, who nodded. "Would you like to try it out for me? I could use an expert opinion."

"He's not old enough," Camilla broke in.

"Nonsense." Pierce patted her hand. "I'd been riding for a year by the time I was his age."

"I don't know, Pierce, I—" Realizing she'd used his Christian name, she said quickly, "My lord, perhaps it would be better if he just looked."

Whitley was a sharp fellow and instantly assessed the situation. "It's a good pony, madam. The young master would get great enjoyment out of it."

She blinked. "Oh, I'm not planning on purchasing—"

"The boy wants a ride, that's all." Pierce cast Whitley a warning glance. Later Pierce could point out to her the advantages to being his mistress, for Jasper as well as her. But no need to spook her now.

Pierce looked at Jasper. "Would you like to ride the pony?"

"Oh, yes, my lord. Ever so much."

"Good, then it's settled."

Camilla's grip tightened on Pierce's arm. "Are you sure he'll be all right?"

"He'll be fine just riding about the paddock, won't he, Whitley?" Pierce said in a voice that conveyed what would happen if the boy was harmed.

"I'll treat him like me own, madam," Whitley said,

obviously used to anxious mamas. He helped Jasper down from the fence, then ordered his youthful helper to fetch the pretty little Shetland from the pen. As Whitley brought Jasper over to the pony, Pierce felt that same persistent nagging at his memory.

It wasn't because he'd bought a horse from Whitley; that had happened in a barn. It was this particular situation—a paddock and a boy going to ride.

"Oh, I do hope Jasper doesn't get frightened," Camilla said. "He's so young."

He scarcely heard her. "Camilla," he said as his mind sifted through his memories. "I think I might have ridden a horse at this fair, too, years ago."

She looked up at him. "What do you mean?"

"When I came here with Mother. I remember it." More of the past came into his mind, and he closed his eyes, trying to summon up the scene. "She told me . . . yes . . . she said she wanted to purchase a real horse for me. Not a pony."

His eyes shot open. "No, that can't be right. It was only after spending so much time at the stud farm that I started enjoying riding. Before that, while I was still at home, I wasn't fond of it and Mother knew that. She would never have considered buying me a larger horse."

"Then why would she have said it?" Camilla glanced over to where Jasper now sat in the saddle, looking like a sultan on the throne, his hat perched rakishly to one side. Apparently reassured that he was all right, she added, "Why would she have had you ride at all, if not to try out a horse for purchase?"

He shook his head. "I don't know. I just remember being led around the paddock while Mother watched." He caught his breath as memories flooded him. "No, she didn't only watch. She argued with her cousin."

"Her cousin?"

"A second cousin, if I remember right." He shook his head. "I'd forgotten all about that. He was standing near the fence. At the time, I didn't think it odd, but now . . . Why was Mother's cousin at the fair? To my knowledge, he didn't live nearby."

"You're sure it was him?"

He nodded. "I'd met him at Grandfather Gilchrist's funeral tea when I was six. One of Mother's aunts introduced us. I only knew him as Mr. Gilchrist. That day at the fair, Mr. Gilchrist stormed off before I was done riding, and when I asked Mother about it she said they were arguing because he wanted to buy the horse, too. Only . . ."

Oh, God.

"Only what?" she prodded.

"I never made the connection before—it was so long ago. But a few days later, he showed up at Montcliff. I heard a servant tell Father that Mother's cousin was waiting for him in the drawing room. Father went in and Mother followed him, and there was a great row with the man. I couldn't hear what it was about."

His stomach clenched, just as it had then. "But I do remember that Father was furious. He threw Gilchrist out and ordered him never to return. Said he wasn't welcome at Montcliff."

Camilla shot a quick glance to where Jasper was waving at her. She waved back as she asked in a low voice, "Did your parents explain what the problem was?"

"I asked Father. He told me to mind my own affairs." A chill swept through him. "Since he was always saying that, I thought it was just grown-up business. He'd always hated Mother's family. But now I wonder if it might have been more than that."

"Why?"

"Because just a few weeks later, I was packed off to school. And I didn't see my father again for thirteen years."

19

❧

Camilla stared at Pierce, worried by the way he'd turned still as stone. Glancing over to where her son was happily riding, she forced a smile for him, but her blood was pounding so fiercely she could hardly keep her countenance. The same idea as before leaped into her head, but this time she felt she should mention it.

"Have you considered the fact . . ." She paused, wondering how someone suggested such a thing to an earl. "Is it possible that—"

"I'm not my father's son?" he finished in a strangled voice.

She nodded.

"I never considered it before." A muscle ticked in

his jaw, once, twice. "But it would make sense. It would explain why he hated me, why he banished me from my home after that day Gilchrist came to see him. Perhaps Mother's cousin knew who the man was. Gilchrist might have tried to blackmail her or threatened to go to the scandal sheets with his knowledge if Father didn't pay him."

"Or Gilchrist might himself have *been* the man."

He sucked in a breath. "I hadn't thought of that."

"Cousins are often thrown together. Look at you and your Waverly cousins. He might have seen her at any family affair."

"Except that I was definitely born after my parents married—ten months after the wedding." He blinked. "Or so I've always been told. But a few weeks might have been glossed over. It wouldn't surprise me to learn that I was born earlier than they said. And that's easier to swallow than the possibility that Mother—"

"I know. It doesn't seem like her to break her marriage vows."

He cast her an earnest glance. "You've considered this before."

She reddened under his gaze. "Only after she told me that your father kept her from you. But you look so much like him."

"That's what everyone says. I can't see it, though. Aside from our coloring being the same, I don't think we look alike in any other way."

She wasn't so sure about that. She'd have to get another look at his father's portrait. And portraits weren't always true, either. "Still, I just can't imagine that your mother . . . would take a lover."

"Nor can I. She would have risked much to have an affair. If I am a bastard, I had to have been conceived before the marriage. And he would have known she wasn't a virgin on their wedding night."

"There are ways to . . . well . . ."

"Yes, I know. To disguise it. Because surely if he'd guessed it then, he wouldn't have waited until I was eight to banish me." He drew in a deep breath. "And there's another flaw in this theory."

"What's that?" she asked. Mr. Whitley was drawing the pony to a stop; it appeared that Jasper's ride was just about over.

"I can see how Father would hold her sin over her to keep us apart, especially if I wasn't his son and he couldn't stand the sight of me. But why did she go along so completely? She never wrote, never visited. I didn't see her for thirteen years."

"Perhaps he threatened to divorce her."

He stared blindly at the horses. "Divorces aren't easy to gain, especially if he had no proof that he'd been cuckolded. And it would have created a huge scandal, even if it could be done. He wasn't fond of scandal, trust me."

"Besides," she said, "given the choice between

a divorce and losing her son, I can't imagine your mother choosing to lose you, especially if the earl wasn't really your father. Although if she knew she couldn't support you . . ."

"All right, let's say he threatened to divorce her and leave us both destitute. She might have done as he demanded to prevent that, but it would only have worked until I was grown. Once I reached my majority, I inherited money from my grandmother, and that would have kept us both comfortable enough until Father died and I could inherit the estate."

"Could he have threatened to disinherit you?"

"No. The estate is entailed, and both it and the title go to his heir. The law says that his heir is the eldest son born into the marriage, and I was born on the right side of the blanket. Even if he divorced her, I would have inherited everything eventually." His voice grew choked. "So why would he let the bastard he hated inherit, while he got rid of the wife he wanted to keep under his thumb? No, divorce couldn't have been what he threatened."

"He must have threatened *something* to make her comply."

"Yes, but what? And why did she *keep* complying even after I had come into my majority?" He swallowed convulsively. "Why did she choose him over me?"

"How do you know that she did?"

His face clouded over. "Because of what she said to me when I was twenty-one and traveled here to confront Father."

"What was that?"

But he didn't answer. He merely nodded to where Jasper was running toward them.

"Mama, Mama, I rode the pony! Did you see?"

"Yes, muffin, I saw!" she said with a tremulous smile. She caught him up in her arms, and tears started in her eyes as her gaze met Pierce's haunted one.

She hugged Jasper tight to her breast. How could a mother ever give her child up? It was unfathomable. It would kill her to lose Jasper.

If it had been *her*, she would have run off with her son and never come back.

Camilla sighed. Easy for her to say. She wasn't a countess with a husband who had riches and power beyond measure.

"Stop squeezing me, Mama!" Jasper exclaimed, wriggling out of her embrace. "I'm not a baby anymore. I rode a pony!"

She let him slip to the ground, though her heart was in her throat. "Yes, you did. You rode it very well."

"Did you enjoy the pony, lad?" Pierce asked, obviously attempting to hide the strain in his voice.

"Oh, yes, my lord. He comes from way up in Scotland, and his name is Chocolate because he likes chocolate drops." As Pierce went over to Mr. Whitley and had a short, murmured conversation with the man, Jasper added, "Do you think he could pull a sleigh, Mama?"

"Probably not by himself," she said absently, preoccupied by Pierce's tale.

When Pierce returned to her side, he looked solemn. "We'd better go back. They'll wonder what has happened to us."

She nodded, but she knew that wasn't why he wanted to return to the booth. He wanted to question his mother. To get answers.

As Jasper skipped ahead of them, she said in a low voice, "I know you want the truth, and I don't blame you. But you mustn't question your mother about this until you can do so in private, preferably back at Montcliff."

"Why?" he ground out. "No matter how I look at it, she made the choice to abandon me, at least after I was grown. Because *he* demanded it. Perhaps she felt some ridiculous guilt over going into the marriage with a babe in her belly. Or perhaps Gilchrist threatened a scandal. Either way, she acquiesced to his separating her from her own child."

"You can't be sure of that. You can't be sure of any of it."

"I know that she didn't fight for me, and if I'm to believe that she wanted to, then he must have threatened her with something. What? Or was she just too spineless to stand up to him? Damn it, I want to know. I deserve to hear the truth."

"Yes, but not now," she chided. "She's part of a community here. Surely you're not so angry at her that you would wish to see her shamed in front of people who respect her." When he said nothing, she added, "And whether you like it or not, you're part of the community here, too. You have to behave with decorum, if only because you're the Earl of Devonmont."

He walked on in silence for a few moments, then scowled at her. "I hate when you're sensible."

She let out a relieved breath. "What a pity. Because I love when *you* are."

"Do you?" He gazed, unsmiling, at her and lowered his voice to a husky murmur that made her pulse quicken. "Last night I wasn't being sensible, and you didn't seem to mind *that* too much."

Feeling the heat rise in her cheeks, she jerked her gaze from his. "That shouldn't have happened."

"Yet it did." He looked as if he was about to say more. Then he glanced down to where Jasper had slowed to listen to them, and he seemed to think better of it.

They walked in silence a few moments, picking their way over the slushy ground and trying to keep Jasper from getting his little shoes too wet in the icy weather. With only a week left until Christmas, there were holly berries adorning every other booth, and pitchmen trying to coax young men into buying gim-cracks and scarves and such for their sweethearts.

But Camilla wasn't feeling very festive at the moment. The impending storm between mother and son had put her in a quandary. She cared deeply about them both. They would expect her to take a side, but how could she?

Pierce stared ahead at the booth offering ballad sheets for sale. "I suppose there's another reason I shouldn't confront my mother before God and everyone."

She glanced at him. "Oh?"

"If I shame her publicly, you and Jasper will suffer embarrassment, too."

"I don't care about that," she said.

"I know you don't," he said irritably. "You never care about yourself. But that doesn't mean I should allow it. I may be a selfish arse, but considering the damage I've done to your reputation already by singling you out in front of the old ladies—" He halted at the ballad sheet booth. "Great God. I have an idea. Wait here."

He disappeared into the booth and came out a short while later with a package wrapped in brown paper. "Come on," he said brusquely. "And let me do the talking when we reach the booth."

That sounded worrisome. But now they were headed into the most crowded part of the fair, and it was hard to converse, especially since the number of fairgoers had increased substantially, undaunted by the winter chill.

Up ahead, she could see Lady Devonmont and the ladies inside the church's booth. They looked to be doing a brisk business in stockings.

As soon as they entered, he took Mrs. Townsend aside and said in a low voice, "Is there somewhere I can hide my package until we leave? It's a Christmas present for my mother."

Mrs. Townsend blinked. "Oh! Give it to me, and I shall put it under my basket behind the table."

"I hope she likes it," he said conversationally as he handed it over. "It's an assortment of broadsides for the pianoforte, since she enjoys playing and singing so much. Mrs. Stuart helped me pick out pieces my mother doesn't already have."

"Oh, yes?" Mrs. Townsend said, and offered Camilla a faint smile.

Camilla tried to look as if she was in on the secret.

Pierce cast the woman a knowing glance. "I did have some trouble extricating Mrs. Stuart from here so she could advise me. Since I couldn't say why I needed her, Mother proved stubborn. You know how she can be."

"I do, indeed," Mrs. Townsend breathed, obviously delighted to be included in the subterfuge. "Your mother worries overmuch about propriety, my lord."

Her heart swelling at his ingenious solution for

tamping down the gossip, Camilla stepped forward to do her part. "I told his lordship that her ladyship would be happy with anything he gave her, but he insisted on the music."

"Certainly," Mrs. Townsend whispered. "Very thoughtful of him."

"You mustn't say anything to her," he cautioned the woman.

"I won't breathe a word—you may depend on me. I'll just put this under my basket now."

As she scurried off, stopping every foot or so to relate this new information to the other ladies, Camilla said, without glancing at Pierce, "Thank you."

"It's the least I could do," he murmured. "Not the best story, I suppose, but it will hold."

"On the contrary, they'll find it convincing. It was clever of you to think of it."

"One might even call it 'sensible,'" he said dryly. He raised his voice just enough to be heard by two ladies standing near. "Thank you for your help, Mrs. Stuart."

"You're welcome, my lord." She pasted a smile onto her lips, bowed to him, and then carried Jasper to the other end of the booth. Now that he'd gone to the trouble to mitigate any damage to her reputation, she wasn't going to ruin it by standing with him and giving rise to more speculation.

She spent the next few hours helping the ladies at

the booth. Maisie took Jasper off again to see more of
the fair, while Pierce disappeared entirely. Was he tour-
ing the fair again, looking at horses and cattle to buy?
Or was he just shopping for Christmas gifts to give his
Waverly cousins?

Or his mistress.

Her stomach roiled at the thought. As far as Camilla
knew, he was still involved with that famous courtesan
mentioned in the scandal sheets, and she had no reason
to think he wasn't eagerly anticipating returning to her.

That possibility was certainly lowering. Still, it reminded her that he had no ties to her and Jasper, no
reason to involve himself with her. The only association
they could ever have was an illicit one. Earls, no matter
how unconventional, did *not* marry paid companions.

And she didn't think she could stand having the
other kind of relationship with him. To be his, but only
in some secretive, shameful fashion . . .

Sweet heaven, she was getting ahead of herself. He
might not even want that. There was nothing keeping
him at Montcliff, so she simply *must* resign herself to his
leaving. Otherwise, she was going to find herself quite
heartbroken when at last he did.

Still, her spirits lifted shamelessly when he saun-
tered into the booth in the early evening. The sun had
set, but the fair was still going, lit by oil lamps and
moonlight. He'd brought a large bag of beef pasties with

him, for which all the ladies were grateful. It was well past dinnertime for most of them, and they hadn't taken a break to eat.

As they shared the food, the ladies discussed when to close the booth. People were still wandering in, though traffic had subsided in the past hour. They'd sold nearly all the stockings, and it was getting quite a bit colder now that the sun had gone down, so it seemed unnecessary for them all to remain there on the off chance that they would sell every stocking. After another hour passed and they sold only one more, they decided to close up.

Pierce had stayed out of the discussion, talking to Mr. Fowler instead. To Camilla's astonishment, the estate manager had spent the entire day helping in the booth. The ladies had been quite impressed, and one of the widows had even flirted with him, which her ladyship had frowned over. Perhaps she *did* have a spark of interest in the man.

Maisie had brought Jasper back not long ago, and after eating his share of beef pasties, the boy sat in a corner playing with Prancer.

As they began closing up, Pierce went over to watch Jasper play. He looked pensive and somber, and said little as they packed up. He accepted his package from Mrs. Townsend with a word of thanks, then gave commands to the servants about moving the items into the two carriages.

Jasper started to whine, but before either Camilla or Maisie could tend to him, Pierce hefted him onto his shoulder, which managed to cheer Jasper enough to stop him from being *too* querulous as his lordship walked back to the carriage beside Mr. Fowler and Maisie.

Her ladyship walked with Camilla, far enough behind the men to be out of earshot. "We did very well today," the countess said. "I believe we raised enough to not only refurbish the church's organ, but perhaps repaint the vestibule."

"That's good," Camilla said. "It badly needs it."

Lady Devonmont glanced ahead at her son. "Did you have fun earlier when you were going about the fair?"

Camilla tensed. "Yes. Although Jasper ran us both a merry chase."

Her ladyship cast her a shuttered look. "I overheard one of the ladies explaining that Pierce took you off so you could help him pick out a Christmas gift for me. Is that true?"

"Of course," she said lightly.

"Come, my dear, you and I both know Pierce is not buying me any gifts."

Camilla thrust out her chin. "You might be surprised."

"I doubt that." The countess lowered her voice. "Take care, Camilla. Judging from London gossip, I gather that my son has long been used to making free with women's hearts. Pierce may be charming, but he's still a rogue."

Because you made him into one by abandoning him.

No, it would be cruel to say such a thing. And it might not even be true. Pierce might be a rogue by nature.

"He's not as much a rogue as you think," Camilla said, remembering the pain in his eyes whenever he spoke of his past. "He has a lot of good in him."

"Yes, but that doesn't mean his intentions toward you are honorable."

"I would imagine they aren't." At her ladyship's look of alarm, she added hastily, "That is, *if* he had any intentions at all toward me. Which he doesn't."

"Are you sure?"

No. But she wasn't about to tell his mother that. "Trust me, you don't need to warn me that a man like him would never marry so far beneath him. I am well aware of that."

"It has nothing to do with your situation in life, my dear. I don't think he cares much about such things." She squeezed Camilla's hand. "And I would personally be delighted to have you as my daughter-in-law. But Pierce doesn't strike me as . . . well . . ."

"The marrying kind?"

The countess sighed. "Exactly."

"He doesn't strike me that way, either," she said with forced nonchalance. "I know the situation, and I'm fully armed. You mustn't worry about *me*."

Her ladyship gazed earnestly into her face. "I don't want to see you hurt, that's all."

"I understand. I'm safe, I swear."

She *was* . . . because even if she did indulge in an affair with him, she would go into it knowing fully what would happen in the end. Knowing and accepting it.

But that was a very big *if*.

It became even bigger when they climbed into the carriage and headed home. Pierce looked grimmer than she'd ever seen him. He didn't speak, just stared out the window as the carriage trundled along.

Jasper fell instantly asleep in her lap, and she was glad of it. She doubted that Pierce—or even his mother—had the patience to deal with a six-year-old's questions just now.

As they approached the estate, her ladyship said, "You should stay for some supper, Mr. Fowler. I know it's late, but it's the least we can offer after all your hard work today."

Before Fowler could answer, Pierce said, in a tone that brooked no argument, "Fowler has a great deal to do for me this evening, since he's been busy elsewhere today."

"But, Pierce, surely it can wait until tomorrow," his mother said.

"No, his lordship is right," Fowler said smoothly. "I'd already planned to return to Montcliff Manor for a couple of hours before I headed home."

It was clear from the quick glance he shot Pierce that the two of them had worked that out before they'd entered the coach. Camilla stifled a sigh. It was going to be a long night.

"Oh, very well," Lady Devonmont said, clearly unaware of the ambush being prepared for her.

As soon as they arrived, Jasper woke up enough to climb down from the carriage. While the rest of them headed inside, Mr. Fowler rode off in Pierce's coach-and-four to Montcliff Manor.

The footman took their coats, and Camilla told Jasper to go upstairs with Maisie to have his supper. "I'll be up in a bit to tuck you in, muffin," she said. He looked too tired to complain that she wasn't joining him.

"I'm sure they held dinner for us," her ladyship said as soon as Maisie and Jasper left. "It may be a bit cold, but—"

"Mother, I wish to speak to you in the study," Pierce interrupted.

Her ladyship blinked. "In the study! About what?"

"About something we should have discussed years ago."

That put her fully on her guard. "I don't think this is the time or place."

"It's either in the study now, Mother," he said firmly, "or else here in front of the servants."

The two footmen who'd been helping them with their coats exchanged furtive glances, and the countess paled. With a tight nod, she swept ahead of him down the corridor that led to the study.

Camilla stood there, uncertain what to do.

Pierce turned to her. "I want you there, too."

"Are you sure? She might be more honest with you if I'm not."

"I doubt that. She told you more of the truth the other night than she's said to me in my entire life." He offered her a rueful smile. "Besides, if you're there, I might actually keep my temper long enough to get at the truth."

"If she's being her usual stubborn self, I may not keep my own temper."

"It's a risk I'm willing to take." He held out his arm. "Come, it's time to ask her the hard questions. I don't think I can do it alone."

"All right." She took his arm, but her heart flipped over in her chest. What did it mean, that he wanted her with him at such a moment? She tried not to read anything into it, but it was hard not to.

As they walked down the corridor, another thought occurred to her. She'd never been in his father's old study. She'd asked her ladyship about it once, and the countess had said she didn't like to go in it. To her knowledge, Pierce never went in it, either. So why had he picked it for this discussion?

When he opened the door and they walked in, Camilla felt an instant chill, and it wasn't just from the lack of a fire in the room. What little furniture there was lay under canvas cloths, and the place looked as cold and barren as a mausoleum. His mother stood with her back to them, staring at the shrouded desk. Pierce visibly stiffened and cast a quick look around, as if even being in the room caused him pain.

Apparently the same was true for his mother, because as soon as he closed the door, she shuddered before she faced them.

When she saw that Camilla was with him, she gave a start. Avoiding Camilla's gaze, she said, "She shouldn't be here."

A dark scowl knit his brow. "I wouldn't be in this house at all if not for her. I wouldn't have spent the past week here, nor would I have considered, even for a moment, dining with you or spending time with you or even going to the bloody—" He caught himself. "She has championed you and fought for you from the beginning. So she at least deserves to know why."

His mother swallowed hard. "Pierce, I do not wish to—"

"Why did your cousin come to the fair to see you twenty-three years ago?" he asked bluntly.

The color drained from his mother's face. "What do you mean?"

"You know what I mean." Pulling away from Camilla, he approached the countess. "I remembered something today at the fair. I remembered seeing you argue with Gilchrist. Barely two days later, he was here at the house and Father was arguing with you about it. And not long after that, I was banished."

He stared her down. "So I ask you again, Mother, why was he here? What did you argue about? What did he tell Father that day?"

She tipped her chin up. "Nothing. Not a blasted thing."

"I don't believe you," he said. "Gilchrist obviously knew *something* about you—or perhaps about *me*—and whatever it was held enough power to give Father a hold over you that caused you to give up your only son. So damn it, I deserve to know what the man said!"

"I did not give you up!" she cried. "Not in my heart. Not for one day."

His eyes were ablaze. "It certainly felt that way to me."

Her face crumpled. "I know. But we can start anew, forget the past—"

"Not until I have the truth from you."

"My cousin said nothing, I swear! You know how your father always was."

"Yes, but he only banished me from this house after Gilchrist came here. That can't be a coincidence." Pierce set his shoulders. "So tell me this. Am I really Father's son?"

Camilla groaned. Pierce knew nothing about subtlety, at least when it came to his mother.

Her ladyship gaped at him, then lowered her brow to a fierce glower. "If you are implying what I think you are—"

"I'm not implying anything," he snapped. "I'm trying to get at the truth. And it seems to me that the one thing Father could hold over your head, the one thing that would make him banish me from this house, is that you bore him some other man's child!"

"Some other man's—" She muttered an oath under her breath. "Anyone can look at you and tell that you're his son!" She drew herself up with all the dignity a countess could muster. "And how dare you accuse me of . . . of . . ."

"I wouldn't blame you for marrying with a babe in your belly, especially given what I've learned of your situation. I only seek the truth—the reason for why Father hated me so much that he sent me away. The reason for why you *let* him send me away, and keep me away until his death. And the only reason I can come up with is that I wasn't his."

Casting him a blistering glance, she turned for the door. "I'm not going to stand here another moment and be accused of such a thing in my own home."

"It's *my* home now, remember?" he cried as he followed her, his face alight with righteous anger. "Mine. The house is mine. The estate is mine. It's *all* mine. You may be queen of this particular part of it, but it's only because *I* allow it. So the least I deserve from you is the truth!"

She paused in her march to the door to glare at him. "And the least I deserve from you, as the woman who brought you into this world, is a modicum of respect."

That seemed to stymie him. He stood there a moment, his jaw taut and his manner stiff. When he spoke again, his voice was laden with pain. "I'm not asking this because of the years that you left me in the care of my relations, nor even because of the letters I wrote to you that remained unanswered." There was a sharp hitch in his tone. "I'm asking because ten years ago, I stood in this very room and told you and Father that I wished to come home so I could learn how to run the place that would one day be mine."

Her face turned ashen.

"I see that you recall that day, too. You may also recall his response." He glanced over at Camilla with anger glittering in his eyes. "My father told me that if I didn't get my 'damned arse' out of his house and his sight, he would have the footmen forcibly remove me."

Camilla's heart lodged in her throat. She could easily imagine a twenty-one-year-old Pierce, determined to demand his due, being confronted by such a blatant rejection from his own father.

How had he stood it? How could he even stand to speak of it now?

With his hands curling into fists, he turned back to his mother. "If you recall, I told him I wouldn't leave unless he let me speak to you alone. He laughed, but he allowed it. He walked out and left us together." His face darkened. "Because he was sure of you, wasn't he? Sure of his hold on you even then."

"Pierce, don't," her ladyship whispered. Her gaze, torn with agony, flitted briefly to Camilla. "Please don't talk about this in front of her. Leave it between you and me. I beg you."

"I won't leave it," he said hoarsely. "Not unless you tell me the reason for all of it. That's the only thing I want. An explanation. *Any* explanation."

Camilla's heart sank. He'd brought her in here only to use as a weapon against his mother. "Pierce, leave it alone," she said in a low voice.

"She won't tell me!" His gaze locked with his mother's. "So I have to *make* her tell me."

"Not like this," Camilla begged.

"If you insist on revealing to her the awful things I said that day, then go ahead." His mother's shoulders were shaking. "But I won't stay here to witness it."

As she turned again for the door, Pierce cried, "If you walk out on me again without giving me an explanation, Mother, I swear to God, I'll leave for London in the morning, and that will be the end of anything between us!"

She halted at the door to glance back at him with

a look of pure torment. "All I can tell you is this," she choked out. "I love you, son. No matter what I did or said during all those horrible years, no matter how things might have appeared to you, I never stopped loving you."

And with that, she walked out.

Camilla whirled on him, unable to blot out his mother's tortured expression. "How could you be so cruel? Clearly she can't talk about this, and you only make it worse by bludgeoning her with words and accusations!"

With her heart in her throat, she headed for the door, wanting to do something, anything, to help his mother face her pain.

"Cruel?" he called out as she reached it. "You have no idea what cruel is."

When Camilla glanced back at him, his face had gone dead and cold. And when he spoke again, his voice echoed hollowly. "You find her words of 'love' convincing because you don't know what went before." He fisted his hands at his sides. "But the last time I stood in this study, the woman you're so eagerly defending told me to my face that she never wanted to see me again."

20

Perhaps Pierce shouldn't have revealed it, but right now he would say almost anything to keep Camilla from running to Mother and pandering to the woman's refusal to face up to what she did. And where else should he say it but in the place of his shame? The place where both his parents had demonstrated how thoroughly they hated him.

Camilla eyed him warily from behind her spectacles. "Your father must have forced her to say it."

"How, damn it? She was alone with me, right here in this study. She looked me in the eye, her face as cold as a corpse's, and said that if I ever came within a mile of the estate, she would have me thrown off of it. She told me I wasn't welcome here and I wasn't to come back. Ever."

He saw the shock on her face and felt a moment's guilt. But damn it, it was time she recognized that he wasn't at fault. Mother had *chosen* to evict him from her life. And he had every bloody right to hate her for it.

Except that he didn't.

Bile clogged his throat. He'd thought he did. He'd thought he had shut Mother out of his heart completely. But now he realized he'd left a window open somewhere, and she'd found it and was trying to crawl back in.

All these years, he'd fought so bloody hard to protect his heart. To be as cold as Mother was. Yet all she'd had to say was "I love you, son. . . . I never stopped loving you," and the wound was torn open again.

How dare she spout such a lie? It wasn't true. It *couldn't* be true. Because if it were, if he'd been unfair to her, if he'd been wrong to despise her . . .

"Perhaps your father was listening, and she knew it," Camilla said, obviously desperate for a way to vindicate his mother. "Perhaps he was waiting in the hall."

"I considered that at the time." He stared at the window, remembering the agony coursing through him when he looked out of it and realized . . . "But then I saw him riding away, as if he hadn't a care in the world, even as she said those horrible things to me."

His throat felt raw. He couldn't stop the words from

flowing as they never had before. "So I took advantage of his absence. I just couldn't believe that she wasn't the same mother who had . . . held me as a boy and comforted me when I suffered from asthma and—"

He choked back a vile oath, struggling to gain control over his riotous emotions. "I grabbed her by the arm and said, 'I can protect you. I have the inheritance left to me by Grandmother. Come with me now, and we'll say to hell with him.'"

Camilla approached him, but he couldn't look at her. He hated her pity almost as much as he hated this weakness, this need to unburden himself to her. To show her what a pathetic excuse for a man he was, that his own parents could toss him aside like so much rubbish.

"And do you know what her response was?" he ground out. "She shoved me away and stood there, hands clenched, while she told me she didn't want or need my protection, that she wanted only to be free of me. Then she walked out."

He stood there as he had then, hearing the crackle of the fire, the distant peal of the case clock. Tasting the bite of unshed tears as it dawned on him that he really had no parents. Not anymore.

"The footmen entered a few minutes later," he said, "but I had already gotten the message. I left. I went back to London, and I began a systematic course of study in the art of pleasure. I got drunk and I gambled and I had a string of mistresses as long as my arm. It was the only way to show them that they hadn't broken me."

The only way to obliterate the memory of that day. For a time, anyway.

But not anymore. Even before he'd responded to Camilla's damned summons, Mother's weekly letters had started to crack his armor despite his refusal to read them. That was the reason for his restlessness. He could see it now.

"Was that the last time you saw her?" Camilla asked softly.

"Until Father's funeral." He whirled on her, steeling himself for anything, but though pity glimmered in her gaze, it was mingled with something greater. Understanding perhaps. Even empathy.

And more words spilled out of him. "So now you see why I assumed it was all about the money. I thought she wanted me back here because she'd decided she had a use for me at last."

Camilla's heart shone in her face. "I suppose you had good reason to think so ill of her. What she did, what she said, was awful." She spoke slowly, cautiously, as if choosing her words. "But surely now that you've spent time with her and seen what she's really like, you realize that matters couldn't have been what you thought, that nothing was as it seemed."

"I don't know a damned thing anymore."

"Then know this." She came up to him, her eyes

bright. "Having sat with that woman for six months and having heard her go on about her fine son for every day of them, I can assure you that she loves you. As I suspect she did then, no matter what she said that day."

"If she loved me," he growled, "she would explain herself!"

"Perhaps. Or perhaps it's *because* she loves you that she won't. She may just be too ashamed of whatever brought her to that pass. I understand why it drives you mad. It drives me a little mad myself, and I know her better than you." She met his hard gaze unabashedly. "But you may have to resign yourself to never knowing the truth."

"The hell I will," he bit out.

"Listen to me, Pierce," she whispered, her voice so full of compassion, it made him tense up.

Because he didn't know if the compassion was for him or for his mother. And it couldn't be both. "If you're going to argue for *her*—"

"I'm going to argue for *you*. Whatever happened in the past can't be erased. And clearly she won't explain it. But she might in time, if you can bring yourself to put your anger aside for a while." She gave him a sad little smile. "Speaking as someone who never had parents, I can promise that even having an imperfect one who loves you is better than having none at all."

He gritted his teeth. Camilla wanted him to forgive and forget. Why couldn't she see that it was impossible?

"You don't understand. *Your* parents were taken from you by a force of nature or illness or . . . or something." It occurred to him suddenly that she'd never said how. Not that it mattered. "Whatever it was, it was comprehensible. You knew from the beginning that you were an orphan, whereas I—"

"I'm not an orphan," she broke in.

He narrowed his gaze on her. "Of course you are. You told me all about the orphanage." As she tensed, his blood began to pound in his chest. "Your letters of reference were from St. Joseph's Home for Orphans." His voice rose. "Are you saying they were lies?"

She didn't flinch from his angry tone. "No, they're all true. I was raised at St. Joseph's, and I worked there later. That's how I found out that I had no parents. Or rather, none who would claim me." With color suffusing her cheeks, she dropped her gaze to her hands. "I'm not an orphan, Pierce. I'm a foundling. And as I'm sure you know, they're very different things."

For a moment, he could only stand there speechless. They were indeed. "Is that why you *lied* to me about it?" he snapped, his heart thundering in his chest.

Her gaze shot up to his face. "I never lied to you. You made an assumption and I let it rest, as I've let it rest for years with everyone. Because I had to. Because it made it easier for me to be hired."

Her words gave him pause. He thought through every conversation they'd had, then groaned. She was right. She'd never claimed to be an orphan. She hadn't spoken of her parents at all, obviously because she didn't know anything about them.

He'd looked at her on the surface, just as he had with the matter of her son. He hadn't delved any deeper, too absorbed with his own pain to see hers.

She went on in a leaden voice. "I suspect that my parents, whoever they were, personally knew one of the people who managed the orphanage and convinced that person to take me, despite my bastardy." Anger flared in her face. "Otherwise, you and I both know I would never have been admitted. Even the Foundling Hospital, with its rich patrons, has been forced to limit the number of babies it will accept. Every charitable institution is afraid that taking in bastards will encourage the lower orders to leap into bed with each other willy-nilly." She snorted. "As if a woman would *choose* to gain nine months of discomfort, would risk losing her life bearing a child, just for one night's pleasure. People are fools."

"They are indeed," he said hoarsely, still trying to comprehend this new facet of her.

She shot him a look of pure defiance. "My point is, my parents wanted to be rid of me from the moment of my birth. I may not know who they are, but I know that much about them. They couldn't get me into the crowded Foundling Hospital, so they got me into the orphanage."

Her voice turned bitter. "Either way, they had to

know I would never be adopted. No one who is willing to take in someone's bastard wants a redheaded, freckled child—they all want pretty children, with blond curls and porcelain skin."

"Camilla—"

"Don't say it!" she snapped. "Don't try to claim that I *am* pretty, that anyone would have been lucky to have me. Don't tell me all those nice things people say to children who nobody wants."

"All right," he said, taken aback. He'd never seen her like this, at least not on her own behalf.

"Even my husband wanted me only for what he could get out of me." She was shaking now, her temper higher than he'd ever seen it. "Your mother may have abandoned you at eight, but you had her until then. And when she gave you up, she made sure you were put in a safe place, a comfortable place, with good people who cared about you. You weren't left to the indifferent care of an institution. The orphanage wasn't a bad place, mind you, but it wasn't a home, either."

Anger and anguish twisted into one thread in her voice. "So don't tell me how justified you are in throwing away a mother who loves you. Whether you accept it or not, you have her in your life now. You have your cousins and your great-uncle." She set her shoulders like a fierce lioness preparing to fight. "I have no one but Jasper."

He stared at her, unable to look away.

All this time, he'd seen her as sensible, forthright, impossible to ruffle. But beneath that sensible exterior she was a cauldron of righteous fury, a roiling mass of seething emotion. She wanted, she needed . . . she burned every bit as much as he did.

She was magnificent.

As if aware of how much of herself she'd revealed to him, she started to turn away, but he caught her by the arms to hold her still. "You have me," he said hoarsely. "You bloody well have me."

Shock lit her face. Then she gave a mocking laugh. "And what is that supposed to mean? You're going back to London tomorrow, and you made it clear you won't be returning to the dower house. I don't have you in any sense of the word."

When she tried to wrest free of him, he wouldn't let her. Instead, he dragged her closer, his pulse pounding madly. "You would if you came with me."

Her eyes widened. "What do you mean?"

"To London. You and Jasper could return with me." When her brow lowered to a scowl, he added hastily, "Hear me out. I could take a house for you, for us. The two of you would be under my protection."

Her gaze turned wary, like that of a cornered hare. "Let me make sure I understand you correctly. You're offering to make me your mistress, my lord?"

"Yes," he said, ignoring the frosty edge she gave to

the words *mistress* and *my lord*. "That's exactly what I'm offering."

He ought to have been surprised that she had leaped right to that conclusion instead of assuming that he meant marriage. But he wasn't surprised. She knew him, understood him, as no woman ever had. So of course she understood that, too.

But that didn't mean she would accept it. He would have a fight on his hands to make her agree.

And he was prepared to fight. He wanted her that much.

This time when she jerked free, he let her go, though he was ready to snatch her back if she tried to flee.

Instead, she went to stand before the dead hearth. "You have a mistress already," she pointed out dully.

"I gave my last mistress her congé before I even came here."

She whirled on him, face ablaze. "So now you need a substitute, is that it?"

"Damn it, no! That's mere coincidence." He approached carefully, not wanting to spook her again. "If all I wanted was a substitute for her, I'd take one from among the demimonde as I always have. But that's not enough for me anymore."

"I see. You want a change of pace," she said bitterly. "You think to try your hand at a respectable woman, someone who might actually care about you. Is that it?"

As always, the depth of her perception surprised him. But she didn't have the whole story by far. "No. That's not it." Then the rest of her words dawned on him. "Wait, you *care* about me?" And why did that make his pulse quicken? It was only words.

Except nothing was ever "only words" with her.

"Of course I do," she choked out. "I certainly care enough not to want to be your temporary diversion."

"You're more than that to me," he said fiercely, and realized, to his shock, that it was true. When had that happened?

"You say that now, but how long will it be before you tire of me?" She crossed her arms over her chest. "Especially when I have a child in tow."

For some reason, that sparked anger deep inside him. "It's not like that between you and me," he bit out.

"Isn't it?" Sorrow glinted in her eyes. "You're hurt and lonely, and you have no one waiting for you back in London. So you've decided I will do in a pinch."

"No. That's definitely not it."

He stalked her now, determined to make her understand. When she blinked and started to back away, he caught her about the waist and pulled her to him. "Don't you see?" he murmured. "We're alike, you and I. We both show a carefree face to the world while we keep our private torments hidden."

She swallowed hard, showing that she knew exactly what he was talking about. "That merely makes us liars."

"To the world perhaps, but not to each other. We see each other for what we are, and understand each other down deep." He lifted one hand to cup her cheek. "*That's* why I want you to be my mistress."

21

Camilla knew she ought to be insulted. But staring up into the face that had become much too dear in the past week, she ached to accept his offer.

And that made him dangerous.

"We aren't alike at all," she shot back, trying to convince herself of it. "You despise respectability while I—"

"Want it? Really?" He searched her face. "Admit it, dearling, the only thing respectability has gotten you is years of waiting on other people's leisure."

She uttered a harsh laugh. "And I wouldn't be doing that with *you*?"

He scowled. "It wouldn't have to be like that."

"Oh, really. Then tell me what it *would* be like."

When he drew breath to explain, she touched a finger to his lips. "You don't have to—I already know."

With his dark eyes alight, he moved her finger aside, only to catch her hand and press his lips tenderly into her palm. "You don't know anything," he rasped, then kissed her wrist. "We would make our own rules."

Her pulse raced beneath his caress despite her determination to stand firm against him. "I doubt that," she said shakily. "Living in the corners of society as I have, I know how these things work. Nobody makes their own rules."

He trailed kisses up her forearm to the soft skin of her inner elbow.

She fought the desire bolting through her. "If I were your mistress, I would see you at *your* leisure. You would send word that you wished to see me whenever you wanted female companionship, and I'd stop everything to be ready for you. I'd send Jasper to his room with orders not to come out, and I'd—"

"No," he said firmly, pausing to stare at her. "We'd hire Maisie. She would take care of him when we were together."

"When we were fornicating, you mean."

Anger flared in his features. "Damn it, don't make it sound sordid. It won't be that way."

"You can't stop it from being 'that way.'" Pulling free of him, she turned for the door, but he caught her from behind, keeping one arm about her waist as his hand swept up to caress her throat, her jaw, her mouth.

He pressed a hot kiss to her cheek. "It will be what we make of it."

"Not for me, it won't," she choked out. "You can play with me for a while and no one will care, but once you're done, I'll no longer be able to find a post as a companion. The only thing left to me will be other liaisons for hire."

"I wouldn't let it come to that." He nuzzled her ear, and a sensual shiver rocked her.

"I'm sure men have been saying that for centuries," she managed to gasp, though every inch of her wanted to turn and lose herself in his arms. Curse him for that. "I realize you're too far above me for a respectable connection, but that doesn't mean—"

"It's not about that," he hissed. "It's not about your station or your birth. For all we know, I might very well be a bastard, too, no matter what Mother claims." He kissed her neck with such tenderness that it melted all the cold parts of her. "But as you well know, marriage can rapidly become a prison which neither party can escape. I've no desire to let it do that to us."

He pulled her around to face him, his gaze boring into her. "What did your respectable marriage ever gain you? Happiness? We both know it did not. A sense of fulfillment? Not that, either."

"It gained me my son," she whispered. "And it's for him that I must remain respectable."

"And sacrifice your happiness for it? He won't thank you for that, trust me."

"He won't thank me for dragging his name through the mud, either."

"No one's name would be dragged through the mud, I promise you." He slid his hands up her arms to grip her shoulders. "We would be discreet."

"I'd like to see you manage that," she countered. "Especially when I'm heavy with *your* child."

He stared at her as if thunderstruck. Then he shook off his surprise. "There are ways to prevent that."

So she'd heard, while working in Spitalfields. But she'd also heard that men weren't fond of such preventatives. "And you, of course, would be perfectly willing to use them," she said, unable to keep the sarcasm from her voice.

"For you, I would. I have no desire to shame you by forcing you to bear my bastards. I know how you must feel about that." His face was alight now, the face of a man who always got his way, at least where his bed partners were concerned. "And as for the son you already have, only think what I can offer him. I can give him more than you ever could on a companion's wages. You know that's true."

She caught her breath. Oh, he was playing dirty now. "Leave Jasper out of this."

He ignored her. "He'd go to the best schools, eat the finest food, have as many damned tin soldiers as he could cram into his room. He'd have servants at his beck and call, and a pony of his own if he wanted. He'd have a chance at being someone important."

Heaven save her, he knew just what would tempt her. He didn't try to offer her great riches or fine gowns for herself—he knew that wouldn't sway her. But for her son, she would do much.

His gaze was full of promise. "I'd give Jasper anything his heart desired."

"Until you tired of me," she whispered.

"Stop saying that!" He fixed her with a glittering stare. "I would never tire of you. How could I?" He reached up to remove her spectacles and set them on the desk nearby. "You're the only one who sees me for who I am, the only one who knows my secret shame and isn't repulsed. Who wants me in spite of it."

"I don't want—" She halted, realizing the trap he'd laid for her. If she denied wanting him, she'd be saying that his "shame" repulsed her, which simply wasn't true. "It doesn't matter that I want you," she managed in a last desperate effort to resist temptation.

It didn't work. Triumph lit his gaze. "It bloody well matters to me."

Then his mouth took hers, and she was utterly swept away. Because she'd been craving his kiss, his touch, his heat, ever since last night.

No, she'd been craving it far longer than that. Fool that she was, she'd spent half her life wanting someone to desire her, to find her irresistible. Pierce was right—she'd learned to hide that aching need from everyone.

Except him. He did see her, with all her imperfections and seething urges, and he still wanted her. It was so enticing that she couldn't resist him. Not right now.

Then it dawned on her, as he rained kisses over her lips and cheeks and brow, that she had a third choice beyond being his mistress or staying here.

She could have him for tonight. Store up every moment with him for the time when he left.

"I want you, dearling," he rasped as he filled his hands with her breasts.

She hesitated, wondering if she was mad even to consider such a thing. But she would regret it if she didn't take this chance. For once in her life, she wanted to know what passion was like, what having a man desire her felt like. She wanted something real to fuel her dreams for the empty years to come.

The choice was easier to make than she'd expected.

She looped her arms about his neck. "I promised Jasper I would put him to bed, but after that . . ."

Fire blazed in his face. "You'll come to my bed."

It was more an order than a question, but she nodded anyway. For tonight, she'd be his.

"Swear it," he growled.

"Don't you trust me?" She stroked back a wayward lock of his hair.

Foolish question. He didn't trust anyone—his mother had made sure of that, whether she'd meant to or not.

Which was probably why he avoided answering the question directly. "I won't risk having you run up to see your son or console my mother and then changing your mind." His brooding gaze fixed on her as he caught her hand and kissed the back of it. "Swear it."

She couldn't breathe, couldn't think. "Very well. I swear I'll come to your room as soon as I've seen to my son."

That answer gained her a hot, ravening kiss that sparked her need for him into a bonfire, even in the chill of the room. When he finished and she was breathing hard and heavy, he reluctantly released her. "Go. But don't be long."

With a nod, she put her spectacles back on and hurried up to her room. As she passed the floor with the bedchambers, she wondered if she *should* check on the countess. It seemed cruel to leave her alone tonight.

But she just couldn't face the woman right now, given what she was about to do. So she continued up to the room she shared with Jasper. She walked in to find him sound asleep and Maisie waiting for her.

"Her ladyship sent a note for you by one of the footmen," Maisie said, looking up from her sewing. "It's over there on the dresser. I'm surprised she didn't bring it herself—she does enjoy being here when you put Jasper to bed."

"Yes," Camilla said as she read the note, relieved but not unsurprised to hear that the countess wanted to be left alone for the evening.

"I suppose she's having another of her headaches and wants you to read to her," Maisie said, obviously fishing for information about what was in the note.

"I have to go," Camilla said, and shoved it into her pocket, hoping that Maisie would assume the reason for it without her having to lie. "I won't be back too late."

"Oh, it don't matter." Maisie yawned. "I'm going to bed soon as you leave. I'm near as tired as the poor lad was."

"I suppose he ran you ragged today."

"Not a bit. He was right happy to be outside, even in the cold. It was a joy to watch him." The maid smiled. "This afternoon, he couldn't stop talking about his lordship and the horses and how he was going to learn to ride a pony. It was very kind of his lordship to say he'd give the lad lessons."

"Yes, very kind indeed," Camilla managed. That was precisely why she couldn't become Pierce's mistress. Once he ended their liaison, it wouldn't just be *her* heart that was broken.

She shook off that thought. Tonight, she was going to enjoy her time with him. Though she would make him do as he promised and use measures to prevent children. "Good night, then," she told Maisie with a twinge of guilt for misleading the poor girl.

As she headed out of the room, she reminded herself that this was how it would be if she went to London with Pierce. She'd always be leaving Jasper with a maid while she went to meet her lover.

But even that observation didn't dampen the anticipation she felt as she rushed down the stairs and headed to his room.

Before she could reach it, the door opened, and he halted on the verge of coming out. He looked startled. "I was going to fetch you. You were taking too long."

She felt a sudden perverse need to tease him. "I was just passing by, my lord, on my way to the kitchen. Since I was hungry, I thought—"

He yanked her inside the room, then shut the door and backed her against it. "I'll take care of your hunger," he rasped, and covered her mouth with his.

Every inch of her responded, leaping to be touched by him. She craved his kisses, relished the heat and pressure of his hard body. She could feel his arousal against her belly, and it incited her own desire. Even the smell of brandy on him and the taste of—

She tore her lips from his. "You had supper," she accused.

He laughed. Jerking his head toward the table behind him, he said, "I told you I'd take care of your hunger."

Sliding out from between him and the door, she walked to the table and her eyes went wide. Somehow, in the brief time she'd been upstairs, he'd fetched enough food for them both: slabs of cold ham and cheese, thick slices of bread, pears and walnuts, and something in a bowl that looked like . . .

"Almond blancmange?" she exclaimed as she whirled on him.

With a smile, he stripped off his coat and tossed it over a chair. "I know how much you like it. And fortunately Cook does, too, so she had it waiting in case we wanted a good supper. I stole it for you." Eyes gleaming, he strolled over to pick up the bowl and slide a spoon into it.

"How very wicked of you," she said as a thrill went through her. No one ever did such things for her. "Though it shouldn't surprise me that you're a thief as well as a rogue."

"Don't forget 'seducer.'" He handed her the bowl, and as she took a bite of the blancmange, he circled around to stand behind her. Tugging her back against his firm body with one hand, he removed her spectacles with the other and set them on the table. "I'm rumored to be quite accomplished as a seducer."

"Are you?" she murmured, and took another bite of blancmange. Then she offered him some, and when he bent his head over her shoulder to eat off her spoon, she twisted her head to kiss his cheek. "Even you, who doesn't like desserts, must admit that it tastes very good."

He caught her mouth in a long, hot kiss, then drew back. "Not as good as you taste, dearling." Her blood quickened, especially when he cupped her breasts and fondled them shamelessly through her clothes, thumbing the nipples into fine points. "Though I'm happy that *you* enjoy it."

"Oh, I do," she said, savoring another bite of blancmange as he slid one hand down over her belly. She undulated against it, wanting it lower. "Keep feeding me blancmange," she gasped out, "and you won't need to seduce me. I'll fall into your bed of my own accord."

He chuckled. "You may not know this," he murmured as he continued his roguish caresses, "but I'm famous for paying my chefs very well." He nipped her earlobe, then soothed it with his tongue. "So even the most celebrated would happily come to work for my mistress. You could have all the rich desserts you could dream of."

She nearly choked on her blancmange. Wily devil. Leave it to Pierce to try tempting her into accepting his offer with a promise of fine food.

But did he really believe he could gain her only by buying her? Did he think so little of himself?

She set the bowl on the table. "I don't need a celebrated cook. I'm quite happy with the usual fare."

He worked loose the buttons of her day dress. "Ah,

but are you happy wearing another woman's cast-off gowns? Because as my mistress, you'd never have to again. You'd have clothes made specifically to show off your spectacular figure."

"I don't need false flattery, either," she said tartly, annoyed that he would stoop so far. "I know I'm plump."

"It isn't flattery, and it certainly isn't false. I like women who feel like women, not lampposts." Sliding her gown off, he began to unlace her corset. His breathing grew rough. "The first time I saw you, I desired you. And yes, you *are* pretty. It would give me great pleasure to dress you in clothes that convinced you of that."

The idea enticed her in spite of herself. Sweet heaven, how could she be that shameful? This was why the local rector always railed against the temptations of the flesh. Because they were so very tempting.

As her corset came free, she wriggled out of it and turned to face him, wearing only her shift. "You said we'd be discreet. But dressing me up and parading me about town would hardly be *that*."

His admiring gaze slid slowly down her, heated, hungry. He tore off his cravat and waistcoat, but his eyes never left her body. "We can be discreet without having to be recluses. London is large—if we choose the house carefully, we can live as we like without fearing that everyone is watching."

More temptation. The idea of being with him, of *living* with him . . .

Ah, but she knew it wouldn't be like that, no matter how much he wished it. Tonight was all they had.

So she would make the best of it. She reached up to unbutton his shirt, revealing a light dusting of dark brown curls as she opened it down to the placket, then pulled the tails from his trousers.

His voice turned ragged. "We could even go shopping and attend the theater, if we were careful about it."

He yanked off his shirt, leaving his chest exposed, and she caught her breath. She'd guessed that he would be muscular and well-formed, but she hadn't guessed it would have such an effect on her.

Kenneth had been a bit scrawny, nothing like the feast of male flesh before her. She wanted to touch, to caress, to rub herself all over him. What a wanton she was.

As if he read her mind, he grabbed her hands and placed them on his chest. A bit embarrassed, she avoided his gaze as she spread her fingers over the now tense muscles, reveling in how they jumped beneath her touch and how his heart raced at her caress.

How that made her own heart race.

He tugged loose the ties of her shift. "We could go to the museums or . . . take a boat along the Thames in the summer . . ."

He trailed off when she slid her hand down to work loose the buttons of his markedly bulging trousers. His breath came in a harsh rasp now, yet he kept talking. "We could even . . . live close enough to the country . . . to keep horses and ride. I'd buy you the finest mount . . . with a beautiful saddle and . . . a neat little curricle for your own use. . . . Then I'd teach you to ride and drive and—"

"Shh," she whispered. She couldn't bear it anymore. "Stop trying to buy my affections." She brushed a kiss over his lips. "You already have them."

His eyes glinted obsidian in the firelight.

"Would I love for you to teach me all that, and buy me new clothes and the rest of it?" she went on, desperate to make him understand. "Yes. But if I became your mistress, it wouldn't be for any of that." Taking his hand, she pressed it against her chest where her heart pounded furiously. "It would be for *this,* for how you make me feel."

A shuddering breath escaped him. "And how *do* I make you feel?"

She stretched up to kiss his mouth. "Like I can fly."

With a groan, he caught her to him and kissed her with such fervent need that she thought her heart might explode. Oh, what was she going to do? She was falling in love with him.

And he didn't want that.

So she gave him what he did want. She let him pull her shift off her, let him carry her to his bed. She let him lay her down and run his smoldering gaze over her while he finished stripping off his clothes. She didn't flinch or blush or turn away from that hot, riveting stare.

Until he was naked. Then she had to look at *him.* And what a sight he was, all lean muscle and fine lines, a sweet symphony of a body that she wanted nothing more than to play.

He reached over to pull out the drawer to the little table beside the bed. "Since I promised you I'd take preventative measures . . ." He drew out a long sheepskin tube, then held it out to her. "Would you like to do the honors?"

She sat up to gape at it. "Do you carry such devices about with you as a matter of course?"

He laughed. "No. But after what happened last night, I figured you might be more amenable to sharing my bed if I could promise to protect you. And you'd be surprised what the tinkers at a county fair have for purchase, if you know how to ask the right questions."

"*That's* what you were doing this afternoon?"

"Among other things."

With a shake of her head, she took the tube from him. "You really are quite a wicked fellow." Though the fact that he was willing to wear such a thing touched her deeply.

"That's what you like about me," he drawled.

"Hardly," she said with a sniff. "I like you in spite of that."

But as she smoothed the covering onto his thick, jutting member, so much larger than her late husband's, and he hardened even more, it dawned on her that their positions resembled those of the characters in that shocking drawing from *Fanny Hill*.

That's when she finally blushed.

With a chuckle, he tied off the tube, then slid onto the bed and pulled her down to lie next to him. "For a widow, you sometimes seem very innocent."

She frowned at him. "Forgive me if I don't have *your* vast experience. I had only the one husband, and he mostly touched me in the dark when I was half asleep. I hardly ever saw him like . . . well . . . this."

His gaze turned positively carnal. "You'd best get used to it," he said in a husky murmur as he filled one hand with her breast. "Because I intend to be naked with you every chance I get."

Then his mouth was on hers—as was his body— and she shut her eyes to savor it, putting her late husband thoroughly from her mind. Pierce whispered admiring compliments about her hair and her breasts and her belly, kissing each part with a mix of heat and tenderness, making her want and need and yearn—

He kissed her between her legs, and her eyes shot open. "Wh-what are you doing?"

When she tried to pull her thighs together, he wouldn't let her. "You need to read more naughty books, dearling." His eyes glittered. "You had your dessert. Now let me have mine."

And he lowered his mouth to her most private part again.

"But . . . but . . . Pierce . . . ohhh . . ."

She'd had no idea. The way he was kissing her . . .

there . . . seemed decadent and wild and . . . so very delicious that she curled her fingers into his hair to hold him close.

His response was to kiss and suck and tease until she thought she'd go out of her mind with need. It wasn't long before she could feel her release building, feel it growing and lifting . . . "Pierce . . . oh, dear heaven . . . please . . ."

"Not yet, dearling." Dark eyes alight, he moved up over her. "This time we'll go there together."

And he entered her with one silken thrust.

Oh, it was magic. He was inside her, around her, driving her once more toward a glorious madness. How would she give this up? How would she give *him* up? He felt part of her. With him, she was herself and it was right. He liked her just as she was.

But he didn't love her, and that would kill her in time. Because she could never be with him, day in and day out, without telling him she loved *him*.

She did. She loved the dear, complicated man. And she knew, just as she knew everything else about him, that he wouldn't want to hear it. So she would show him tonight, instead.

As he drove into her over and over, she kissed his chin, his throat, his mouth . . . anything she could reach. She wrapped her legs about his hips when he urged her, and she gave herself up to the act that until now she'd always thought awkward and embarrassing. Because with him, it was neither of those. It was like . . . like . . .

"Are you flying yet?" he rasped as he thundered into her, each stroke bringing her nearer loftier heights.

It *was* like flying. Exactly. "Yes . . ." she choked out. "Oh, Pierce . . ."

"Fly then, dearling," he murmured as he drove her higher and higher. "As high . . . as you can . . ." He stared down at her, his eyes darkening with an emotion she'd never seen in them before.

Longing. She recognized it because that's what she felt, too.

He brushed his lips against hers, then whispered, "Just make sure you take me with you . . ."

And with one great plunge, he sent her soaring into the heavens.

She clasped him to her as he, too, reached his release, and for one precious moment, they vaulted into the highest heights together, wrapped in each other's arms without a care in the world.

Then slowly they tumbled to earth. And to her surprise, that was precious, too—for although he rolled off her, he didn't turn over and go to sleep. He drew her close, then held her and kissed her and made her feel like something more than a bedmate.

And as he nuzzled her neck with infinite tenderness, the words she'd fought not to say just spoke themselves.

"I love you," she whispered into his ear. "I love you, Pierce Waverly."

22

To Pierce's shock, his heart sang at the words. He would never have expected them to sound so wonderful. Then again, he hadn't expected sharing a bed with Camilla to be so wonderful, either.

It made no sense. He'd been with plenty of women—more experienced women, younger women, more accomplished women. He'd shared the beds of actresses and whores, opera singers and duchesses, and never once had it been an act of such sweetness that it damned near brought him to tears.

Never once had any of them said those words to him afterward.

Oh, God, didn't he know by now that love was just a word? That it meant nothing?

Except that he couldn't believe Camilla would lie to him. He knew who she was, from tip to toe. She would never say such a thing lightly.

But that didn't mean it was real.

He drew back to stare at her. "Don't."

The pain in her eyes was swiftly covered by belligerence. "Don't what? Love you? Or *say* that I love you? I can stop the latter, but I can't stop the former. It's too late for that."

With his blood pounding through his veins, he took her hand and kissed it. "Look, I know that you think you feel something—"

"I don't *think* I feel anything." She snatched her hand from his. "I know what I feel, Pierce. Don't try to tell me otherwise." Pulling out of his hold, she sat up to throw her legs over the side of the bed.

He looped his arm about her waist to keep her there, then pressed a kiss to her back. "Don't go. Not yet."

She sat there, her body stiff against his arm, but as he sat up beside her, she let out a long, shuddering breath. "I'm sorry. I knew you wouldn't want to hear it. But I couldn't help myself." A wry note entered her voice. "It's been the curse of my life that I speak my mind even when I shouldn't."

"That's what I like about you," he assured her. Even when what she said set him on his ear. He stared down at her bent head, feeling a welter of confused emotions, not the least of which was hope, damn it. "But I can't . . . I don't . . ."

"I know, my lord," she said, the formal term cutting him to the heart. "It just had to be said."

She started to rise from the bed, but he pulled her down onto his lap. "It's not what you think." When she wouldn't look at him, he turned her face up to his. "I'm not capable of loving anyone."

She cupped his jaw, her hand infinitely gentle. "I don't think that's true."

"Ah, but it is."

He debated a moment, but the melting look in her eyes decided for him. She deserved to know what sort of man she was taking up with. Reaching over to open the little drawer by the table, he drew out a much-creased and worn letter and handed it to her.

When she cast him a quizzical glance, he said, "It's the last letter my mother ever wrote me at school, right after I was sent away."

Paling a little, she opened the fragile parchment and read the lines that had been etched on his soul for years. The lines that ended with *And always remember, I love you very, very much. With many kisses, Mother.*

"I kept it at first to sustain me through the difficult

times." His voice hardened. "Then I kept it to remind me how little the words mean."

She glanced at him, tears filling her eyes. "I'm not lying to you when I say them, and I suspect that neither was she."

"Perhaps not," he managed. "But that makes it even more obvious that love is just a meaningless fiction. At least I'm wise enough to understand that. And I can't feel something I don't believe in. I might have believed in it once, but not anymore."

"Because of your parents abandoning you, you mean."

"Not just that." There were times he hated how deeply Camilla saw into him. "But I've experienced too much in my life, witnessed too many unhappy marriages, and . . ." He forced a smile. "It's like Jasper believing in flying reindeer. Once you're around real deer enough to know they don't fly, the magic disappears."

"On the contrary," she said softly. "Believing in love isn't like believing in flying reindeer. It's like believing in rain. Or summer. Or Christmas. Love is real and steady and absolutely essential to any kind of life. Not believing in it doesn't make it any less so."

Fighting the seductive appeal of her words, he rasped, "For me, it does, and that's what matters."

He braced himself for more of an argument, but

she merely shook her head at him. "I know. That's why I didn't intend to say the words."

The regret in her voice knifed through him, and he caught her by the chin so he could kiss her, soft and deep. "It doesn't change anything. Wanting you, having you want me, is more than enough for me."

"Is it?" She stared into his face, her eyes luminous in the firelight. Without her spectacles, she looked even more like a maiden waiting for love.

And it hit him suddenly how unfair he was being, to ask her to give up a future with any other man just to be his mistress.

But she'd had her chance at marriage, and she hadn't liked it. That's what made the two of them so perfect for each other. They were peas in a pod and wanted the same things, whether she admitted it or not.

Didn't they?

"Camilla, I—"

A knock came at the door, and he froze. A glance at the clock told him it was long after midnight. No servant would be up here at this hour.

Camilla leaped from his lap. "Oh, Lord, Maisie must have guessed I was here. Something must be wrong with Jasper!" Guilt suffusing her features, she hurried to put on her shift, then her drawers.

Swiftly, he rose and began to dress, too.

The knock came again. "Open the door, Pierce!" his mother's voice commanded. "I wish to speak with you!"

As the blood drained from Camilla's face, he cursed under his breath. The main rooms downstairs in the dower house had special servants' passages, but none of the bedchambers did. There was no escape.

"I'll be there in a moment, Mother!" he called out as he jerked his trousers on. Somehow he had to draw her away so Camilla could leave without being seen.

Camilla was still frantically gathering up her clothes and grabbing her spectacles when the door swung open, and his mother entered.

Bloody hell. He'd forgotten to latch the door.

Mother took in the scene with a look of pure horror. "I knew it!" she cried. "I went looking for Camilla, and Maisie said she'd thought she was with me. So I went to the drawing room and the study and found no trace of either of you. That's when I knew." Her gaze met his accusingly as Camilla stood fixed in the middle of the room. "How could you?"

"My lady, please, it's not how it seems," Camilla said.

"No?" she choked out. "Because it appears to me that my son has just finished seducing you."

Pierce glared at her. "How dare you—"

"You have every reason to be angry with me, Pierce," his mother went on fiercely. "But to use Camilla as a weapon against me is—"

"A *weapon*?" Only with an effort did he keep from tossing her bodily from his room. "Not that it's any of your concern, Mother, but she *chose* to be here. We chose to be together."

"A woman in Camilla's position is unable to choose such a thing," his mother protested. "Do you really think she could refuse you? You're her employer, so any association of that kind between you gives you all the power, and you know it."

He stiffened. He did know it. And the worst of it was he would do it again if he had the chance.

"You paint your son more ill than he is, my lady," Camilla put in. "He never demanded anything of me, never took advantage. I really *did* choose to be with him. I know you probably think it very wrong of me, but—"

"I don't blame you, my dear," his mother told her softly, then nodded to Pierce. "I blame *him*."

That was the last straw. "You have no right to blame me for anything, ever," Pierce hissed as he advanced on her, not caring that he wore only his trousers. "You gave up the right to dictate to me when you abandoned me."

"I did not abandon you!" Mother cried. "I acted in your own interests."

That was a new twist, and the ludicrousness of it infuriated him. "Oh? How so?"

Her lips tightening, she glanced away and said nothing more.

His temper rose into fury as the festering sore of twenty-three years erupted. He bore down on her with ruthless intent. "Were you acting in my interests when you ignored the letters where I begged to be allowed to come home? Or when you kept me from learning how to run the estate I would one day inherit? Or even when you shattered every real feeling I ever had by telling me—"

He broke off with a curse. "I refuse to do this anymore. I don't care what your reasons were. Nothing you say can make up for what you did." He turned to where Camilla was watching them both, her expression clearly torn. "Camilla, go gather your things and Jasper's. We're leaving for London now."

His mother turned ash white, which gave him a moment's twinge of conscience, but he ignored it. She had no say in this. She'd given up that right years ago.

But Camilla hadn't moved.

"Go on, dearling," he commanded her. "I know it's late, but you and Jasper can both sleep in the carriage. Bring Maisie, too, if you need to."

She swallowed hard, then said, barely above a whisper, "I'm not going with you."

He gaped at her. He couldn't have heard her right. "Of course you are."

"I can't," she said, her voice a little firmer. "My place is here."

"Your place is with me!" he ground out.

A tear escaped her eye, then another. "Pierce, you have to understand—"

"No!" he cried as the bottom dropped out of his

stomach. "Damn it, no, I don't have to understand a bloody thing!"

She couldn't be doing this. He wouldn't let her.

He strode up to grab her by the arms. "You belong with me. We belong together. You owe her *nothing*, no matter what you think."

Tears were streaming down her face now, and she clutched her pitiful bundle of clothes closer to her chest, as if to use them as a shield against him. "It's not about your mother."

"The hell it isn't! You're choosing her over me, because you've got some idea in your head that being at her beck and call is more respectable, more—"

"I'm not choosing either of you," she said in a tortured whisper as she pulled free of his grip. "I'm choosing my son."

That caught him by the throat. It was an argument he felt powerless to refute. But he tried anyway. "You know he'll be better off in London."

"As the scorned son of your mistress?"

He glowered at her. "No one would *dare* to scorn him, or you. Not with my power and fortune behind the two of you."

"And after we no longer have you?" she asked softly. "What becomes of us then?"

Her logic was inescapable, and he hated her for it.

"Or what happens when you marry?"

"I will *never* marry," he vowed.

Tears sparkled in her eyes. "You say that now, but you can't promise it."

He scowled. "If you want promises from me, then come with me to London. I'll have my solicitor draw up whatever legal document you require to ensure that you—"

"It has nothing to do with money!" she cried. "I can't risk your coming in and out of Jasper's life at your leisure. Small children don't understand such things. You of all people should know that."

The words hit him like a blow to the gut, making him want to strike back. "I know that you said you love me. You *claimed* that the words were real."

Though the blood drained from her face, she didn't waver in her stance. "They are, and I do. Which is precisely why I can't go with you. I love you too much to be just your toy for a while."

"You wouldn't be my toy, damn it!"

But he could see from her face that no argument would sway her. Once Camilla made up her mind to do something, she stayed the course, even if that course drove a stake through his heart.

How *dare* she show him heaven for one brief, glittering moment, and then snatch it away, leaving him alone once more?

Always alone.

"Fine," he choked out, steeling himself against the hurt that rent his heart.

She thought to force him into marriage, did she? Well, the days when he could be jerked about by other people's whims were long gone. Never again would anyone force him into doing anything.

"To hell with you." He looked beyond her to where his mother had gone still as death. "To hell with both of you. I'm leaving this house, and I'm not returning. So I hope you're both very happy together. Now get out of my room."

When they just stood there, staring hollow-eyed at him, he marched toward them. "Out, damn you!"

His mother fled at once, but Camilla paused in the doorway to glance back at him. "I know you're angry, Pierce, and I understand why. Your parents tore a hole in your heart when they abandoned you, and you've been trying to mend it ever since. That's why you've had a string of mistresses—not because you wanted to show your parents they hadn't broken you, but because you kept hoping to find someone who really did care about you."

"Shut the hell up!" he cried, fighting the truth in her words as furiously as he fought to ignore the compassion on her face.

"Well, you've found that someone. I truly do love you. But until you put the past behind you, you won't be free to love me or anyone else." She hitched up the bundle of clothes in her arms. "If you've learned anything from your parents, it ought to be this—love works only when it's mutual. Otherwise, eventually it becomes exactly what you call it—a meaningless word. For both parties."

Then she walked out.

He stared blindly at the door, willing her to come back through it, to change her mind, to throw caution to the winds.

But he knew better. She would never do that. Not for *him*. No one ever did.

And it was time he stopped waiting for it.

Camilla stood in the countess's sitting room as the house was thrown into an uproar. Pierce had given orders for his coach-and-four to be readied, and the entire cadre of servants had been roused to do all the myriad tasks required for a trip.

His mother wouldn't look at Camilla, and Camilla wasn't certain if it was embarrassment or disgust that kept her so distant.

At the moment, she didn't care either way. She was numb from the inside out. She should have known that her heart-stopping plunge into pleasure would end like this. Anything that wonderful never lasted.

Ruthlessly, she stifled the tears that kept threatening. She refused to cry in front of her ladyship. That would come later, when she was alone. No doubt, regret would come with it, too.

But right now she didn't regret her few stolen

moments with Pierce. They would sustain her for years to come.

They would have to. Now that she knew what love was like, she didn't want to go through it with anyone else. She didn't think she could bear this pain more than once.

Tears threatened again, and she lifted her handkerchief to blot them before they could fall.

"Perhaps you should have gone with him," the countess said in a ragged whisper.

The words, sounding like a dismissal, startled her. "Will it be so hard for you to endure my presence now?"

"No! Never, my dear, never. But I hate to see him go off alone." Her ladyship seized Camilla's hand and squeezed it. "And I hate to see you so unhappy."

The countess's words made Camilla want to cry even more. She squeezed her ladyship's hand back. "I'll be fine."

One day perhaps. But at the moment, it didn't feel as if she'd ever be fine again.

"I suppose you did the right thing. It wouldn't do for Jasper—"

"No, it wouldn't," Camilla said firmly. It wouldn't do for her, either. Spending her life as Pierce's sometime lover would have drained the heart out of her.

"He shouldn't have asked it of you," her ladyship said. "It was very wrong of him."

"He was just being Pierce."

And yet . . .

She kept seeing the look of betrayal on his face. He'd been sure she would go with him, especially since she'd been foolish enough to tell him how she felt about him.

Of course, then the wretch had tried to use that against her. Anger coursed through her, and she choked it down. What else had she expected? That he would profess his undying love? She should have kept her feelings to herself.

The door burst open, and Maisie rushed in with a wide-awake Jasper in her arms. "What's going on, mi-lady? The poor lad woke up in a fright at all the noise."

Lady Devonmont drew herself up, becoming her usual restrained self once more. "His lordship is leaving."

"In the middle of the night? But why . . . what . . ." Maisie glanced to where Camilla stood, now dressed but with her hair still down about her shoulders and her eyes teary, and Maisie's lips tightened into a line. "I see."

"You are not to say a word about this," the countess commanded. "Not to anyone, do you understand?"

"Of course, milady," Maisie said fiercely. "I would never do anything to harm you or Mrs. Stuart."

Camilla cast the maid a grateful smile.

Sudden silence descended on the house, and her ladyship sighed. "He must be gone now."

"Yes." Camilla's stomach plummeted. Oh, how would she bear it?

Jasper reached for Camilla, and she took him from Maisie. He stared up at her sleepily. "Why did his lordship go away, Mama? And why didn't he say farewell to me?"

"I'm sure he wanted to, my dear boy," Lady Devonmont put in, "but he was in a very big hurry. He has a lot of important matters requiring his attention in London, you know."

Jasper stared at the countess. "Because he's the great earl, you mean."

"Yes, exactly," Camilla choked out. The great earl who equated believing in love to believing in flying reindeer. Because if he believed in love, he'd have to put the past behind him, and he just couldn't.

"But what about Christmas?" Jasper asked. "And what about Blixem? He said he'd give me Blixem when we got home, and he forgot."

"I'll give you Blixem," her ladyship answered. "Don't you worry about that."

"And if you'll recall," Camilla added, "his lordship did say he wouldn't be here for Christmas. He has to go to Waverly Farm."

"I remember." Jasper pouted. "I just thought he might change his mind."

Thank heaven Pierce had left when he had. Right now Jasper was merely intrigued by the man, but many more encounters and his leaving would have hurt the boy deeply.

Rubbing his eyes, Jasper stared into her face. "Does this mean I don't get to learn to ride a pony? His lordship said there was a Welsh pony in the stables, and I could learn to ride it."

"And you shall." Lady Devonmont's voice was firm. "I'll speak to Mr. Fowler about it tomorrow."

"I don't know if I want to anymore." Jasper laid his head on Camilla's shoulder. "It won't be the same without his lordship. Will it, Mama?"

"No, muffin, it won't," she choked out.

Nothing would ever be the same again.

23

Pierce tried to sleep on his way back to London, but it was impossible. He couldn't cast Camilla from his mind. At first all he could do was rage at her for her small-mindedness. How could she not see the value of what he offered? And how could she claim Jasper would be harmed by their association? He would never hurt the lad. Never!

Jasper would gain advantages beyond her wildest imaginings: schools and money and—

And after we no longer have you? What becomes of us then?

He clenched his hands into fists. The words ran-kled. Yet as his temper cooled, his rational mind reasserted itself, and he recognized that her words were fair. She had every right to worry about the future. Her idiot husband had died unexpectedly, and she and Jasper had been left with nothing. It could happen to Pierce just as easily.

All right, perhaps that was true. But he would make provisions, *legal* provisions.

It has nothing to do with money! I can't risk your coming in and out of Jasper's life at your leisure. Small children don't understand such things. You of all people should know that.

He did. God, how he did.

His heart pounding, he stared out the coach window at the pre-dawn darkness. The snowy fields glowed white beneath the waning moon, reminding him of the day he'd left home for school, not knowing it would be his last day at Montcliff for years to come.

And he realized with a jolt that if Camilla had chosen him over Jasper, she would be no better than his own mother, who'd chosen Father over him.

Or had she?

He'd scoffed when Mother had said she'd acted in his own interests, but now he had to reconsider that possibility. If Father had held something over Mother's head, as he and Camilla had postulated, what if it really *had* been something having to do with him? Pierce couldn't see how that was possible, but then, he couldn't see straight when it came to the past.

Camilla had recognized that.

I truly do love you. But until you put the past behind you, you won't be free to love me or anyone else.

Try as he might, the words kept thrumming through his brain. It was easy for her to say—she didn't have his past.

No, he thought wryly, she merely lived with the daily realization that her parents hadn't wanted her at all. That she'd been born destitute in ways he couldn't begin to understand, even with his own painful situation.

He let out a long breath. No wonder she couldn't accept his offer to make her his mistress. She yearned to be wanted for herself, as she never had been, and what he was offering was a poor substitute.

But could he offer her more? Did he dare? Or would he be better off not risking it?

He still had no answers by the time the coach arrived at his town house shortly after dawn. The servants were prepared for him since he'd sent word ahead, but even their presence couldn't liven a place that felt like a tomb after the bustle and cheer of the dower house. He hadn't realized until now how sterile his life had become, with his mistress relegated to her own lodging.

Indeed, even before he'd gone to Hertfordshire, his most pleasant days had begun to be the ones spent with his cousins and their friends the Sharpes. What did it say about him that he increasingly found enjoyment only with happy couples and relations?

He ought to go to bed—he hadn't slept in twenty-four hours. But he was too restless to sleep. And a few moments playing the pianoforte in his drawing room gave him no comfort, either.

The brandy decanter tempted him briefly, but he'd gone that route three days ago. It had been oddly unsatisfying.

Thinking that losing himself in work might be the best alternative, he headed for his study. But as he stood behind the desk, sifting through the pile of mail that Boyd had left for him, he was arrested by the sight of the infamous box of Mother's letters.

Pierce's throat tightened as he stared at them.

Then he sat down, dumped out the box so that the very first letter was on top, opened it, and began to read.

My dearest son,

You cannot know how much I have missed you all these years. You probably have trouble believing that, but it is the absolute truth. Being with you at the funeral, even with you so very angry at me, made all the rest of it bearable.

May I say that you were dressed very well? I was glad to see it. Your great-uncle always said that you wore a fine coat better than any man he knew, and I quite agree.

The nine-page letter went on in that vein, mixing her observations of him from the funeral with information she had apparently gleaned from his great-uncle. He hadn't known that his uncle wrote to her, but it wouldn't have mattered if he *had*, for apparently she hadn't written back to Uncle Isaac, either, since she made no mention of it.

But here and there her letters to Pierce contained a reference to this or that anecdote Uncle Isaac had written about him. Some events she described had so faded into the distant mists of his memory that he was astonished anyone remembered them, especially her.

As he tore through letter after letter, she commented on her daily life, but the accounts always rambled into memories she'd stored up of him from myriad sources. Some were gleaned from the newspapers—in one letter she waxed on for pages about how Eugenia wasn't worthy of him—and some were taken from his great-uncle's and the late Titus Waverly's letters.

Occasionally she would recount something that Fowler had told her of Pierce's work at the estate. She even offered advice, and he realized with faint amusement that although he hadn't read any of it, it had still filtered to him through Fowler, and he'd often taken her advice secondhand.

It took him several hours to read all of her letters, and when he was done, he sat back with a tightness in his chest. Years of tales of him were recounted, some that he couldn't believe she'd even heard about. It was as if she'd stored up his entire life for the day when she could relive it with him. The day when she could be with him again.

And he had spurned the gift without even giving it a glance. Why? Because she wouldn't explain herself or her actions.

She didn't do it in the letters, either, just as Camilla had predicted. There were no references to his years of banishment, no mention of that horrible day in the study. She barely spoke of Father at all. It was as if the man had disappeared from her thoughts and memories on the day of his death. Clearly, there'd been no love there.

Yet love for her son shone in every word.

He sat there with the last letter in his hand, his blood thundering and his eyes misty with tears, and read the last line. It was the same last line of every single letter in the box:

> *Even if you can never forgive me, my son,*
> *know that I will love you until I die. And*
> *beyond, if God would allow it.*

He stared blindly across the study, and Camilla's words came to him.

Your mother may have abandoned you at eight, but you had her until then. And when she gave you up, she made sure you were put in a safe place, a comfortable place, with good people who cared about you. . . . So don't tell me how justified you are in throwing away a mother who loves you.

Mother *had* loved him. He could see that now.

Camilla had said that the very fact of her love might have to be enough for him. That he might never know the truth about why she'd banished him for so many years.

But could he put the past behind him and just go on, build a relationship with his mother outside of the past?

He didn't think he could. Not because he didn't want to but because he didn't think *Mother* could, either. No matter how they tried to ignore it, those years of pain would taint every encounter.

If Camilla was right, however, and Mother would never reveal the truth, then he'd have to discover it on his own. He knew more now than when he'd gone off to Hertfordshire. He might even know enough to get him started solving the puzzle.

Because it was time he got to the bottom of things. Since Mother wouldn't reveal it, he would unveil it. It was better than sitting around brooding over Camilla, better than parsing his wreck of a life for what he might have done differently.

And he knew just the man to help him do it, too.

A few hours later, fueled by coffee and a fresh purpose, Pierce was being shown into Sir Jackson Pinter's grand new office in Bow Street.

The famous former Bow Street Runner had been knighted for solving the twenty-year-old murder of the Sharpe siblings' parents. Thanks to that—and other celebrated cases—he was now chief magistrate. But as far as Pierce knew, he still did investigative work. At least Pierce hoped so. Because if Sir Jackson couldn't find out the truth, no one could.

But only when the former runner greeted him with a decidedly cool manner did Pierce remember that the fellow didn't *like* him. Unbeknownst to Pierce at the time, the woman who was now Sir Jackson's wife had briefly used Pierce as a pretend suitor in part of a scheme to thwart her grandmother's edict of marriage.

He'd forgotten that rather sticky point.

"Have a seat, Devonmont," Sir Jackson said with a jerk of his head toward the chair before his desk.

As Sir Jackson sat down, Pierce did the same. "You look well," Pierce said, figuring he'd best smooth the past over if he could. "Marriage suits you."

A smile stole over the man's face, softening what were generally rather harsh features. "Marriage and fatherhood. I have a son now, you know."

"I heard. Congratulations. Did he come out brandishing a pistol?"

Sir Jackson blinked, then laughed. "No, but if Celia has her way, he'll be learning to aim one by the time he's three."

"If anyone could teach him how to shoot, it's your

wife. And if anyone could teach him *when* to shoot, it's you."

"Thank you, my lord." Looking a bit more genial, Sir Jackson settled back in his chair. "Now tell me, what brings you to Bow Street?"

Pierce got right to the point. "Actually, I have need of your services to find out information about a cousin of my mother's."

"Your estranged mother?" Sir Jackson said.

"You know about that?"

"Aside from the fact that the Sharpes are notorious gossips, I . . . er . . . did a bit of research into your background for Celia."

"Ah." Pierce wasn't surprised. He wasn't even annoyed. Since Sir Jackson seemed a bit embarrassed by it, he might be willing to make up for it by helping Pierce now. "Well, that's all water under the bridge." He arched an eyebrow at Sir Jackson. "As long as you're willing to take the case."

"Willingness has nothing to do with it, I'm afraid. I don't do that sort of work anymore. Between serving as chief magistrate and being asked to supervise a number of criminal investigations, I have no time."

Pierce sighed. "I was afraid that might be the situation."

"However," Sir Jackson continued, "I've passed off the private investigations part of my work to a new fellow. He's very competent, worked for me for years, and has now struck off on his own. And you're in luck—he just happens to be here today, questioning some fellow in our custody. If you can wait a minute, I'll have him fetched."

"Thank you," Pierce said.

Sir Jackson rose and headed for the door. "You'll like the man. He was a Harrovian like yourself, though in a younger class, I believe. His name's Manton. Dominick Manton."

And before Pierce could react, Sir Jackson was out the door.

Manton? The brother of George Manton did investigative work? How the devil had that come about? Viscounts' sons, even younger ones, didn't do work for hire. And certainly not *that* kind of work for hire.

He vaguely remembered Dominick Manton—a sullen, quiet chap with a passion for dogs and mathematics, who was two years Pierce's junior. While George had stalked about bullying all the younger boys, including Dominick, his little brother had sat in the corner reading tomes by Sir Isaac Newton. Strange fellow.

But as Sir Jackson brought Manton in, Pierce had to acknowledge that he'd grown up well enough. Nor did he much resemble his brother. George, now the Viscount Rathmoor, was beefy and hard-faced, though handsome enough to have snagged himself a very wealthy wife. The last time Pierce had seen Rathmoor, the man still had a body like a mastiff, all head and brawn.

Manton, however, had a body like a Labrador—leaner and sleeker, with intelligent eyes. His black hair was unfashionably short, and a light scar crested one cheek, giving him a rakish appearance.

"My lord," Manton said after Sir Jackson introduced them.

Pierce found the formal address ironic, considering they were both gentlemen. "You may not recall, but I went to school with you and your brother."

The tightening of Manton's lips at Pierce's mention of Rathmoor told Pierce a great deal. The brothers clearly didn't get along.

Which was fine by him. Anyone who hated Rathmoor was a friend of Pierce's.

"I remember," Manton said. "You had asthma."

"For a while, yes."

"If you gentlemen don't mind," Sir Jackson broke in, "I'm expected at a meeting down the hall. But you're welcome to talk in here if you like." He sighed. "The only thing I hate about being chief magistrate is all the damned meetings."

Pierce chuckled. "Not as exciting as running after nefarious criminals, I would expect."

"Not even as exciting as eating supper," Sir Jackson said wryly, before he disappeared out the door.

Once again, Pierce took a seat in front of the desk, but Manton took the chair next to his.

"What can I help you with, sir?" he asked.

Pierce found it easier than he expected to lay out what he wanted from Manton. With Sir Jackson he might have been less forthcoming, since the man was now related indirectly to Pierce's cousins.

But Manton, with his efficient manner and thorough questions, put him at ease.

When Manton had finished asking everything he needed to know, he said, "So you want me to find out what I can about this Mr. Gilchrist and the rest of your mother's family, especially her relationships with all of them. Is that correct?"

"Yes. And I'll pay you whatever it costs to have it done quickly. Preferably before Christmas."

The man started. "That *is* quick. Today is Thursday, and Christmas is next Monday."

"I realize that." But he couldn't bear the idea of returning to Montcliff without knowing the truth. Nor could he bear spending Christmas with the Waverlys without knowing the truth. It felt important to know it as soon as possible. "Do your best. It should help that all of Mother's relations live in London."

"Yes. Little Britain, though a shabby community, isn't that big. And I know a tavern owner on Aldersgate Street, near where your mother used to live."

It dawned on Pierce that the man hadn't taken any

notes during their entire interview. "You remembered all that without writing it down?"

Manton nodded. "I never write anything down. I remember everything I hear, word for word."

"That's quite a talent."

"It comes in handy. But it can be a damned nuisance sometimes, too—all that information buzzing around in my head when I want to sleep."

"I can imagine."

Manton stood. "Well, then, if that is all, you'll be hearing from me soon."

Pierce stood, too, and held out his hand. "Thank you. I know it's not the most interesting of cases, but—"

"Actually," Manton said as he shook Pierce's hand, "this should be a nice change of pace. I spend most of my time looking into the backgrounds of prospective applicants for various posts, confirming their former places of employment, their birth records, and such. Much less interesting work."

Pierce stared at him. "Do you ever investigate a foundling's parentage, something of that nature?"

"No, but I could, if I had enough information to begin."

"Then I believe I have a second case for you. You see, my mother's companion . . ."

As he filled Manton in on the details of Camilla's background, he told himself he was only doing it for her sake. He wanted to help her, to give her some knowledge of the family she'd lost.

It had nothing to do with his own curiosity about her past. Nothing to do with wanting to be prepared for whatever surprises might lie in wait for him if he happened to marry her.

Marry her?

Ridiculous notion. He had no intention of marrying anyone. Marriage was for men who intended to bear heirs.

It's the only way to strike back at her for what she did. If you don't marry and don't have children, then she has no grandchildren to look after her in her old age.

He groaned. Camilla was right. And he no longer *wanted* to strike back at his mother. Not that way, in any case.

But did he want to marry? Did he want to risk giving up the hard-won measure of control he'd gained over his life? That was the crucial question. And he just didn't know the answer.

One thing was certain—Camilla would never agree to anything less than marriage. And he began to think that life without her might be worse than life as a married man.

The morning after Pierce left, Camilla wandered about in a fog. Her ladyship slept very late after their long night, and Jasper did, too, but Camilla couldn't. She kept replaying everything she'd said to Pierce. Should she have tried harder to keep him here? Said something different?

But what could she have said? He was too damaged by the past to be reasoned with. How was she supposed to break through that?

Now the three of them sat in the drawing room, along with Maisie. It was early afternoon. Jasper was gilding almonds under Camilla's supervision as Maisie and her ladyship made paper cutouts of reindeer for the Christmas tree.

Though neither Camilla nor her ladyship felt like preparing for Christmas, they had to. Jasper was looking forward to it, and they needed something to keep their hands and minds occupied. Otherwise, they would both fall into a gloom from which neither was liable to emerge anytime soon.

One of the footmen appeared in the doorway. "Mrs. Stuart, there's a Mr. Whitley here to see you. He asked for his lordship, but when I said that my lord had gone to London, he said he would speak with *you*."

"Who is Mr. Whitley?" her ladyship asked.

"I don't know. The name does sound familiar, though." Camilla frowned in thought. "Wait, that was the name of the horse trader from the fair. What would he be wanting with me?"

"I don't know," Lady Devonmont said, "but we should definitely find out. Do send him in."

The footman looked uncomfortable. "He asked that I have Mrs. Stuart come into the garden, my lady."

"This grows more curious by the moment," the countess said. "Come, Camilla, let's go find out what this is all about."

"I want to go!" Jasper cried, always eager to be outside.

So all four of them followed the footman out into the garden, where Mr. Whitley stood waiting for them in a fine suit.

And he had the Shetland pony with him.

"Chocolate!" Jasper cried as he raced over to the pony.

"Good day, madam," Mr. Whitley said, smiling. "I brought the pony over just as his lordship asked."

Camilla paled. "I believe there's been some mistake."

"No mistake. The earl said it was a Christmas present for the lad. Told me to see Mr. Fowler about payment today, and I did. It's already paid for."

"Oh, but—"

"Just take it," Lady Devonmont said in a low voice. "If it worries you, I'll pay for it." She squeezed Camilla's arm. "It's worth it to see the boy so happy."

Jasper was petting Chocolate and talking to him

nonstop, and the pony was enduring it all with what Camilla thought was a great deal of patience.

"I'll fetch a groom for him," the footman said, and hurried off.

"Well, then, I wish you joy of him," Mr. Whitley said with a tug of his forelock to her ladyship. Then he left.

"I had no idea," Camilla said. "It seems wrong to accept such an extravagant gift, especially now, given what has happened between me and Pierce."

Her ladyship told Maisie to go keep an eye on Jasper, then said to Camilla in a low voice, "I think perhaps my son feels more deeply for you than he can admit."

"Because he bought Jasper a pony?" Camilla said skeptically. "It's just part of his campaign to make me his mistress."

"I don't think so. In all the time he's been taking mistresses, he's never been involved with anyone who had a child. The women have all been cold, glittering females flitting from protector to protector, not your sort at all."

"That doesn't mean anything. I just happened to be handy."

The countess shook her head. "I saw how he looked at you last night. It's not the way a man looks at a conquest." She drew in a deep breath. "I think you should go talk to him in London."

Camilla gazed into the woman's face. "There's no

point. Not unless you come with me and tell him what he needs to know. Until he can put the past behind him, he can't go on, and he's never going to do that as long as you don't set things right."

Her ladyship was quiet a long moment. "What if it didn't set things right?" she finally said. "What if it made them worse?"

"How can they possibly be worse than they are now?"

"He could still come back here," the countess said, worrying her lower lip with her teeth. "He might relent in his anger, especially for you."

Camilla shook her head. "I don't think so. I think he's had enough." She tucked her arm in the countess's. "At least tell *me*. Then I can judge how he would take it."

Lady Devonmont stiffened. "You'll despise me."

"He told me what you said to him that day in the study, and I'm still here, aren't I?" Camilla's tone was gentle. "I'm willing to give you the benefit of the doubt. Because unlike him, I can see beyond the past to how much you love him."

Tears started in the countess's eyes. "All right. I'll tell you what happened."

24

Pierce kept as busy as he could during the next couple of days, while he waited to hear from Manton. The night after he'd met with the man, Pierce went to his club, but he kept running into men who unwittingly reminded him exactly how much of an arse he'd been for the past several years.

Everyone had heard of his break with Eugenia, so they were eager to find out who his next mistress would be. Was he considering the French opera singer Minette, with the fine tits? Or Nelly Banks, whose low beginnings were matched only by her astounding ability in bed?

For the first time, their coarse remarks annoyed

him, especially in light of the fact that he'd meant to bring Camilla to London as his mistress. No wonder she'd refused. Even without moving in his circles, she'd known what it would mean for her and, by extension, for Jasper. And she had too much integrity to want the boy sullied by such slurs.

It began to shame him that he'd even considered it.

After spending the next day with his secretary, going over the previous week's correspondence, Pierce attended an afternoon performance of the opera, but his heart wasn't in it. He kept comparing the voices of the female singers to Camilla's, and all of them came up wanting.

Worse yet, in the theater lobby he ran into Eugenia. She'd already found a protector, whom she paraded in front of Pierce in what appeared to be an attempt to make him jealous.

He felt nothing, even when she and her new gentleman friend paused to talk to him for several minutes. Hard to believe that he'd ever been enamored of her. Now she seemed brittle as ice, her sophistication like a table that had been lacquered so many times, one could no longer see the luster of the wood.

But watching her try to rouse a response in him did remind Pierce that with him gone, Camilla was now free to take up with any damned chap near Montcliff who fancied her, especially since there was no longer any need for secrecy about Jasper. She could find a respectable husband, a farmer or a shopkeeper—or even the handsome new doctor in Stocking Pelham.

That thought succeeded in rousing his jealousy. Indeed, the idea of a horde of country doctors beating down Camilla's door so annoyed him that when the opera was over, he chose to walk home rather than ride in his carriage, hoping that the biting cold and brisk walk would clear his head.

But it merely lowered his spirits further. Since it was the night before Christmas Eve, the city had taken on a festive air. Mince pies were displayed in all the bakery windows, mistletoe was hung wherever young people congregated, and carts had begun to enter the city laden with evergreens and the occasional tree. Apparently the custom Mother had followed for so many years was beginning to catch on.

Were Mother and Camilla preparing *their* tree? Were they even now hanging evergreens on the mantel and winding them up the banisters? Jasper must be beside himself with excitement over the impending holiday.

Pierce missed the boy. No, he missed them all, every damned one of them—Mother and Maisie and Fowler. He even missed Cook, with her no-nonsense meals of beef and onions.

Most of all, he missed Camilla. And the ache of missing her, which he'd thought would diminish over time, only got stronger with each day.

He was so lost in thought that he didn't hear the voice hailing him from the street until a phaeton practically ran him down. It was his cousin Virginia's husband, Lord Gabriel Sharpe. Only Sharpe would drive an open phaeton in the middle of damned winter.

"What the devil are *you* doing here?" Pierce asked as Sharpe offered him a hand up into the phaeton.

"Looking for you." Sharpe turned the phaeton and started back for Pierce's town house. "I'd been waiting at your not-so-humble abode, but when your carriage came back without you, I gave up and headed for home. Then, as luck would have it, I spotted you on the street." Sharpe slanted a glance at him. "Good thing I did. You were so distracted, I daresay you would have gotten yourself run over."

"The only person I was in danger from was *you*," he grumbled. "Why were you waiting for me, anyway?"

"My wife sent me, what else? You know Virginia. When she didn't hear from you about whether you were coming to Waverly Farm for Christmas, she got worried. She thought perhaps with our moving into our own property outside town and your uncle Isaac marrying my grandmother . . . well, you might think you weren't welcome."

Camilla's words flitted through his mind again: *And when she gave you up, she made sure you were put in a safe place, a comfortable place, with good people who cared about you. . . .*

A lump stuck in his throat. "Your wife worries too much," Pierce said.

"As I tell her practically every week. But she ignores me, especially where you're concerned."

At his arch tone, Pierce bit back a smile. "Don't tell me you're still angry over the time I pretended to court her."

"Certainly not. I know you did it to be sure of my intentions." He grinned at him. "Besides, she has convinced me that she knows you for the arse you are, so I have nothing to worry about."

Though Sharpe was just trying to get his goat, the remark sobered him. He really *had* been an arse, and for quite some years. He'd spent nights in a drunken stupor, gambling to excess merely because he'd known it would land him in the newspapers. He'd seduced actresses and toyed with young ladies' affections so the gossips would excoriate him, and in the process had left a trail of wreckage behind him.

And for what? To strike back at his parents? It hadn't done that. It had merely obscured the past even more. He could have spent his time more usefully, but he'd been too angry to see the forest for the trees.

He was damned well seeing the forest now.

"You *are* coming for Christmas, aren't you?" Sharpe asked as he pulled up in front of Pierce's town house.

Down the street, carolers were regaling a household with a warbling version of "Here We Come A-

Wassailing." His neighbors had clearly been busy this evening decking the outside of their houses with greenery, and the pungent scent of fir wafted to him on the night breeze.

"No," he heard himself say. "I'm going home."

Home?

Yes, home. He'd been banished from it for so long that he'd grown used to thinking of it as something denied to him. But it wasn't anymore.

Sharpe turned to gape at him. "You don't mean Montcliff?"

"I do. I mean to spend Christmas with my mother and her companion." *The woman I intend to marry.*

She deserved better than a life as his mistress. He could never drag her down into such a situation; he saw it now. And marriage didn't have to mean becoming some besotted fool like Sharpe and giving up control over his life. He could still protect his heart.

She won't settle for that.

She would have to. It was all he had to give.

Sharpe was looking at him oddly. "But I thought you and your mother didn't . . . er . . . get along."

"We didn't. But now . . . well . . . it's a bit hard to explain."

"Trust me, I understand 'hard to explain.' I have a family full of 'hard to explain,' as you well know." Staring ahead to where his horses were champing to be off, he frowned. "When will you leave?"

"Tomorrow morning, at first light."

Sharpe brightened. "Then you'll have plenty of time to stop at our place in the country. It's right on your way, and we're not leaving for Waverly Farm until late in the afternoon." When Pierce drew breath to protest, Sharpe said, "Virginia will never forgive me if you don't at least come by. You haven't even seen our new home yet. For that matter, you haven't even seen the baby."

Pierce winced. He'd forgotten that Virginia had recently given birth to their first child, a baby girl named Isabel. "All right. I'll stop in on my way to Hertfordshire."

The next morning, Christmas Eve, Pierce arose early and ordered the servants to pack up his bags. The very prospect of heading to Montcliff lifted his spirits, which told him he was doing the right thing.

But just as he was shrugging into his greatcoat, Manton arrived. He had information for Pierce, he said, and some of it couldn't wait until after Christmas.

Blood pounding in his ears, Pierce brought the man into his study and prepared himself for anything.

"First of all," Manton said after they'd exchanged the usual pleasantries, "I tracked down a few of your mother's relations, including your mother's second cousin Edgar Gilchrist."

Pierce blinked. "You spoke to him."

"I'm afraid not. He died a few years ago, but I was able to talk to his widow."

"He was married?"

"Yes." Manton shifted nervously in his chair. "But she said he only married her after he'd given up all hope of being with your mother."

Pierce sucked in a breath. Camilla was right— Mother *had* been involved with Gilchrist. "His wife knew about him and Mother?"

"Oh, yes. She gave me quite an earful. All about how your mother was the siren who'd broken his heart and ruined him for any other woman. According to her, he courted your mother behind your grandfather's back. It started when she was sixteen and he was twenty."

"Sixteen!" That stymied him. She'd married Father at eighteen. "How long did Gilchrist court her?"

"Up until the time they attempted to elope, shortly after she turned eighteen."

Great God, that was a serious courtship. "Attempted? How, exactly?"

"Well, as best I could determine from the man's wife, who'd been admiring him from afar all those years, your mother and Gilchrist ran off to Gretna Green and actually got across the border, before her father caught up to them and made them come back. One of your mother's other relations confirmed that. The family managed to hush it up, and it rapidly became apparent why, when the earl proposed to your mother."

"Ah, yes," Pierce mused aloud. "By then, the earl

must have agreed to pay off Grandfather's debts in exchange for Mother's hand in marriage."

"That would explain why she married him."

No, Pierce thought with a sinking in his stomach. *The babe in her belly explains why she married him.*

Gretna Green was a long way off, after all. Plenty of time to consummate the wedding before it took place. Then she would have been too ashamed to admit to her father that she wasn't chaste. Or perhaps she *had* admitted it, and Grandfather Gilchrist hadn't cared. After all, he already had an earl waiting in the wings.

Or had he? "Did Mother know the earl before she eloped?"

"Yes. Apparently the reason your mother and Gilchrist ran off in the first place was that the earl had taken a fancy to her, and since her father didn't approve of her marrying Gilchrist, the couple feared they would never get to marry unless they eloped."

"Did my father—" He checked himself. "Did the earl know about her connection to Gilchrist?"

"That, I could not discover. All I know is that he met your mother at some grand ball during your mother's come-out. According to Gilchrist's wife, a friend of the family even then, the earl was instantly smitten and pursued your mother relentlessly. When she ran off, he was told she was visiting relatives, and as far as Gilchrist's wife knew, he believed it."

"But then Gilchrist came along years later and

threatened to tell my father that she'd borne him a bastard," Pierce mused.

Manton snorted. "A bastard? If that's what you're worried about, my lord, you can set your mind to rest. The earl was engaged to your mother for six months before they married—it took that long to prepare the large wedding that your father insisted upon. Unless Gilchrist found a way to get around her father and see her during that time—which I seriously doubt, considering their previous attempt at elopement—you are almost certainly the earl's son."

That's what Mother had claimed, too. He'd thought she might be lying, but perhaps she hadn't been.

Still, if Mother *had* shared Gilchrist's bed while they were eloping and Father found her unchaste on their wedding night, he might have suspected her of infidelity later with *someone*. Father had to have believed Pierce wasn't his, despite all evidence to the contrary. That was the only explanation for why the man had despised his own heir.

But it still didn't explain why Father had spurned him only after Pierce turned eight. Had Gilchrist tried to blackmail Mother by threatening to tell Father that he'd been the one to take her innocence? Given the Gilchrist family's predilection for gambling, perhaps the man had needed money and had thought that a way to gain it.

And if Mother had stood firm against his threats,

then he might have gone to Father, threatening a scandal if Father didn't pay him off.

But then what could Father have been holding over Mother's head to make her cut off her son so completely? Knowledge of some botched elopement wouldn't have made any difference in their marriage.

Unless . . .

A cold chill passed through him. "Are you absolutely certain that Gilchrist and my mother didn't make it to a church or even an 'anvil priest' in Gretna Green?"

Manton's eyes narrowed. "Gilchrist's wife said they didn't."

"What else *would* she say? If Gilchrist *had* managed to marry my mother, even in one of those havey-cavey Scottish weddings, and it became known, his marriage to this other woman would be entirely void. She would be left with nothing."

Manton's gaze locked with his, reflecting the same horror Pierce felt. "And your mother's marriage to your father would have been entirely void as well."

"Exactly. Except that my mother wouldn't have been the only one left with nothing."

As the full ramifications of that hit him, Pierce's heart plummeted into his stomach. At last he knew what Father had held over Mother's head. And perhaps even what Gilchrist had told Father that day at Montcliff.

Pierce rose, his mind racing. If his theory was right,

it changed everything. He had to see Mother. He still had a couple of stops to make on the way out of town, and he'd promised Sharpe . . .

That was one promise he must keep. The Waverlys were his family, too, after all, and he was just beginning to realize how important a part they had played in saving him from his father's wrath.

"Forgive me, Manton, but I have to go."

Manton rose as well. "Of course, my lord."

"You will keep this to yourself, I assume." With a sudden sick feeling in his gut, he remembered that Manton's brother had always hated him. What if Manton—

"You have nothing to fear from me," Manton said fiercely. "My clients always have my complete discretion. Sir Jackson would never have recommended me to you if he didn't trust that."

"True," Pierce said tightly, only slightly reassured.

"Besides, I know better than you think how family arrangements can destroy people's futures." Manton looked as if he were debating something, then added softly, "My father had another family, a mistress and two illegitimate children—my half brother and half sister. It is because of them that I am estranged from my brother. Father left them provided for, but George refused to honor the agreement. It has wreaked havoc on all our lives."

Pierce instantly understood why the man was telling him this family secret. Manton clearly knew that the best way to reassure a man that his secrets were safe was to offer one of his own.

Feeling more easy about Manton, Pierce turned for the door, and Manton said, "Did you wish to hear about the other investigation you charged me with?"

"Other investigation?"

"The one concerning Mrs. Stuart."

"Ah, right." He'd forgotten about that. It felt like years since he'd asked Manton to look into her background. And now it seemed rather . . . sordid.

"I don't have much to tell you," Manton went on. "When I spoke yesterday to the couple who run St. Joseph's Home for Orphans, they were evasive. They admitted that she'd worked there and had an exemplary record but said they had to check their files concerning how she'd ended up there. They said they would report to me this morning about whether they could even speak of the matter. That's one reason I'm here. I thought you might wish to attend the meeting with me."

So he could find out if Camilla was the daughter of a whore or a princess? He didn't need to know that, because he already knew he wanted her in his life.

It didn't matter who her parents were. It didn't matter how she'd come to be at St. Joseph's. Pierce knew the kind of woman she was, inside and out. She was the kind of woman who stood up for those who wouldn't or couldn't stand up for themselves. The kind of woman who took delight in a simple pastry, who could tease a lord about naughty books in one moment and defend the man's mother in another.

The kind of woman who still believed in love. And who apparently had been fool enough to fall in love with *him*.

The least he could do was accord her privacy in her personal affairs. She had never asked him to find out who her parents were, and she could have discovered that herself when she worked at St. Joseph's, if she'd wanted. So he was far overstepping his bounds by pursuing this. He certainly hadn't asked about it for her sake. He had done so for his own, so he could feel safe in marrying her.

Well, no more. If any problems ever arose out of her murky background, they would face them together. Assuming she gave him that chance.

When he saw her, he would tell her that if she wanted Manton to pursue the matter, he would arrange it. But it would be her private affair. Because it truly was none of his concern.

"No," he said. "I don't need to be there for the meeting. And neither do you. I'll pay you for what you've found out so far, but unless I'm directed otherwise by Mrs. Stuart, we'll leave the past in the past."

"Whatever you wish, sir," Manton said, a decided note of approval in his voice.

Clearly they were both in agreement on this—there were some Pandora's boxes that should never be opened.

"What do you think?" Lady Devonmont asked as she held up a delicate figurine in the early evening of the night before Christmas. "Too extravagant for the tree?"

Camilla gazed at the glass angel and remembered Pierce's words about angels and devils. Perhaps if she'd never looked past the flip words to the clear heartache behind them, she wouldn't now be sitting here with her own heart bleeding.

"Camilla?"

"Hmm? No, not too extravagant." She stared at the countess. "We should have gone to London. He shouldn't be alone for Christmas."

The countess sighed. "He isn't *in* London, my dear, and he's certainly not alone. He's at Waverly Farm. And it's better this way. I'm willing to take some risk in telling him all, but . . . I can't bear to do it amid all the madness at the Waverlys'. There's more of them now, and I'm sure they think I'm—"

She pasted a determined smile on her face as she turned back to the boxes of baubles. "It doesn't matter. But I would rather have him to myself when I talk to him." She cast Camilla a long glance. "And you said you didn't want him thinking you were interested in being his mistress."

"I know. We made the right decision not to go. It's just—"

"Mama, Mama!" Jasper cried as he ran in ahead of Maisie. Bored with the tree decoration, he'd gone out earlier to feed Chocolate sugarplums. "Someone's coming!"

Camilla's heart leaped into triple time, and she surreptitiously smoothed her skirts. "His lordship has returned?"

Maisie flashed her a pitying glance. "It's not his carriage. Though it's quite a fine one, I don't recognize it."

"Well, then," the countess said smoothly, "let's go see who it is."

The four of them headed out toward the entrance hall, reaching it just as two people entered. It was a gentleman about Pierce's age and a woman of about the countess's age, dressed entirely in deep mourning, down to her ermine fur muff. A very odd couple, who looked a bit startled by the foursome coming to greet them before they could even be announced.

The countess came forward with a smile. "Good day, sir. I am Lady Devonmont. May I help you?"

He gave a bow, and his gaze flicked briefly over Camilla and Maisie. "My name is Dominick Manton, and this lady is Edith Perry, the Viscountess Hedon."

Lady Hedon gave a quick nod to everyone. Camilla couldn't tell if it was because she was haughty or shy. Mr. Manton, a rather handsome fellow with eyes of a remarkable green, seemed oddly uncomfortable with his surroundings, too.

He nervously scanned the entranceway. "I was hoping to find Lord Devonmont here. I was told, when I met with his lordship at his town house this morning, that he was heading here directly."

"His lordship is coming! His lordship is coming!" Jasper burst out.

"Jasper, we have guests," Camilla chided him. "Hold your tongue."

"Yes, Mama." But his smile didn't fade.

Camilla's heart began to pound, and her ladyship cast her a look of mingled panic and joy as she said to the man, "Are you sure he—"

"His servants told me that he was, and I saw his equipage being loaded. Plus, he said he had to head off. But perhaps I was mistaken in where he was going."

"Perhaps," Lady Devonmont said. "Is there something *I* can do to help you?"

Mr. Manton glanced to Lady Hedon as if for direction.

"I see no need in waiting for his lordship," she said, her eyes darting from Maisie to Camilla, and then settling on Jasper most oddly.

"Very well." Mr. Manton smiled at them all. "I assume that one of you other two ladies is Mrs. Stuart?"

Camilla blinked, then stepped forward. "I'm Camilla Stuart, sir."

As Lady Hedon's wan cheeks grew even more pale, Mr. Manton said, "Is there somewhere we can speak privately, madam?"

Camilla looked to the countess, who said, "Why don't you take the small parlor, dear? I'll have refreshments sent in."

"You are Mrs. Stuart's employer?" Lady Hedon asked, obviously bewildered by her ladyship's manner.

Camilla couldn't imagine what business it was of hers but was gratified when her ladyship said, "I think of her more as a friend than an employee."

"That's good," Lady Hedon said, to Camilla's surprise.

Camilla led the guests into the little parlor, burning with curiosity to know what this was all about.

After everyone was in the room, Mr. Manton closed the door. "Before I explain myself, Mrs. Stuart," he said, "I wish to assure you that I didn't intend for this to happen. After his lordship asked me to look into . . . er . . . how you came to be at St. Joseph's—"

"He did *what*?" she asked, not sure whether to be outraged or touched. It vastly depended on his reasons.

"Oh, he thought better of it later," Mr. Manton hastened to add. "He told me to halt my investigation until he could speak to you about it, but by then the wheels were turning."

"What wheels?" she echoed, thoroughly at sea.

"What Mr. Manton is trying to say," Lady Hedon

put in softly, "is that some months ago, after my husband died, I went to St. Joseph's looking for you, but they weren't sure where you worked anymore. So when Mr. Manton came to the orphanage this week asking questions, they arranged to meet with him and then hastened to me to ask if I wished to be there. I said yes, of course." Her tone grew arch. "Mr. Manton didn't show up for the meeting, so I went to his office, but—"

"I beg your pardon, my lady," Camilla said, becoming more bewildered by the moment. "But who exactly are you, and why are you looking for me?"

Lady Hedon swallowed, then stepped forward to seize Camilla's hands. "I, my dear, am your mother."

25

Christmas Day

It had been snowing now for hours. It was melting almost as soon as it hit the ground, but it still made travel more difficult. And Pierce had only himself to blame for his being so late.

His stops in London had taken more time than he'd expected, and then he had stayed far too long at Virginia's. Uncle Isaac and his new wife, Hetty, had shown up for the occasion, and he'd been forced to attempt to explain what was going on between him and his mother, which he hadn't done very well.

There was too much he had to leave out, too much

he couldn't say until he had more answers. He'd talked briefly with his uncle, hoping that he could shed some light on the past, but Uncle Isaac could say only what Pierce already knew. When Pierce was eight, Mother had asked Titus to raise him with his other children, and Titus had agreed.

After Titus died, Uncle Isaac had been asked to take up the mantle, and he'd done so, hoping that Pierce could be like an older brother to Virginia and the late Roger. Pierce had done his best with that.

Indeed, it was precisely because Virginia was like a sister to him that he'd had so much trouble getting away. And baby Isabel hadn't helped matters any. The child was so amazingly winsome. He kept holding her, thinking that he and Camilla might have a little girl, too. And marveling that for the first time, the thought of having a child didn't completely terrify him.

But he shouldn't have lingered so long with his cousins because he'd been forced to drive through the night. It was nearly eight o'clock on Christmas morning, and his coach-and-four was only now approaching Montcliff.

Were they at breakfast? he wondered as the carriage halted and he leaped out, carrying a box in his arms. Mother and Camilla tended to rise early, so he wouldn't be surprised. And it was Christmas morn, so Jasper had probably been up with the chickens.

He strode into the house and stamped the snow

from his boots but found it oddly quiet. "Where is everyone?" he asked the footman who took his greatcoat.

"Her ladyship is in the drawing room, milord. And Mrs. Stuart—"

"Thank you," he said, hastening off in that direction with his box. They were undoubtedly all in the drawing room, if that's where they'd put the tree.

He couldn't remember what they'd said about that, but Mother used to put it there.

Evergreens were draped on every available space, but for the first time in years, the smell of fir and cedar didn't plague him with bad memories. Not now that he understood so much more.

He walked into the drawing room, then halted. Mother was sitting at the table alone, drinking tea and eating toast. The tree was nowhere in sight, but its absence didn't register nearly as much as Camilla's.

She must be getting dressed or something, which was just as well. What he had to say to Mother would best be said in private.

"Pierce!" she cried, a smile breaking over her face. She rose, then seemed to remember the circumstances under which they'd last parted, and her smile faded a little. "We . . . didn't expect you."

"I tried to get here for Christmas Eve, but I stopped at Virginia's and—" He was babbling, for God's sake. Fighting for calm, he set down his box and went over to her. Might as well get right to the point. "Mother, I don't know how to tell you this, but since you refused to tell me anything about Gilchrist, I had an investigator look into your friendship with him."

He expected her to try to escape the conversation, as always, but she just stared at him, her eyes wide. "I see. And what did he learn?"

"That before you married Father, you attempted to elope with Gilchrist."

She swallowed, then nodded.

"So I figured out what Father was holding over your head—the fact that you'd married him while already married to Gilchrist."

"I did *not!*" she cried. "I was *never* married to Edgar. And Walter knew it, too. His blasted investigators couldn't find one shred of evidence that I was ever married to Edgar because I *wasn't!* We didn't get that far."

"Then why—"

"Because your father never needed any proof to use something to his advantage," she said bitterly. She began to pace, her color high. "You know how Walter was. He felt his honor was besmirched. He told me that if I didn't send my 'bastard' away and never see him again, he would drum up whatever evidence he needed to prove a prior marriage. He would pay witnesses and he would stop at nothing."

Tears sparkling in her eyes, she halted to gaze at Pierce. "And he was just the man to do it, too. He would have disinherited you entirely! You would have lost everything—the title, the estate, your legitimacy!"

"I wouldn't have cared," he choked out, his throat tightening convulsively. "I would have had you. I would have had one parent, at least."

"You say that now, as you stand in one of the several properties you inherited, with the weight of your title behind you," she pointed out raggedly. "But you wouldn't have thanked me if I had let that bitter, resentful man plunge you into poverty and disgrace at the age of eight."

She lowered her voice to a hiss. "I slid from riches to poverty as a girl, my boy. I knew what it was like. And I didn't live in disgrace, as you would have had to do. No. I wasn't going to let *my son* endure any of that just because my jealous husband had some foolish notion that you weren't his. You have *no* idea how cruel life can be."

He stood there, buffeted by her words. Life had certainly been cruel to her. Who was he to sit in judgment on what methods she had taken to protect him? He had never been a woman, entirely dependent on the men in her life. Men who'd failed her, one after another.

Still, there were things he didn't understand. "So I really *am* the earl's son."

She fought to regain her composure. "I told you before—of course you're his son. You were born ten months after we married."

"There wasn't any leeway in that? Because if there wasn't, I don't understand why he thought me a bastard." That was the crux of it.

Apparently, it was the crux of it for her, too, for she'd gone white, and she wouldn't meet his eyes.

"Mother?" he prodded.

She started pacing again, this time wringing her hands. "You just couldn't leave it alone, could you? You had to start stirring up the past, looking under rocks."

This time he refused to let his temper get the better of him, though she was sorely trying his patience. "What do you expect?" he said quietly. "You stood there in the study and told me to my face—"

"Because you were going to ruin everything!" she cried. "If I had weakened even one moment, if I had let you know how I felt and you had started coming round, he would have done as he threatened. I could see it in his face. He would have cut us both off out of sheer spite. The money you inherited from your grandmother? Gone. Your position in society, your inheritance, your title? Gone! And all because I—"

She broke off with a sob.

His heart breaking to see her so overwrought, he walked up to pull her into his arms. "Shh, shh, you don't have to tell me." He held her trembling body close, cursing himself for bringing her to this pass.

"I do have to tell you," she whispered. "Camilla was right about that." She lifted a tear-streaked face to him.

"But if I had guessed for one moment what my stolen afternoons with Edgar would cost me . . ."

And that's when it hit him. They'd been wrong about her. She *had* risked it all; she *had* stood up to his father. She'd had an illicit affair with her cousin—her lover—and had paid the price. A very high price.

So had he.

That's why she wouldn't tell him this before, why she wouldn't admit the whole truth. Because she felt deeply ashamed. And obviously deeply guilty, too.

She ducked her head and pulled away from him. "Your father . . . was very enamored of me. And at eighteen I found it rather flattering, even though I was still in love with Edgar. Even though I had . . . given myself to Edgar."

Mortification reddened her cheeks. "When your father discovered on our wedding night that I was not . . ." She swallowed. "I made the mistake of confessing all, admitting to having run off with Edgar. But I told your father—and I believed it—that I was past my youthful indiscretion. That I would be a good wife to him. And he forgave me."

Her voice hardened. "Or so I thought, for he sometimes taunted me with it privately. It was like a burr under his saddle in the early years of our marriage. But we had you, and I tried to be content." She cast Pierce a quick smile. "You were the only bright spot in those years."

Pierce could hardly breathe. He knew what was coming, and he knew he should stop her from telling it. But he couldn't. She needed to tell it as much as he needed to hear it.

"Then I went to your grandfather's funeral, and Edgar was there."

"I remember," he said hoarsely. "That's when I met him, when I was six."

"We were as much in love as ever, and I was so unhappy with your father—" Her breathing grew labored. "We started meeting in a town not too far off. Your father drank a lot, as you may remember, so I would go riding when he was passed out, and . . . well, you can guess the rest."

"He found out," Pierce said, his blood thundering in his ears.

"Yes. After that day at the fair." Her expression grew rigid. "I'd begun to realize how much I was risking, and I'd stopped going to meet Edgar. But the blasted fool wouldn't be cautious. He came to the fair, hoping to see me and persuade me to run away with him. I told him I couldn't—it would mean giving you up." Her tone turned brittle. "Because a woman may leave her husband, but if she does, she can never take her children with her."

And he had worried that marriage meant giving up control of his life? What had he been thinking? A woman gave up far more in a marriage than a man ever could.

"We argued, and Edgar left, and I thought that was the end of it." She stared off beyond him, as if looking into the past. "But someone saw us, someone who knew who Edgar was. And that person, whoever it was, mentioned to Walter about seeing me with my cousin at the fair."

She pressed her fingers to her temples. "That's when all hell broke loose. Your father sent footmen to bring Edgar to the house, and told Edgar that if he ever came within a mile of me, he would kill him."

A shudder racked her. "And then he went on a rampage, convinced, no matter what I said, that we had been seeing each other all along. That's when he took the notion into his head that you weren't his."

"He never did think me worthy of his fine bloodlines," Pierce said acidly.

"I don't think it had anything to do with you, my dear. He could see that I loved you, and he knew I didn't love *him*. And he hated that. It was an easy leap for him to say that I must love you because you were Edgar's child."

That made a horrible kind of sense to Pierce. In every memory he had of his father, even as a young child, it had been Mother and him against Father. That had to have rankled.

"So after he dealt with Edgar, he laid down the rules for me. I was never to see Edgar again. I was never to go anywhere without my husband. And I was not—"

She choked back tears. "I was not to see my . . . 'bastard' child. In exchange, Walter would allow me to send you off to school and relations. If we didn't have another child, he would allow you to inherit. But I was not to write to you or speak to you. He allowed me that last Christmas with you only because the school wouldn't take you until after the holidays."

Her gaze met his, glittering with tears. "I treasured every moment of that Christmas. And even after you left, I kept hoping that once you were away, he would relent. But when he discovered I was sneaking letters out to you, he told me that if he ever saw that again, he would do as he threatened—claim I had been married before and in one fell swoop make you illegitimate."

Pierce stood there, fists clenched, wishing his father were alive so he could kill him with his bare hands.

When the tears began to fall and she patted her pockets, apparently looking for a handkerchief, Pierce stepped forward to give her his.

She took it gratefully. "He was determined to *make* me be the wife he wanted. He knew I would do anything to keep you safe, and he used that. I think he was terrified that if I ever got you to myself, I would run off with Edgar and he would never see us again."

"Why didn't you?" he rasped, his own tears clogging his throat.

"And have your inheritance denied you because that . . . that evil wretch thought you weren't his? Not on your life." She lifted her chin, her gaze fierce. "I could endure the blasted devil if it meant keeping you from losing everything. And your children and your children's children."

His children's children.

Great God. That's why she'd been so hateful to him that day in the study. Because she had seen beyond him to a future that went down generations, a future she'd been bound and determined to save for him. Always stubborn to a fault, she was not going to let Pierce "ruin everything" in a fit of pique at his father. Not after what she'd already suffered to gain it.

The fire suddenly went out of her face. "So now you know. You were punished because I was an adulteress."

And she clearly believed he would hate her for it. But how could he? It was monumentally unfair that she had been forced to give up the man she loved because her father couldn't control his gambling. That she'd suffered because she'd confessed all to her husband on her wedding night.

Snatching something precious for herself shouldn't have brought her to this. "I don't blame you for what you did."

"You should," she choked out. "If I hadn't taken up with Edgar again—"

"Father probably would have found some other reason to suspect you. Men like that often do." He pulled her into his arms, his eyes burning with unshed tears. "I don't blame you for wanting a few moments of happiness in such a miserable marriage."

"Even if it meant that you—"

"Yes," he choked out. "Even then." He held her close, his heart in his throat. He still thought she would have been better off throwing Father's rules in his damned face and running off with her true love, taking him with her.

But that was a man's way of thinking. He wasn't a woman. He wasn't a mother, who would do anything for her child.

"I wish you'd told me sooner," he whispered into her hair.

"And have you learn . . . that I was a vile adulteress? That I risked your entire future for . . . for a sordid affair?"

"With the man you'd always loved?" He drew her back to stare at her. "It wasn't you who banished me, Mother. It was Father. And I think I'm wise enough to place the blame squarely where it belongs." He swallowed. "Though I wasn't always." He brushed a tear from her cheek. "I'm sorry I didn't read your letters. It was wrong of me."

Tears threatened to overthrow her again. "You're here now. That's all that matters." She stepped back and forced a bright smile as she dabbed at her eyes. "And it's Christmas! I have you for Christmas. At last."

He choked down his own tears. "Yes, you do," he

managed. "And you always will." Before she could start crying again, he added, "Which reminds me, I brought you a couple of presents. But one in particular I wanted to give you privately."

He went over to where he'd set down the box and brought it back to her, then opened it to reveal all her letters. Unsealed. "I want you to know that I read every one, from beginning to end. I only wish I'd read them sooner."

"Oh, Pierce . . ." That brought the tears back, and he had to set down the box to hold her again and comfort her until she stopped crying, all the while cursing himself for not starting to repair their relationship the very day of Father's funeral. For being so angry that he hadn't looked beneath the surface.

Once she got control of herself and pulled back from him again, he glanced around them with a frown. "But where is the tree? I thought it would be in here, and young Jasper would be fighting to get at it by now."

"Oh no, it's in the nursery," she managed as she blotted her face again. "Jasper begged us to put it there once he saw it all decorated." She beamed at him. "He and Camilla are up there now, with Lady Hedon. I came down to give them some time to themselves after we opened our gifts this morning."

"Who the devil is Lady Hedon?"

Her smile faltered. "You didn't know? It was your man Manton who brought her here—oh, right, he hadn't had the chance to tell you." She took a heavy breath. "Lady Hedon is Camilla's mother."

Pierce stared at her, thunderstruck. "Her mother."

"Yes. Thanks to you, Manton found her." She gave a small frown. "And now I'm going to be hard-pressed to keep Camilla here. The woman wants to take her back to London and make her part of her family."

Pierce turned to the door. "The hell she does!"

His mother caught his arm. "Don't spoil this for her. She has a chance to make her own way for once. To be her own person. Lady Hedon is a widow with no other children and plenty of money, and she says she wants to leave it to her daughter. Camilla will be able to live as a lady, with her son alongside her."

"You mean, instead of living a life of degradation and shame as my mistress."

Mother colored. "Exactly. She deserves better."

"I know," he said tightly. She deserved much better than what he'd offered. She deserved what Lady Hedon was apparently willing to offer—freedom. The right to live her life as she chose. He should let her have that.

And he would, if that's what she really wanted. But he prayed to God that it wasn't. "You'll be happy to know that I've seen the error of my ways. I've come to offer Camilla marriage."

He would have thought that would make his mother ecstatic, but she merely stared at him with a worried frown. "Why?"

He blinked. "Because I want to marry her, of course."

"Yes, but *why* do you wish to marry her? If it's just because you think that it's the only way you can have her in your bed—"

"No!" He stopped, then said more firmly, "No. That's not why."

It dawned on him—that really *wasn't* why. He did want her in his bed, of course; he'd always wanted that. But there were other things, too. He liked that she smiled at his wit, even when he was being an "overgrown child," and that she listened to him with an intensity that showed she cared what he said.

Yet it went beyond enjoyment of her very amiable self. For the first time in his life, he was willing to give up a bit of control to be with someone forever. To be with *her.* Because he didn't mind giving up control to the woman he knew he could trust absolutely. With his life, his soul . . . his heart.

"I want to marry her because I love her," he told his mother.

"Well, then," his mother said with a brilliant smile. "That's a different matter entirely, isn't it?"

He damned well hoped so.

26

The Christmas tree sparkled in the nursery corner where they'd placed it. With the candles lit, Lady Devonmont's ancient glass baubles glittered from every branch, reminding Camilla of a bejeweled music box she'd seen once in a London shop.

She glanced over to watch as Lady Hedon showed Jasper how to tie a ribbon into a bow. This was what she'd always wanted—a family. And now she had it. Yet something was missing.

The viscountess—her *mother,* of all things—caught her staring and smiled. "I still can't believe I have a grandson."

"And I still can't believe I have a mother," Camilla choked out.

She'd expected to feel more of a connection, an instant visceral recognition of the person who had borne her. But Lady Hedon still felt like a stranger. Far more than Lady Devonmont did.

When Jasper took the bow and ran off to show Maisie, Lady Hedon said quietly, "I didn't want to give you up, you know."

"Yes. You said that last night."

Lady Hedon cast her a sad glance. "But you don't believe me."

"On the contrary. Working at the orphanage, I've seen how hard the world makes it for a woman having a child outside the confines of marriage."

"I was so young, only sixteen," Lady Hedon said, wistfully watching after Jasper. "My parents gave me little choice. It was either relinquish you or be cast out." Her clasped hands tightened into a knot in her lap. "And having grown up very sheltered as an earl's daughter, I didn't know how I would take care of myself and an infant, too."

"I understand," Camilla said, though she was really only beginning to. After hearing Lady Devonmont's horrific story, she no longer felt qualified to sit in judgment of other women's decisions about their lives.

She did have one question she burned to ask her

mother. The entire time since last night that they'd spent coming to know each other, she'd wanted to broach it, but it was a delicate subject, and since Lady Hedon hadn't brought it up yet . . . "If you don't mind me asking," she blurted out, "who is my father?"

Lady Hedon blushed. "I am almost ashamed to tell you. When I do, you will know exactly how much a slave to my passions I was." She hesitated, then said, "He was one of my father's footmen." Pain slashed over her face. "And he happily took a nice sum of money from Papa to make himself scarce."

"I'm sorry," Camilla whispered.

"I'm the one who's sorry. I wish I could have given you better news on that score, but I don't even know where he is now. I haven't seen him since the day Papa paid him to leave."

Camilla reached over to squeeze her hand. "It's all right. One parent is more than I had two days ago."

Camilla started to pull her hand back, but Lady Hedon caught it and held it. "I never stopped thinking about you. My late husband and I tried to have children but couldn't, and though I would have suggested looking for you then, I would have had to admit what he never realized—that I wasn't chaste when we married."

Thank God she hadn't admitted it—he might have been the cruel sort of fellow Lady Devonmont's husband had apparently been.

"In any case, he . . . he wasn't the sort of man who

would have wanted to take in my . . ." She sighed. "He was a very upright sort. Don't mistake me, he was a good man, and I loved him, but I just couldn't tell him *that*. I couldn't risk my marriage."

Camilla understood all too well after Lady Devonmont's tale. Was it any wonder that Pierce couldn't find any path to happiness when he had such a skewed blueprint to follow?

Pierce. She sighed. *He* was what was missing.

As if she'd imagined him, the door to the nursery opened, and his painfully familiar voice said, "There you are, lad. I was wondering where you'd gone off to."

"Lord Devonmont!" Jasper cried, and ran over to him. "Look, Mama, who's come for Christmas!"

"I see," she managed, trying to keep her heart from shining in her eyes as they all rose to greet him.

There was a shadow over his features and a hint of uncertainty in the way he stared at her. She didn't know what to make of that, but she took some reassurance from the fact that Lady Devonmont stood beside him beaming. Had he talked to her already? Had she told him all?

Pierce lifted Jasper into his arms, but his eyes never left Camilla. "Merry Christmas, Mrs. Stuart."

"Merry Christmas, my lord." She dared not say more. She was afraid her every word would trumpet her feelings.

"I understand that we have guests," Pierce said.

With a groan, Camilla realized she'd been so flustered that she hadn't made the necessary introductions.

As she did so, she could feel her mother's eyes on her. No doubt she was curious about why the atmosphere between Camilla and his lordship was so charged.

"I'd like to thank you, sir," Lady Hedon said, looping her hand through Camilla's arm. "If not for you sending Mr. Manton to St. Joseph's, I would never have found my daughter."

"You're welcome," he said, his voice now decidedly strained.

"I got a lot of Christmas presents, my lord!" Jasper said, always wanting to be the center of attention.

"Did you, indeed?"

"Oh, yes! Her ladyship gave me a box of brand-new tin soldiers, and they even have a fort! And Mama gave me a stocking to hang by the fire, that she made all by herself, and it's full of nuts and oranges and sugarplums. Oh, and she gave me a wooden boat, too. And Maisie gave me a cap for Christmas and it's like the one in the poem and I'm supposed to wear it when I sleep and—"

"I brought you a Christmas present, too, my boy," Pierce said, staving off what was promising to be a long recitation.

"Oh no, my lord, please," Camilla protested. "You already gave him a pony. And you really shouldn't even have done that."

"Nonsense. Besides, this is just a small gift." Setting the lad down, he motioned a footman forward who was carrying several wrapped boxes. Pierce pulled one out and offered it to Jasper with a flourish. "Here you go."

Jasper looked to her. "Can I open it, Mama?"

"Of course," she said.

Tearing off the paper, Jasper pulled out what looked like a framed picture. He stared hard at it, then broke into a smile. "It's the poem, Mama!" he cried, running over to her. "Look, it's the poem about St. Nicholas!"

It was indeed. Pierce had gotten someone to write it out on vellum and then frame it.

"Now, it will be preserved for whenever you want to read it," he told the boy.

Camilla's heart caught in her throat. "It's a very lovely gift," she choked out. "What do you say, Jasper?"

"Thank you, my lord!" Jasper said. "Thank you very much!" Then his face fell. "I don't have a present for you." He glanced over at his eight tin soldiers, lined up in front of the tin cup that was serving as a sleigh. "Unless you want my old soldiers."

Pierce walked up to ruffle his hair. "You keep those. But there *is* a gift you could give me." He lifted his gaze to Camilla. "I'd like to steal your mother for a short while, if you don't mind. I won't keep her long. Is that all right?"

Jasper bobbed his head. "I'll stay here with Maisie

and her ladyship and my grandmama. I have a grand-mama now, you know."

"I heard," Pierce said tightly.

"I never had a grandmama before." Kenneth's par-ents had been long dead when Jasper was born. The lad smiled over at Lady Hedon. "She's nice."

Lady Hedon chuckled. "And you, my boy, are quite the little charmer. In fifteen years, you'll be breaking every heart in London. Now come here and sit with your grandmama and show me your new poem, while your mother goes to speak to his lordship."

Pierce held the door open, and Camilla went out with him, her heart hammering so hard she was sure the world could hear it.

He led her down the hall a short way to where a big box sat. "I brought you a present, too," he said.

She wanted to cry. "Pierce, you can give me and Jas-per as many gifts as you like, but it's not going to change my mind about—"

"I know. That's not what I'm trying to do." He ges-tured to the box. "Just open it."

With a lump in her throat, she opened the box, then stared in bewilderment at what was inside. It was a miniature sleigh with handles on the back, for a doll or a—

Her gaze shot to his.

"It's for the children I hope we'll have. At Montcliff. If you'll consent to be my wife."

When she just stood there, gaping at him, hardly able to believe her ears, he added, "You told me once that I make you feel like you could fly. Well, I'm hoping perhaps we can fly together as one big family. You, Jasper, our children—"

"Your mother?"

"Yes, her, too," he said, his eyes misty. "She told me everything. I'd already figured out most of it, yet when I heard it from her, I realized that you were right—about a great many things, but one in particular. I *was* trying to punish her by not marrying. All I ended up doing, however, was punishing myself, denying myself the family I'd never had, because I was sure that if I tried to gain it, I would fail. And I knew I couldn't endure that pain a second time."

She was crying now, silently.

"Hearing how much she risked for me made me see that love has risks at every turn. She risked so much for love—love of Gilchrist, love of me, love of the children I haven't even had yet. So I told myself that the least I could do to honor that sacrifice was risk my own heart."

He smiled and reached up to rub her tears away. "There was only one problem with that," he said, his voice hoarse with emotion. "I'd already lost my heart. I think I lost it the moment you showed up in my bedchamber, demanding that I give my mother her due, telling me that absurd tale about how you would readily jump into my bed because I was 'rumored to be quite good at that sort of thing.'"

"And justifiably so," she managed to tease through her tears.

"You see?" he rasped. "That's why I love you, Camilla. You are the only woman who simply laughs at me when I try to be an arse. And somehow, in doing so, you make me not want to be an arse at all."

"You're not an arse," she said, lifting her hand to cup his cheek.

He covered her hand with his. "Oh, I am sometimes. And I know that you have other choices now that you have a mother who wants to make you an heiress, and you are free as a bird for the first time in your life. I realize what an incredible gift she is offering you. But if you marry me, I promise to spend the rest of my life giving you every possible chance to fly."

"I don't want to fly, my love," she whispered, sure that her heart would explode at any moment. "Not unless we fly together."

The smile that broke over his face was so unguarded that it made her want to drag him downstairs and right into bed. But she settled for letting him pull her into his arms and kiss her as if she were the only woman in the world. The woman who'd miraculously captured his heart.

When he had her pulse racing and her toes curling, he tucked her hand in his elbow and said, "Now let's go tell Jasper that he's just gained himself a papa and another grandmama."

She gazed up at him with a happy smile. "That might actually render him speechless."

He eyed her askance. "I would sooner believe that reindeer fly." Then his gaze warmed until she could see his heart, his true feelings, shining in his eyes. "But after today, I might actually believe that, too. Because if I can fall in love, dearling, then anything can happen."

Epilogue

A year and a day later, Pierce sat in the big chair in the nursery at Montcliff Manor with Jasper, dressed in his nightshirt, in his lap. His wife sat opposite them, nursing their two-month-old daughter, Gillian, while Maisie, who'd proved to be an excellent nursery maid, was tidying up.

Beyond them, the tree in the nursery sparkled and gleamed in the firelight. It was one of three at Montcliff this year, with a larger one in the grand drawing room downstairs and one at the dower house.

It was amazing how Montcliff Manor had become so dear to him. But it didn't take long for him to realize that it hadn't been the house that was cold and sterile. It had been the people in it.

The nursery was an excellent example. His father had built it with an eye toward having an heir one day to supplant Pierce. The fool had fitted the room with austere paintings and a tall table and unforgiving chairs that would make any child squirm.

Camilla had thrown all of that out. Now cheerful scenes of boys riding ponies and children gamboling through a wood hung on the wall. The chairs were smaller and adorned with brightly colored cushions, and the table was lower to make it easier for little ones to write.

Pierce chuckled. Father was probably turning over in his grave to see it being inhabited by the likes of Jasper—the son of a vicar and a foundling, and little Gillian—the daughter of his despised son and a foundling. Every time Pierce thought of his and Camilla's children profaning Father's holy empire, running joyously about the estate, he felt a certain smug satisfaction.

Perhaps Mother was right. All the years of pain had been worth it just so they could both beat the old bastard in the end.

"I suppose you want me to read the Poem again," Pierce said to Jasper. That was what they all now called "A Visit from St. Nicholas."

"Oh no, not tonight, Papa," Jasper shocked him by saying. "This is the night *after* Christmas, so I wrote a new poem for it."

Pierce blinked. "You did? When did you do that?"

"This afternoon, while Grandmama Devonmont was here. She helped me." As he unfolded a sheet of paper, he said, "Are we going to Grandmama's house for Twelfth Night?"

"I imagine that your grandmother would march over here and box our ears if we didn't."

Camilla snorted. "As if she would ever 'box' anyone's ears."

"She used to make me sit in the corner when I was a boy," Pierce pointed out. Strange, how the memories of his childhood had become less painful and more treasured in the past year.

"You probably deserved it," Camilla said with a twinkle in her eye.

"Me? I was a model child."

"Like *me*," Jasper said.

"Exactly," Pierce agreed as his wife rolled her eyes.

She claimed that he spoiled Jasper, and perhaps he did. But he certainly didn't spoil the lad one whit more than Grandmama Devonmont did. Or, for that matter, Grandmama Hedon, whom they were going up to London to visit next month.

"All right," Jasper said as he smoothed out the paper. "Here's my poem. ' 'Twas the night after Christmas and all through the manor / Not a creature was stirring, not even a grandmama.'"

"Your grandmama didn't mind that you called her a 'creature'?" Pierce interjected.

"She wanted to be in the poem. And I didn't want to put a mouse in there; they scare Mama."

"Ah, right. Go on."

"'The baby was nestled all snug in her crib, / While visions of sugarplums danced on her bib.'"

Camilla's lips were quivering, and Pierce had to bite his tongue to keep from laughing.

"'And Mama in her 'kerchief, and Papa in his cap—'"

"I don't wear a cap to bed," Pierce pointed out.

"You do in the poem," Jasper said, as if that explained everything. "'Had just settled down for a long winter's nap / When out on the lawn there arose such a noise / That it woke up the boys.'"

Pierce raised his brows. "You have a baby sister."

Jasper cut a sly glance up at him. "And now I want a baby brother."

Camilla began to cough.

Pierce grinned over at her. "I think that can be arranged."

"You do, do you?" she said coyly as she got up to put the now slumbering baby in the crib.

Jasper paid no notice and went on. "'When what to my wondering eyes should appear—'"

"Wait a minute," Pierce said, lowering his voice to keep from waking the baby. "You skipped ahead."

"I know. I couldn't think of anything for that stuff about the 'breast of the snow.' It's silly." Jasper took a deep breath. "'When what to my wondering eyes should appear / But a really big sleigh and eight giant reindeer.'"

"Why did the reindeer get so big?" Pierce asked curiously.

"So they'll be like *our* deer." He gazed up at Pierce. "You know, the ones in the pen. Besides, if St. Nicholas is carrying presents, he needs *lots* of room. A miniature sleigh isn't nearly big enough."

"Excellent point," Pierce said.

Jasper folded up the paper. "So that's it."

"What about the rest of it?" Camilla asked in a whisper as she came up to perch on the arm of Pierce's chair.

"Mama, the Poem is *really* long. It took me all afternoon to write this part out." He snuggled closer to Pierce. "Okay, now you can read me the real Poem."

"Oh no, lad," she said as she picked him up and headed off. "No more stalling. It's time for bed."

Jasper cast Pierce a beseeching glance over his mother's shoulder, and Pierce threw up his hands with a rueful smile. He knew better than to gainsay Camilla when it came to bedtime.

Besides, once the children were in bed . . .

A short while later, he had *her* in his lap as they sat

in the drawing room looking at the tree. This one had ribbons and bows and lit candles, as well as a number of new baubles from the London shops. Camilla wasn't one to spend buckets of money on anything, but she did like a pretty Christmas tree almost as much as his mother did.

He propped his chin on her head. "Fowler informed me today that he is planning to ask for Mother's hand in marriage. I think he was rather surprised when I told him I'd be delighted to have him in the family."

"He certainly waited long enough in getting around to it."

"You know Fowler. It took him six months after our wedding to work up the courage to ask her to go for a walk, and another two months before he progressed to asking her to ride with him. If I hadn't prodded him into inviting her to accompany him to that harvest assembly last fall, he would probably still be riding with her every day and giving her long, yearning glances at dinner. That man courts at a snail's pace."

"Not everyone can court at *your* manic pace," she teased. "Though I'm not sure I'd call it *courting*. More like a transparent attempt to get beneath my skirts."

"It worked, didn't it?" he said with a grin.

"Yes." She shifted in his lap so she could look up at him. "As did my transparent attempt to reform you."

"You did not reform me," he said stoutly. "I reformed myself."

"Oh, you did, did you?" she asked as she looped her arms about his neck. "I had nothing to do with it?"

"Hardly. Every time I looked at you, my thoughts were decidedly *un*reformed." He lowered his gaze to her mouth. "They still are."

"Are they, indeed?" Her eyes gleamed. "Do tell."

He brushed a kiss over her lips. "'Twas the night after Christmas, and all through the place / The only ones stirring were the lord and his mate."

"That is an awful rhyme."

"Shh, I'm not done." He rose with her in his arms, and headed for the door. "They went off to nestle all snug in their bed / While visions of lovemaking danced in their heads."

She eyed him suspiciously. "Is this the naughty version of the Poem?"

"No." He stared down into the face of the woman who'd become dearer to him than life. Who made his life richer and fuller and decidedly more interesting with each passing day. "It's the version for men who are in love with their wives."

She smiled up at him, that same love shining in her face. "Then carry on, sir."

"And Mama, quite naked, and I naked, too—"

"Pierce!" she cried, half laughing, half chiding.

"Oh, all right," he said as he carried her up the stairs. "I suppose it *is* the naughty version."

Turn the page for a special look at
the second delightful romance in the new
Duke's Men series

When the Rogue Returns

by *New York Times* bestselling author
Sabrina Jeffries

Coming Spring 2014 from Pocket Books

By the time Victor Cale arrived at the Theatre Royal he was fit to chew nails. He'd started his investigation of "Mrs. Franke" at her shop on Princes Street, hoping to speak to her seventy-year-old partner, Angus Gordon. But the place was apparently closed on Saturdays, which was interesting. Shops were closed just on Sundays, not on both Saturday *and* Sunday. Not unless they made very good money.

Judging from what those who ran the neighboring shops had to say, that was the case. Indeed, the other shopkeepers found Mrs. Franke a fascinating subject for gossip. Some praised her talent as a jewelry maker. Others commented favorably on her willingness to contribute to charitable causes. A few speculated about her past—whether she was Gordon's illegitimate granddaughter, why she had chosen to settle in Edinburgh, what battles her supposedly dead soldier husband had fought in.

None of them knew where she lived. Or knew anything about her family, beyond the fact that she was a soldier's widow. Or knew even if she attended church. To hear the denizens of Princes Street tell it, Anna Franke's life began when she arrived at her shop in the morning and ended when she left it at night.

They all did agree on one thing, though—that Rupert, the Baron Lochlaw, was sure to marry her within the year. He visited the shop with great regularity, he spoke of her in glowing terms, and he was often seen staring after her like a lovesick puppy. She would be a fool not to accept any offer he made.

And Mrs. Franke was no fool.

Victor gritted his teeth as he entered the theater, an unprepossessing building with only a statue of Shakespeare for adornment on the outside. The very thought of his wife attempting to marry that green lad made him want to smash a hammer through one of the marble pillars inside the theater. She was *not* going to commit bigamy, for God's sake, even if it meant exposing his own past to the world.

The Theatre Royal was surprisingly lush inside, and very small. Only thirty or so private boxes lined the walls, probably half of what was in a London theater. It took only one word with an usher, and Victor was promptly shown into the spacious Lochlaw box.

The Dowager Baroness Lochlaw rose to greet him

with a kiss to each cheek, making sure he got a good glimpse down the front of her very low-cut gown. Her heavy perfume swirled about his head like steam rising from a harem's bathing room, but the only woman he had eyes for was Isa. His wife. Who thought she could get away with pretending to be Mrs. Franke, a widow.

Isa was standing at the other end of the box under a sconce, perusing a program with her ladyship's son. She frowned as the lad tried to explain to her certain English words.

Lochlaw looked only marginally better dressed than he had earlier. There were no holes in his coat sleeve now, but both his cravat and his hair were rumpled, and the creases in his trouser legs had already started to vanish.

But Isa was a goddess in human form. She had her hair ornamented with ostrich feathers and a glittering diadem, probably made of imitation diamonds but no less beautiful for it. If that was an example of her handiwork, it was no wonder she and her partner did well.

Her gown was far simpler than the baroness's heavily furbelowed one—white taffeta embellished with green piping, short puffy sleeves, and a respectable neckline—but the little it revealed and the way it nipped in at her waist reminded him of the last time he'd taken a gown off her. Slowly, with the reverence of a hesitant new husband.

Now he wanted to rip it off her with his teeth. Then

cover her soft, pale body with his and explore every inch with his tongue and hands and cock. He wanted to bury his mouth in the enticingly shadowed valley between her breasts, lick his way down her slender belly to the dark brown curls that covered the sweetness below . . . and drive his cock inside her until she begged him for more.

He fought an erection.

No wonder Lochlaw had stars in his eyes whenever he gazed at her. No wonder Lady Lochlaw saw Isa as a threat.

Just then the baron looked up and spotted him. "Ah, there you are, cousin!"

Lochlaw headed for him, but Isa stayed in place, her eyes widening and her mouth flattening into a tight line that he wanted to kiss until it softened.

God, what was wrong with him? Ten years ago, she had left him to deal with the police alone, to make apologies for her even as he was uncertain whether she'd stolen the royal diamonds. She had abandoned him without one look back.

And all of that seemed to melt away when he saw her. What a fool he was.

Yet he must continue to play this foolish role of the baroness's cousin, at least until he could figure out what Isa was up to.

"Good evening," he said as Lochlaw reached him. He nodded in Isa's direction. "Nice to see you again, Mrs. Franke."

She nodded, a flush rising to her cheeks. Was *she* thinking about their nights together? Their very short week of marriage?

"I'm glad you've come," the baron said. "The opera is about to start, and they frown on anyone entering after it begins."

"Opera?" Victor said, stifling a groan. "I thought we were seeing a play called 'The Iron Chest.'"

"They refer to it as 'a musical play' in the program," Isa said. "But some of the reviews deemed it 'operatic.'"

Her gaze met his, soft with memory, and he was catapulted back to Amsterdam. Her sister and brother-in-law had dragged them to the opera once. He and Isa had only been able to afford the worst seats, and they'd spent most of it whispering together since neither of them had liked the singing. His opinion of opera hadn't altered since then, despite his attending a couple of others with his relations in London.

A bell rang, and Lady Lochlaw took Victor's arm to lead him to the two chairs sitting side-by-side in front of two more. Lochlaw seated Isa in the chair directly in front of the baroness, then took the one in front of Victor for himself.

As the orchestra tuned up, Lady Lochlaw leaned over to Victor to whisper, "You see what I mean about that woman being vulgar? That tiara is the height of bad taste; I daresay the diamonds in it aren't real."

He could tell from Isa's stiffened back that she heard every word.

"That *is* what she does for a living—make imitation diamonds," he whispered back. "And as I recall, in London many women wear tiaras to the theater."

Lady Lochlaw sat back with a sniff. A moment went by, during which time the music began. Then she leaned close again. "Clearly she knows nothing about opera. Why, she pronounced the word 'aria' like 'area.'"

Just as he was about to point out that Mrs. Franke wasn't a native speaker of English, Lochlaw half turned to hiss, "Quiet, Mother. I want to hear the music."

And that was that.

Thank God, because Victor didn't think he could tolerate many more of the baroness's snide comments. But he did understand her reaction. Isa outshone her as a rose did a weed, despite the wealthier woman's finery and expensive jewels. That had to gall her.

The first act of the opera turned out to be not as bad as he expected. For one thing, it had a decent story, with some interesting political notes. And for another, from his vantage point he had a good look of Isa in profile. He could feast his eyes as much as he liked on her glorious hair, her delicate ear, her glowing cheek.

He knew it was foolish to do so, but he let himself dwell on the times he'd kissed her just there, where her pretty neck met her shoulder, or had run his tongue down the hollow of her throat. By the time the first act ended, every part of him ached to touch her.

As the interlude began, they all rose.

"How did you like it, Mrs. Franke?" Lady Lochlaw

asked, casting Victor a conspiratorial glance. "The contralto's *aria* was lovely, don't you think?"

A mischievous gleam shone in Isa's eyes. "I didn't really notice. I was too busy admiring the gorgeous necklace she'd purchased from my shop. It sparkled so nicely in the gas light."

Lady Lochlaw's smug smile vanished. "Did it have real gems? Or imitation?"

"You mean you couldn't *tell*?" Isa asked sweetly. "How odd. I would have thought it obvious to a woman of your discernment."

Victor nearly bit his tongue to keep from laughing. A servant entered just then with a tray of champagne glasses, which was a good thing since Lady Lochlaw looked fit to be tied. Feeling decidedly cheery, Victor took a glass for himself. But when the baron handed Isa one and she smiled up at him engagingly, Victor's mood suddenly soured.

"So, Mrs. Franke," he said in a hard voice, "what made you decide to leave the Continent for Scotland?"

She took a sip of champagne, her eyes darkening. "The death of my husband. I wanted to escape the bad memories."

"Of his death?" he bit out. "Or of your marriage?"

"Both," she said pointedly.

He gritted his teeth. So that had been an illusion, too. All the while he'd been besotted, she'd been resenting their marriage. Damn her for having hidden it so well.

Lochlaw had begun to frown, and even her ladyship looked wary, but Victor ignored them. "What was wrong with your marriage? Was he cruel to you? Did he mistreat you?"

"Neither," she shot back. "But then, he didn't have to. He just acted as if I were his pet. That was the problem. He never told me anything of himself or his family, never let me see inside him. After he was gone, I realized I never really knew his character at all."

That wasn't the answer he'd expected, though on that subject at least, she spoke the truth. He had *not* let her see inside him. He'd been afraid that if she learned the dirty secrets of his childhood, she would bolt.

In the end, she'd bolted anyway. "Perhaps you weren't married long enough to take his measure."

"Perhaps. But that's all the more reason I was stunned to learn how much he'd lied to me, how much he'd pretended to be one thing when he was quite another."

What the devil was she talking about? "You make him sound like a villain," he growled.

"See here, cousin," Lochlaw interrupted, "this conversation is becoming very rude." He cast Isa an uncertain glance. "Don't you agree?"

"Your cousin is perfectly aware that it is," Isa said. "But I'm happy to tell him whatever he wishes to know." Setting her glass down, she came toward Victor. "Still, Mr. Cale, we needn't bore Rupert and his mother with such nonsense. Perhaps you'd like to take a tour of the theater? I understand there are some very fine statues in the lobby."

"And I'll go with you," Lochlaw broke in with a scowl.

Lady Lochlaw put her hand on her son's shoulder. "No, you will not." When he glowered at her, she added, "You can't leave me here alone, dear boy. What would people think?"

"I'm fine, Rupert," Isa said as she took the arm Victor offered. "Your cousin and I will take a little walk and be right back. I need to stretch my legs anyway."

Ha—he'd succeeded in provoking her! And this time he would make sure she gave him some solid answers. During the play, he'd spotted an unoccupied box a few boxes over. He would lead her there so that they could have some privacy for this discussion.

As soon as they were in the hall, she said, "Speaking of lies, are you really her ladyship's cousin?"

He debated what to say. He wasn't ready to tell her what he'd been hired to do, since that might spook her into fleeing. "You're the one who remarked that I never told you about my family," he said evasively. "You're right. I didn't."

"So you really expect me to believe that you're cousin to a Scottish baron." Her voice turned acid. "And not that you're insinuating yourself into her life for some devious purpose."

They'd reached the other box, and he dragged her inside and pulled her behind a pillar where no one could see them from the theater. Thrusting her against it, he braced his hands on either side of her shoulders to glare down at her.

"My devious purpose is to unmask my wife," he growled. "You can hardly blame me when I find you frolicking with the likes of Lochlaw."

"*Frolicking?*" she exclaimed, half laughing. "Are you mad? I keep telling you, Rupert and I are just friends!"

"You're either blind or a fool." He lowered his head. "He watches you incessantly whenever he thinks you don't see. He stares at you with such yearning . . ." He muttered a curse. "Perhaps *you* consider him a mere friend, but I assure you, he does not. I'm a man—I can damned well tell when another man covets my wife."

Her stunned expression told him that she truly hadn't realized that the young man's feelings for her ran that deep.

Then she steadied her shoulders. "Even if you're right, even if he does have an interest in me, why do you care? You don't want me, so—"

"Don't want you?" he said incredulously before he could stop himself. His eyes fixed on her mouth, and his heart began to thunder in his chest. "Now, you really are a fool."

Then, driven by the rampant need that had been boiling up in his blood ever since he'd first seen her this afternoon, he seized her mouth with his.